There's nothing
sexy man who
for you—in
And if you are

Royal AFFAIRS

PRINCESSES
& PROTECTORS

Fantastic novels from bestsellers
Lucy Monroe, Raye Morgan
and Day Leclaire

THE Royal AFFAIRS COLLECTION

Royal AFFAIRS
DESERT PRINCES & DEFIANT VIRGINS

SARAH MORGAN · SUSAN MALLERY · KIM LAWRENCE

Royal AFFAIRS
PRINCESSES & PROTECTORS

LUCY MONROE · KAYE MORGAN · DAY LECLAIRE

Royal AFFAIRS
MISTRESSES & MARRIAGES

DAY LECLAIRE · JENNIE LUCAS · LAURA WRIGHT

Royal AFFAIRS
REVENGE SECRETS & SEDUCTION

JENNIE LUCAS · ROBYN DONALD · DAY LECLAIRE

Royal AFFAIRS:

PRINCESSES
& PROTECTORS

LUCY MONROE

RAYE MORGAN

DAY LECLAIRE

Mills & Boon, an imprint of Harlequin (UK) Limited, Eton House,
18-24 Paradise Road, Richmond, Surrey TW9 1SR

ROYAL AFFAIRS: PRINCESSES & PROTECTORS
© Harlequin Enterprises II B.V./S.à.r.l. 2011

Forbidden: The Billionaire's Virgin Princess © Lucy Monroe 2008
Jack and the Princess © Helen Conrad 2003
The Forbidden Princess © Day Totten Smith 2007

ISBN: 978 0 263 88751 8

026-0711

Harlequin (UK) policy is to use papers that are natural, renewable
and recyclable products and made from wood grown in sustainable
forests. The logging and manufacturing processes conform to the
legal environmental regulations of the country of origin.

Printed and bound in Spain
by Blackprint CPI, Barcelona

Forbidden: The Billionaire's Virgin Princess

LUCY MONROE

Lucy Monroe started reading at age four. After she'd gone through the children's books at home, her mother caught her reading adult novels pilfered from the higher shelves on the book case…alas, it was nine years before she got her hands on a Mills & Boon® romance her older sister had brought home. She loves to create the strong alpha males and independent women that people Mills & Boon® books. When she's not immersed in a romance novel (whether reading or writing it) she enjoys travel with her family, having tea with the neighbours, gardening and visits from her numerous nieces and nephews. Lucy loves to hear from readers: e-mail Lucymonroe@Lucymonroe.com or visit www.LucyMonroe.com.

Don't miss Lucy Monroe's exciting new novel,
***For Duty's Sake*, out in June from**
Mills & Boon® Modern™.

For all the readers who wanted Hawk's story. Thank you for writing to me. And with special thanks to Mills & Boon for letting this, my twentieth story for them, be part of their amazing one hundred years and still going legacy!

CHAPTER ONE

LINA MARWAN stood on the edge of the bridge, her eyes shut as she searched for her center.

A slight breeze caressed her sun warmed skin. It was a beautiful day to be alive. She released the railing and nothing stood between her and open air…a fifty-foot drop to the rushing waters of the river below.

Adrenaline coursed through her at the thought of what she was about to do. Her breaths came in short pants and sweat formed on her temples and palms. She curled her fingers into fists and then released them several times as she forced her lungs into a more relaxed rhythm.

Loud voices from behind her disturbed the peace she was trying to attain. Opening her eyes, she looked back over her shoulder and saw him.

Sebastian Hawk.

The last person she expected to see at this moment in her life. The last man she expected, or wanted, to see ever again. Before, or after, death. God wouldn't be so cruel as to put her and the deceitful bastard in the same part of heaven.

Well, there was nothing for it. He was here and it would only be a matter of seconds before he convinced the officials holding him off the bridge into letting him come for her.

She faced forward again, spread her arms like wings and let her body fall forward as the sound of Sebastian's roar echoed off the ravine's rocky walls.

Soaring through the air like a bird diving for its prey, memories from eight years before flooded Lina's mind in a reel-to-reel play of her time with Sebastian Hawk.

Headed toward the University Center, Lina rushed across the quad. She was late for the meeting, but it couldn't be helped. She'd had to ditch her bodyguard. Again. He was reading a book on Ancient Egypt on the ground floor of the library. He believed she was in a study group meeting in one of the rooms on the second floor. If the poor man knew how many hours he spent in the library while she was elsewhere, they would both be in a lot of trouble.

He was easy to fool. Too easy for her ego. In his mind her high grade point average attested unequivocally to many hours spent studying. She did study, just not nearly as much as he believed. However, like her father and far too many other men from her country, her guard did not believe a woman could get the grades she did without putting a huge effort into the task. All of the guards in her current security detail were similarly afflicted in their thinking.

When she had discovered the benefits to this particular formerly annoying trait she had been grateful for her father's insistence on supplying her bodyguards from her home country for the first time.

Raised in America since she was six, she'd often chafed at the attitudes exhibited by her Marwanian guards. Then she had arrived at university and discovered how easy it was to gain temporary freedom on the pretext of studying. She grinned. Life might not be perfect, but it certainly was fun.

Her grin changed to a grimace as she ran into a rock wall dressed like a man.

She bounced backward, landing right on her bum in the grass. "Ooof."

"Are you all right?" Oh, wow. The rock wall had a voice that made her insides ping.

She looked up…and up…a couple of inches over six feet of *rippling* muscle, until their eyes met. His were gray. A dark, mysterious gunmetal gray. Though, right at that moment, their expression was perfectly readable. They were lit with concern. For her.

Nice.

Her smile returned and she stuck her hand out. "Fine. Thanks. Give me a lift?"

His lips quirked. "Certainly." He reached toward her and their hands connected.

Starbursts might have gone off, she wasn't sure. Because the momentum from his tug landed her body against his and her senses went supernova. Her dazzled brain registered that his mouth was still curved in that half-curve. She wondered what he'd look like with a full-blown smile. Devastating, probably. She probably wouldn't survive it.

"You sure you're okay?" he asked, looking really concerned now.

And darned if she didn't *really* like that. "Wonderful."

"You don't need help to remain standing?"

"No." Did she look like she needed help?

"Then, maybe you'd like to let go? Not that I mind the close contact." Warm amusement laced his words.

"I should...let go I mean." But her body made no effort to move backward.

He laughed. "My name is Sebastian Hawk."

Ulp. His laughter sent shivers through her as she found herself mesmerized by the absolutely gorgeous smile that accompanied it. Okay, so she'd survived a close encounter with his smile, but wasn't so sure about her mental faculties.

This man was very destructive to rational thought processes.

"And you are?"

Right. Very bad for normal brain activity.

"Oh, I'm Lina Marwan." She never used her complete name Lina bin Fahd al Marwan anymore.

"It's a pleasure to meet you, Lina," he said as he gently set her away from him.

She had to fight the urge to press forward and reconnect. Was this what it felt like to be attracted to a man? If it was, she could now be glad she'd spent her teen years at an all-girls school. Unlike her classmates, she'd never had the opportunity to spend time with boys her own age during school breaks. Her family kept too close of tabs on her for that.

In the year and a half since she came to university,

she'd hugged a couple of boys, friends she met in her secret pursuits, but they'd never affected her like Sebastian Hawk. She'd always wanted to know what it was like to kiss a boy, but only in the abstract. Now she wanted to know the very concrete reality of kissing Sebastian Hawk.

The craving was so strong, her lips twitched. Sebastian's gray gaze was knowing—as if he could read the unfamiliar desire surging through her.

The tower clock chimed the quarter hour across the quad and Lina's body jolted with memory.

"Shoot. I'm late. I hope I haven't missed my chance to sign up for the kayaking trip." She still hadn't worked out completely how she was going to get away from her bodyguard and family for an entire weekend, but she was determined to go on this trip.

"You kayak?" Sebastian asked in a surprised tone.

"It's one of my favorite things. Not that I get to go as often as I like." She started walking briskly toward the University Center.

He kept pace with her. "When did you learn?"

"In high school." There were benefits to being the *female* offspring to a Middle Eastern king.

Sure, at first, when she'd been sent away from all that she knew, she'd felt abandoned. But as she'd grown older, she'd realized her parents' lack of interest in her daily life was to her benefit. They were very conservative and that attitude influenced their Americanized relatives they'd placed her with at the tender age of six.

However, she still had more freedom living with her relatives than she would ever have had at home. And she'd gotten her first taste of real freedom when she'd gone to boarding school in seventh grade. The exclusive, all-girls prep school was far from the typical American middle and high schools, but she'd been allowed to do things there she would never have been able to do when living with family. Things like kayaking.

"I see. I thought the kayaking trip was a three-day get-away."

"It is. Are you going?" she asked, unable to stifle the hope in her gaze as her eyes remained locked with those of the tall, dark-haired hunk.

She felt the same adrenaline rush she got when competing in a race. Man, this being attracted to a guy thing was nothing like she'd expected it to be. It was almost scarily consuming. As exciting as taking a kayak out on white water. Maybe even more so.

Hawk had to bite down on an ugly four-letter word.

The diminutive princess was just full of surprises. The first had been when he'd seen his newest charge hurrying across the quad when she was supposed to be safely ensconced in the library studying with a small group of female friends. The plan had been for him to confer with her bodyguard and then arrange to "bump into" the princess on her way out of the library later.

It was a good thing he'd seen her, or he would have been just as ignorant of her true whereabouts as her hapless guard. The man needed to take a course in security from Hawk Investigations.

"I don't kayak," he said to her, "but I'd like to learn." Which was a total lie. He had no desire to learn, but he had experienced canoeing. Even if it wasn't his favorite thing, it was close enough to the other that he was confident he would make a good showing of himself on the water.

A man did what he had to for his job. And Hawk's current assignment was sticking close to Princess Lina bin Fahd al Marwan.

Her smile was dazzling. "If we hurry, maybe we'll both still get a chance to sign up for the trip."

Options clicked through Hawk's mind. One, he could prevent her from making the meeting at all. Two, he could scuttle any chances she had of going on the trip with a single phone call. *Or* he could follow his instincts and go on the trip with her.

Her obvious attraction to him would make it easy to arrange for her to miss the meeting, but *this woman* would probably find a way to sign up for the trip regardless. Lina Marwan, as she called herself, was nothing like the shy, quiet, studious, nineteen-year-old he had been led to expect.

Did anyone in the princess's life know who she really was and how she amused herself?

The answer was no doubt in the negative, which was why he also did not want to scuttle the trip entirely.

He'd been hired as extra security during a time of increased risk for the Royal Family of Marwan. However, if his interaction had the benefit of allowing him to help her security detail enhance her overall safety—so much the better. He had to identify the ways she circumvented it in order to prevent her from doing so in the future.

Letting her make the trip while he accompanied her

to ensure her safety, would give him the opportunity to see what measures she took to avoid her security detail.

He made all these determinations in the space of seconds.

"Lead the way," he said with a smile.

She nodded, but instead of increasing her pace, she stopped, her dark brown gaze fixed on his lips.

"Lina…"

"Uh, yeah, right…go." She made a visible effort to look away. Flipping her long black ponytail over her shoulder, she started jogging toward the University Center. "The meeting was supposed to be upstairs."

His long strides matched her speed with little effort, but his body heated in reaction to the enticing bounce of her feminine curves. The attraction was definitely mutual, which should make his job that much easier. He wouldn't have to pretend an interest to stay close to her. Though his original intention had been to strike up a friendship, being just slightly more than friends would be an even better "in" to the princess's life.

However, he would only take it so far. He didn't do long-term and for so many reasons, Lina was not a candidate for a short-term affair. Not only was she the daughter of a client and herself his assignment, but she was a princess from a part of the world that placed a lot of importance on a woman's virginity. It wouldn't be fair to the princess to take their association beyond friendship and mild flirting.

Although he had a sense of honor that would not allow him to use the innocent, he was *not* above using her attraction to him.

Lina stopped in front of an athletic-looking blond man who had been coming down the steps in front of the U.C. "Hey, Bob. Did we miss the meeting?"

"Yeah, but no biggie. All we did was pass out info sheets and take names."

"Can we still sign up?" she asked enthusiastically.

The jock put his hand on Lina's shoulder and squeezed, his smile practiced and more than a little flirtatious. "Anything for you, sweetie."

Another curse fought for release from Hawk's mouth. Did she have a boyfriend her family didn't know about, too?

"Great." The diminutive princess bounced on the balls of her feet. "Sebastian's a new kayaker. I'd like him assigned with me..." She turned to look at Hawk. "I mean if you don't have an issue with a woman teaching you."

"No, I'd like that."

"Hey, Wayne could train the newbie and then you could be *my* partner," Bob suggested.

"*The newbie* would prefer to partner his new friend." It was the *only* way the princess was getting out on the water. A bodyguard could hardly do his job from the shore or another boat.

"Oh, I'm sorry. We didn't mean to talk about you like you weren't there." Lina's doelike eyes shone with genuine repentance. "I hate it when people do that to me."

He supposed, considering the strongly conservative and male centered family she came from, she'd had a lot of experience with it, too. "No problem." But the look he gave Bob told the other man not to mess with him.

From the expression on the college boy's face, he got the message, but didn't look happy about it. Again Hawk wondered if the relationship between Bob and Lina was closer than merely friends with a mutual interest in kayaking.

"Look, I'll sign you both up, but I'll need your contact details," Bob said to Hawk. "I've got Lina's. In fact, I already signed you up, babe. I was going to bring you the info sheet in World Politics."

Lina smiled at Bob, her eyes lit with gratitude and excitement. "You're the best. Thanks."

Bob slipped his backpack off his shoulder and dug out a notebook. "Here, just put your stuff in here." He didn't let go of the notebook when Hawk reached for it, though. "You are a student here, right? This trip is only open to students at the university."

Lina frowned, but her expression cleared when Sebastian said, "I'm in the MBA program across the street."

"Oh. Okay then." Bob let go of the notebook.

Hawk took it and flipped through the pages until he came to a list of names under a handwritten title, "Kayaking Trip." He pulled his pen out of his pocket and took pictures of the list of names under the guise of clicking the pen open. He added his name and cover contact information to the bottom of the list.

He would have someone at Hawk Investigations run a report on the names on the list to make sure none of them represented a threat to Lina's safety.

He wondered how she planned to dupe her bodyguard for an entire weekend, but he had no doubt, whatever her plan was, she would succeed. A princess who had managed to become an expert kayaker *while* going to the exclusive boarding school she had attended without her family's knowledge was adept at getting around their strictures for her life.

Bob looked at his watch and then at Lina. "We've got almost an hour before class. Do you want to get coffee with me at the Starbucks on State Street?"

She bit her bottom lip and looked sideways at Hawk, then nodded. "Can we get our coffee at the cafeteria, though? I need to pick something up at the library before class."

Hawk almost laughed out loud. She had to pick something up all right...her bodyguard. "You don't mind if I tag along, do you?" he asked. "I could use a cup of coffee myself."

Lina's mouth curved into another blinding smile. "No, of course not. You'll have to let me buy, though. It's the least I can do after running into you in the quad."

"You're the one that ended up on the floor. I think I should buy."

Bob shook his head. "Whoever wants to buy, let's go. I need my fix of caffeine."

"Were you up studying late again last night?" Lina asked him.

"You could call it that."

She smacked his arm lightly. "You are so bad. Who was it this time? The sexy sorority girl with a boyfriend at a different school or the gymnast?"

"I'm not seeing the gymnast anymore. Her coach told

her one more late night and lack of focus the next day and she was off the team."

So, Bob was a player. And Lina knew it. The question was, did he plan on adding Lina to his list of conquests? Not on Hawk's watch, he wouldn't. Her family had hired his agency to see to her safety and he would do so. On every front. What she and the jock-boy did when Hawk finished with the case was not his problem.

He studiously ignored the tightening in his gut that occurred at that particular thought.

The student cafeteria coffee wasn't bad. They even had an espresso machine. Not that Hawk drank specialty coffees, but both Lina and Bob did and from the hum of pleasure Lina emitted as she took her first sip, Hawk assumed it was good. He'd won the argument about him paying, but then he had expected to.

He wasn't in the habit of losing—at anything.

"Are you going to the environmental demonstration tonight?" Bob asked Lina as he leaned back in his chair, his gaze following a curvy coed cross the dining room.

"I'm not sure, but I'll try to be there."

"There's a rumor the Young Republicans are going to show up to heckle us."

"Well, if they do, they'll be heckling half their membership. Environmentalism isn't the partisan issue big politicians say it is. There are conservationists on both sides."

"If you say so."

"You know I do."

"Are you a political science student?" Hawk asked Lina, already knowing the answer, but wanting to get *her* to tell him more about herself. How much honesty was she willing to give?

"We both are," Bob answered for her. "Lina's a fence-sitter, though. She won't identify with either of our major parties."

Lina simply shrugged, but didn't mention what Hawk assumed was her real reason for not identifying with either party. She was a citizen of Marwan, not the United States.

"I'm not a Young Republican and it kills my dad." Bob's satisfied smirk said a lot about why *he* leaned to the left politically.

Lina sighed and shook her head. "I swear you go to the rallies simply out of reactionary rebellion."

"Didn't you tell me once that you decided to study politics because your dad told you not to?" Bob asked pointedly.

The princess nodded, not looking the least bit phased. "It was a little more complicated than that, but his negative reaction to my interest in the subject did spur me on. However, how I react to what I've learned in my studies is the result of personal convictions. I hold beliefs different from my family, but not because I want to get a rise out of my dad. I doubt he'd even deign to notice, but my family's political beliefs have had a strong and sometimes negative impact on my life."

"In what way?" Bob asked.

Lina merely shook her head and changed the subject. Apparently Bob was not a close enough friend to be aware of Lina's position as daughter to a desert king.

CHAPTER TWO

OVER THE NEXT WEEK, Hawk learned that, though Lina could be described as nothing less than *involved*, she had no friends that knew the truth about her. In fact, while she had many people she spent time with, she had none Hawk would classify as close friends period. At least the report about her he had received had been correct in that regard. Even if it had been wrong about so much else.

And *nothing* in the report had prepared him for the growing attraction between them. He had thought it would be something he could use to stay close to her, but discovered quickly that it was far more a detriment than a benefit in regard to doing his job.

How could he protect her when he was distracted by how her ebony hair shone in the sunlight? His fascination with her waist-length hair had been born the first time he saw her wear it down. It looked and felt like silk. And how did he know how it felt?

He couldn't stop himself from touching it. And Lina didn't seem to mind. While she shied away from a lot of physical touch from others, keeping hugs short and one-

armed with even her female acquaintances, she leaned into
Hawk's touch. Not that he had touched her...that way. But
he wanted to. Badly. His fingers actually ached to brush
against the luscious curves hidden under her clothing.

It wasn't that she wore anything overtly sexy, but it
was the way she moved, with an innate sensuality he was
certain she had no idea she possessed.

Like right now, she was sitting across from him at the
Starbucks her friend Bob had first mentioned. The way
she held her head in attention while Hawk spoke high-
lighted the delicate curve of her neck and drew his gaze
down to breasts that were molded lovingly by the cotton
of her T-shirt. He was pretty sure she wasn't wearing a
bra. Or the one she had on was so thin she might as well
not be wearing it, because for the last several minutes her
nipples had been hard. His mouth was watering for a taste
of the sweet flesh.

"Sebastian?" she asked in a soft...almost uncertain
voice.

His gaze shot from her breasts to her face and he felt
himself going red. When was the last time that happened?
He was a twenty-seven-year-old millionaire in his own
right. He'd left blushing boyhood behind too long ago to
remember it, if indeed it had ever been a phase for him.
"Yes?"

"I...uh...I wondered if you wanted...um..."

"Yes?"

She was silent for several seconds, chewing on her
bottom lip, looking too damn delectable. Then she said
all in a rush, "Maybe we could go for a walk down State
Street."

"Sure. If you've got the time." Once again, her regular bodyguard believed that she was studying. This time, at home.

When Hawk had learned Lina knew how to bypass the security and leave the apartment she shared with a chaperone next to the one that housed her security detail, he'd been ready to strangle somebody. Her bodyguards were at the top of Hawk's list. How many times had the princess left her home unprotected? Hawk had not revealed the security breach to the family retainers, though.

He was operating under the assumption that the threat to her family could be from within and he wasn't taking any risks. He would give a full report with detailed suggestions for improving security for the princess when this situation was over. He had another operative from his staff at Hawk Investigations watching Lina's building when he slept. And she was supposed to be sleeping. With the feisty princess one could never be sure.

Normally he would have the entire case assigned to his operatives, but Hawk had made his investigative agency an international contender and multimillion dollar company by knowing when it was prudent to take a personal interest in a client's needs. He'd certainly made the right call this time.

Lina moved close to him as they walked along the tree-lined street near the capitol building and, of its own volition, his arm snaked around her petite waist.

It was only natural considering his role, but it felt *too* good. Not only was she a client (even if she didn't know he was her paid protector), but Hawk didn't do affectionate gestures and warm fuzzy feelings. His liaisons with women were just that. Commitment free, exchanges of pleasure without any false protestations of emotion. He didn't even have female friends. He had no interest in getting serious with a woman. In any guise. Ever.

Every woman he had known had been devious in her own way. The woman who had given him birth had pretended maternal interest until the day she found a more lucrative benefactor than his father. She'd dumped them both and had contacted Hawk exactly twice in the intervening years. Both times she had wanted to use him. He'd let her the first time, but known enough to send her packing the second.

His grandmother was just as mercenary, though she'd stayed with Hawk's grandfather. He didn't know if the men in his family sucked at picking out women to share their lives with, or were simply unlucky. Either way, he'd managed to follow family tradition twice before establishing a firm rule about the type of relationship he was willing to have with the feminine sex.

Which was none at all. Not with the women related to him and not with the women who occasionally shared his bed.

While the things he felt around Lina were more intense and harder to control, he *had* to control them. Because she was no different than the other women in his life he should have been able to trust.

She lied to her security detail and family on a regular basis. Would she be any more trustworthy in a relationship?

He didn't think so. After all, she hadn't yet told him

the true nature of her life. They might not be in a relationship and she wasn't even a candidate for a brief liaison. But she didn't know that. As far as she knew, their flirtatious friendship could go anywhere. Yet she still maintained the deception about her life.

And that life—her existence as a princess—was one reason the depth of his desire for her was so completely unacceptable. Even if she wasn't his assignment, an affair would carry too many complications with it.

Not only was there the whole virginity thing, but Lina herself was not the type of woman to be content with a little, or even a lot, of between the sheets pleasure. She was more the type to believe in everlasting love and the whole fantasy that went along with it.

He might not trust her. He may be more cynical than other men still naïve to the ways of women, but Hawk wasn't about to be the cause of Lina's shattered fantasies. That would happen soon enough. Life would see to it.

Not even a princess was immune.

On top of all of that, Hawk had worked too hard to build his company into an international power player in the industry. He wasn't risking its reputation for a woman. No matter how enticing she was.

Flashing faster than instantaneous replay, scene after scene of her time with Sebastian rolled across the movie screen in Lina's mind.

Sebastian had offered to drive her to the kayaking excursion in his car. A Dodge Viper, the same gunmetal gray of his eyes, the powerful sports car didn't have room for anyone else. So they would spend the ninety-minute drive to the campground alone. She found her attention occupied by his profile and the way his powerful thighs bulged in his jeans, rather than the admittedly gorgeous scenery out the window.

She'd spent endless hours thinking about this man, trying to decide if he was as interested in her as she was in him.

She had no experience and no one she felt comfortable going to for advice. That left her with her own opinion based on…well nothing. Okay, there'd been the gossip from other girls in high school, but none of it seemed to apply. Sebastian wasn't pushing for sex or copping a feel every time they were in a remotely private place.

She thought it was probably because he was older, a graduate student who already had some experience in the business world.

She was pretty sure he desired her, though. The way he looked at her at times made her brain melt. And other bits as well.

She'd tried reading women's magazines, but they all touted open communication in a relationship. Did that mean she was supposed to just *ask* him?

She would rather pick up on nonverbal clues. And she was convinced there were some.

Sometimes, his eyes would gleam with something that responded to the ache deep in her womb whenever he was around. But he had never acted on it and they had been seeing each other for three weeks now. They hadn't had any dates per se, but he'd been around pretty much constantly since she'd run into him in the quad.

Since he did not seem like a big joiner, the fact that he was at meetings she'd never before seen him at or rallies she was pretty sure he had no personal interest in, she had to assume *she* was the reason he showed up. Which meant he wanted her, right?

It amazed her, really. That a man like Sebastian would be interested in Lina Marwan was pretty incredible. She was accustomed to people being drawn by her royal status, but like the rest of the students at the university, he had no way of knowing she was a princess. But he liked her…maybe…

He was everything she had dreamed of finding in a boyfriend, not that he was actually her boyfriend.

She sighed. Sebastian gave her a questioning look. She smiled a little and shrugged. Thankfully he didn't ask her what she was thinking. She might just blurt it out and embarrass herself unbearably.

He was so gorgeous; he was assertive without being domineering. He listened to her, maybe even better than her brother. He was smart and driven—his going for an MBA showed that. And he was intense in this really, super sexy way. Was it any surprise she was falling for Sebastian Hawk in a big way?

The problem was that sometimes she was convinced that all he wanted was friendship.

She was so bad at this whole male-female thing. Her lack of practical experience was becoming a real nuisance. If she had been like the other girls who attended the female-only academy she had, she would have at least had a chance when not in school to meet people of the opposite gender. To learn to *flirt* for goodness sake. Though she had to admit that even if she had the opportunity, the male dominant nature of her family had made her wary around men and she probably would have shied away from any sort of interaction.

That caution combined with the reality that in order to date it would have meant further deceptions, or the indignity of being subjected to not only a bodyguard, but a chaperone as well, had also kept her from pursuing or responding to the pursuit of any guys since she'd arrived at university. Until Sebastian.

Of course, it helped that he was willing to spend time with her doing the things she already arranged for involvement in.

Only…for this man, she would do whatever it took to see him personally. She just wished she knew *what* to do with him.

Not that lack of experience had ever stopped her from trying something that she wanted to. She was not the demure, ornamental—aka useless—piece of feminity her father believed her to be.

Sebastian was so different from the men in her family. He never dismissed her thoughts as unimportant simply because she wasn't heir to a throne or provincial position. He wasn't surprised by her intelligence and he didn't seem to think her political science major was a waste of her time. Not that he knew why she had chosen that major, but he acted like he believed she could, and most likely *would*, do something valuable with her education.

That was her hope.

She'd spent her childhood separated from her home, only to see her parents and siblings one week out of the year when she flew to Marwan and stayed in the royal palace with them. She did not remember her parents ever touching her with affection, and knew for a fact her father had never once given her any recognition as anything but his inferior female offspring.

She refused to spend her adult life feeling and *being* insignificant. She wanted to make a difference in the world and not merely as the attractive, well mannered appendage on some man's arm.

"You're pretty quiet over there," Sebastian said.

"I was thinking how different you are from the men in my family."

"Yes?"

"Yes."

"In what way?"

"You don't discount me simply because I'm female."

"Who does that?"

"My father. To some extent my uncle. Others."

"Your brother?"

She didn't remember mentioning her brother, but she must have done so. She gave one of the rare smiles that occurred when she thought of her family. "My brother is different. He has been raised to be just like my father, but he's not. You can't tell on the surface, but he does special things to let me know."

"Like what?" Sebastian's obviously genuine interest encouraged her to be more open with the truth than she would have normally.

"He spends time with me."

"Don't your parents?"

"My mother does...sort of." Though the sessions spent training Lina for her station could hardly be classified as mother-daughter bonding time.

"Not your father?" Sebastian didn't sound surprised or disapproving, simply curious.

"No. He's far too busy to spend quality time with a mere daughter." Though, according to her sister, their father made limited time available to his daughter still living in Marwan.

"That bothers you?"

"Wouldn't it you?"

He looked a little startled and then shrugged. "I suppose. But in my case it was my mother that couldn't be bothered to see me. My dad is and has always been pretty busy with his business interests, too, though."

"And that doesn't upset you?"

"Why should it? I'm busy with my own life."

"So, you don't think a family should spend time together?"

"You mean the dream of dinners together and family camping trips every summer?"

"Something like that."

"If you're born into a family like that, I'm sure it's nice. But if you aren't, you have to accept your circumstances and move forward."

"Or change them."

Again, he looked surprised by her comment.

"How would you do that?"

"Me, personally? I plan to marry someone who believes family is as important as I do or I won't marry at all. I will spend time getting to know my children, if I have any. No son *or* daughter of mine will grow up feeling expendable."

"You think you are expendable to your parents?"

"I know I am."

"Why do you say that?"

"I came to the U.S. at the age of six because my mother's older sister had been unable to conceive and it was decided that she would be given the honor of raising me. I only see my parents once a year, for a week." She never ever gave details of her life to people, but Sebastian was different. She trusted him.

"And your brother?"

She smiled again, warmth filling her at thoughts of her brother. "When I'm staying with my parents, he makes sure we eat at least one meal together each day. And we talk. He asks about my life and *listens* to my answers. He praises me for my grades and other things. He's the only person in my family who knows that I was on the kayaking team at school. He also makes sure he comes to visit me every time he is in America. My father flies to Washington, D.C., at least twice a year, but he's never once made the additional effort to come see me as well. Even when he and my brother are traveling together and Hasim makes arrangements to do so."

"I'm sure he's confident that you are well taken care of by your aunt and uncle."

"I am. I don't want to denigrate them in any way to you. My aunt is sweet, if a bit reserved, and my uncle is much more open to new ideas than my father, having been raised himself in Canada. He was a third son.

Though sometimes family attitudes still show, I was allowed to attend university only at his insistence. If it had been up to my parents, I would have gone to a finishing school in Europe." Even after her father had agreed to her university education, Lina had taken the added precaution of pursuing United States citizenship as soon as she turned eighteen.

It had taken her two years and had been the reason she'd learned to ditch her bodyguard as well as how to get out of her home undetected. She had two sets of papers. Her Marwanian papers, which she used traveling under the aegis of her country's ruling family. She also had legitimate U.S. passport and citizenship papers, which her family knew nothing about.

As a Marwanian citizen, her father had had final say over anything and everything in her life, no matter what her age. That was not true for all Marwanian women, but as a member of the ruling family, she could not legally act without her father's permission. However, as an adult U.S. Citizen, her freedoms were numerous including the right to refuse to return to Marwan if it became necessary.

"But your relationship with your parents makes you unhappy?"

"My *lack* of a relationship. Like I said, if I have children, I want a different life for them."

"I am sure you will succeed at whatever you set your mind to."

She gave him a glowing smile. She was definitely falling in love with this man. "Thank you."

* * *

When they arrived at the cabins the kayaking group was staying in, Hawk noticed only one other car there. It turned out to be Bob's. He and three more members of the group were still unloading. Hawk made sure that he was in one of the bedrooms of the cabin Lina was staying in. He noticed that Bob did, too. In fact, they were sharing the room. Which worked for Hawk. He was a fan of efficiency and this would allow him to keep an eye on both the princess and her wannabe hook-up.

Lina was sharing her room with one of the other coeds. A blonde who looked like a pinup and talked like G.I. Jane. Lina told Hawk when they were reconnoitering the lake (well he was surveying their environment, Lina was just walking) that the blonde was former military and had just started university this semester.

Hawk had known *that* from his agency's reports. What he hadn't known was that Lina's admiration for the other woman's independence and lifestyle bordered on hero-worship.

"She's been to seedy bars in more countries of the world than I've even visited."

"And you see this as a good thing?" Hawk asked.

Lina's laugh was joyous and too damned appealing to his libido. "Yes. My life has been so sheltered. A weekend like this is as about as adventurous as I've ever gotten."

"But you want more adventure?" Hawk asked with a sinking feeling. If her family didn't beef up Lina's security, she would get that adventure. She was too resourceful not to.

"Yes. I want to travel. I want to do things...help

people. See the world, but not as a member of…um…the privileged classes. As someone trying to make a difference."

"You make it sound like you want to join the Peace Corps."

"That's one of my dreams, but I doubt I'll ever realize it."

Hawk had to take a deep breath or choke on his surprise. A princess in the Peace Corps? He didn't think so. "If you can't have a dream, find a practical replacement." Like donating money to worthy causes. That was something a princess could do without causing a political incident.

Lina stopped walking and stared out over the lake, her expression thoughtful. Hawk stopped, too…but he watched his princess. Her golden skin glowing in the sunlight, her perfect features shone with a beauty that took his breath away. Of its own volition, his hand reached out and brushed her hair away from her face.

She shifted slightly so their eyes met, her velvet-brown irises drawing him in, her smile tempting him to taste her lips. Her head tilted; his dipped until their lips barely brushed. Electricity jolted through him at the contact, freezing time around them. Neither moved. They did not deepen the kiss, but nor did they move apart. Both stood in a paralysis of feeling he knew he had never experienced and suspected she had not, either.

They were only linked physically in two places—his lips barely touching hers and his hand still against her cheek—but he felt the connection in a place deep inside that he had not even known existed.

"Hey, you two." Bob's voice brought Hawk abruptly to his senses.

Yanking his hand away from her cheek, Hawk stepped away from Lina.

What the hell was he doing? He hadn't even heard Bob's approach. This was totally out of line. He would fire an operative for being so sloppy. If Bob had been a threat, Lina could be dead right now. Cold chills chased along his skin.

He was here to protect Lina, not make love to her. Or moon over her like some lovesick calf. He was not the mooning type.

Maybe he needed a vacation. One filled with discreet liaisons that would rid his mind of his...*the* princess's image.

One thing he knew with certainty. The idealistic pocket-size Venus was turning out to be a weakness he could not afford, "Hi, Bob." Lina's voice was softer than normal and her eyes were unfocused.

Hawk had to suppress a groan. This *thing* was getting totally out of hand. *It already was*, a taunting voice whispered inside his head. Bob gave them both a knowing look. "This is supposed to be a sports trip, not a romantic getaway."

Sebastian glared at Bob. As if jock-boy wouldn't take advantage if he got the chance. And he'd have a hell of a lot less scruples about it than Sebastian did.

Lina looked away, her cheeks going an adorable pink.

"Was there something you wanted, Bob?" Hawk asked. Trying to forget that the word adorable was not usually part of his vocabulary and that he had applied it to a client.

"Just thought I'd check the lake out. We'll start out on the smooth water tomorrow morning. Assess everyone's skill level, then move to the river after lunch tomorrow." He gave Hawk a significant look. "That is provided we're all ready to move to the river."

Hawk was about to assure the other man that *he* would be ready when Lina spoke up. "If Sebastian isn't comfortable enough for moving water, I'll stay on the lake with him in the afternoon."

And just like that, Hawk's plans for proving his proficiency changed. "If you're sure you won't mind," he said.

Bob frowned. "That's hardly fair to you, babe. I'm sure one of the other experienced kayakers would be willing to stay with him."

Hawk noticed Bob didn't volunteer.

Lina's features set in what was becoming a familiar look of stubbornness. "Don't be silly. I invited Sebastian to come on the trip. I promised him I would teach him and I will."

Which was exactly what she did. Hawk's previous experience canoeing made learning the balance and movement of the kayak easier, but Lina was also a good teacher and could take most of the credit for his proficiency by afternoon. He was careful to dump into the water a couple of times though to lend credence to his request to stay on the lake for the rest of the day.

They all ate lunch together in the biggest cabin. Lina was animated and grinning most of the time, praising him for his efforts and complimenting the others on their techniques. She and her roommate got into a discussion of what their most challenging kayaking course had been. And that's when he learned that Lina had come very near to drowning once, sending a sick feeling through him.

Her senior year of high school, while on a very difficult race course, another kayaker had dumped. She'd bumped her head and hadn't come up. Lina dove into the white water to save her. Both girls had come close to drowning, but Lina had managed to get them to shore.

Hawk experienced an unexpected, unfamiliar, and not to mention totally irrational fear as Lina recounted her story. That fear did not dissipate when Lina looked on with wide-eyed wonder and no small amount of interest when her G.I. Jane roommate recounted shooting the rapids on the Yangtze River. Damn...if Lina's family didn't do something soon, she was going to get herself killed in her search for adventure.

She needed a husband to watch over her.

Heaven knew her father, uncle and their hired security weren't doing a good enough job. Unreasoning black anger washed over Hawk at the thought of a protective male in Lina's life that was not him. He dismissed the image of Lina in some faceless man's arms with a vicious precision he refused to analyze.

CHAPTER THREE

HE AND Lina finished on the lake before the others returned from the river and she suggested going swimming.

"Haven't you spent enough time in the water?" Hawk asked, having to admit privately that he had enjoyed his time on the water more than he ever had in the past.

Lina shrugged, smiling. "I love water. Maybe I should have been born a dolphin."

"Oh, no. I think you make a perfect woman." Hawk had to stifle a growl. He should not have said that. Things were getting out of hand with his princess. But he couldn't deny the warmth that shot through him as her smile increased wattage. "Thank you," she said happily without a hint of a woman's usual coyness at such a compliment.

They pulled the kayaks up onto the shore, took off their slim life vests and jumped back into the water. At least he did, but when he turned to see where Lina was, she was on the beach still, peeling off the Neoprene suit she'd been wearing to kayak in. The very brief bikini she wore underneath made the air stall in Hawk's chest.

Damn. She had a luscious figure. Her breasts were a

little oversized, her waist tiny above the flare of her hips, her legs toned and smooth. And that damned scrap of cloth that passed for bikini bottoms showed way more skin than it covered and clung to the perfect curve of her backside. She kicked the wet suit aside and walked back into the water.

She stopped a few feet from him, her head cocked to one side, her doe-brown gaze questioning. "Something wrong?"

"Uh—" He had to clear his throat. "No. Nothing. You sure you don't want to wear your Neoprene to swim in? It's warm for spring, but not exactly hot out here."

"I'm fine." But she shuddered with a full body shiver, belying her words. She smiled self-deprecatingly. "Well, I'll warm up swimming, anyway."

Her body was covered in goose bumps, but it was the hard nubs of her nipples behind her scant bikini top that drew his gaze.

And held it.

He watched in inescapable fascination as the wet lycra of her swimsuit did nothing to hide how the already hardened pebbles tightened into fine points.

"Sebastian…" The husky desire mixed with confusion in her voice was a potent aphrodisiac.

She wanted him and didn't know what to do with that need. What man would not be drawn by that combination of innocence and feminine awakening?

She did not move, her body frozen there, half in the water. Her breathing increased to pants, further revealing arousal so unfamiliar to her. Her small hands fisted at her sides, her knuckles turning white.

Had any woman exhibited such intense desire for him?

Perhaps it was the result of Lina's innocence. Hawk hadn't had a virgin since high school. He had a strict policy of keeping his liaisons limited to experienced women who weren't looking for a relationship much less a lifelong commitment.

So, what the hell was he doing looking at Lina like a wolf did his prey?

He forced his gaze to lift to hers. And it was worse. The evidence of her interest in him shone brightly in her doe-brown eyes. Damn it.

Unblinking, her gaze fixed to his, she bit her bottom lip and damn if he didn't want to replace her teeth with his.

If he didn't do something soon, he was going to end up giving her her first time right here in the lake. His entire body vibrated with the need to go to her.

It took every ounce of his formidable self-control to turn and dive into the cold water. When he came up fifteen yards from the shore, she was only a few feet behind him.

Treading water, she grinned. "You aren't supposed to dunk yourself, don't you know that?"

"Oh, really?"

"Yes, really." Without further warning, she launched herself toward him.

Her hands pushed against his head and he let himself go under as his training took over and he used her momentum to get her into a hold she had no hope of getting out of. He brought them both up, breaking above the water to the trill of her laughter.

Her smile was unrepentant. "Now, that's how you're supposed to get dunked."

"You sure about that?"

"Of course. It's in the rules."

"The rules?"

"You know, the playing in the water rules?" she asked, her eyes lit with a mischievous spark.

"I don't know those rules."

"Why is that I wonder?"

"Maybe because I don't play."

"Everybody plays."

"Not me."

"Then I suppose I'll have to teach you how."

His mind immediately latched onto several images of things he would like to teach her. And not a single one of them was anywhere as innocent as playing in the water.

"You're doing it again."

"Doing what?" he asked, genuinely confused.

"Looking at me like you want to eat me."

He stared at her, for once speechless.

She laughed as she kicked out of his now lax hold. When she was several feet closer to the shore, she stopped and faced him, her chin just above the waterline. "What does that mean? The look."

"I..." He didn't know what to say to diffuse the situation. Sure as certain not the truth.

She took another couple of steps backward so the water wasn't so deep around her. Her head cocked to one side and she looked at him like a chemistry lab experiment that wasn't going the way she expected. She started chewing on that way-too-kissable, full lower lip of hers again.

Then she nodded as if making some kind of internal decision. "Look, I'm not very experienced at this sexual attraction thing. Okay?"

He nodded because it seemed like she wanted a response.

"Good. Some guys…especially ones a few years older than me, would be put off by that."

"Uh…"

"Don't worry about it. I'm glad you're not, but the problem is, I don't know what stuff means. Like that look you were giving me…" Her voice trailed off and she looked away, clearly uncomfortable with the direction of their conversation.

For which he felt profound gratitude. "Do you really want to talk about this?"

"Um…no…I just—"

"You're doing fine."

"I am?"

"Yes." That, at least, was safe to say.

"Oh, good then…I…"

He took advantage of her preoccupation and dove for her, figuring that her idea of water play had to be better than talking about the overwhelming attraction between them that should be *anything but* on his side. She expelled her air in a shocked gasp as she fell backward under his weight.

Without thought, he sealed his lips over hers, breathing his air into her lungs as they went under the water together.

He twisted his body and brought them both up again, breaking the connection of their mouths as water ran in rivulets down their faces.

She shook her head, laughing. "That was wild."

He tried to dunk her again, but this time she was ready for him and slipped out of his grasp. They played like that until she was gasping, "Uncle, uncle...I give, I give."

"I'm not your uncle, but I'm glad to hear you recognize my superior water playing skills."

"Funny, funny." She sighed and relaxed, linking her hands behind his neck. Then, she wrapped her legs around his waist. "That's better. You wore me out."

"Poor you," he choked out, trying to maintain some semblance of distance with her attached to him like a limpet.

Was he the one who had thought playing in the water was safer than talking? After fifteen minutes of her hands gliding over his body as she attempted to pull him under the water, he was hard as a rock and twice as hungry for her taste. And now, apparently she considered him her resting place. The position of her legs around his waist was way too tempting for the precarious control he had over his libido.

"It might just have a little to do with the fact that you are almost a foot taller than me."

"What?" he asked, having totally lost the train of their conversation. Hell, he was in a different depot entirely.

"The reason you won our water fight. You're bigger than me...it gives you an unfair advantage in the deeper water."

"You should have kept us in the shallow water then. It's all about strategy."

"I'll remember that." Her gaze flicked to his lips...and stayed there. Her small pink tongue darted out to lick her own lips as they parted in unconscious but unmistakable invitation.

That one small move was the final nail in the coffin of Hawk's control and he did what he'd been wanting to do since they got in the water. He leaned down and took her bottom lip between his teeth. He sucked on it gently as she made a soft, surprised sound.

That sound went through him like an electric shock and his arms locked around her, pulling her body fully against his. She fit like she'd been created to be just there.

Her eyes opened, their chocolate depths glazed with passion. She was so beautiful...so perfect in her arousal.

He gave into the silent plea in her gaze and kissed her, taking her mouth fully with lips, teeth and tongue. She whimpered, her body writhing in unconscious abandon against him. He memorized her body with his fingertips, touching every centimeter of skin he could reach.

She broke her mouth from his, wildly turning her head side to side. "Sebastian!"

"It's okay...let me touch you. You were made for my touch." He paid little attention to what he was saying, his words a natural outpouring from his desire.

However, there remained a small flicker of awareness in the back of his mind. That marginal ability for rational thought was surprised and maybe even a little worried at the possessiveness of his own words.

"Yes." She pressed into his hands, her own kneading his neck like she didn't know what to do with them.

He had just enough presence of mind not to encourage her to return the caresses.

He cupped the indent of her waist, marveling at the perfection of the curve. Even with the conservative protection of her family, it was unbelievable to him that she remained so untouched. Her natural sensuality and beauty were an irresistible aphrodisiac.

She kissed him back with unfettered passion while her body trembled with a need he was only too greedy to fulfill. However, he would not make love to her for the first time in the middle of a lake. There were many ways to satisfy the conflagration burning between them that did not require him buried in her virginal body. And if it took the last shred of his sanity, he would do those things rather than claim her body irrevocably as his.

He moved them a little closer to shore until the water lapped against his chest and then he peeled her arms from around his neck. She whimpered in protest.

"It is all right, little beauty. Trust me. I will give you what you are craving."

"Please, Sebastian." She looked at him with needy innocence.

She had no clue what she was asking for, or what he could give her. But he would show her…if nothing else, he would hold the distinction of being her first sexual teacher. He could not have more…they could not have more, but this he would have.

He flipped her around so her back was to his front and

he leaned down so his mouth was against the shell of her ear. "I am going to make you feel so good, princess."

"P-princess?" she gasped out.

He stiffened in shock at his slip, but then decided to go with it. The term princess was used by a lot of American men as an endearment. He reasoned that she was Americanized enough to know that. "You are my princess."

Damn, there went that possessiveness again. He decided to go with it too. For now.

Her head fell back onto his shoulder. "Yes, your princess."

"Put your arms around my neck again."

She nodded, but he had to help her get her hands locked in place. She was that out of it…because of him. He made no attempt to stifle the sense of pride that she gave him.

He gently bit her earlobe while one hand caressed her stomach below the water. "Perfect."

She undulated against him, her body brushing his steel hard shaft. Pleasure shuddered through him despite the layers between them. He had never reacted so strongly to such a limited touch, but he had no such plans to restrict his own contact.

He undid the lower strap on her bikini top with his unoccupied hand, running his fingertips along where the strap had touched her. She shivered and made an inarticulate sound.

"Like that?" he asked in a whisper right against her ear, knowing his breath would send further shivers through her.

"Oh, yes." She paused, panting. "You're not…" Her voice trailed off as he traced the bumps of her spine. "It's…it feels…I…"

"Good?"

"Yes, good…so…"

He caressed the nerve-rich center in the small of her back and her whole body convulsed.

"Oh, Sebastian! How are you…what…"

He chuckled at her incoherence.

"Not funny." Her voice was low and filled with want. "Amazing."

He smiled and kissed along her neck, tasting her sweet skin. "Surprised your body is so sensitive?"

"Yes." Her fingers dug into his neck. "I didn't know it could feel like this from you touching only my back."

"Is my princess's front feeling neglected?" he teased.

"I…" But she didn't say whatever she'd planned, merely turned her head from side to side on his shoulder as he squeezed and caressed her backside.

"Ah, Lina. You are so responsive. I want to touch you all over."

"O-okay."

Unwilling to deprive himself of the pleasure, he leaned his head forward so he could see down the front of her. Then using both hands, he peeled her wet swimsuit away from the generous curve of her breasts. Drawn into tight nubs, her dusky nipples came into view. He cupped both mouthwatering mounds, allowing his thumbs to brush over the distended nipples.

She gasped and turned her face into his neck, her body

going rigid and then languid, but her grip on his nape did not falter.

He gently pinched her nipples and *she bit him*. It was so primal and unexpected that he felt himself harden in his swim trunks, aching to be out of confinement. His teeth gritted against his own desire, he continued his manipulation of her breasts and luscious nipples. He wanted to taste them so badly, but he knew if he turned her to face him, he would lose what was left of his restraint.

He knew Lina would do nothing to stop him if he stripped her and took her right here in the water. She was mindless with her pleasure and all the new sensations her body was experiencing. He was not in the habit of being the voice of reason for two people. For that matter, he was usually only too happy to take what was on offer.

But Lina wasn't like his other women. Not only was she a virgin, but she was a client. She would think sex meant happily ever after, but he didn't do permanent. Damn it, even if he was stupid enough to be tempted, she was a princess. Her father would never allow her to be with Hawk. Not short-term and not long-term. For all the independence she thought she had gained for herself at university, her father's word was law in Lina's life. Hawk could not keep her and trying would only lead to pain. Despite knowing this, he knew his control was more precarious than it had ever been.

His right hand slipped downward, traveling in ever moving circles until his fingertips brushed the top of her bikini bottoms. He ran his index finger along her skin just inside the waistband.

She went still, her breaths ceasing.

He stopped when he was just above her never before touched mound. Then, *oh so slowly*, he allowed his hand to go beneath concealing fabric until he cupped her between her legs.

Her thighs tightened convulsively, trapping his hand where it was. "You...I...what..." Her words came out broken and breathless.

"Shh...let me touch you, Lina. It's what we both want."

"I..."

"You want me to make you feel good."

"Yes."

"Relax your legs for me, princess. Let me in."

"In?" she asked, her voice laced with sultry confusion.

"In," he commanded. He moved his fingers just enough for her to taste the pleasure to come.

"Yes...." she hissed, her legs relaxing.

He carefully pressed his middle finger against her pleasure center, rubbing just the tiniest bit against the already swollen knot of nerve endings at the top of her labia.

She cried out against his neck, her lower body bowing toward his touch.

"That's right," he praised as he drew tiny circles on her sensitized clitoris before delving below to allow one fingertip to touch just inside her, she was warm and very wet.

Her lips and teeth were working on his neck again as animalistic little sounds came from her throat.

She was so close...and he had every intention of taking her over.

Using the heel of his hand, he stimulated her pleasure button while he caressed her silky wet lips with his fingers. Increasing the pressure on her nipple, he pressed his lower body against her and felt his own pleasure rise to irretrievable levels.

They climaxed together, her scream mixing with his primal yell in a sound that satisfied a place deep in his soul he had never even known was there.

She went limp against him, her hands falling from his neck. Only his hands kept her from slipping into the water. He felt a warm wetness on his neck that was not from the lake and her breath hitched in an unmistakable tell.

"Are you crying, my princess?" he asked.

"A little."

"Why?" Had she not been ready for this introduction to sexual pleasure?

"That was so amazing. I've never felt this close to anyone in my life. It's so good it almost hurts."

Her words acted like a falling ice glacier to his senses. Those were definitely the words of a woman looking for more than physical satiation from a man. She wanted to go into emotional waters neither one of them could navigate.

Damn it all to hell and back again.

"Hey, guys, having fun?"

Bob's voice came as an almost welcome interruption. If he could discount the fact that yet again Hawk's here-to-fore infallible reputation was at risk of being destroyed. No matter how amazing it had been.

Lina's body went rigid and he realized how exposed she

must feel. He was grateful they were facing away from shore for her sake, but felt like a complete idiot in regard to his charge to protect her. In every way, he had failed. Doing the only thing he could to mitigate the damage, he gently dropped her into the water and covered her fumbling with her top by turning to face Bob. "How was the river?"

"Awesome. You two will have to try it tomorrow... unless you're still too nervous to go on moving water."

Hawk ignored the taunt. He had bigger things to worry about than that jock-boy's slur to his pride. Like the fact that Bob had made it to the lake without Hawk even noticing he was in the vicinity. Again.

What he had just done with Lina was stupid from every side. He had not built up his agency to top international status by making mistakes like this. Or any mistakes for that matter. He'd proven time and again that he was every bit the businessman that his father was without the other man's weakness when it came to women. His mother wasn't the only woman to manage a better payout than most stockholders from his father's companies. The senior Hawk had once told his son he could afford bad judgment when it came to his feminine company.

Only Hawk had always wondered how the older man's pride could stand it. He knew the two times he'd almost been taken for a ride had been enough for him and since then he'd had a perfect record.

That wasn't going to change now.

Not for Lina.

Not for anyone.

So, he'd better get his damn libido under control.

* * *

Lina played with the food on her plate, trying not to stare at Sebastian and mostly failing miserably. How could he sit there so calmly, chatting with the others after what had happened that afternoon?

Looking at him, you would never know that he'd given her the most intense and mind altering experience of her life.

Which was best. Right?

If he acted all possessive and physically affectionate, she would probably run for the hills. Emotional intimacy was not something she was used to, not to mention the physical closeness.

The truth was, the way she'd responded to Sebastian's touch scared the life out of her. Even right now, just being in the same room with him was making it hard to breathe normally, much less focus on the conversation going on around her.

He didn't seem to have any such problems.

What did that mean?

Suddenly their eyes met and the look he gave her made her toes curl. Okay, so he was just better at masking his feelings. Which, considering the experience she had in that regard, said a lot for his self-discipline.

Which was just another thing to love about him. Um…admire. She meant admire, right? She didn't love him. Not yet. She might be falling, but she wasn't past the point of no return, was she? Oh, gosh…*was she*? Love was a truly scary emotion. When you loved people, they had the power to hurt you. Hadn't she learned that with her own family?

Echoes of the pain she'd felt when she finally realized

her parents would not be coming to take her home still lingered in the deep recesses of her heart. She'd idolized her father, the king. So handsome, so powerful, so revered by everyone in Marwan. She'd adored her beautiful, always composed mother. At the age of six, she had not yet realized that her feelings of affection were not returned.

She'd missed them so much when she'd first come to America. She'd cried herself to sleep every night, though never in front of anyone else. She'd already learned that much control by the tender age. She'd longed for her big brother and younger sister. Lina's heart had cracked more and more each day she remained in her aunt and uncle's home without her parents requesting her return until it had finally shattered on the day she'd accepted that the family that she loved did not love or need her. She'd been careful not to open her heart completely to anyone since.

Not to her aunt, who treated Lina like a gift she had never expected to have. Not to her uncle who treated her better than her father ever had. Oh, she was affectionate to them, even loved them…but not as deeply as that innocent six-year-old had loved her parents.

Out of self-preservation, she'd never let herself feel that deeply again.

Until now.

CHAPTER FOUR

LINA surged up from the table, picking up her far-from-empty plate.

"What's up, Lina-girl?" Bob asked.

"I…uh…I'm not hungry. I think I'll go for a walk."

Sebastian stood. "I'll go with you."

"No!" She took a deep breath. "I mean, finish your dinner. I feel like my own company right now." She forced a smile to mitigate the rejection.

Sebastian frowned. "It's not safe to walk in the forest alone."

Lina's roommate, Jennifer, stood. "I'm finished eating and could use a walk myself."

"Okay," Lina said quickly. In her current state, the other woman's company was definitely preferable to Sebastian's.

And from the determined glint in his eyes, Lina had a feeling she wasn't getting out of the cabin alone. She'd spent her life coming to know what battles to fight and which ones to give in gracefully on. This situation called for partial surrender. Frankly she just wanted out of the cabin and his presence. Like now. Right this minute. Having the quiet former soldier along would not be a hardship, even if Lina *preferred* to be alone.

How many times in her almost twenty years had she been forced to choose the lesser of two evils?

Sebastian nodded his approval, like it was necessary. So, maybe not *so* different from the men in her family.

Lina immediately felt guilty for the thought. Sebastian did not treat her like a puppet without a brain.

"So, you and Sebastian a couple, or something?" Jennifer asked in her blunt manner as they stepped off the cabin's porch and headed toward the woods.

"Uh…something. I think."

"That doesn't sound like you're all that sure."

"I'm not. I'm, uh, pretty inexperienced with guys and relationships, I guess."

"Seriously? Because you could be a model or some-thing with your exotic looks."

"Look who's talking."

Jennifer snorted. "Yeah. Plenty of guys in the military mistook me for a dumb blonde and lived to regret it."

"Tell me about it." Except the living to regret it part, though she was pretty sure that when it came to her, the king of Marwan would have a rude awakening one day.

"I bet." Jennifer looked up at the star-laden sky. "It's gorgeous out here."

"Yes, it is."

Jennifer started to go toward the lake and Lina said, "Let's go this way."

The other woman gave her a measured look in the

moonlight, but obediently took a path that went in the opposite direction to the lake.

"So, does Sebastian treat you like that?"

"Like I don't have a brain in my head?"

"Yeah."

"No. In fact, he's one of the few men in my life who really listens to me and takes my opinions and thoughts seriously."

"Sounds like a good guy."

"He is."

"But you aren't sure about him?"

"Like I said, I'm pretty uneducated when it comes to the man-woman thing."

"Do you want to talk about it?"

Lina considered how odd it was that she would be having this discussion with the tough ex-soldier, but then shrugged. She'd take what she could get in the way of a friendly ear. "Love scares me," she said, surprising herself with her candor.

"You'd be pretty dumb if it didn't, in my opinion."

"People you love can hurt you."

"Even when they don't mean to." Jennifer sounded like she knew what she was talking about.

Lina sighed in agreement.

"The thing is, they can also bring more joy into your life than anyone or anything else."

Lina hadn't had a lot of experience with that. Even her beloved brother was a source of both pain and joy in her life. She missed him so much sometimes. "Really?"

"Yeah." Again that tone that said Jennifer had enough personal experience to back up what she said.

"What if he doesn't love me?"

"Sebastian?"

"Who else?"

Jennifer laughed. "Right. Falling in love is a risk, but it's one I'm not sure you can avoid. Even when you want to."

"You don't think we can control our emotions?" Lina's mother would disagree. Vehemently.

"Not when it comes to true love. If you're falling in love, the only chance you have of derailing your feelings is to not see him. And even that doesn't always work."

"I don't want to stop seeing him."

"Then I think you're screwed."

Lina was startled into a laugh. "Not yet."

"Oh? He's not pushing you too fast? That's a good sign," Jennifer said, proving she knew exactly what Lina had been thinking.

Both women burst into laughter. "I can't believe I said that," Lina gasped.

"I can." Jennifer went serious. "So, you're nervous about your feelings for Sebastian?"

"Terrified, more like."

"What scares you the most?"

"That he doesn't love me, too."

"So, you *do* love him?"

Lina bit her lip and watched the beam of her flashlight play along the forest floor. Then, she took a deep breath and nodded as she let it out. "Yes."

"I figured. You watch him the way I watch my fiancé."

"You're engaged?"

"Yes. To a national from my last posting. He's applied for a student visa and should be here with me next year."

"I bet you miss him."

"Like a lost limb. Yes."

"How did you know you were in love?"

"I couldn't imagine my life without him in it. At least not without a lot of pain."

That sounded familiar. "How did you know he loved you?"

"He told me. I mean, he showed it, too, but I'm a pretty literal person. I didn't read the signs until he admitted it out loud."

"What were the signs you didn't recognize at first?"

"The way he put my needs first."

Sebastian had certainly done that. Her experience with him that afternoon had been the most intense emotional moment of her life. The way he'd touched her had been so perfect, so unselfish.

She might lack practical experience in the relationship area, but even she knew that the way Sebastian Hawk had put her pleasure first with no thought to his own was not common.

"What else?" she asked.

"Even though I was a highly trained, not to mention tough, soldier, he was really protective toward me. He worried about me."

"Like making sure you didn't walk alone in the woods at night?" And that wasn't the only example of Sebastian's protectiveness toward her. Not by far. He seemed to have a real thing for her personal safety, always lecturing her on going out alone, walking places she should drive (in his opinion anyway).

Jennifer smiled. "Yes."

"Hmm…"

"There's the sex thing, too."

Lina stumbled at her new friend's continued bluntness. "Uh, yes, there *is* that."

"So, was it good?"

"We didn't have sex," Lina said, louder than she'd intended.

"But something *did* happen?"

"Yes."

"And?"

"It was indescribable."

"Good. Sexual compatibility is a big component to a strong relationship."

"I think maybe we're too compatible." Lina had behaved in a way she had never expected of herself. Her depth of feeling that afternoon scared her as much as the prospect of being in love with Sebastian.

"Trust me, there is no such thing as too compatible. If he makes you feel like fireworks are tame by comparison, you're a lucky woman."

"But how can I know if he felt the same?"

"Was he out of control?"

She thought of the fact that Sebastian had touched her in a semipublic place, something she was sure he would not normally do, and nodded. "To a certain extent."

"But he maintained enough control to be what you needed?"

"And then some." Lina was glad for the darkness

because her cheeks were burning. "You think that means he loves me?"

"Could. You sound like you have a hard time believing it."

"I am."

"Why?"

"I, um…I'm used to being seen as who I am in reference to my family. The thought of him loving me for who I am…just plain Lina Marwan…" Not a princess from a super wealthy royal family. "It's just way outside of my usual frame of reference."

"So, you're from some really rich family, or something?"

"Yes."

"You do a good job of coming off just like any other coed."

"Thanks."

Jennifer laughed. "I guess you work at it."

"Definitely." The other woman could have no idea how difficult that feat was, either. Ditching her bodyguards was nothing compared to keeping them in the background so that no one knew she had them trailing after her all of the time.

Deep in thought, Lina followed Jennifer back to the cabin. What would happen if she told Sebastian she loved him? Was that something she was supposed to do? Or was she supposed to wait for him to declare himself? She should have listened more closely when the other girls at school talked about their adolescent relationships. At least she'd have some frame of reference.

What if Sebastian *did* love her? What did that mean

for Lina and the rest of her life? She knew her parents had every intention of choosing her husband and arranging the marriage. She doubted they would even consider her opinion before negotiating the prenuptial contract on her behalf. She would be lucky to meet her future husband before the engagement was announced.

So, what would her parents do when they discovered she'd chosen her own future mate? Oh gosh. She was getting way ahead of herself. Just because Sebastian liked kissing and touching her didn't mean he saw a future together. That much she did know from listening to the other girls in school.

Sexual attraction did not equate to love. It was a lot easier to tell her brain that than to get her heart to accept it.

Regardless, the very fact that she wanted to date him was going to send her family into a tizzy. Considering the depth of her feelings for him, she didn't know how long she could keep this secret. She had more impetus to do so than ever before, but she also craved his company more than she could get away with in her current schedule of ditching her bodyguards.

Why did life have to be so complicated? She was a princess, but far from making her life easier, that status only made it almost impossible to follow her own dreams. It wasn't fair, but then she'd learned long ago that life rarely was.

Over the next few days, Sebastian showed just how in tune with her state of mind he was and how much he respected her feelings. He'd been treating her with a careful distance that helped her deal with her confused emotions and the lingering mortification she felt from almost getting caught in a hugely compromising position.

As much as she liked it, she wasn't comfortable with the overwhelming nature of her burgeoning sexuality. Remembering how wantonly she had responded to Sebastian's touch was only mitigated by her memory of the praise he'd given her for that response. The fact Bob had only missed seeing her half naked body because of Sebastian's quick action left a feeling of shame she could not quite rid herself of.

Her mother would be furious if she knew. Heck, even her more tolerant aunt would be horrifically disappointed in Lina's lack of control.

She'd talked about it to Jennifer; the woman had become a good friend in a very short time. The ex-soldier told Lina she was repressed. Lina had to agree, but she didn't know how to change that. She'd spent her entire life having it drilled into her that she had to maintain control of her emotions at all cost. Amidst the miasma of feelings besetting her, one thing had become clear to Lina: the only way to completely control her reaction to Sebastian was to stay away from him. And she wasn't willing to do that.

So, against her lifelong training, she was determined to ignore the niggles of guilt and shame that did not want to let her go. She might not be able to help the fact that she was every bit as repressed as Jennifer accused her of being, but she did not have to give into that aspect of her nature any more than she had to accept her father's view of her identity and value in life.

Part of her wished that Sebastian would push the

physical intimacy, but he had been careful not to pressure her sexually. And she had to admire him for that. She really did. It would just be easier if he made the first move. Only she got the feeling he was waiting for her to decide what she wanted and then to tell him.

Despite the distance he'd maintained since the afternoon on the lake, she did not feel rejected. If anything, he spent more time with her and was attentive to her in every way, even as he kept his physical distance.

Lina had always prided herself on not being a coward. She'd taken risks over and over again to try new things, to experience life beyond the box others tried to build around her because of her status as a princess. Sebastian and the way she felt about him was definitely worth taking another risk.

She would have to make the first move and no matter how much her repressed nature cringed at that idea, she would not be cowed by personal hang-ups.

The river rushed toward Lina, growing from a ribbon in the distance to a sparkling expanse, as details from the last time she'd seen Sebastian came into focus.

Lina had arranged to meet Sebastian at Jennifer's apartment. She would have liked to use her own, but living with a traditional chaperone chosen by her aunt made that impossible. She was not yet ready for her family to know about Sebastian and had no intention of ever divulging the level of intimacy she hoped to attain with him on this "date."

She'd managed to get approval for spending the night

with Jennifer after her security staff ran a background check on Lina's newfound friend. She'd been shocked they agreed to leave her at the apartment without a security detail watching, but was grateful.

Jennifer, being a true friend, had made plans to be gone for the evening. Lina was free to follow through on her determination to make the next move in her relationship with Sebastian.

She had spent more time stressing over what to wear than she had planning and cooking their traditional Middle Eastern dinner. She'd given up on her current wardrobe in despair and invited Jennifer to go shopping with her.

Since the other woman knew at least some measure of truth about Lina's background, they were even able to do the shopping trip under the auspices of Lina's security team. She'd never gone shopping with a girlfriend before and found that the tough ex-soldier was in no way immune to the delights of the mall. They had spent hours trying on clothes, visiting cosmetic counters and shopping for just the right accessories.

Lina's outfit was definitely sexier than anything she had ever worn before, but it was not skanky. Or so Jennifer assured her. The thin, scoop necked silk sweater by Jones New York clung to her generous curves, as did the low-rise medium wash jeans she'd bought to go with it. She'd taken her shoes off and her bare toes peeked out from the flared hems. A belt of dark leather medallions attached with copper colored grommets rode her hips over the camel colored sweater.

Both Jennifer and the sales associate had assured Lina it was a casual, but sexy look.

The clothes were also comfortable, which was just as well since she was practically crawling out of her skin with nerves from what she planned to do.

CHAPTER FIVE

SEBASTIAN arrived only a minute, or so, after Jennifer had left. Thank goodness. Lina's stress level would never have stood up to a long wait. His knock was firm and confident. Like the man.

Lina opened the door with a smile that only felt slightly forced. "Hello, Sebastian."

He didn't smile, but she was used to that. She'd learned he did so rarely, but since she'd noticed that his smile seemed to be reserved pretty much exclusively for her, she didn't mind at all. His expression was anything but cold, though. His look practically singed her.

So, the shopping trip had been worth it.

"Hey." He looked around the small apartment. "Where's Jennifer?"

"She's not here."

"I thought we were having dinner."

"We are."

His eyes narrowed. "But not *with* Jennifer?"

"Um, no. I thought we could use some time alone."

Something flickered in his gunmetal gaze. "That's not necessary, Lina."

She bit her lip, took a deep breath and firmed her resolve. "I think it is."

He sniffed the air. "Something smells good. What are we having?"

She allowed the subject change. "I've prepared B'stellela, traditional Middle Eastern salad, apricot chicken, vegetable cous cous, braized beef kabobs and fresh mango for dessert."

"Wow. Sounds delicious. I didn't know you were such a gourmet cook."

She relaxed a little at his praise. It was only as she'd been reciting the menu that she realized he might think she'd gone overboard on it. "I'm not, but I enjoy preparing food for the people I care about."

She'd never cooked for her parents, though. Only her aunt and uncle and her brother when he came to visit. She'd even made B'stellela for her sister on occasion when she'd been in Marwan. But getting time in the palace kitchens was trickier than managing time without her bodyguards.

Sebastian's visage turned even warier and it was at that point she realized that had been his mien since arriving in the apartment. What did he have to be concerned about? Had she misread his interest in her? Hard to misread a man touching her more intimately than she'd ever been touched before, she thought. No, something else had to be making him react this way.

Or she could be misreading him completely.

Deciding they could both use a break from the tension, even if it was all in her head, she said, "Would you like something to drink before we eat?"

He made a visible effort to relax his shoulders. "Sure."

So, not in her head.

She nodded and went to pour him a glass of Absolut she'd gotten Jennifer to buy for her. "Why don't you sit down and relax with this while I put the food on the table?"

"All right." He looked down at the oversize pillows she'd set up in front of the coffee table. "Here?"

"Yes."

"So, we're going all out authentic with tonight's dinner?"

"Yes, I hope you don't mind."

"Not at all."

She hoped he still felt that way when she informed him they would be eating with their fingers just like such a meal would be consumed in Marwan.

He took a sip of his vodka and his eyes widened. "It's very strong."

"Yes. My uncle says this makes other vodkas seem like drinking water."

"You are not drinking any?" Sebastian asked with obvious displeasure at the thought of her doing so.

"Of course not." She wasn't fond of the taste of alcohol and she'd been raised to believe that setting a good example for others was of paramount importance, even for an incognito princess.

Drinking alcohol when she was not of age would certainly be considered a poor example to set.

"Good."

"Thank you, Officer Do-Right."

He had the grace to look chagrined. "I'm sorry. I did not mean to sound like your father."

"My father would assume I would never consider drinking a man's beverage, but my brother would question me."

A faint smile creased Sebastian's features. "Then I apologize for sounding like your brother."

"Do not worry, Sebastian. I do not in any way think of you like my brother." She did not wait to see his response to that bit of honesty, but beat a hasty retreat to the kitchen.

He was putting his glass down after taking what looked like a hefty drink when she returned with the B'stellela. She set the pastry covered in powdered sugar and stuffed with egg, lamb and cooked vegetables down on the low table before lowering herself to the cushion beside him. Then she lifted the silver water pot over the bowl for finger washing.

He must have been to the Middle East at some point or at least dined at an authentic restaurant because he put his hands out for her to run the water over without hesitation. He then returned the favor for her and they both dried their hands on the tea towels she'd placed at either side of the silver bowl.

She pinched off a piece of the stuffed pastry and lifted it to his lips. "Taste."

Something dark moved in his eyes and he opened his lips for her to feed him. His tongue brushed her fingers as he took the bite.

Sharp tingles of electric charge arced up her arm and she gasped, her gaze locked with his.

"It's very good."

"Thank you."

She fed him another bite. He looked like he was going to refuse it, but at the last second his mouth opened again. Once more she felt the velvet tip of his tongue. Oh, man. No wonder Jennifer had recommended feeding each other. It was incredibly erotic.

"I can feed myself," he said when he finished chewing.

"But I like feeding you." She really did. She'd never done anything like this before and she liked it as much as the other new things she had experienced with him. It was all so wonderfully intimate. It made her feel close to him...like she belonged with him.

He seemed to have an internal battle and then he took another sip of his drink. He put the glass down again and took a pinch of the phyllo pastry. "You will have to allow me to return the favor."

She nodded, her mouth suddenly too dry for speech.

He presented the bite to her lips and she took it, tasting the spicy saltiness of his fingers as a subtle flavor under that of the sweet-savory pastry. She sucked his fingertips as he slowly withdrew them from her mouth.

He groaned. "You don't know what you are doing to me, Lina."

"I hope I do," she whispered.

He looked pained, but took another bit of pastry to feed her. She did the same and they fed each other simultaneously.

"I shouldn't be doing this," he said in an agonized voice after the third such synchronous bite.

"It's all right, Sebastian." She brushed his lower lip with her forefinger. "This is right."

He shook his head, but just swallowed rather than saying anything.

"Would you like some more vodka?" she asked softly.

"No. I definitely should not drink any more of that witch's brew."

She giggled. "Oh, my uncle would be so offended at that description."

"Are you going to tell him?"

"No."

"I've never met your family." He said it casually, but for Lina it was anything but an indifferent topic.

"Do you want to meet them?"

"I just think it is interesting that I have never met anyone from your family as much time as we spend together. For me, there's just my dad and he lives on the East Coast. But you've mentioned your brother, sister, parents and your aunt and uncle."

"None of them live near the university."

"You live alone then?"

"Uh, no...I've got a roommate." That was one description for her chaperone. "She's terribly nosy. That's why we're having dinner here rather than in my apartment."

"I see."

She doubted it. Few people had to tolerate the level of intrusion into the privacy of their life as royalty, but that was the cost of being who she was. Or so she'd been told over and over again since birth. She shook off the thought and smiled. "Are you ready for the salad?"

"Salad is good."

She took the remaining pastry away and returned with the salad and a small bowl of bread pieces. They fed each other again, but the traditional salad was messy and they ended up laughing more than anything else. She served the three elements of the main dish together on a single oblong platter with the two meats on each side and the cous cous in the center.

The apricot chicken was sweet and tangy, and for the first time in the hundreds of times she'd eaten it, it had a strangely aphrodisiaclike quality. Or something did because this time when bits of the sauce dribbled onto his chin, all she wanted to do was lick them off...not laugh. Not even sort of.

It seemed to affect him the same way because he actually leaned toward her before groaning and wiping at something at the corner of her mouth with his thumb.

"This is my favorite meal, but I have never enjoyed eating it as much as right now," she admitted in a voice laced with awe she made no attempt to stifle.

She didn't mind him knowing he had such a profound impact on her.

His eyes devoured her with such intensity that her body shook. His jaw tightened, but he said nothing.

"It's the company," she dared to say, leaning just slightly forward.

A strangled sound came from his throat and he jumped up. "I need to..." His voice trailed off as he headed to the bathroom.

Deflated, Lina slumped on her seating cushion. Maybe she'd been wrong. Maybe Sebastian *didn't* want her. At least not anymore. Had her reaction in the lake disgusted him, but he'd been too polite to say so? Only it seemed that he had been trying very hard to get exactly the response she had given him.

Bits of lectures from both her mother and her aunt rang in Lina's ears, condemning her embracing her newfound sensuality. She looked down at her clothes and noticed that in her current sitting position the shadowed valley between her breasts was on display. Feeling the disappointed gaze of both her mother and her aunt even though the women were miles—and in the case of her mother an ocean—away, she yanked the top up, covering the cleavage.

Then she stumbled to her feet, her limbs still suffering the effects of arousal. Quickly clearing the low table of food, she silently berated herself for foolishly believing she and Sebastian had something special.

Something he wanted to keep and explore as much as she did.

He came out of the bathroom as she put dessert on the table, this time with forks to eat it with. She wasn't risking making an idiot of herself again. She'd poured two glasses of sweetened mint tea as well and placed them beside the dessert bowls as Sebastian sat down.

Instead of taking her place beside him, she took a position on the sofa across the coffee table from him.

His brows rose in question, but she ignored the silent communication. If he wasn't going to verbalize the question, she wasn't going to embarrass herself by answering it.

"Are you all right, Lina?"

"Fine." She took a bite of mango that tasted like sawdust in her mouth.

"Why are you sitting up there?"

Oh, now that was just mean. Like he didn't know. She frowned at him. "I felt like it."

His expression was pained. "I see."

"I'm sure you do." She looked down at her dessert and asked, "Would you prefer coffee to the mint tea?"

"I would prefer you were sitting beside me again."

"Right."

"Damn it, Lina."

Her head came up and she glared into his eyes. "What? I got the message, all right? I can't help it if I need the physical distance. Pointing it out is hardly tactful and it would be a kindness if you would simply drop the subject right now. It won't happen again, I assure you."

"What won't happen?" He looked genuinely confused and not a little frustrated himself. "Nothing *has* happened."

Her attempted seduction was nothing? That was an even more demoralizing thought than what her family would think of her behavior. "Right. *Nothing important* has occurred here tonight."

He said an ugly word and she flinched.

"I apologize," he muttered.

They ate in silence, neither one finishing their fruit before pushing the bowls away. She took the cue and got up to clear the table, forgoing the final ceremonial hand washing after dinner. He'd obviously done so when he was in the bathroom and she'd washed her hands in the kitchen sink when she was clearing the main course.

Since they'd used forks, they didn't need to do so again and she wanted to avoid any semblance of additional intimacy.

So many thoughts and feelings were rushing through her that she couldn't make sense of any of them. She didn't know if his hasty retreat to the bathroom was an all-out rejection, or not.

Sebastian stood and helped her carry dishes and cutlery into the kitchen. She filled the sink with water and soap to wash the dishes. She'd planned to do it later, but now she needed something to keep her hands occupied.

He joined her at the sink and began rinsing the dishes as she placed them in the second sink, then drying them.

"You don't need to help. This will only take me a minute." She'd washed all the cooking utensils before he arrived.

"I don't mind."

She stifled a sound of annoyance. She needed a break from his presence, but he seemed singularly obtuse to that fact.

"These are beautiful dishes," he said. "Are they yours?"

"Yes." They were from the traditional set of china her aunt had given her when she moved into the apartment with her chaperone.

"Are they family heirlooms?"

"Not heirlooms, I don't think, but they're from my family's home country."

"Where is that?"

"Marwan."

"Like your last name."

"Yes."

"That's pretty interesting."

"I guess." She wasn't telling him all her secrets, especially tonight of all nights.

"Is it a common name in your country?"

"Not too common, no."

"Does that mean you are someone special in your country?"

"*My* country is the United States, but if you mean Marwan…no, I'm really no one special there." Not special enough to keep around, not important enough to have a voice in her family or anything else.

"You sound angry."

"No." Sad and disappointed by that reality, but not angry. Not anymore.

His hands on her shoulders, he turned her to face him. "Look at me."

She shook her head, her gaze firmly fixed on his chest. Which was not conducive to her peace of mind, but it was better than meeting his eyes.

He tipped her chin up. "Lina."

"What?"

"Tell me what is bothering you."

"Please, Sebastian, drop it."

His thumb brushed over her lips. "I can't." And he sounded really bothered by that fact.

She bit back a whimper at his touch. "I know that you don't want me. And that's okay. Really. I just. I feel stupid."

"Stupid? Oh not stupid, princess. Never that. If anything, you are too intelligent."

Not believing the compliment for a minute, she shrugged. As she did so, she realized that somehow he'd moved even closer because her breasts brushed against his upper abs. Her nipples tightened against the silk sweater. If he looked down, he could not miss the evidence of her weakness. She prayed he did not look down.

"Why do you think I don't want you?"

"I can't believe you are asking me that. Do we have to talk about this, Sebastian? You may not have feelings for me, but I thought we were at least friends. Why would you want to humiliate me?" she asked, unable to keep the tears fighting to break free out of her voice.

His hand on her shoulder tightened. "The last thing I want to do is humiliate you."

"Then maybe you should go in the other room." She swallowed. "Before I humiliate myself."

"You want me."

"You can't doubt that after the afternoon at the lake."

"I could say the same."

"I'm not the one who jumped up and ran to the bathroom when we almost kissed…and it's not as if you've done anything since the kayaking trip. I thought at first you were giving me space, letting me come to terms with my feelings, but now I realize you simply didn't want anything more from me…that way, I mean." Tears she'd been battling since before dessert broke free and trickled down her cheeks.

He closed his eyes. "Don't cry, princess."

"I'm not." She didn't even blush at the blatant lie.

His eyes opened and met hers. "You really don't think I want you?"

She sniffed, blinking away the moisture from her eyes. "It's obvious. Can we stop talking about this now?"

"Yes, we can stop talking now." Then with a groan that sounded like a dam breaking, his mouth smashed down on hers, his lips taking possession of hers with passion that felt both angry and desperate, but most of all... genuine.

He broke the kiss and rested his forehead against hers, his breath coming in gasps as ragged as her own. "I don't want to hurt you, sweetheart."

"Wanting me hurts me?" she asked in confusion.

"There are reasons this thing between us can't go anywhere."

"What reasons?" Then not even waiting for an answer, she said, "No, I don't believe you. That's a copout. I've been told all my life there are reasons I can't pursue my dreams, but I fought then and I'm willing to fight now. To fight for us."

"You can't always fight."

"I don't believe that...unless...are you married?"

He barked out a harsh laugh. "No."

"Engaged?"

"No."

"Seriously involved, or committed to someone else?"

"No."

"Then whatever you think this insurmountable obstacle is, we can overcome it."

"You don't understand."

"So, make me understand. After." With that she kissed him, not willing to listen to him tell her why they shouldn't want each other. It was enough that they did.

He was perfect for her and she would convince him that she was just right for him.

If she'd thought his initial kiss was volatile, it was nothing compared to his response now. He literally lifted her off her feet, pressing her body tightly against his as his mouth ate at hers in a devouring so hot, her lips felt like they were on fire.

He was moving, but she couldn't make herself care where they were going. When her back hit the wall, she merely tightened her hold on his shoulders. Her legs spread of their own volition, making room for him in an invitation she'd never offered before but which felt wholly natural. He was quick to accept, maneuvering her so that his steel-hard erection pressed directly against the apex of her thighs. Sparks of pleasure shot through her and she moaned.

"You're killing me," he growled against her ear before nipping at the tender lobe and then laving it with his tongue.

She couldn't get her mouth to form words, so she let her body answer for her, undulating against him as much as she could considering her position between his big, hard body and the equally unforgiving wall.

He licked along her neck, sending shivers all through her. "You taste so good."

"Better than dinner?" she managed to tease. Go her.

"Better than anything," he ground out in a voice that held no amusement, only pure male animal hunger.

How had she gone her whole life without feeling this way even once before? But the answer was obvious. She had not yet met Sebastian Hawk and no one else could or would make her feel this good…this needed. The tension was building inside her again…like it had at the lake. She could feel the overwhelming pleasure climbing toward the inevitable peak, but she wasn't ready for it.

She wasn't ready for this to end and she wanted to bring Sebastian pleasure, too. She knew he'd found his release at the lake, or at least she thought that was what his shout had meant, but she wanted to see him this time.

To see his face in the throes of passion beyond his control. She needed that.

An annoying beep tried to impinge on her consciousness, but she ignored it in favor of touching Sebastian's neck and back, mapping and memorizing the play of his sculpted muscles under her fingertips.

With a curse, he suddenly let her go and stepped away from her as he fumbled for the phone in his pocket.

CHAPTER SIX

SHE tried to burrow back into his arms, but he shook his head, a look of disgust on his face as he pushed her away.

Hurt and confusion at his blatant rejection mixed with the cauldron of emotions churned up by his kiss and she slumped against the wall.

He turned away from her and flipped his phone open. "Hawk here."

How could he sound so dispassionate after what they'd just been doing?

He was silent for several seconds as he listened to his caller speak. Then he turned back to face her, his face set in impassive lines. "So, the threat has been neutralized and my assignment here is done?"

Another silence while he listened, this one much shorter.

"My final report will be ready the day after tomorrow. I have several recommendations for more effective security."

Another layer of confusion clouded Lina's brain as she tried to make sense of Sebastian's conversation in light of who she knew him to be.

"Right, arrange with my assistant for a time to meet and I'll present the report in person."

Another short silence.

Sebastian said, "I'll be on the first flight out tomorrow."

He said something else and flipped the phone shut.

Trembling and a feeling of nausea growing, she swallowed against the dryness in her throat. "Flight out? Where are you going?"

He grimaced, as if the conversation was distasteful, but other than that no emotion showed in his expression. "I'm returning to my home office tomorrow."

"Home office? I thought you were a graduate student."

"That was my cover."

"Cover? Are you an FBI agent, or something?" She didn't know how well she would handle having a relationship with someone who had a job like that. It *would* explain why he had hesitated to take their relationship to a deeper level, though.

"Or something."

"What?"

His hands fisted at his sides, but that was the only indication he was uncomfortable with this conversation. "I own an international investigation and security firm that specializes in the high end market."

Lina's stomach cramped as a suspicion started to form. "You mean like catering to royalty?"

"Some. Hawk Investigations has a clientele predominately comprised of the extremely wealthy."

"I see." But she didn't and wasn't at all sure she wanted to.

"Do you?" he asked sardonically.

"I don't know," she admitted.

"Your family received death threats and it was decided you needed additional security. It was your uncle's idea, that rather than pulling you out of university until the threat was neutralized they hire additional protection."

"Someone threatened my aunt and uncle?" she asked, fear for their safety lacing her voice.

"No, your father. Each of his children was named as a potential causality if he did not change his stance on a certain political agenda."

"Why wasn't I told? Why the cloak-and-dagger?"

"Since your studies weren't to be interrupted, it was felt that apprising you of the situation would do you more harm than good." Sebastian's voice was even, expressing no emotion whatsoever.

And she didn't know how he managed that. She felt like he'd taken a tazer to her heart. Heaven knew it hurt so bad, she didn't know how it kept beating.

"You mean my father thinks I'm so weak minded that if I had known about the threats, I would not have been able to keep my attention on my studies." She said with a bitterness for more than the paternal arrogance.

"His head of security did not tell me the details of the motivation behind their decision to make your added protection clandestine."

"You just do what you're told, right?" Well, this explained why her security men had allowed her to spend the night at Jennifer's without hanging around. They knew she was already being watched.

"That's my job."

"And you always do your job without voicing an opinion," she said with sarcasm. She refused to believe Sebastian was anybody's yes-man, even her father's.

"I agreed with the stipulation. If my agents and I were simply added to your security detail, we would have gained nothing but extra bodies between you and the threat, but by maintaining the appearance of friendship and or complete invisibility we were able to watch not only you, but your security detail as well."

"What, you thought one of them might be a traitor?"

"It's been known to happen."

She couldn't argue that. Didn't even want to. Didn't want to keep talking at all. There was too much pain inside of her and it was going to find its way out soon. "So, everything was a big deception. You weren't my friend...my anything."

"The deception was necessary."

"No, it wasn't." Pain lanced through her, but she wasn't going to let *that* comment slide. "You could have told *me* the truth."

Except it was obvious he agreed with her family that she wasn't smart or strong enough to be kept in the loop on what was happening in her own life. She felt like an idiot all right, but for trusting Sebastian. Maybe her family was right...she certainly hadn't shown good judgment of character when it came to him.

Heck, she'd let herself fall in love with a man who was lying to her in order to do his job.

"You lied to me, over and over," she whispered the accusation, the vise on her heart squeezing tighter. "I fell for you and it was all a lie. Everything."

"*I* lied?" he asked with clear censure. "And you have been so up front and honest with me, *princess*."

For the first time, the word did not sound like an endearment.

She stared at him, grateful for the wall at her back. She was sure her legs would not support her otherwise. "What were all those questions about? *Do you live alone? Why haven't I met your family?*" she mocked. "My gosh, you probably know more about my life than I do." Her voice was rising to a dangerous register. For the first time in her life, she was nearly shouting. "I thought you liked me for *me*, not because of my family's wealth or position. I can't believe how stupid I've been."

"Stop acting like the injured innocent, Lina." His voice was ice-cold. "You say you fell for me, but you never once told me the truth about yourself. I gave you a chance tonight to be honest, to trust me and you sidestepped it. Just like you have every other opportunity since we met."

"I didn't want where I come from to prejudice your opinion of me," she cried out. "Besides, the fewer people aware of my true identity, the less a security risk to me. *You* should understand that."

"That might have flown in the beginning, but we've known each other for weeks. You planned to offer me your body tonight, but intended to continue to withhold the truth. If you had *feelings* for me, you would not consider me a security risk. You certainly don't mind circumventing other measures meant to protect you when you find it convenient."

"It's not the same, *everything* about you is a lie. I

do…did…care about you, but there was no relationship on your side. Just a job." Didn't he understand how much that hurt her? How wrong that was? But then, like her father, Sebastian obviously believed the ends justified the means.

For just a second, the blank mask slipped and anger blazed out of his dark gray eyes. "Just like a woman to have a double standard about honesty. You are like every other woman I have known Princess Lina bin Fahd al Marwan. Your protestations of heartfelt emotion carry as much weight as the other *truths* you have chosen to share with me."

"That's not fair, Sebastian. I had my reasons."

"Like you have your reasons for lying to your family and your security team. Does it matter to you that the men on your detail will most likely lose their jobs once my report is filed with your father's head of security? Did you once consider your family or the poor saps responsible for your safety when you were busy lying to them all so you could have *your freedom*?"

She couldn't breathe. He didn't know her at all. She'd thought he'd understood her, but that was just another deception. However, it wasn't that knowledge that was shredding her heart right now. The men in her security detail weren't bad. They had lives, families…she could not stand to see them fired.

"You can't file a report that gets them in trouble." She didn't care if she sounded like she was begging. She was. She'd never do it on her own behalf, but for *the good of* men who relied on her family's goodwill for their livelihood she would not let her pride stand in the way.

"You should have considered that before learning to circumvent the security measures your family had put in place."

"I didn't know I was being watched by a second detail, did I? I would never have done anything to get them into trouble."

"And you don't think that if something happened to you on one of the numerous occasions you'd managed to ditch your bodyguards that they wouldn't have been fired? Or worse?"

"No one knows who I am here. I'm not at risk."

"You're beyond naïve if you believe that."

So, just like every other man in her life, Sebastian thought she was lacking brainpower. So much for his earlier comment on her intelligence. She didn't have the time to worry about that right now however. "Please, Sebastian, you can't file that report."

"I don't have a choice. I take my job seriously."

She looked down at the floor, hugging herself for comfort that was never there. She had to convince him to keep some things out of that report. "What if I promised not to do it again?"

"Not to do what exactly?"

She thought quickly before speaking, knowing that she would feel compelled to keep any promise she made to the letter. No matter what *he* thought of her honor. "What if I promised not to do any of the things that I've done to ditch my bodyguards again?"

He snorted and her head snapped up. "What?" Then she answered her own question before he could. "You don't think I'm capable of keeping a promise."

"Like you kept your promise to be honest with your security team?"

"I've never made such a promise. I've never even claimed such a thing. It is not my fault they assume I'm too dumb or docile, or both, to arrange for a slice of personal freedom in my life."

He still looked unconvinced.

It shouldn't surprise her, but it did...and it hurt. "Look, even if our supposed friendship was nothing but smoke and mirrors, you must know me well enough by now to realize I would never do anything intentionally to hurt someone else, particularly the people dependent on me for their livelihood."

"Yet, you put the jobs of your entire security team and your chaperone at risk, not to mention your uncle losing face with your father once it comes to light that he is ignorant of big chunks of your life."

"*I never thought I would be caught.* It wasn't on purpose."

He shook his head.

"Please, Sebastian."

"You promise me you won't lie to your security detail or your family again nor will you argue against the new measures and I will consider making suggestions for your increased security without revealing why I think they are necessary."

"I promise." She certainly wasn't going to want the freedom to try dating again for a very long time. She never wanted to hurt like this again.

"I promise not to deceive my family or retainers when it comes to my personal security," she clarified.

She wasn't promising never to withhold the truth from her family again. She lived a whole life that they would never understand, particularly the little detail that she was now an American citizen.

His look anything but approving, Sebastian nevertheless nodded. "Agreed."

He refused to leave until Jennifer returned and another bodyguard had been called to watch Lina's friend's building.

It was all Lina could do to keep it together in front of him. The only way she could even remotely manage the pain was to pretend he wasn't there and pretend her mother was. It would probably seem childish to someone else, but Lina had never cried in front of her mother—at least in her memory.

The mere thought of her mother witnessing her ignominious rejection was enough to keep external tears at bay. It didn't decrease her emotional agony, though. In fact, the idea that her mother might be aware of Sebastian's employment and the nature of his cover for a way into her life intensified Lina's sense of utter betrayal. She might not be crying on the outside, but her heart was crying tears of blood.

Lina's bungee cord bottomed out and her hands brushed the water before the ricochet snapped her up again. She flipped her torso up and started undoing her harness before the final bouncing stopped. Diving into the water on the next downward plunge, she immediately started swimming for shore. She couldn't believe Sebastian was back.

He was no longer simply the hands-on owner of the largest detective and security agency in the world, but ran his deceased father's business holdings as well. Not to mention chairing multiple nonprofit boards. She had a hard time comprehending that even her father had the power to command the personal attention of business tycoon Sebastian Hawk on a case.

She was *not* surprised the king of Marwan had engaged Hawk Investigations when rather than accept the edict she marry a man she had never met, his recalcitrant daughter disappeared. After all, hadn't the agency done a bang-up job eight years ago? Not only had Sebastian kept her safe, but he had recommended certain changes in her security that had severely limited her ability to have a life outside of her studies.

Thank goodness for Jennifer. Without her, Lina's remaining years at the university would have been miserable. Once those years were over, however, it had been those same security measures that spawned her first all-out rebellion against her family. That rebellion had resulted in a relaxation of the strictures surrounding her, but it had also led to a near break between her parents and her aunt and uncle. Once again dismissing Lina's own will and intellect, the royal couple blamed the Americanized relatives for their daughter's unwillingness to conform.

Yet despite her insistence on a certain amount of autonomy, her parents had still assumed she would be willing to marry a man of their choosing. The level of their sheer arrogance left her breathless. Then and now.

She reached the shore.

"Awesome jump, Lina. You ready to go again?" Aaron slapped her on the back...or was it Adam? She couldn't remember. He was ground crew, that's all she knew for sure.

She shook her head. "I'm going to have to forgo any more jumps today. Can someone give me a ride back to the hotel? Um...right away?"

She wasn't naïve enough to believe she could outrun Sebastian, but she definitely didn't want to have the coming confrontation in front of a group of strangers.

"You okay? Something happen on the jump?"

She shook her head. More like *someone*. "I'm fine. I just need to get back to the hotel."

"Hey, no problem. I'll take you," he said with a flirtatious smile before calling out his plans to the other ground crew.

The Jeep ate up the miles between the jump site and Lina's hotel.

Aaron...Adam...whatever...downshifted and took a tight curve coming out of the canyon on squealing tires. "So, you going back to the hotel...it got anything to do with the suit yelling his head off on the bridge?"

"Sebastian doesn't yell."

"Artie said the guy's got a set of lungs on him. Near to made Artie jump off the bridge when he pulled the gun."

"He pulled a gun?" Lina asked with genuine shock.

"Yeah, but you'd already jumped. The guy...Sebastian

you said…he cursed better'n any sergeant Artie ever had in the Army, he said."

"How do you know?"

"Artie called from the bridge when the guy took off in his car. Thought he might be headed down to us."

"He might have been." But even Sebastian couldn't drive the distance by road as fast as she had plunged on her bungee cord.

She was however slightly surprised they hadn't run into each other at the junction out of the canyon.

"This Sebastian dude your boyfriend, or something?"

"Or something."

When she didn't elaborate, her blond driver just shrugged. "Hey, I can respect your privacy."

"Thank you."

"You want me to tell Artie you won't be taking the job with the outfit after all?"

Startled by the blonde's perception, she said, "If you don't mind."

"No problem. You going to need transportation into the city?"

Seeing a sleek black Jaguar parked outside her room as they pulled into the small hotel's parking lot, Lina's spine stiffened. "No, I don't think that will be necessary, but thanks for the offer."

The Jeep came to a stop beside the Jaguar. "Looks like your 'or something' beat us here. You want me to come in with you?"

Lina couldn't help smiling at that. There were lots of good people left in the world and she had to remember that. Even if her own family was happy to sell her out to the god of political expedience.

She turned to face him and put her hand on his arm. "Thanks, Aaron—"

"Adam."

She grimaced. "Sorry."

"No problem."

"I really appreciate the offer, but I'll be fine. Sebastian's not here to hurt me." Not physically anyway.

"Good luck with your life, Lina. You ever want a job, you come on back. Artie is plenty impressed with you. I am, too." There was no mistaking the interest in Adam's eyes, but Lina felt no responding feminine pique.

She hadn't felt anything like that since the night eight years ago when she discovered she was nothing but a job to Sebastian Hawk. Goodness knew she'd tried, but it was as if her libido had turned off and she had no idea how to turn it back on.

In some ways, her lack of sexual interest in the men who had dated her had made life easier. She hadn't gotten hurt again and she'd had more time and energy to devote to her causes than she would have otherwise.

She leaned forward and kissed Adam on the cheek. "Thanks."

He turned his head and kissed her back—on the lips. He wasn't aggressive and she didn't feel threatened, but she didn't feel anything else, either. Nevertheless, she smiled before grabbing her pack from the backseat, where she'd left it that morning, and got out of the Jeep.

Sebastian was waiting in the open door to her room when she turned from the still running four-wheel drive.

He was indeed wearing a suit, or at least what was left of one. He'd discarded the jacket and tie, having rolled the sleeves of his crisp white shirt up to reveal his tanned, muscular forearms. His no doubt designer label slacks had been tailored to fit his hips and long legs perfectly.

Lina's mouth watered while her hands itched to reach out and touch.

What was happening to her?

She'd spent eight years as close to asexual as a woman could get and all of a sudden her hormones were on a roller coaster that rivaled the scariest ride at Six Flags Amusement Park.

It took all of her training in hiding her emotion, to maintain a blank expression as she faced the man who had haunted her dreams for almost a decade. "Hello, Sebastian."

His left brow lifted sardonically. "You don't sound surprised to see me."

She shrugged, as if the very sight of him wasn't sending a plethora of signals to nerve endings she hadn't been aware of in eight years. "I could say the same. I could have run."

"I would have caught you."

"Probably." Her initial flight hadn't been well planned after all...more an act of rebellion than anything else. She had nothing in place to help her disappear with a hunter like Sebastian seeking her out.

That did not mean she *couldn't* disappear. Just not right this minute.

He stepped back into the room, indicating she should join him. She went without argument. Why not? Privacy was exactly what she wanted for their upcoming discussion. It also didn't hurt to lull him into believing she was as docile as her family believed she should be.

A quick double honk behind her had her turning and waving off Adam as he drove away.

Sebastian closed the door, turning the security lock as well. "I'm glad to see you being so reasonable."

"You expected anything less?" she asked, trying to ignore the sense of the room being too small now that he was in it.

"I have personal experience with how little credence you give duty to your family and crown. I admit, I expected a lot more trouble from you. You didn't even try to get your boyfriend to rescue you."

The words hurt, but she refused to let him see that. The truth was that his opinion shouldn't matter. The fact that it had the ability to impact her made her furious...with herself. "Perhaps I don't buy into the belief that my filial duty extends to marrying a man I have never met and moreover one who has been dubbed the *Playboy Prince.* That does not mean I'm interested in getting an innocent bystander embroiled in my situation."

"I see the years have not changed you."

"Really? In what way?" she asked in masochistic compulsion.

"You are still putting your own comfort above that of the people who depend on you."

"Oh, right...because the people of Marwan are going to be devastated if I don't marry the younger son of a neighboring sheikhdom."

"Your father believes it is best for his country."

"Maybe it is, but since Marwan stopped being *my* country more than two decades ago, I fail to see why I should sacrifice my life for political expedience."

"You are still a princess in Marwan."

She shrugged, not willing to continue the argument standing there in nothing more than a damp T-shirt and shorts over her still wet swimsuit. "As fascinating as this discussion is, I need to take a shower and put some dry clothes on."

Hawk watched Lina disappear into the small bathroom, her hands filled with clothes she'd pulled from the drawer of the cheap dresser that also served as a television stand. The room had a window, but it was too small for even Lina to get through. Though he wasn't taking any chances.

"Leave the door open," he ordered.

She didn't answer, but she also didn't close the door.

Damn. He almost wanted her to disobey…to argue. So, he could have the pleasure of subduing her? What the hell was the matter with him?

And what was up with her? The Lina he remembered was not this acquiescent. He'd said she hadn't changed, but the truth was—she had. He didn't like it, which made no sense.

The fact that she made no attempt to run, or involve her blond boyfriend in trying to get rid of Sebastian was the behavior of a docile woman. His princess was anything but that. Or at least she had been eight years ago.

One thing hadn't changed in all that time. The reaction

of his body to her presence. He'd had a hard-on since she climbed out of the Jeep and it was only getting more urgent as his senses took in the sounds and smells of her showering.

CHAPTER SEVEN

SHE used the same shampoo and body wash she had when they first met. The scents were unmistakable. He could hear the splashes of water as she washed herself and damned if he didn't want to strip off his own clothes and join her. This was not the way he'd planned to react to her when he agreed to take the missing persons case personally.

Her father was angry and not a little worried at Lina's disappearance. In an unprecedented move, the king had come to Hawk's office. His security advisor had accompanied him, but the king had done all the talking, practically begging Hawk to find his daughter.

Seeing another proud man brought to this point had moved Hawk, but he was too honest with himself to pretend that was all that had influenced his decision to come after Lina. He'd never forgotten the weeks he'd spent guarding her. There were still nights he woke up with the scent of her skin a memory so real he reached for her in the bed.

She was never there, and never would be, but he had

to be the one to bring her in. To deliver her to her family to marry the *Playboy Prince*. Okay, so he didn't understand why King Fahd bin Latif had arranged Lina's marriage to a sheikh who didn't seem able to keep his scandals out of the newspaper, but it wasn't Hawk's job to judge the actions of his clients.

He'd taken on an assignment and he would see it to completion.

And maybe he'd get the chance to have the conversation she had denied him the last night they saw each other and one attempt he'd made via the phone since.

He owed Lina an apology, maybe even an explanation. If he could go back, he wouldn't change his actions—at least not that he'd walked away. He'd had no choice. Her place in the royal family of Marwan dictated that reality. However he would have been more honest with her after the first kiss, instead of relying on self-control that had turned out to be weaker than he thought.

He also would have explained that his attraction to her had not been a deception, but the real deal. That even if they couldn't have a future he would rather part as friends. But he'd been totally disgusted with himself and his failure to control his libido. He'd taken it out on her, being cold and judgmental—he'd had to try and keep control—when he should have been apologizing.

A part of him had realized it then and that had only made it worse.

He found himself doing it again today. He'd been livid watching her kiss that damn water bunny and had expressed his anger in disdain he wasn't sure he even felt.

He'd taken on a job and he would see it to completion, but was it really such a bad thing for a twenty-first century woman to want to choose her own husband. Even a princess?

The sound of the shower curtain sliding back had Hawk's head snapping up. He looked through the cracked open door, knowing he would not see anything. Lina would no doubt finish dressing behind the door.

Only he hadn't taken the vanity mirror into consideration. The open door had stopped it from steaming up and the reflective surface gave a perfect mirror image of Lina drying her delectable little body. He should turn away, he knew he should. But he couldn't make himself do it.

She was so beautiful. Her honey colored skin glistened with moisture where she had not yet reached with the towel. Droplets of water dripped off the ends of her hair to roll down her generous breasts, some curving around her beaded nipples, others rolling right over the tips.

He wanted to go in there and lick those drops of water right off her and had even taken two steps forward before he caught himself. He stood rigid, locking his muscles into immobility and watching with uncontrollable fascination as she continued to dry off. She turned and bent over, exposing her heart shaped backside and the shadow of her most feminine place.

He groaned.

She stilled. "Did you say something, Sebastian?"

"Uh…no." If he didn't move, she was going to catch him watching her like an adolescent getting his first peek at a female body.

Gritting his teeth, he shut his eyes and forced himself

to turn away and take several steps toward where he knew the bed was. He opened his eyes once he felt the bed against his shin. He sat down and only considered the lack of wisdom in choosing this particular spot once he was already there.

Once she came out of the bathroom, he was not going to toss her onto the bed and ravish her within an inch of her life…or his. *He wasn't.*

Lina dressed quickly, but clothing herself acted as no barrier between her and the feelings that Sebastian elicited in her. The shower hadn't helped, either. The feel of hot water cascading over her body had acted as a catalyst to sensations she had long ago given up on.

This was so incredibly wrong.

She'd dated several men since graduating from college, men *worthy* of her affection and desire. And felt nothing for any of them.

Then Mr. Sebastian Hawk walks back into her life and within milliseconds she's reacting to him as if he'd never been away, had never betrayed her.

Sebastian had used her once and she had no intention of falling for him again. But then what she was feeling right now had nothing to do with love. It was one hundred percent physical. It had to be. There was nothing left over from her love for Sebastian. She'd loved a lie anyway. It wasn't as if anything about the man had been real eight years ago.

And she could keep reminding herself of that important truth, but it wasn't going to do a darn thing to dampen the fire lit deep inside her. Which just proved that it *was* entirely carnal in origin. Her emotions knew better than to react to the man's presence.

Apparently her body wasn't quite as wise.

She pulled her long hair up into a ponytail. She could barely see the highlights while it was wet, but dry it glinted with blond, red and light brown streaks mixed with her natural black. Her mother hated it. Her aunt loved it and Lina liked it enough to have her roots touched up every six weeks.

Wondering what Sebastian would think of it dry and trying to ignore the traitorous thought, she walked out of the bathroom. He was sitting on the bed, a pained expression on his face.

"You all right?" she asked begrudgingly.

The blank mask she'd learned to hate the night she discovered his duplicity settled over his features. "Fine. You ready to go?"

"Go where exactly?"

"Playing word games with me, Princess?"

"No. I assume you plan to deliver me to my family, but considering the fact that we are twenty-six hundred miles from D.C. and at least a four-hour drive from any sort of municipal airport, I'm assuming we've got at least one stop between here and there."

"I didn't say your family was in the States."

"You didn't have to. My father may think I'm incapable of keeping up with world events, but I'm not. Nor am I oblivious. The fact that the king of Marwan and his entourage are currently staying in our nation's capital is hardly a state secret." And if he thought he was taking her to Marwan, he was delusional.

"You're right. Your parents, not to mention your fiancé, are waiting for your arrival in D.C."

"I assume they are staying at the Embassy?" Her father was fanatical about security and did not trust hotels or even U.S. government provided housing. The Marwan Embassy was large enough to not only house him and the royal entourage, but had several more guest rooms besides all the ordinary facilities for hosting other government dignitaries.

"Yes."

"So?"

He looked a question at her.

"Where exactly are we going now?"

"You think I should tell you?"

"I get that you fall in with my father's draconian belief that he should be able to dictate my future as well as who I share it with, but are you so tyrannical that you don't think you perhaps owe me the most basic of courtesies? Namely telling me where I should expect to spend the night?"

"Knowledge is power, Princess, and I'm not in the habit of giving that commodity away."

"Stop calling me that."

"It's your name."

"My name is Lina."

"But you are a princess."

"And you are a cold-blooded Neanderthal, but I show you the respect of using your name regardless."

"Fine, *Lina*. Are you ready to go?"

"I need to pack, but I would still like to know where we are going."

His look told her she could go right on wanting answers. He wasn't giving them away. Fine. If that's the way he wanted to play it. She wasn't ready to tip her hand by going all stubborn on him. She could guess their destination anyway. She figured they were headed for the airport in either Reno or Lake Tahoe. Tahoe was closer, but its airport was much smaller. Considering the type of rental car he had, there was a better chance the agency he'd rented from had a drop off at the Reno airport. Not that that sort of thing would be a major hurdle for a man with Sebastian's resources, but business tycoon or not, he was a fan of efficiency.

Okay, so maybe she'd read an article…or ten…about him over the years.

The only thing she couldn't be sure of was whether or not he'd take her directly to the airport or to a hotel. She started packing her things in a Gucci duffel bag her aunt had given her for her last birthday. She hadn't brought much with her when she'd flown the coop and it only took a few minutes to pack her possessions. She shoved the used swimsuit in the outside pocket of the backpack that matched her duffel bag.

She'd laughed when she'd opened them and smiled now at the memory. Her aunt knew her pretty well and managed to give her gifts she would use, even if they were wildly more expensive than anything she would buy for herself. She had far more important things to do with her money.

She slung the backpack over her shoulder and grabbed the duffel bag. "I'm ready to go."

"That's it? No arguments…no demands to tell you

where I'm taking you before we leave the room?" He sounded truly befuddled by her submissive façade.

Good. A confused enemy made an easier enemy to outwit. "Nope. No arguments."

His eyes narrowed, but he didn't say anything further. He took her duffel from her with such a natural movement, she let him have it. There was no reason to hold it back anyway. Everything important was in a money belt concealed under her clothes.

He tossed the duffel in his trunk and she noticed a black case in there as well. So, he wasn't checked into a hotel nearby, not that she'd expected him to be.

They arrived in Reno late that evening. Hawk took Lina to the luxury villa, high in the hills on the outskirts of the city, that his agency had arranged for them. He hadn't apprised King Fahd that his daughter was in custody yet. Hawk was a superstitious soul when it came to his baby, Hawk Investigations, since giving an incorrect report to a client a year ago, he did not report in until he was absolutely sure of his facts. It had been one of his operatives that had taken the pictures of the wrong twin, but that did not mitigate Hawk's sense of responsibility about the false report.

He used the code his PA had texted him on the drive to disarm and open the door. He let Lina into the house and went back to the car for the cases. He doubted she would run in the dark up here in the hills. It was one of the reasons he'd requested this location for their accommodations.

Lina was in the kitchen getting a glass of water when he came back inside.

"I set the house alarm, so don't open any doors or windows."

She rolled her eyes. "You really think that's necessary."

"It pays to be cautious."

"Well, no one would accuse you of being sloppy."

"So…."

She turned to face him, taking a sip of her water. "Yes?"

"No arguments about how I shouldn't be taking you back to your family. No appeals to my democratic beliefs about human rights and liberties?"

A brief flash of anger burned in her doe-brown eyes before it banked and she shrugged. "What would be the point? I learned all I needed to know about how much you respected my privacy and personal rights eight years ago. You showed me then that you would do or say anything to get the job done. I fully expect you to do the same this time around."

While he understood her cynical view of him, it still stung. And it shouldn't. Her opinion of him should not matter at all, but just like eight years ago—she was already becoming more than just an assignment. "I'm not the one letting people down here, Princess."

She frowned. "Neither am I."

"So, the security company that lost your father's account because of your little flit and the guard that lost his job…how do you not see yourself letting them down?" Damn it, what was the matter with him? Maybe

Lina wasn't living up to what her family considered her responsibilities, but she wasn't a criminal.

"First, the company having my father's account is not my responsibility, it's theirs. Second, I made sure the security guard was compensated for losing his job," she said, ticking the items off on her fingers. "And if you check, you'll discover he already has a new one with better benefits."

"What do you mean he's been compensated? Did you pay him off to look the other way?"

Her body stiffened with affront. "I did not. I wouldn't compromise someone else's integrity like that. I arranged for payment after the fact."

"Like you supposedly arranged for another job offer?"

"Exactly."

"You expect me to believe that after he lost you, he had no problem getting a better job?"

"It all depends on how you define better. I found out that Rodney didn't really like being a bodyguard, but he didn't think he had any other marketable skills since he got out of the military. I encouraged him to take classes at the local college when he wasn't watching me. When it came time to part ways with him, he was educated enough to qualify for a job he really wanted. With the proper recommendation of course."

"Which you gave him."

"Yes."

"Wow."

Lina's look said she thought he was being sarcastic, but he wasn't. He was really impressed. She'd cared enough about her bodyguard not only to get to know him, but to have a backup plan for when she took a flit. "How long have you been planning to run?"

"Believe it, or not, it wasn't a plan. The timing just worked out for Rodney to move on the same time I did. I was planning to encourage him to go for the other job anyway."

"Still the social activist, huh?"

"You've read my file, so you know the answer to that."

"Your file says that you work for an environmentalist group and spend your few off hours volunteering at a shelter for runaway teens."

"Technically I no longer work for the organization."

"You can do just as much good in your role as princess, maybe even more." He wanted to believe that. Lina without her causes wouldn't be his princess at all.

"Is that supposed to make me feel better about having my life hijacked?"

"No one is hijacking your life."

"Really? So, my father would be fine with me walking out of here? You wouldn't follow me?"

Unreasonable anger tinged with guilt surged through him, but he kept his voice even. "You know that's not true."

She simply looked at him as if to say that her point had been made.

"Your father is worried about your safety. Leaving behind your security was not a smart move, Lina." Hell, the truth? Even if he just now realized it, was that half the reason he'd come after her himself was because he'd been worried about her.

She crossed her arms under her breasts, lifting them

in purely innocent enticement. "My father's only concern for me is my ability to further his political agenda. As for leaving behind my security detail, I believe we had this discussion once before. If no one knows who I am, then there can be no threat to my safety."

"If you believe that, I've got several thousand police reports where women are victimized for you to read."

"Oh, please. Every other woman lives in the same world as those police reports and ninety-nine-point-nine percent of them don't have bodyguards."

"You are not those women."

"What makes me so different?" she demanded.

"You're a princess. You were raised in a privileged environment."

"And I've spent the last five years living a normal life. I'm no more at risk than any other woman out there."

"That's not true." And her refusal to see that she couldn't hide from who she was did not bode well for her future.

"It's a moot point and this discussion is a waste of both our time. Where am I sleeping?"

According to information from his PA, there were two bedrooms, a fully functioning office and a game room upstairs.

"In one of the bedrooms on the upper floor."

"You're going to let me pick my own room?" she asked in a voice tinged with false surprise and mockery.

Damn it. He was just doing his job. "Yes, you can pick whichever room you want," he managed to get out between gritted teeth.

He followed her up the stairs, grabbing both her duffel

and his bag before she had a chance to. She walked straight into the bedroom on the left at the end of the hall without even giving the other a glance. He followed her and dropped her duffel on the bed.

"Thank you." Her voice was soft and so damn alluring.

He didn't back away when she turned. He couldn't. He wanted to take in her scent, to feel her warmth even if he was determined not to touch her. "You're welcome. Our flight is in the afternoon. We'll be leaving for the airport right after an early lunch."

"Noted." She looked up at him, her dark eyes filled with deep thoughts, but she didn't say anything. Nor did she move away.

"What?"

"I always wondered…"

"What?"

"Was it *all* part of the act?"

His body jolted with shock. Maybe he should have expected that question, but he hadn't. He wanted to explain himself, but just like eight years ago—he wasn't sure what to say. It was the main reason he hadn't pushed harder for a chance to talk.

He didn't pretend not to know what she was talking about, even if it might have been the smarter thing to do. "No."

She bit her lip and nodded, backing away from him. "Thank you. I don't think I want to know which parts."

It was his turn to nod. He'd regretted few things in his life as much as he had his lack of control with Lina. He had been totally disgusted with himself that final night.

He couldn't believe he'd allowed himself to get lost in her physical presence again. Once more, his libido had put her at risk and he'd been sick with himself.

His self-disgust had made him harsher with her than he had meant to be when revealing the truth of his assignment. He'd had eight years to come up with a multitude of different scenarios for the revelations of that night, not one of them leaving his princess looking so damn wounded and betrayed.

She'd moved over to the window and stood looking out at the darkened desert. He didn't know what she could see, but doubted it was the view she was focused on anyway. He walked up behind her and placed his hand on her shoulder.

She shivered and he wanted to pull her body into his, but he had more self-control at thirty-five than he had had at twenty-seven and he didn't do it. "I'm sorry, princess."

"For?" she asked in a voice husky with emotion she was obviously trying to hide.

"I should never have let things get out of hand between us. I compromised your safety twice with my inattentiveness."

She laughed, but the sound was hollow. "You're sorry you didn't do your job right?" She shook her head as if trying to clear it. "Don't worry about it. As far as I could tell, you did it perfectly."

"I'm also sorry I hurt you." There, he'd said it. And it could go down in the record books because he could count on one hand the number of times he'd apologized in his life and this counted for two of them.

"Is that why you took this job? So you could tell me you were sorry?"

"Yes, partly. I don't do fieldwork any longer."

"You're too busy with your multitude of other business interests."

"It sounds like you've been keeping up with me."

"You know what they say. It's important to know your enemies."

He felt something tighten in his chest. "I'm not your enemy."

"You aren't my friend."

"I was once."

"So you could keep an eye on me. That's not friendship, that's an overdeveloped sense of responsibility where your job is concerned."

"I liked you, Lina. I respected you."

The harsh sound that came from her throat was all disbelief.

"I did. I still do. You've done a lot with your life, most of it without anyone's encouragement or help."

"That's not true. My aunt and uncle have stood behind me."

"I'm glad there are people in your family you feel you can trust."

She said nothing.

He fought a sigh. This apology thing was so not his gig. "I should have told you the truth about who I was once I realized how hard it would be to keep my hands off you." Try impossible. He forced himself to drop his hand from her shoulder and move back.

She nodded. "Thank you."

He didn't know what to say to that so he said nothing.

"Is that what you wanted to tell me when you called that time?"

"Yes. And when I tried to talk to you the night you learned the truth."

"You had already said a lot."

"Believe it or not, princess, that was a bad night for both of us."

Her shoulders tensed.

"If you respected me so much, why did you accuse me of not caring about the people who depend on me?" She turned to face him, for once her expression open for reading. Skepticism and unhappiness marked her features. "You made the same accusation tonight."

He had and she'd put him firmly in his place. "I made assumptions then and now about your lack of concern. Eight years ago, I thought you knew the effect your actions would have and did not care."

"But I didn't know. It never occurred to me that my bid for personal freedom might cost someone their job."

"Because you were overly confident in your ability not to get caught."

"A wealth of confidence should be something you understand."

He found himself almost smiling at that. "Yes."

"You made the same assumption this time."

"And I was wrong."

"It doesn't matter, though, does it? You still think I owe my father my life and my happiness."

"I thought you believed that line of reasoning was useless to argue with me." But damn it, she was wrong.

What he believed was that she had no choice and she would be happier if she made the best of the life she'd been born to.

She seemed to wilt. "It is. I'm tired, Mr. Hawk. Do you mind if I go to bed?"

CHAPTER EIGHT

LINA woke up just before sunrise.

She'd slept surprisingly well considering how disheartened she had been when she went to bed. Sebastian had given her an apology with one hand and snapped away any comfort that might bring her with the other. He might like *some* things about her and even respect her to an extent, but when all was said and done—the man still believed she had no right to an opinion about her own future.

In that way, he was exactly like her father. For a man raised not a part of any country's nobility, he certainly had a medieval view of what it meant to be born a princess.

Well, no matter what her father and his agent provocateur regarded as truth, she didn't agree with them and she was not going to be forced into marriage to a man she didn't know, obviously didn't love because of the former and had little hope of doing so considering his womanizing reputation.

Actually she'd researched her supposed fiancé pretty

thoroughly, almost as intensively as she'd researched
Sebastian Hawk over the past eight years, and she
thought she and Amir could be friends. They both chose
to live modern lives outside the normal sphere of their
royal families. He was called the *Playboy Prince*, but
he'd never gotten a woman pregnant and refused to stand
by her, or had an affair with a married woman, or even
broken an engagement.

He dated. A lot. But he also oversaw his family's
holdings in the U.S. and did an excellent job with them.
He didn't dismiss his responsibilities in favor of play, nor
did he ignore the needs of the less fortunate. The Faruq
al Zorha businesses in the States donated more than
fifteen percent of their profits each year to worthy causes,
and not simply politically expedient or popular ones.

Her impression of him was so favorable that she had
considered meeting and getting to know him more than
once, but in the end she knew it would be useless. She
wanted love in her marriage, or she preferred to remain
unattached. If she had children, she was determined to
give them a different upbringing than she had had. No
matter how much her aunt and uncle had loved her, Lina
had never been able to completely dismiss her parents'
rejection.

They'd simply given her away. She'd been a thank you
to the childless couple for their loyal service to her father,
just as if she had been a prize stallion or other possession.

At the age of six, she had not been able to stop her
parents from treating her like an object rather than a
person, but she was twenty-seven now—an adult fully

capable of influencing her own destiny. Her father needed to learn that people were not commodities and if she was the only one willing to teach him that particular lesson, so be it.

She got out of bed and walked quietly to the adjoining bathroom, thinking Sebastian was probably still sleeping and not wanting to wake him. She could use some time to herself this morning to get her thoughts sorted and plan her next move.

She was so focused on her inner reflection that she had stepped inside the bathroom before she realized two things at once. The first, the light was on and she hadn't been the one to flip the switch. And the second, Sebastian stood there naked, preparing to step into the shower.

Her brain short-circuited as her body reacted in a way it hadn't to any stimulus since she was nineteen.

For as intimate as they had gotten when she was in college, she had never seen him naked. She'd never seen any man without his clothes on and it was a revelation. Bronzed skin stretched over sculpted muscle *all over*. Dark silky whorls of hair covered his chest and torso, arrowing down to his manhood. That particular appendage fascinated her and she reached out to touch it without thinking. Her fingertip barely grazed the tip. The skin was surprisingly smooth, like satin. As she watched, the flesh grew rigid, flushing with color.

It was big. Much larger than she had expected. Men and women had been copulating for millennia, so she had to assume the fit wasn't a problem, but she couldn't quite imagine how that would be true. The now hard shaft bobbed under her gaze, curving up toward his taut stomach and Sebastian made a sound halfway between a groan and a sigh.

It was the first sound either of them had made since she walked into the bathroom. Yet the spell of silence surrounding them did not break further.

She was too entranced to even look up at his face. She wanted to feel more of that satin-smooth flesh. Was it as warm as it looked?

Without realizing she'd done it, she had moved closer so his body was mere inches from her own. She could smell his male musk. Was that what arousal smelled like? It was heady, like a drug. Sucking her bottom lip between her teeth, she gave into the urge to touch and brushed her fingertips over the heated flesh. It was hot and both so very soft and incredibly hard...like pulsing stone under a velvet covering. Her fingers curled of their own volition around him. He was too thick for her fingertips to touch her thumb, but he felt just right in her hand. She still couldn't imagine him fitting inside of her, but the pulsing pleasure between her thighs told her she wanted to try.

A pearly drop of wetness formed on the tip of his penis and her nostrils flared as she took in this new scent. So incredible. She took a deep breath, a tiny moan escaping her throat as her body reacted.

Sebastian pressed his forehead to hers. "You need to stop this, princess." His voice came out a hungry growl that went directly to her core.

"Why?" she asked.

"Because if you don't, I'm going to pick you up and carry you to my bed and I won't be letting you out of it until I've touched and tasted every centimeter of your skin."

That sounded good to her.

He made a pained sound and it was then that she became aware of how tightly wound he was, his entire body rigid with tension. His big hands were curled into tight fists at his sides. A fine tremor shook him and she knew he was fighting what was happening between them with everything in him.

"Please, princess. We can't do this." He sounded so desperate; she could not ignore his plea.

She pressed her hand down his shaft just once before pulling it away. A guttural groan came from deep in his chest. She knew she had to step back from him and return to her own room, but she didn't want to. She wanted to revel in this feeling, to experience an aspect of her femininity that had been missing since his betrayal eight years ago.

She tilted her head back so that their eyes met, then her gaze flicked to his mouth. Would his lips taste the same? Was she sure she remembered that flavor right? Would his kisses affect her the way they had when she was nineteen? She had to believe they would because everything about him brought about an intense response in her.

"Kiss me," she whispered in the air between their lips.

Hawk's lips were eager to do just that, but he knew that even the most chaste kiss would lead to him taking Lina to his bed. He couldn't do that. She was an assignment, not a girlfriend. Technically she was engaged to another man. All of the reasons that had existed eight years ago for not giving in to his urges continued to be valid. She was still a princess. He was still determined not to make a fool of himself over a woman. She was still a nonrunner for a short-term affair. There was still no possibility of a future between them.

Plus one.

It took him several long seconds to work up the strength to gently push her away. Even that touch felt like it burned him; it made him want more. But more was something he was determined *not* to have. "No, sweetheart. We can't." Then he said the one thing that for him was irrefutable. "You belong to another man."

It was as if an ice storm had blown into the room, it got so cold.

Lina's gaze could have frozen lava as she put more distance between them. "Even if I had agreed to marry a man, I wouldn't belong to him like a pet dog. We might conceivably belong to each other in an emotional sense, but my commitment would be just that. A commitment, not a contract of indenture. And in *this* case, I did not agree to marry anyone. I am not engaged and I have made *no* promises of fidelity. If I had, rest assured I would not be in this bathroom with you."

With that, she spun on her heel and left, slamming the door behind her.

Lina was so angry she could spit nails. That arrogant prehistoric *male*! How dare he imply she belonged to Amir? Okay, so, according to Sebastian, she *was* engaged to the sheikh. But she wasn't, darn it. She wasn't! And she wasn't going to be.

But even worse? Was the realization that she was a virgin at twenty-seven and it looked like the only man she wanted…might ever want…to change that was in league with her father to treat her like she was a possession, not a person.

How could this be? She had her theories about why she was…well for lack of a better word, *frigid* and not one of them included the prospect that she was a one-man woman and he was her man. Or at least her chosen physical mate.

The very thought made her stomach churn. The last thing she wanted was to be irrevocably connected to a man who had betrayed her the way Sebastian had done. Moreover, he was so much more like her father than she would ever have believed, even after the debacle when she was nineteen.

No, that couldn't be it.

She'd only tried dating a couple of times in college, both at least a full year after the last time she'd seen Sebastian. The results had been less than auspicious. Her new security measures had resulted in her being outed as a princess and that had subsequently led to her inability to be sure the men wanted her for herself.

After her minor rebellion and the loosening of her security, she'd tried dating again, but even when she was fairly sure she was being dated because the man liked her, there was always a tingle of doubt. What if he had been hired by her father to keep a closer eye on her like Sebastian had been? To this day, she wasn't sure any of her dates had been purely legit.

Which probably said way too much about insecurities she'd rather not face.

But Sebastian's betrayal had destroyed her ability to trust. Both her own judgment and in the honesty of men who expressed interest in her.

She'd always assumed that she needed to be able to trust a man in order to feel the things that Sebastian had brought about in her so many years ago. Well, that theory had been blown to Hades because of all men, she certainly didn't trust *him* now. Yet there was no denying the way he impacted her senses. Or was that her hormones?

It certainly wasn't her heart. That particular organ was off-limits to him. Forever.

So, what did all this mean for her status as a virgin? Did she have no hope of ever having a normal physical relationship with a man?

Prior to Sebastian's reentry into her life, she'd convinced herself she was fine with being alone...with being sexually innocent. That was before he reawakened her sensual self. She still wasn't entirely sure she could trust that aspect of her nature, but she recognized it was one she missed. No matter what her mother's opinion would be on the subject.

The prospect that a man who had betrayed her held some irrevocable sway over her libido was completely unacceptable.

A man who had the audacity to believe she *belonged* to the man her parents had chosen for her without her input.

The sound of a growl surprised her and she realized it had come from her. He made her *so* angry.

No way was she going to let him hold her sexuality hostage.

So, how did she fix it? She already knew that trying to do something with another man wasn't going to work. At least not while her body was still tuned to respond to Sebastian.

She'd always kind of thought that if she ever fell in love again, not that she really wanted to—the whole pain and betrayal thing had really soured her on the concept—but that she would be as turned on by whoever she loved as she was by Sebastian.

Now, she wondered if her unresolved attraction to Sebastian was actually blocking her from feeling anything physical *or* emotional for another man. Her memories of the pleasure she'd experienced with him were all wrapped up in an uncomfortable shame she'd stuffed deep inside rather than deal with. The first time at the lake, she'd been so wanton in her response that she had not even realized that Bob had come up on them. Even her doctor hadn't seen her completely naked since she was a very tiny child. The thought that Bob had almost seen her breasts exposed had been extremely disconcerting.

In fact, it still was.

Then the night she learned of Sebastian's betrayal forever linked sensual pleasure with emotional pain and why hadn't she seen that before?

Because she hadn't cared enough to analyze; because she'd been safer avoiding any sort of intimacy in her life. Her parents' rejection had hurt her more deeply than they could possibly understand. Sebastian's had simply confirmed to her battered heart that it was better off lonely than taking a risk on allowing someone else to hurt her the same way.

How ridiculous that she had allowed the very people she did not want influencing her having more sway over her actions and feelings than anyone else.

This had to be changed.

Again, she wondered how to do that. She couldn't do much about the love thing right now since there was no one in her life she was even close to having that kind of attachment to. But her ability to embrace her physical nature was something else.

If she had sex with Sebastian, losing the last vestiges of her innocence and virginity, wouldn't that break through whatever mental barrier had been holding her back since she was nineteen? It had to.

She knew Sebastian wanted her and that made her feel for the first time in a long time. The only question was: how did she get Sebastian to have conjugal relations with her when they were at odds more than anything else?

She could try seducing him, but that hadn't worked the first time around. It had only taken a single phone call to derail her plans as well as what she'd thought was their relationship. Besides, she wasn't super fond of subtle manipulations. She'd much rather be up-front about what she wanted. She refused to play the games of deception that Sebastian now said he was sorry for.

She turned the problem over in her mind until a decent plan began to form.

* * *

Hawk disconnected the call with his assistant and put his computer into standby. It had been three hours since his confrontation with Lina in the bathroom. The house alarm was still on, so he had left her to her own devices while he caught up on work. Staying out of physical proximity was the safest course of action, but breakfast would be delivered soon and he had to disarm the security system to let them in.

That required being in visually confirming distance of Lina's presence. She hadn't acted like she was getting set to run again, but then she was too smart to telegraph her intentions that way.

And after what had happened before his shower, he had to acknowledge that he had no clue what she was thinking.

He would never have expected her to touch him like she had. Unwelcome arousal and pleasure poured through him at the memory. He had never been so close to coming from a single touch in his life. Hell, he'd almost climaxed from the way she was looking at him. He'd wanted to kiss her so bad; he'd almost given into her soft order. Only a last remnant of sanity had stopped him. But, man, had he pissed her off when he'd said she belonged to the sheikh.

However, her reaction had not shocked him nearly as much as his own. As he'd said the words, they left an acidic burn in his mouth. Her fury was nothing compared to the urge he'd had to hurt someone. Namely Sheikh Amir bin Faruq al Zorha, the man Lina's father had contracted for her to marry.

He should never have taken this job on. Lina had

rocked his world right off its axis eight years ago and it
was happening all over again. The situation certainly
wreaked havoc on one of his most closely held beliefs.
That Sebastian Hawk did not have a heart and if he did,
it certainly wasn't going to get wrapped up in a woman's
wiles.

Hawk knocked on Lina's door, but got no response. He
called her name, but that elicited no response, either, so
he opened the door, hoping he would not find her in the
process of changing. But the room was empty. He didn't
find her in the game room, either. Since he'd come from
the office, he assumed she must be on the lower level and
went downstairs to find her. After searching the ground
floor rooms and calling her name twice, his tension level
had racked up to dangerous levels. Lina was not a house-
breaker; she did not have the technical knowledge to
bypass the alarm system. At least her file had said she
didn't, but then her file eight years ago had neglected to
mention her interest and proficiency in kayaking.

The garage was empty but for his rental car. Where
was she?

He opened a door he had assumed the night before
belonged to a closet, only to discover that the house had
more amenities than he'd realized. Lina was relaxing in
a bubbling spa, listening to an MP3 player. Her eyes
were closed and she was leaning back, exposing the delectable column of her neck. Her swimsuit clad breasts
were mostly hidden by the churning hot water, but he
could see enough of the upper swell to make his mouth
water for a taste and his libido go zing.

He walked around the circular, recessed hot tub and laid his hand on her shoulder.

Her eyes opened slowly and a smile that could be labeled nothing short of sensuous curved her lips. "Hello, Sebastian."

He gently tugged the speaker bud from her left ear. "Breakfast will be here soon."

"Oh, are we having it delivered?"

"I'm not the cook you are."

That smile flashed across her lips again. "I would be surprised to find out you could cook at all."

"I can keep myself from starving, but that's about it."

"I guess it's a good thing you're a millionaire so many times over, then. You can afford to have all your meals catered."

"I have a housekeeper in New York."

"I'm not surprised."

"I was surprised to discover that you've been living by yourself for the last four years."

"As alone as I could get with a security detail monitoring me 24/7."

"It was a clever setup, actually."

"It was the best I could do to ensure a measure of privacy and maintain the level of security my father's advisors recommended."

"You designed the security plan?"

"Yes. I researched and found the American security company as well."

"I'm impressed." And he was. She'd arranged to have a physical bodyguard watch her whenever she left her apartment, but when she was home she was monitored by less intrusive video surveillance. Her security team maintained an apartment in her building so they were on the spot without actually being in her face.

The setup would not have worked if she had an active social life, but according to her file, she didn't. She dated so rarely that even her father wasn't worried about her getting involved with an inappropriate man. Of course, the king was totally clueless about Hawk's attraction to and for Lina.

Her volunteering was as scheduled as her hours at work. Basically she'd been living as regimented a life as her parents could wish.

"Why are you so against marrying the sheikh?" he blurted out, but wanted the answer enough not to retract the question.

She cocked her brow in question.

"Your life is not exactly a hotbed of different experiences and experimentations. You would have more freedom married to your father's choice."

"Freedom to do what was expected of me. My life may not seem all that exciting to you, but I spend it doing what is important to *me*. I love my job and the time I spend volunteering. It's fulfilling."

"You could do similar things as the sheikh's wife."

"Right. I want to spend my life *doing*, not making politically expedient visits to visible charities so that I am a credit to my husband."

The doorbell rang and Hawk straightened. "That's breakfast. I'll let them in. Meet me in the dining room?"

"Okay. I'll be there in a few minutes."

The sound of her stepping out of the hot tub followed

him out of the room. He ached to turn around and see her in the revealing swimsuit, but he knew his willpower was not up to that kind of temptation.

CHAPTER NINE

LINA walked into the dining room wearing a short T-shirt that did nothing to hide either her gorgeous curves or the fact that she still wore her swimsuit. Revealing a slice of honey-colored skin, the hem didn't even reach the top of her bikini bottoms.

"Can we eat outside? I wanted to go out on the deck earlier, but the alarm was on." She smiled winningly at the server setting the food up on the table. "We can move the food ourselves. It looks delicious."

The young man looked at Lina with a besotted expression that irked Hawk. "I don't mind moving it at all. No problem." He started gathering dishes and headed toward the French doors that led outside.

"I didn't say I wanted to eat outside," Hawk said mildly...he thought.

But the server flinched and froze halfway to the door.

Lina just grinned. "Come on, Sebastian, don't be a spoilsport. Even big business tycoons have to take the time to stop and smell the roses sometimes."

He frowned at her. "I'm not overly fond of flowers."

She laughed. Even the server cracked a smirk.

Hawk sighed, giving in. "All right, we'll eat outside."

"Great." Lina spun and headed outside, making it to the door ahead of the server so she could open it for him.

He smiled his thanks, his gaze traveling over Lina's scantily clad body with unmistakable pleasure.

Hawk stifled a growl and followed them.

As expected, the outdoor furniture was immaculate and ready for the server to place the food. Hawk automatically pulled a chair out for Lina and she took it with another smile that only the most conservative would *not* call flirtatious. What the hell was going on?

She'd been furious with him earlier and now she was treating him like she had before he'd revealed his true reason for making her acquaintance eight years ago. Well, not exactly like…she'd grown up and was a lot more overtly flirtatious now.

Confused, he sat down and tried to figure out what had changed with her while he waited for the server to finish putting the food out. The younger man chatted with Lina as he set dishes on the table and poured juice in crystal glasses.

At one point he was bold enough to touch Lina's hip. "Cute ink."

Hawk's hand snapped out and grabbed the younger man's wrist before he even thought. "Don't touch."

Lina frowned and the server put his other hand up in a placating gesture. "I was just pointing out I liked her tattoo."

Lina had a tattoo? No way. Hawk would have noticed.

He let go of the other man and barked to Lina, "Let me see."

She rolled her eyes and stood up, cocking her right hip as she did so. "See?"

Damn. There it was. Right over her hipbone. A tiny cartoon animal no bigger than a quarter.

"Can I sit down now?" she asked with exaggerated patience.

"Don't on my account," the server said with a laughing leer.

Hawk gave him a stare he reserved for employees on the verge of being fired, but Lina met the other man shamelessly riposte for riposte until he was done putting their food out.

"Thank you," Lina said before Hawk had the chance.

Though he wasn't sure anything but a snarl would come out of his mouth if he opened it. And right that second, he felt like doing anything *but* expressing gratitude to the guy.

"No problem," the server said. "Just page me when you're finished and I'll come back to clean up."

"Great, will do," Lina said when Hawk remained silent.

The server nodded and left.

"You were awfully snarly with him."

"You're assuming I'm not like this all the time."

"That's true. I only know of you what you chose to project eight years ago and most of that was probably a façade." She sounded pleased by that assumption, rather than angry.

"The only role I played was that of a student. The rest was me."

She looked at him speculatively. "I wonder."

"You think I'm lying."

"I think you are unaware of how much of yourself you kept under wraps when we were together before."

"What do you mean?"

"You're an intense man, Sebastian. You hid that intensity most of the time eight years ago, but it's been on display pretty much nonstop since yesterday."

"If you say so."

"I do."

To change the subject, he asked, "A tattoo?"

Lina shrugged. "It seemed appropriate at the time."

"Why?"

"It's the Road Runner. He should be a victim, prey…right? But he's not. I needed a reminder I wasn't either, that I didn't have to fit the mold made for me, no matter how hard it seemed to live outside of it."

"When did you get it?"

"The month after you left."

For no reason he could fathom, he felt guilty. It was an unfamiliar emotion and even less comfortable one. When unsure of your defense, go on the offense. It worked in business, why not interpersonal relationships? Not that he had a *relationship* with Lina, but even he couldn't deny she was more than a simple client. "Did you have to wear your swimsuit in front of the catering staff?"

"It was only one server and he didn't seem to mind."

She started to eat, making a small moan of pleasure as she tasted the crab Benedict.

"Do you enjoy flaunting yourself in front of susceptible men?" He was aware that he sounded like someone's stern father, but couldn't seem to shut up.

Lina just chuckled. "He was pretty susceptible, wasn't he?"

Hawk tensed, his jaw clenching.

She reached out and brushed his forearm. "Relax. I was just kidding. We were both being friendly. That's all."

Even through his suit jacket and shirt, his body reacted with a jolt to her touch. "Friendly plus half dressed equals flirtatious."

"Whatever you say."

He only wished.

She said, "I wanted to go back into the spa after breakfast, so I didn't want to change, but if it bothers you that much, I'll go put something else on."

"It doesn't bother *me*." As the words slipped out, he realized they were a mistake, but he couldn't call them back.

"So, it only bothers you for other men to see me with a little skin showing?"

"It's a hell of a lot more than a little," he growled, digging the hole deeper.

But she just shook her head. "You know what I think?"

"What?"

"You're projecting your own feelings onto him. You're assuming because you want me that he does, too."

"I didn't say I want you…and why wouldn't he?"

Her laugh was free, sweet and too damn sexy for his libido to stay in check. He'd been semihard since tracking her down in the spa and now his slacks fit like a pair of cycling shorts a size too small.

"Oh, you want me. I saw proof of that earlier this morning."

"It's called a morning erection. All men get them."

"Statistically speaking, that's not actually true, but don't try to tell me your reaction this morning wasn't you getting excited."

"Lina!" Her earthy comment shocked him to the core.

"What? You think that just because I haven't dated a lot, I'm hopelessly naïve?"

"According to your file, you're innocent."

Her perfectly shaped brows rose above a mocking brown gaze. "Was our little interlude at the lake or at Jennifer's apartment in that file?"

"Of course not."

"Well, then…"

"You've had increased security since then."

She shrugged. "I won't argue the point."

"Because there isn't one to argue." It was more important than it should be—read that *not at all*—for her to confirm that she hadn't had a string of clandestine lovers.

"But," she went on without acknowledging his comment, "let me just point out the lack of practical experience, if I *did* lack it, would not stop me from reading up on the subject."

"You've read books about sex?" Okay, maybe he shouldn't be so shocked, but his sweet, innocently sensual Lina reading sex manuals? It was shocking, but more all too arousing a thought.

"Sure. Why not?"

He didn't have an answer, so he didn't attempt one. They ate in silence for several minutes. Lina seemed perfectly at ease, but Hawk kept thinking about all the things she might have read about.

She delicately dabbed at her lips, put her napkin on her plate and pushed it away. "Have you informed my father or his advisors of my location?"

"Why? Are you hoping to convince me to let you go?" He frowned at the thought, for once unsure what he would do if faced with that kind of test to his commitment to his assignment. Nevertheless, he said, "I won't do it. Even after what happened this morning."

"You mean what *almost* happened?" she asked teasingly.

"You touched me."

"And you liked it."

He opened his mouth to speak, but nothing came out. She laughed. Again. "No denial?"

"You aren't going to convince me to dismiss my promise to your father with sex."

"The thought honestly never crossed my mind."

Thank goodness for small favors.

"The truth is, I'm hoping to strike a bargain."

"I just said—"

"Not for my freedom. Even if you were willing, you don't have the power to offer that. Not really. You could withdraw your services, but my father would simply hire someone else."

"That's true." And he was glad she realized it. The thought of some other man escorting her back to her family—using means Hawk didn't want to consider—sent black anger through him.

"But you can give me something I want."

"What?"

"To start with, time."

"Lina…" he said warningly.

"Not too much time…just a few days."

"And what do you think you have to bargain with?" Curiosity about what it might be ate at him. Was she going to offer her body in exchange for that time? The prospect was way more appealing than he wanted it to be.

"My compliance."

Her answer stunned him. "I have you. I don't need your compliance."

"Are you sure about that?"

"You will probably call me arrogant, but yes."

Flicking her silky cascade of multicolored hair over one shoulder, she cocked her head to one side. "How do you intend to get me on the plane?"

"I have a letter from your father giving me permission to use whatever means necessary to insure you do."

Lina blanched, but looked no less confident. "And in Marwan, that letter would carry a lot of weight, but we aren't in my father's country."

"It's your country, too, princess."

"No, it is not." She sounded so sure, not at all like a petulant child rebelling against her parents.

"You can't wish away your place in the world."

"No, but I can and did take legal action to change it."

"What do you mean?"

"I am a U.S. citizen."

"Living in this country, even for most of your life does not make you a citizen."

"No, but applying for citizenship and passing the test does."

An ugly word came out of his mouth.

"If you attempt to take me on a plane, or anywhere else for that matter, by force, you risk being faced with kidnapping charges."

"Your father—"

"Has diplomatic immunity. You don't. And while his word may be law in Marwan, his letter of authority isn't worth the paper it's written on when it applies to a U.S. citizen here in the States."

"You're lying."

"I'm not, but you are welcome to check. I'll even give you my social security number to make it easy for you."

"You don't have an SSN."

"I do. I got it when I became a citizen."

"This is not possible."

"But it is."

"If you are a citizen, why did you come with me yesterday?"

"Because I know I have to face my family."

"Why run in the first place?"

She looked away, an expression he couldn't decipher on her face. "You wouldn't understand."

"Your father knows nothing of your dual citizenship."

Heck, Hawk couldn't be absolutely sure that she wasn't bluffing, but something in her eyes told him she wasn't.

"It's not dual. I gave up Marwanian citizenship to become a U.S. citizen."

"Why?" In Marwan, she was a princess. In America, she was just another woman from a wealthy if conservative family.

Not that her action really changed who she was. Lina was still the daughter of a powerful king who expected her to marry the man he'd chosen for her. If she refused, she would cause a break with her royal parent that would most likely be irreparable.

Hawk had always maintained that his mother's disloyalty and lack of maternal love did not bother him, but the truth was, if he could have her in his life without her using him…he would. The absence of any real family since his father's death had caused him more than one brooding moment in the past few years.

"Marwan does not offer dual citizenship. My father's family has always expected absolute loyalty from their people."

"It's your family, too, princess."

She shrugged, her face going neutral.

"I can't believe your father is not aware of your change in citizenship."

"It's not something he would have anticipated. The security team wasn't watching for it, neither were the paper pushers."

"You flew right under their radar," he said with unquenchable admiration.

"Yes."

"You couldn't have done it with the new security measures."

"No. It was seeking my citizenship that caused me to go looking for ways to circumvent my security team in the first place."

"You had your citizenship when we first met?"

"Yes."

"Why did you do it?"

"I knew one day I would need the leverage." She sighed, frowning with a sadness he hated to see. "I don't expect you to understand. You've made your feelings about my so-called duty clear, but when my parents tossed me away, they lost the right to dictate my life. Not that I'm convinced they had it regardless."

"They didn't toss you away."

"Call it what you like, they sent me to live in America. I chose to become an American."

"So, you said you wanted to bargain with me for your compliance?"

"Yes."

"Besides time, what do you want?"

"You, Sebastian. I want you."

CHAPTER TEN

LINA WOULD HAVE LAUGHED at the expression on Sebastian's face if she wasn't so nervous. She'd done a good job so far of hiding her emotions, but the mask was going to start cracking soon if she wasn't careful.

"What the bloody hell do you mean, *me*?"

"It's quite simple, really," she forced past the dryness in her throat. "I want sex with you...more than once, which is why I want time."

"I'm not a gigolo," he ground out, sounding highly insulted.

"And I'm not offering to pay you to have sex with me."

"You might as well be."

"Don't be such a prude. Whether you want to admit it, or not, you want me." She took a deep breath and let it out. This was harder than she imagined, and she hadn't thought it was going to be a cakewalk. And she hoped to God she was right. "And I want you. For two normal people in a situation less melodramatic than this one, that would most likely end with them in bed together."

"Are you saying you don't think I'm normal, princess?"

"What, a super wealthy man who runs not only a plethora of businesses, but his own internationally renowned detective agency? Nah, that's as normal as it gets."

He shook his head. "You aren't serious about this."

"Like I'm not really a U.S. citizen?"

The sound that erupted from his throat was pure frustration...of the male variety.

"Look, it's not like I'm really asking for something you don't want to give. Think about it, Sebastian." She stood up. "And while you are at it, why don't you page that cute server so he can come back and clean up?"

She peeled her T-shirt off as she walked away. It didn't hurt to give him a glimpse of what she was offering. Lina had a hard time accepting her own bold actions, but then she'd never shrunk from going after what she wanted.

Right now, she needed freedom.

And it was a type of freedom only he could provide. A sexual liberation that unfortunately, it seemed like only this man could give her.

No matter how much she teased him about the hot server.

The other man had touched her hip and it hadn't affected her as much as the way Sebastian had *looked* at her when she stood up to show him her mini-tattoo.

She'd only been sitting in the bubbling hot tub about five minutes when Sebastian came storming into the room. "What about your sheikh?" he demanded in a cold voice.

"For the last time, he's not my fiancé...not my

sheikh...not my anything. What you and my father choose to believe does not in any way alter reality. And in reality I never gave my consent, either implied or otherwise, to my father choosing my future spouse."

"You knew he believed he had the right to do so."

"He also believed he had the right to give me away as if I was nothing more than a possession when I was six years old. I didn't agree with that and I don't agree with this."

"You just want sex?" he asked with bad temper. "You aren't expecting this to become something more?"

"Don't worry, Sebastian. I fell for you eight years ago because I thought you were a different kind of man. Don't concern yourself...I could never fall in love with a man so much like my father, no matter how great the sex is."

"Then why the hell do you want it?"

"My reasons are none of your business. The question is, are you willing?"

He cursed.

"Crudely put, but that's the idea, yes."

He glared at her and darned if that didn't turn her on. Her reaction to this man was just too weird. She wanted him pretty much all the time...no matter what his mood. She'd worry about what that said about her if she didn't know how much she *didn't* react to other men. She figured this was a unique response to this man she would not have to worry about once they parted ways.

But she wanted him out of her system. She wanted to be over him. For real this time. And if it took living out the sensual fantasies he sparked in her overactive imagination, then so be it.

He said something under his breath that she couldn't make out.

"What was that?" she asked.

"I said, I can't believe this."

"Really?"

He looked at her like she'd lost her mind. "Really."

"What's so hard to believe?"

"That you are trying to blackmail me into having sex with you." He spoke slowly, like trying to explain himself to someone who wasn't very bright.

She didn't take offense. Sebastian Hawk was one hundred percent pure alpha male. He was accustomed to being in control of any situation that involved him. With the drop of her bombshell about her citizenship, she'd taken away some of that control and he had to be royally ticked off.

"It's not blackmail. It's a bargain. And frankly, you're getting the better side of the deal. There is nothing that says I have to cooperate with you at all, but I have my reasons for doing so. In exchange I want something that if you were honest with yourself and me, you would admit you want as well."

"You're damn audacious."

"You don't think a princess should be bold?"

"You want the truth?"

"It would be nice, yes."

He looked at her for several silent seconds, making her want to squirm under the scrutiny. However, she maintained her nonchalant air…barely.

Then a half smile tipped one corner of his mouth. "I find your honesty and willingness to go after what you want arousing."

Her gaze flicked to the suit slacks tented below his waist and she felt a blush climb up her neck. "I see."

He laughed shortly. "I guess you do. I'm not sure why this whole situation is so tempting to me."

"Um...because you *do* want me?"

"Perhaps, but there is something about an innocent being so brazen that is very exciting to a man like me."

"You are so sure I am innocent?"

"You talk a good game, princess, but you blushed when you looked at my erection and that says more about your lack of experience than all the bold statements you might make."

She bit her lip, the betraying blush once again heating her skin. "I suppose it doesn't hurt to tell you."

He cocked his head to one side as if waiting for her admission.

"I am still a virgin." There was no reason to spell out just how inexperienced she was. He didn't need to know that no other man had ever touched her as intimately as he had eight years ago.

He nodded.

She sighed.

He laughed again. "Trust me, that is something you want me to know."

"Why?"

"You mean after reading all your books on sex, you don't know?"

"You'll be more careful?"

"I would have anyway, on the chance…but yes."

She'd guessed that…which could have been a dumb assumption to make, but at least now he knew. "So, we have a deal?"

"That depends."

Her heart stuttered in her chest. Was he agreeing? "On what?" she asked with an embarrassing squeak.

He took off his suit jacket. It was slate-gray, obviously an English designer…and why she was noticing that, she didn't know. Maybe because if she focused on the fact he was undressing…that was what he was doing, right? Well, if she focused on that, she might hyperventilate.

He loosened his tie and she bit her lip, wanting very much to ask him what he was doing, but afraid of the answer. What if she was assuming things again and his intent was just to get more comfortable. The spa room was warm after all.

"Lina?"

"Yes?" There went that revealing squeak again.

He unbuttoned the top button on his crisp white shirt. "What exactly are the terms of this deal?"

"Um…terms?"

"Yes, Lina, terms. I'm a businessman. I want to know exactly what you expect in return for your cooperation."

"I already told you." Was he really going to force her to spell it out?

"You want sex. I got that, but you also said you wanted time. How much time are we talking about?"

She swallowed, trying to wet her suddenly parched throat. "I hadn't really considered." Which was the truth, she just knew that one night wasn't enough. But as she admitted that, she felt silly. She was the one who had offered the bargain in the first place, she should have figured out the terms to begin with.

She just knew this was going to put her at a disadvantage.

"I think understandably, I'm not comfortable with an open-ended arrangement. Your father is expecting results." And he knew he couldn't give her anymore.

"And you're not about to have your professional reputation besmirched." Just like eight years ago.

"I would prefer not to, no."

"Um…" She licked her lips. "A week…seven days."

"That's too long. Your father knows I expected to find you before then."

"Just because you expect something to happen, doesn't mean it will."

"It does for me."

"So, this time you can be disappointed."

"I did find you, princess."

"My father doesn't need to know that."

"I have a responsibility to him—he's my client."

"Yes, your responsibility is to make sure that you find and deliver his daughter to him. You can't do that if I refuse to comply…not without facing serious legal charges. So, technically this week *is* what is necessary to fulfill your obligation."

"Three days, princess."

Whether it was the final tenuous link to her belief in romance, or simply her nerve to keep haggling, something broke inside her. Along with the break came anger.

She was tired of his denial of a need that anywhere matched her own, but she was past the point of being willing to argue about it any longer. "Fine," she said with cold precision. "If you think we can burn the fire out between us in two nights, then I bow to your superior experience in this area."

His eyes widened. "I expected a counteroffer, princess."

"Then you miscalculated."

"I see that."

She climbed out of the hot tub and walked over to her towel on the bench. Drying off, she ignored him.

"I said three days, not two nights, Lina."

She didn't bother to look at him as she shrugged. "Same thing."

"No, technically, it is not. Three days constitutes the same number of twenty-four hour periods. Starting now, that would constitute three nights as well."

Something lightened inside her that he was maximizing the amount of time they had together, but she didn't allow herself to get all warm and fuzzy. After all, *he* was the one who had argued against a week.

"Duly noted," was all she said as she grabbed her T-shirt from earlier and slipped it on.

"Where are you going?"

"To take a shower."

"We can start there, but I would prefer to spend some time together in the spa."

She looked up then, to discover that he had removed everything but his slacks and the fly was open on them, revealing black silk boxers tented over his hardness. He should have looked vulnerable like that, only half-dressed and asking her if she wanted to go back in the hot tub with him. But he didn't. He looked as commanding as always.

And really, he hadn't asked about the spa, had he? He'd simply stated what he wanted.

"Is that a request, or an order?"

"What do you want it to be?"

Her heart started trip-hammering. "I…"

He moved until he was standing right in front of her and cupped her cheek. "Do you want me to take charge, princess?"

"Is that what your sex partners usually ask for?" she inquired breathlessly.

"There is no room for what others do or do not like here, Lina." His hand trailed down her neck and rested on the side of her breast, not moving, but his thumb a hairsbreadth from touching her nipple.

"I want…"

"Yes, baby, what do you want?"

"I like the hot tub."

He smiled. "That's good, but that's not what I asked."

She swallowed, feeling nervous and yet conversely powerful. He'd asked what she wanted, hadn't tried to convince her one way or another. Despite everything, something inside her craved the chance to trust in this man. "What I choose…does it last the whole three days?"

"Let's just make it for the time while we're in this room."

"Okay."

"Okay, what?"

"I want you to take charge." Her heart was nervous…her mind wasn't so sure…but her body knew with a primal instinct she could not dismiss that they both needed this.

The tiny flicker of relief in his gray eyes confirmed it.

His thumb covered the tiny distance to make contact with her nipple. Despite the two layers of cloth between her skin and his, she felt the touch like an electric jolt that reached not only that one spot, but her other breast tingled as well and she felt an intense pulse of pleasure between her legs.

"Are you sure, princess?" And something in his expression said he was asking about more than him being in control.

She sucked her lower lip between her teeth and looked deeply into his eyes. Along with that subtle message, all she saw was desire, pure and honest sexual need. "You won't try to deny your sexual need for me anymore?"

"No."

"Or hide behind a man who has no claim on my life?"

"No." This was practically growled and the flash of anger that darkened his features surprised her.

So, Sebastian didn't like the idea of her with her father's chosen, either.

"For three days…seventy-two hours…there is only room for you and me." Which was a far cry from acknowledging that she had no obligation where Amir was concerned, but it was better than nothing.

On some level Sebastian had to realize the sheikh had no legitimate claim on her. If he hadn't, Sebastian would not be touching her right now. His sense of personal honor was too great, no matter how strong his sexual interest in her.

She would have to be content with reading the message into some things that simply were not going to be said.

"Then, I am sure."

His lips tilted in one of his rare smiles. "Good."

She appreciated the fact that he had not asked her if she was certain she wanted him to be her first lover. Again, his actions spoke more eloquently than his words. His lack of belaboring the point of her virginity told her that he respected her enough to accept that she knew her own mind.

She would not deny that a small part of her wished this was happening on her wedding night, but she accepted that if she could not get over Sebastian, chances were she would never have one of those. She certainly had no intention of sharing such a thing with Sheikh Amir.

Sebastian leaned down to kiss her. It was barely a brush of lips, but it somehow sealed their deal. Both the three days and her assertion she wanted him to take charge right now.

He grasped the hem of her T-shirt. "I'm going to take this off."

She nodded, raising her arms so that he could remove it easily.

She had worn a swimsuit in front of him on several occasions, but she felt more exposed as her top got dropped to the floor and the suit was revealed this time.

His gaze traveled over her, making contact like a touch and she trembled. "You are so beautiful."

"Am I?" It was not something she thought of herself.

"Yes." He reached out to trail his fingertips from her temples down her body until he reached her hips. Then he stopped. "You are the most alluring woman I have ever met or seen."

The praise was over the top, but she had no doubts of his sincerity. Sebastian was not the type of man given to empty flattery.

Her tummy fluttered. "I'm glad you see me that way."

"And I'm glad you want me anything near like I want you."

Finally he had admitted it out loud. She had no idea how much she'd needed to hear the words until they came out of his mouth and her knees gave way in relief.

His hold on her hips tightened and he pulled her closer to him. "You okay, princess?"

"More than," she admitted, feeling his honesty deserved her own.

"I'm going to kiss you then I'm going to take off your swimsuit top. And I'm going to look at you like I wanted to do eight years ago."

"Yes," she said on a breath of sound.

He made good on his words, closing the distance between their mouths with slow inevitability that had her entire body straining for the kiss by the time their lips met. Her body melted into his as she tasted the flavor that had haunted her dreams for too long. His tongue dipped into her mouth and then retreated. She whimpered a protest, but he just nipped at her lower lip.

"Sebastian."

"Be patient, for me. I'm going to make this so good

for you, but I need you to cooperate." He didn't give her a chance to respond, but renewed their lip-lock.

It was so good. His lips molded hers, moving and sending waves of pleasure through her. Needing an anchor in the swirling fog of her senses, she reached up to grab his shoulders and touched hot, silky *naked* skin over rigid, bulging muscle. Her eyes flew open to find his had never closed. He was staring down at her with dark, piercing ardor.

She moved her hands down his chest, asking with her gaze if it was all right to touch. His answer was another flick of his tongue against her lips. She took that as approval and she explored the hair roughened contours of his chest.

So strong…so hot…he was such a perfect example of masculine power. Her fingertips slid over his nipples. They were hard. She'd read that for most men, they were erogenous zones. She played a little, circling, lightly scraping her nails over the pointed nubs.

He groaned and stepped back, grabbing her wrists so she could no longer touch him.

She looked at him questioningly.

"You know what comes next."

She remembered what he'd said and her heart fluttered. "Yes," she whispered.

He smiled, approval shining in his gunmetal gaze.

She took a deep breath and let it out as he released her wrists. Then, he reached behind her to unhook first the bottom, then the top strap of her bikini top. It fell away from her body, dropping to the floor and making a small wet plop as it landed. Neither of them looked down to see, though.

Her eyes were glued to his and his look was set on her newly revealed flesh with tactile strength.

"How do you do that?" she asked, perplexed.

"What?"

"Touch me with your eyes."

He shook his head. "I don't know. I only know that watching you is like a feast for my senses."

"Don't you want to touch?" she dared to ask.

"Oh, I definitely plan on touching you, princess, but right now I want to look."

"That's all?" she asked, her voice catching.

"For the moment."

She said nothing, did not know what she should say if she did speak. She had told him he could be in control and the truth was, it was exciting her beyond anything she would have believed possible to have relinquished the power of decision-making to him. She really did need this.

Her body kept telling her that no matter what had happened with him in the past, or what might happen in the future, she could trust him. It wasn't logical, but at present, she didn't care a penny for logic.

She just wanted to keep feeling what she was experiencing right this moment in time.

She did not know how long she stood under his burning surveillance. Time became elastic, seconds could have been minutes and vice versa. Nothing existed for her but his eyes on her. Her gaze flicked over him, noting the changes watching her elicited in him.

His jaw hardened as if he was biting back words and his body tensed, the bulge in front of him unbelievably growing. A wet spot formed on the black silk of his boxers where the tip of his manhood pressed against the fabric.

She'd read about pre-ejaculate...she'd seen it that morning, but knowing that merely studying her visually was causing it now, gave her a strong sense of feminine sensual power.

She'd given him control, but that was precisely the point. She'd *given* it to him and her willingness to trust in him, to his perusal, was inflaming him. That knowledge felt almost as good as his kisses.

"I want to see all of you before I start touching you," he said in a guttural voice.

CHAPTER ELEVEN

LINA licked her lips nervously and took a breath before speaking. "Okay."

"Take off your bottoms."

"*Me?*"

"You."

"But—"

"If I do it, I'll touch you and I'm not ready to do that yet."

"You look ready to me."

He laughed, releasing a measure of the tension building between them. "Too ready. Now, do as you're told, princess."

"Maybe I shouldn't. I don't think princesses are supposed to take orders."

"You are *my* princess…for now…that means you can take my orders."

"If I want to."

"I thought we established that you did."

She smiled, letting her actions speak for her as she went to push her bikini bottoms down her hips.

Considering her background, she should have felt self-conscious baring herself to him, but she didn't. All she felt was an eagerness to witness his reaction to seeing her as no one else had in her adult life.

She was not disappointed. A sound came from deep in his chest somewhere between a growl and a moan. His eyes narrowed, but his pupils dilated with arousal and his already tense body went rigid as if he was physically having to hold himself back from touching her.

She shook under his scrutiny, moisture making itself known between her thighs. Aching with sensation even though they were not being touched, her nipples tightened so that she could feel their pebble hardness in the softly circulating air of the room. In the end, it wasn't him that moved, but her, her feet taking her closer to him of their own volition.

"Stop."

"I can't," she said as she took another step.

With a sound that was torn from his throat, he reached out the remaining gap between them and grabbed her shoulders, then pulled her toward him with barely leashed savagery. His mouth slammed down onto hers with erotic force, his tongue taking instant possession of her interior. Her tongue battled for supremacy with his while her lips moved against his in instinctive pleasure that was in no way limited by her lack of experience.

Okay, so maybe she'd practiced a time…or twenty… on her hand, but still…it felt so right and man, was it good. He didn't seem to mind her aggression, either. In fact, if the way he grew progressively more uncontrolled was any indication, he liked it a lot.

She liked it, too, but she *loved* the way it felt when her bare breasts rubbed against his chest. It was the most amazing sensation and her lips actually went slack as she concentrated on enjoying it. Sebastian didn't stop kissing her, though, forcing her lips to mold to his even though she wasn't consciously doing so.

She was focused on moving in small increments. Side to side. Up on her tiptoes and down again. Back just a little bit and then forward until she was pressed firmly against him. All of it felt brilliant. So, she did it again. All of it. His lips owning hers while she used his body to explore new sensations with her own.

Had she really reached the age of twenty-seven without ever feeling this before?

How?

But the answer was more disturbing than satisfying. No other man in her life had been him. Which was why she was doing this, she reminded herself. So, enjoy it, already. Right.

She found that she liked it best when her nipples barely brushed over his when she was going side to side, so she did that several times until the emptiness growing in her womb grew so acute she cried out in inarticulate need against his marauding mouth.

He seemed to understand, though, because he pulled his lips from hers and brushed them over her forehead, then her cheeks. "Shh...princess, it's all right. I'll take care of you."

"I need something, Sebastian. Please."

"I know what you need."

"Yes."

"Do you trust me?"

Instinct answered over her brain's automatic negative. "Yes."

And that word felt far too right.

"Then just stand there. Let me bring you down a little."

"I don't want to come down," she whined. Oh, gosh…when was the last time she had whined? It was not her. But then neither was this needy wanton.

"Yes, you do."

She looked at him and read his sincerity in a gray gaze gone almost black with his own need. She took a deep breath and let it out slowly. "Okay."

He nodded.

She smiled despite her unfamiliar but acute sensual hunger.

He stepped back…only a few inches, but enough to break body contact. He cupped her face and looked into her eyes. "Just breathe for me, princess."

It was then that she realized she was panting in short shallow breaths and she had to concentrate on breathing in and breathing out. The severe, almost painful arousal coursing through her began to scale back slightly.

It wasn't like she lost her desire, but she became aware of the whir of the overhead fans, where before all she could hear was his inhalations and exhalations. The sound of the hot tub jets running as it maintained temperature encroached on her consciousness.

She looked around her, seeing the opulent room with new eyes. The recessed spa bubbled gently in one corner and the smooth as glass water of the indoor-outdoor pool glistened in the other. Now that the outer doors had been opened, she'd been able to open the divider that made the pool accessible to the outside and she could even hear the fall of the oversize fountain in the center of the outdoor portion.

"If you want me to cool down a little, maybe we should go in the pool rather than the spa," she said.

Sebastian's smile was so sexy, it undid the last few seconds of her calming down process. "Good idea, beautiful."

"So, you're going to take off your pants?" she asked with undisguised interest.

"After you get in the water."

She pouted.

He laughed. "Do you have any idea how adorable you are when you do that?"

She shook her head. She never pouted, so how could she? Did he really think she was adorable? But his continued smile said he did indeed. Wow.

"So, you want me to get in the water?"

"Yes."

"And you *are* going to join me, right?" She had no desire to "cool down" alone.

"Of course, princess. What would be the fun otherwise?"

"Okay then." She turned and walked to the steps that led down into the water. Though she knew it was heated and had dunked her hand in it earlier to test the temperature, finding it perfect, it now felt chilly against her overheated skin.

She forced herself to descend into the pool until the

sound of fabric sliding against skin arrested her. She spun to face him, barely keeping her balance on the bottom step. Sure enough, his pants were already in a puddle of expensive fabric on the floor of the room. He pushed his boxers down past his hard-on and it bobbed up toward his belly. Was it bigger than it had been that morning?

She gulped. It certainly looked like it.

He started walking toward her and she nearly choked on her own breath. Still, his body was amazing. In motion, it was a work of art. A masterpiece at that.

"You're watching me like you want to devour me."

"Maybe I do."

His body jerked and he stopped. "Don't say things like that with that beautiful as sin mouth. You are going to give me ideas you are not ready for."

And it was then that she realized how her words could be taken. Oh. "Who says I'm not ready? You think I don't want that?"

He groaned. "Please, princess…be quiet, for just a minute."

She shrugged in acquiescence, but then turned and dove into the water, swimming to the end of the indoor section of the pool. It wasn't very long, but it was long enough…to give him a glimpse of her body in motion. If it affected him like it had affected her to see him then her silence wasn't going to have the impact on his escalating libido that he wanted.

Some part of her insisted she push his limits. She was aching to consummate their relationship…uh…*deal*. It was a deal, not a relationship and she so had to remember that, but the internal reminder sent a pang of pain through her heart.

Strong hands grasped her around the waist and she went swishing backward through the water until her body landed against his. "There are consequences for teasing a hawk."

"Are there?" she gasped out.

"Yes."

"What are they?"

"Hawks are predators, what does that make someone they catch?"

"Prey?" she asked in a whisper.

"Exactly."

"I think I want to be your prey, darling Sebastian."

His body shuddered. "Say that again."

"That I want to be your prey?"

"What you called me."

"Sebastian?" she teased.

He just growled into her ear and she shivered.

Then she went still. "Darling."

"I like that." He sounded confused and not a little bothered by that fact.

She laid her head back on his shoulder. "I do, too."

He turned her to face him. "I have never wanted another woman as much as I want you."

Again he sounded bothered and she did not comment on the surprising admission. Or at least she did not plan to, but words just sort of came out of her mouth. "If only you had wanted me that much eight years ago."

Then none of this would be necessary.

If a tiny voice deep in her mind questioned that assertion, she chose to ignore it.

"I did."

She shook her head. "No. You walked away."

"You didn't have anything to blackmail me with back then. Well, you did, but you didn't realize it."

Her head spun...was he only touching her because of the deal? That's what he'd said. He'd also said she could have attempted blackmail eight years ago.

Then she realized with perfect clarity what he was talking about. Eight years ago, she'd been so devastated by his betrayal, she had not even considered that he had betrayed her father as well. Or at least his own work ethic by touching her as intimately as he had.

It had been a couple of years before she'd been able to analyze the situation with enough distance to give Jennifer's earliest comments on the situation any credence. From the first time Lina had poured her broken heart out all over her friend, Jennifer had insisted that the whole thing could not have been merely a job to Sebastian. Because a man like him would never compromise a sexual innocent in order to do his job, especially if that job involved protecting her.

That realization had healed a tiny portion of the hurt that had shattered Lina's heart and self-confidence. Not enough to make her open to trusting another man, but some.

She scrutinized Sebastian's face, trying to read his expression, trying to understand the coldness creeping through *her* as his words forced another moment of clarity.

She could not decipher his expression, though—or at least make herself believe what she needed to about what he was feeling. He wanted her, a lot. According to him. And well, she believed it because his physical reactions had been blatant. But also, according to him, he would not be acting on that desire without her bargain. Which she had known and yet something inside her had refused to really *know* it, or maybe to accept it as truth.

She'd convinced herself that despite his words, this thing between them was bigger than both of them, not just her. Only now, for whatever reason, his words were sinking into her brain in a way that they had not before. Maybe because he was saying the same thing despite what they had done and the massive evidence of his arousal.

Maybe because he was finally admitting his desire for her in words and yet still denying that he would have acted on it without being forced. Perhaps because he was finally speaking the truth she had been able to discern all along, she felt compelled to believe him about *everything*.

She couldn't hide from the ugly truth. She couldn't live with it, either.

No matter what she'd thought she was ready for. No matter what kind of compromise to her principles she'd thought she could tolerate. Regardless of what she'd thought she wanted, she knew in that instant that she did not want Sebastian as the result of a deal.

She might never get over him, but if she couldn't have him because he truly wanted her…then she could not have him at all.

She pushed away from him and because he was not expecting it, she slipped easily from his arms. She propelled herself backward until she was to the steps.

She stopped with her hand on the rail. "This was a mistake. We can fly out this afternoon as planned. I'll go to D.C. and meet with my father."

Shards of pain were cutting into her, but she refused to go down emotionally like she had eight years ago. At least this time, Sebastian had not lied to her. She had lied to herself.

And, ultimately, isn't that what had happened when she was nineteen? She'd believed he felt the same emotions she was experiencing, not because he'd said he did, but because she had wanted to. He'd betrayed her friendship, but he hadn't betrayed her love. She'd done that all on her own.

And she wasn't going there again. Not for freedom from her sexual repression. Not for *anything*.

"What the hell are you talking about?" Sebastian demanded. "And where the hell are you going?"

"Back to my room…to get dressed and pack."

"What?" he practically shouted. "Why?"

"I don't want to blackmail you into having sex."

"That's not what you were saying a few minutes ago."

"I…" Could she explain and get out of there without losing it? She had to try. Her pride wouldn't allow otherwise. "I thought you wanted me."

"I do want you, damn it."

"Have you noticed you swear a lot when you get upset?"

"What the bloody difference does that make?"

"Um…none. Just noticing, that's all."

"Don't try to change the subject. You promised me heaven and now you are backing away, ready to leave me in hell. Are you scared, princess? I told you I wouldn't hurt you."

"No. It's not that." She still wanted him. Her body was literally aching to return to his arms.

"Then what is it?" His eyes narrowed dangerously. "Is this payback for eight years ago?"

"No! Of course, not."

"Then why are you over there and I am over here?" His body tensed for movement. "To hell with that." Then he exploded into action.

She'd only taken a single step backward before he was *there*, grabbing her waist in a firm grip.

He pulled her toward him and deeper water once again, only stopping once they were on the verge of going outside. "Now, explain. Use small words and short sentences so there's no possibility I'll misunderstand."

Oh, wow…he was really mad, angrier than she'd ever seen him. And yet his hold on her was not bruising and she felt no fear for her person at all.

"I'll go to D.C.…you don't have to have sex with me to gain my cooperation."

"And if I want to make love to you regardless?"

"But you don't. You just said you're only touching me because I blackmailed you into it."

"I also said I wanted you more than I've ever wanted another woman."

"But you wanted me that way eight years ago. You didn't touch me then because I didn't force you into it."

"Lina!"

"*What?* That's what you said."

"I know what I said."

"So, um…you can let me go." She didn't say please, but she wanted to. She needed to get away from him before she begged him to make love to her anyway.

And ended up hating herself.

His head lowered until their foreheads touched and he sighed, a long drawn out sound that caused a pang in her heart. "No, baby, I can't."

"You can't let me go?"

"No."

"Why not?"

"Because I need to make love to you."

"But you said—"

"I know what I said," he interrupted. "I was strong enough to walk away eight years ago without finishing what we started. I might have been strong enough this time without your deal, but then again, maybe I wouldn't have been. I do know that we've gone too far to turn back now…unless you really don't want this."

She pulled her head back so she could look into his eyes. "So, this isn't about the deal. You want me? Even though you know I'll return to D.C. with you regardless."

"Yes."

"And you don't begrudge me three days?"

"I wouldn't begrudge a whole week, but I think we're safer sticking with our original plan."

She didn't ask what he meant by safer. She thought she already knew. And she agreed. She had an awful suspicion that the time they spent together would lead to craving more and more and more. And the longer it lasted, the stronger the craving would get.

If he was being brutally honest, she could, too, if only to herself. And she could admit that this wasn't only about getting over a sexual fixation that might very well afflict her for the rest of her life. It was about sharing something she would never have the chance to experience again with the one man who had ever gotten deep enough into her heart to matter.

She might fall in love again one day, but she knew it would never be like it was with Sebastian. Their connection was something special and no matter what he felt, or didn't feel, she could acknowledge that—inside herself at least—where the admission was safe.

"So, three days."

"Three days."

Then he kissed her and the watershed of emotions she'd just gone through fed the passion he'd sparked earlier until her insides felt like a raging inferno of unsatisfied longing.

The slip-slide of their naked bodies together in the water was amazing. She undulated against him, learning a whole new series of pleasure points. His hands were all over her, mapping her skin, branding her with his touch.

She didn't realize they'd been moving until she felt the cool water of the waterfall showering her skin. They were outside. She tried to make herself care, but she couldn't. This felt right...natural.

The knowledge in the back of her mind that there was an eight foot tall brick privacy wall all the way around the backyard helped. So did the fact that the closest neighbor was at least a quarter of a mile away. She was going to assume the caterer had either already come and gone, or Sebastian had not paged him to return yet.

She had no doubt that her three-day lover was too possessive to allow another man the possibility of seeing her naked. He'd been much too disturbed by the server seeing her in her swimsuit with a T-shirt over it.

So, she relaxed…mentally anyway…and let herself wallow in the feelings he was causing. Her body screamed with pleasure and need. And this time even a dunk in a mountain fed stream wouldn't cool her off.

He swam with her, their lips still locked together, until they reached the steps in the outer pool. Then he swept her into his arms and carried her out of the water.

She broke the kiss to ask, "Where are we going?"

He nodded toward a decadent wrought-iron double lounger under a Roman canopy in the middle of the emerald green grass.

"Oh," she breathed.

He smiled, the look indulgent and warm. She was careful not to read anything more into it than masculine desire. She wasn't going to lie to herself again.

He laid her carefully onto the overstuffed oyster shell cushion and then joined her, covering her body with his.

"Have I told you how beautiful and downright sexy you are, princess?"

"You might have mentioned it." Her voice was croaky and filled with want.

He kissed his way down to her breast. "It deserves more than a mention."

"Thank you. You're the sexiest man I have ever known."

"Glad to hear it." Then his mouth curved around her distended nipple.

He laved, then sucked, then circled the sensitive peak with his tongue before doing it all over again while his hands were busy touching her all over.

She reached for him, but he grabbed her hands and placed them over the ornate white iron bar at her head. "Keep them there, princess."

"But I want to touch you."

"You agreed to let me call the shots."

"In the room. We're outside now."

"I want you to hold onto the bar. Will you do that for me?"

She couldn't deny him, realized she didn't even want to. "Yes."

If she'd thought his touching before was intense, it was nothing like what she experienced now. He caressed, traced, licked, nibbled and teased every inch of her skin until she was a quivering mass of nerve endings ready to explode.

Then he spread her legs with gentle hands and leaned forward to touch his tongue to the most intimate part of her.

She screamed and came and shook as her body immediately began the climb toward another climax. As he lashed her pleasure spot with his tongue, his finger explored her inner recesses. She felt a pressure…some pain…but it only heightened her pleasure high. Then a second finger joined the first and he pressed them deeply inside, gently massaging a barrier she knew denoted her virgin status.

As she went supernova the second time in less than a minute, he pressed forward and a sharp pain mixed with her euphoric pleasure.

When he withdrew his fingers, they had blood on them. She saw it through the haze of her satiation and she knew what it meant. He had broken her barrier...claimed her in a way no other man would ever be able to.

A primitive part of her she had not even known existed was fiercely glad.

He surged up until his body covered hers. He pressed his hard penis against her tender flesh, but did not attempt to breach her opening. Instead he thrust against her, his length sliding along her clitoris from root to tip with each pelvic movement.

"What...? I...this..." She couldn't string a coherent thought together, but she knew this wasn't what was supposed to happen.

Only it felt so good and he seemed to be enjoying it as well. His face was contorted in ecstasy as his thrusts increased in speed and pressure. Her body had been so starved for this that she found herself careening toward another climax.

When it came, she heard him shout and felt warm wetness against her belly.

Everything was so intense, she felt like she might pass out, but she clung to consciousness, not wanting to miss a moment of the pleasure.

Sebastian said something against her temple that she could not make out.

"What?" she asked in pleasure slurred tones.

For one second he looked totally freaked out before his usual game face slipped back into place and he shook his head. "Nothing."

"If you say so."

"I want to do this again."

"It's a good thing we have three days."

Something dark crossed his countenance, but he nodded. "Yes."

CHAPTER TWELVE

HAWK tracked Lina down in the living room. She was curled up on the oversize suede leather sofa dozing. He'd left her alone to answer some e-mails and make a few phone calls, but he'd ended up closing down his computer before the in-box was empty and ignoring an important call from Japan in order to find out what she was doing.

It was an addiction.

Not just making love, but simply being in her company.

He enjoyed it. Too much.

For the first time in his life, he considered the possibility that he was in love. With a woman promised to another man. How lacking in intelligence was that?

Only Lina didn't consider herself engaged and because she didn't, he didn't, either. On the first day they were here, she'd said he was like her father. Maybe he was. *In some ways*, but not all ways and certainly not to the point that he was willing to force his princess into a marriage she didn't want.

He'd been a fool to think he could do so from the beginning. No matter what he'd said to her, he realized now that deep in his heart he had agreed to come after Lina himself so that he could once again protect her. This time from her family if need be. How could he have been so unaware of his own motives not to have seen it? Okay, so he was a very stubborn man and he had stubbornly insisted that he was never going to fall prey to love.

Only he had.

And the hell of it was, he didn't even mind.

If only he could believe Lina's family, or even she herself, would respond to his feelings with as much acceptance. She'd said she could never love him because of his similarities to her father, but he was hoping to change her mind. It didn't help that she still referred to their lovemaking as sex, holding a part of herself back from him. He felt it and it made him crazy, which led him to try to break down the barrier. The only way he knew to do so was to make love.

Again.

Not that they'd actually had intercourse, but they'd done pretty much everything else. He'd told her he wanted to wait until she had healed a little inside before attempting to penetrate her. He didn't want her first time with their bodies completely joined marred by soreness from her broken hymen.

And he was determined to make it their first time, not their last. It was going to happen tonight, their final agreed upon night together.

But right now, he just wanted to be with her. Sappy?

Maybe. But true. And he was a big enough man…
finally…to admit it. Okay, it also helped to know she was
a U.S. citizen. What had been flat out impossible in his
mind eight years ago, not shown with the light of hope
to his rapidly changing heart.

If her father did not have legal control over her, it was
just possible Lina and Hawk could have a future.

He sat down near her feet and her eyes fluttered open.

She smiled…a wide-open expression filled with love,
he was sure of it. Then her look shuttered and her
welcome turned down a couple of notches.

He stifled his sigh of frustration. This was his fault and
he was going to fix it. He'd made a mistake eight years
ago when he'd walked away and he'd made a mistake
four days ago when he came after her with the intent of
taking her back to her family.

He planned to rectify both mistakes in an unmistakable way.

"You said I wouldn't understand why you ran, even
though you knew you didn't have to. I'd really like you
to explain it to me now."

"Why?" she asked, her voice still husky with sleep.

He reached out and brushed his fingers through her
long hair. "Because I want to know you better…to understand everything about you."

She laughed. "Women aren't that easy to understand,
don't you know that? That would take a lifetime."

"Maybe. Would that be so bad?"

Her soft brown eyes widened, but then she shook her
head. "You're joking."

It was his turn to say, "If you say so." One of her

favorite phrases that he'd figured out pretty quickly meant she wasn't going to argue, but didn't necessarily agree.

She frowned.

He smoothed the line between her eyebrows with his fingertip. "Tell me why you ran."

"I was scared."

"Why? You're a U.S. citizen."

"And my father is a king. I was afraid of what he might do to try to force me to his will…I was afraid of what I might do in some final ditch effort to gain his approval."

"So, you ran in order to shore up your reserves."

"And to force him to send someone else after me, someone who hopefully wouldn't have diplomatic immunity."

Clever. And effective. "Your plan worked."

"In unexpected ways."

"Was it really so unexpected? You had to know he wouldn't use the security company who had lost track of you to begin with."

She sat up, staying close, letting their bodies touch as she settled into her favorite seat in the corner of the couch. "You're right. I think I may have even subconsciously expected him to contact you. After all, it had worked before."

"But you were still disconcerted by my arrival." Not that she'd shown it overtly, but he'd figured it out eventually.

"I think you will always disconcert me, Sebastian."

"And you will always drive me to distraction."

She grinned. "Is this where the kissing starts?"

"Actually it's where I remind you that we are going out tonight and you need to get dressed."

"We went out last night." She chewed on her bottom lip, something she did when she was thinking, or trying to get her courage to the sticking point. "I would rather stay here with you than go anywhere."

"Where I want to take you is a very special place."

"It couldn't be as special as spending time alone with you."

"I'm glad to hear that, but this is important to me. Please, princess? For me?"

"I don't have anything to wear."

"If you go upstairs to our room, you'll find that you do. It's on the bed."

"There was a delivery while I was napping?" she guessed.

"Yes."

"You really want to do this?"

"More than anything in my life."

"That sounds serious."

"It is, Lina. Very serious."

"Okay, I'll go get dressed, but you have to let me dress alone, or we won't make it out of the house."

"Already taken care of." She was right and he'd known it before she said anything, so he'd put his tux in the second bedroom—the one she'd slept in the first night—and planned to dress in there.

Lina had spent three days falling in love all over again, or admitting to herself that the love she'd felt for

Sebastian when she was nineteen had never died. She had also spent those days forcing herself not to play mind games, or trick herself. She was determined not to fool herself into believing he cared about her when all he wanted was sex.

Only he *hadn't* just wanted a bedtime playmate. He'd asked her more questions like the one on the couch downstairs than she could count. He'd spent hours digging into her psyche and letting her return the favor. Just like eight years ago, only this time he had no cover story to maintain, no reason to pretend to want friendship—a *deep* friendship—with her.

Even so, each moment of the past three days, she'd been aware that he was actively pursuing a plan that could result in her married to another man. Or at least she'd believed that was his desire. He certainly wasn't acting like a man who expected the woman he was sharing his body with to move on to someone else.

In fact, he often made comments about the future that implied they would be spending it together.

She'd been adamant about making herself dismiss each and every one. Now she had to wonder if this time, she'd been actively fooling herself into believing that the man she loved wanted to let her go.

Oh, man…that kind of thought just led to heartache and pain. Yet Sebastian was not acting like a man who was going to hurt her. Not even sort of.

She pulled a tissue wrapping from the dress on the bed and gasped. Eight years ago, in one of their many discussions in the coffee shop on State Street, she'd mentioned to Sebastian that when she got married she wanted to wear her aunt's wedding gown. It was a white beaded, formfitting gown that would have looked in place on a 1940's starlet.

That dress was lying on their bed. Next to it was a pair of white satin heels in her size and a tiara. Not like something she'd ever worn in Marwan. Her father was a desert king and tiaras weren't de rigueur over there. But it was the kind of thing Sebastian would buy for *his* princess.

Tears burned her eyes as she wondered if she had enough courage to take one more chance with the man she was destined to love until the day she died.

In one of those sweeping moments of clarity that usually scared her half to death, she realized she didn't have the courage *not* to.

But first…she needed him to answer a question.

She found him in the room next door. He was fiddling with his bow tie, looking more nervous than she'd ever seen him.

He looked up when she walked in. "You don't like it?" he asked, his voice tight with emotion she had no trouble deciphering.

It was fear.

"I love it. You had to know I would."

He swallowed. "I hoped."

"I need you to answer a question."

"Anything for you, princess."

"I am your princess, aren't I?"

"Yes."

"That wasn't my question."

"I figured."

"Why?"

"Why what?"

"Why walk away eight years ago? Why almost walk away this time? Why the proposal? That's what this is, isn't it?" she asked, indicating the precious beaded fabric over her arm.

"That's a lot more than one question."

She didn't say anything, just waited.

His hands twisted in his tie and he yanked it off. "I'll have to use another one."

"I'll help you with it…if you answer my questions."

"Eight years ago, I believed you were under your father's legal control completely. I knew…or believed… we couldn't have a future. And frankly, that relieved me as much as it hurt."

"How come?"

"I told you about my mom."

"Yes."

"She wasn't the only woman in my life to teach me that love, affection even, is a weakness my pride cannot afford."

"Do you still believe that?"

"No."

"What happened to make you so sure of it before?"

"I've only had two other semi-serious relationships. The first tried to sue me for palimony after I broke it off once I'd discovered she had another man on the side. And the second dumped me for someone higher in the food chain."

"So, you thought all women were like that?"

"At least the women the men in my family are attracted to. Both my grandfather and my dad had lousy taste."

"But you don't."

His smile was brilliant and beautifully open. It made tears come to her eyes because she realized it was an entirely new expression for him. "No. I have excellent taste." A flash of pain shone in his eyes. "I only wished I'd realized that eight years ago."

"But back then you were convinced my father would and could do whatever he needed to break us apart."

"Within reason, yes. As distant as he's been with you, he is a man of honor. He won't break the law to get his way. You're no longer a citizen of his country, he can't legally order you to do—or undo—anything."

She realized Sebastian had been a lot more impacted by her father's position than she'd ever given credit. And not because he was in awe of it, but he saw it as a potential to hurt her. In his own way, her lover had been trying to save her further heartache eight years ago.

"You tried to talk to me twice."

"I couldn't let you go completely."

"I never let you go, either."

"I'm glad."

"Say it."

He grimaced.

"If you want me to wear this…you have to say it."

"Another deal?"

"Nope. This time it's pure blackmail."

He walked forward, took her into his arms and she was surprised to find he was trembling. Their eyes met.

He cupped her cheek. "I love you, my princess, today and every day throughout eternity. You are everything I ever dreamed a woman could be and more."

She wanted to tease him about being so corny, but she was too busy swallowing tears of joy. Finally she sniffled and said, "I love you, too."

"Marry me?"

"Yes."

Sebastian waited at the front of the exclusive wedding chapel for Lina's uncle to walk her down the aisle. Contacting the couple who had raised her had been a calculated risk. There was a strong chance that they would tell Lina's father of Sebastian's plans and the king and his entourage would show up to try to stop them.

But he also knew it would mean a lot to his princess to have the older couple there. So, he trusted in their love for Lina and called them.

And they'd come through. Not only had they been willing to take the private plane he had arranged for them to arrive in time, but they had brought the dress Lina now wore.

She looked like a vision…an incredible too wonderful for him but he wasn't letting her go vision. She'd pulled her long, black hair into an intricate knot on top of her head and then placed the tiara in the perfect spot. The dress accentuated her gorgeous curves and the heels lent a swing to her walk that sent his temperature straight toward the heavens.

When her uncle placed Lina's hand in Sebastian's, he

felt as if his life had finally reached where it was supposed to be.

She smiled and his heart squeezed.

"Thank you," he said with fierce conviction.

The minister cleared his throat. Lina's aunt and uncle both chuckled, but she just gazed at him with a wealth of love. "For what?"

"For loving me enough not to give up."

"You're welcome. Thank you for loving me enough to come after me."

"The pleasure was entirely mine."

The rest of the ceremony was a blur of emotions and promises that rang true to the very depths of his soul.

Afterward, they had a celebratory dinner in a little known restaurant at the top floor of one of the larger downtown buildings. It was reserved for high rollers and visiting royalty. Sebastian thought his princess qualified.

His princess. For the rest of his life. Contentment poured through him in waves.

And those waves turned into a tsunami of passion when they got back to the house.

They were naked in their bed. He was poised above her, having brought her to completion once already. He throbbed with the need to be inside his wife.

He pressed until he had barely breached her most intimate flesh. "Until death."

"Until death," she repeated and lifted herself, impaling herself on him.

"I love you," he cried out as he came. "Lina, you are my life."

"Love, love, love..." she chanted over and over again

as she climaxed around him, lending her pleasure to his until the circle was complete.

They were one, never to be torn asunder. He would make sure of it.

EPILOGUE

THE king of Marwan made threats and postured, but in the end, it was surprisingly easy for Sebastian and Lina to convince him to accept their marriage. It helped that she had the total support of her surrogate parents, not to mention her adopted citizenship.

The Marwanian king was not happy, but he was far from stupid. Definitely savvy enough to realize the kind of embarrassment his daughter's new allegiance could cause his country if it became public knowledge. Which it surely would if he fought against the fait accompli of Sebastian and Lina's marriage.

Her uncle had pointed it out just in case his brother-in-law was having a dense moment.

Lina had simply stated her case and then gone silent with a look Sebastian recognized as rock-hard recalcitrance. Apparently her brother recognized it, too, because he advised her father to leave be.

Sebastian ended up being good friends with the future king of Marwan, which pleased his wife so much that she experimented with some things she'd read about while studying up on human sexuality.

He made a mental note to please her often, but then that's what a man did for the woman he would love into eternity and knew with no shadow of doubt would love him just as long.

Jack and the Princess

RAYE MORGAN

Raye Morgan has spent almost two decades, while writing over fifty novels, searching for an answer to that elusive question: just what is that special magic that happens when a man and a woman fall in love? Every time she thinks she has the answer, a new wrinkle pops up, necessitating another book! Meanwhile, after living in Holland, Guam, Japan and Washington, DC, she currently makes her home in Southern California, with her husband and two of her four boys.

To royalty everywhere:
May they live on in our dreams
And stay out of our politics!

Chapter One

Scaling the wall of a mansion and slipping from a balcony into an upper-floor room was probably a unique way of interviewing for a job. But Jack Santini was a pretty unique guy, and he decided it was the reasonable way to go. And all went well until he got to his destination. He hadn't expected to find a young woman in the room, much less in the bed, in mid-afternoon. As he came in through the open French doors, he was as surprised as she was.

He couldn't afford to have her scream and bring the household down on top of him, so he followed his instincts and grabbed her quickly, covering her mouth with his hand while he whispered in her ear.

"Take it easy, honey. I'm not going to hurt you."

She didn't struggle. Her first start of alarm faded quickly, and though he could feel hear heart beating

wildly, she was looking at him sideways, more with
wide-eyed interest than with fear. She was a pretty
one, with shiny golden hair that curled around her
face and huge blue eyes framed by thick black lashes.
For just a moment he was intensely aware of how soft
and rounded she felt, and his head was filled with her
fresh, sunshine scent. But he shook it off. Years of
training held him in good stead and he quickly regained his professionalism.

"You think you can stay quiet for me?" he asked
her, his mouth against her ear.

She nodded and he loosened his grip, waiting just
a few seconds to make sure she wasn't bluffing before
completely releasing her. Springing up off the bed, he
went to the door and listened, ready to leave as
quickly as he'd arrived. There were people in the hallway, chatting back and forth. Probably maids cleaning rooms. He combed a hand through his thick black
hair, frustrated. He was going to have to get past them
if he was going to end up downstairs in the business
office without triggering any sort of alarm.

That was his goal. He'd come to interview for the
job as head of security for this estate. He liked to take
a direct approach and test out what was going on,
which is why he'd come into the property the way he
had. His experiment was showing him that security
here needed a lot of work.

But his test wasn't over. He still had to arrive at
estate manager Tim Blodnick's desk without being let
in the front door. He was anticipating the look he

would see on Tim's face when he appeared out of
nowhere. The next few minutes after that look would
determine whether he took the job or not. Even
though he was desperate as hell for something to pull
him out of the swamp he was stuck in, he wasn't
about to sell his soul. Time would tell.

The best thing would be to show up in front of
Tim's astonished face in about two minutes. But the
voices still echoed up and down the hallway, sounding casual, in no hurry. He couldn't leave the room
until they'd gone. Stymied, he glanced back at the
girl on the bed.

She was sitting back against the headboard, watching him, her eyes very bright. She looked wary but
not really scared, and he supposed that was a good
thing, although rather unusual. One yell from her and
he would seem foolish instead of exceptionally
expert, which was what he was going for. He was
lucky she was staying calm.

''Where are you taking me?'' she asked him, acting
more like someone on the brink of an adventure than
anything else.

He turned fully and looked at her, noticing again
that she was one of the prettiest girls he'd seen in a
long time. An employee, probably. The room was
sparse, with nothing more than a simple bed, a
straight-backed chair and a small dresser. There were
no decorations, no fancy drapes. The house itself had
the look of a fairy-tale castle from the outside. If she
was part of the family who lived here, he would think

she would have fancier digs. At the most, he expected she might be a visiting granddaughter of the old couple Tim had mentioned lived in the place.

"I'm not taking you anywhere," he reassured her, starting back toward the door. "I'm getting out of here as soon as the coast is clear."

Her pretty face took on a puzzled frown. "Wait a minute. Didn't you come to kidnap me?"

He spun and stared at her, both hands raised. "Whoa, hold on. I'm not kidnapping anyone." He frowned, put off balance by her odd reactions. "Why would I want to kidnap you?"

Her chin lifted as though she was gathering pride around herself. "Because I'm the princess, of course."

A princess. Oh, sure. He relaxed. She certainly looked like one, though, sitting there in her lacy nightgown with her hair tumbling around her face. She could have been right out of a picture in a Victorian novel. Too bad she also seemed to be a little nuts. Either that, or she was just pulling his leg.

"A princess," he said wryly. "Right. And I'm Robin Hood."

Robin Hood. Karina Alexandera Roseanova, Princess of the Royal House of Nabotavia, mulled that over and it made her smile. This very imposing man would fit perfectly into the role of the bandit with a heart of gold. He moved with a strength and agility that made her marvel, and he had the right audacious attitude for it, as well.

She knew he was mocking her, but that didn't bother her at all. In fact, it made this encounter all the more interesting. She hardly ever got this close to such an attractive man—especially one who didn't know who she was. He was scoffing at the idea of her being a princess.

He didn't know!

This gave rise to all sorts of intriguing possibilities. She didn't get the chance to come across as a regular person very often. In fact, her life was often monotonous, although seldom ordinary. For her to sit here and contemplate being kidnapped and not be frightened by the prospect should have been bizarre, but somehow it wasn't. She knew very well that one of the main reasons they had to have such extensive security here at the estate was exactly because there *were* Nabotavian rebels who might think grabbing the princess would give them leverage of one sort or another.

There had been a coup in Nabotavia shortly after she was born. Her parents had been killed in the fighting, and she and her three brothers had been whisked out of the country for safekeeping. Ever since, fears that one of them might be grabbed and taken hostage in order to manipulate events back in the old country had been a constant backdrop to their lives. She knew she ought to take the risk more seriously, but she was tired of spending her life jumping at every strange sound and distrusting everyone who looked at her too long.

She'd lived that way for years; had endured being moved from one boarding school to another just when she'd finally made friends, because there might be a threat. She'd spent her summers in places so unpopular, no one under fifty could be seen on the streets; and had sat through long dinners where her aunt and uncle and other relatives moaned and groaned about living in exile, while she dreamed of just being close enough to real life to see men who didn't wear dentures.

And now a gorgeous specimen of the most virile masculinity had been dropped right into her lap.

She watched as he went back to the door and pressed his ear to it, listening, it seemed, to see if the coast was clear. Remembering how it had felt when he'd held her in his arms, she shivered, even though she knew very well it had only been for emergency purposes. She hadn't had much male attention in her young life. That feeling was one she was going to cherish for a long time.

And she was going to need it, knowing the future she had in store for her. A shadow passed over her face as she thought of it, but she pushed it away quickly. She had the rest of the spring and most of the summer before her fate would be sealed. She meant to enjoy that small window of freedom to the hilt.

"You know..." she began, but he motioned for silence and she obeyed.

"Just a minute," he murmured, listening at the

door and getting impatient. The maids were passing very close, laughing over some shared joke. If only they would get out of the hallway. At this rate he was going to be late, and the effect of his entrance wouldn't have nearly the same impact.

"Well," she began again, from right behind him this time.

He spun around, shocked that she had gotten up out of the bed and come so close without his noticing. He must be losing his edge. And guys in his business who lost their edge usually lost a lot more in the process. He was going to have to watch it.

"Shh," he warned her sternly.

She blinked and complied with his warning, going on in a stage whisper. "If you're not here to kidnap me, what are you here for?"

"Get back on the bed," he told her gruffly, feeling slightly dizzy from the sense of her warmth so close. He was tall and muscular, and suddenly he felt every bit of his manhood as he looked down at her delicate features. The white lace of her nightgown was edged by a threaded blue satin ribbon, emphasizing her femininity. She came to his shoulder, but her figure was slender. She looked light as a feather. Still, the outline of her breasts was clear through the lace, full and rounded and...

The bottom threatened to fall out of his stomach, like going fast over a dip in the road, and he had to look away quickly to keep control of his reactions. He'd just told her to do something, but he'd forgotten what it was, and she wasn't doing it, anyway. He frowned, trying to recapture his sense of reserve.

"You're not trying to burglarize us in broad daylight, are you?" she demanded as she thought of it. "Or maybe you're casing the joint?"

He had to look at her again at that one. She'd said it oddly, and he suddenly realized she had a very slight accent. "'Casing the joint?'" he repeated, his tone shaded with just a little ridicule. "You've been watching too many old movies."

"And you're avoiding the question."

He supposed she deserved to know the truth. "Listen, you've got this all wrong. I'm not burglarizing anything. I'm just testing the security system on this estate, evaluating how tight it is."

She rolled her eyes. "'Just testing.' Right." She said it in a direct copy of the way he'd responded when she'd mentioned being a princess. "And I'm the chimney sweep."

He couldn't hold back the slow grin she evoked. She was darn cute, if annoying, with her tousled locks and her pert attitude. "Okay, chimney sweep," he said. "Because that really is what I'm doing. Just give me a minute and I'll be out of your hair."

The word triggered something between them. Her hand went involuntarily to smooth back her curls, and his gaze followed, caressing the golden cascade of hair for a moment, then sliding down to take in the way her breasts filled the bodice of her nightgown before he met her gaze and realized she'd noticed the way he was looking at her. Her huge blue eyes widened, and without saying another word, she reached out and took up a light robe that was slung across the back of a chair, slipping into it and pulling it together in front.

He felt his ears burn and wondered why. Suddenly, incredulously, he knew. Dammit, he was blushing.

That was what getting mixed up with women did for you. It was Eve with the apple every time—sweet temptation that you had to pay for, big-time, later on. With a soft, internal groan, he turned back to the door. There was still noise in the hallway. Without bad luck, he would have no luck at all.

"They'll be gone in a few minutes," she told him calmly. "They're a pair of chatterboxes."

"Maids?" he asked.

She nodded. "They would be in here right now, only they think I'm asleep. I'm just getting over the flu."

He glanced at her again, realizing that his attention was being drawn back to her repeatedly because she was just so good to look at. "I was wondering what you were doing in here at this time of the day."

She gazed at him levelly, her head to the side as she scanned him. "Since you figured out that I'm not the princess, what do you think I am?" Raising her arms, she turned before him, her eyes crinkling with amusement. "What do I look like to you?"

He would hate to say. She would probably slap his face if he were honest about it. "I don't know." He shrugged, put on a forced frown and went to the window, looking out at the rolling green lawn that was her view. You couldn't see the street from here, but he could see the tall wrought-iron fence that guarded the property. Everything else was trees. You would have thought this was out in the country somewhere. You couldn't really tell they were in the middle of Beverly Hills. "Maybe a nanny for the little kids or something," he said back over his shoulder.

"You think I look like a nanny?" She seemed pleased as punch, turning to look in her mirror as if to confirm his opinion. And that just confused him all the more.

"You *do* work here, don't you?" he asked, just to make sure.

"Oh, yes." Turning back, she nodded wisely. "I work very hard, in fact."

"Do you? What do you do, exactly?"

"I...well..." She avoided his gaze, her attention skimming over the room. "You might say I'm a sort of companion to...to the princess." She gave him an impish grin. "There really is one, you know. And to the duchess."

"The duchess? What duchess?"

She turned to stare at him rather majestically. "Do you mean to tell me you broke into this house and you haven't any idea who lives here?"

"I haven't a clue."

"You see, that's your problem. If you did better

research before you set up your breaking-and-entering projects, things might go more smoothly.''

He knew she was trying to tease him, but he shrugged again. ''It doesn't matter. My old friend Tim told me he had a job for me as head of security. I'm in real need of a job right now. He gave me the address and I came on over.''

She drew in a quick breath. ''So you're going to work here?''

''Maybe.'' He frowned at her, realizing she was going to be one of his charges if he did get the job. It was evident she needed a few lessons in how to protect herself. ''You know what?'' He jabbed a finger in her direction. ''If I do, you're going to be one of my first cases. I'm worried about you.''

''Me?'' she squeaked, wide-eyed. ''Why?''

He leaned toward her and she took a step back. ''You don't really know who I am or what I'm doing here,'' he said accusingly. ''You should be hysterical about now. Why aren't you?''

''Oh, please.'' She waved his question away. ''I'm afraid hysteria is not my style.''

His eyes narrowed thoughtfully. ''You're taking this all too casually. Just for future reference, if a man ever comes bursting into your room again, I want you to scream this house down.''

''Shall I do it now?'' she asked obligingly.

''No!'' Taking a quick step in her direction, he almost grabbed her, until he realized what he was doing and stopped himself. ''No, not now.''

She gazed at him with ill-concealed amusement. "So you're the only man allowed to come in off my balcony. Is that it?"

He resisted the urge to grin at her, knowing very well it would be disaster to let her think he could treat her as a friend. "You got it. If I become head of security here, there are going to be some changes made."

"Well, I guess so." She was teasing him in earnest now. "After all, old Mr. Sabrova never came into my room without knocking first."

"Who is old Mr. Sabrova?"

"The previous head of security. But then again, I don't think he could have made it up here even if he'd put a ladder up to the wall. He was pretty old. But a very nice man," she hastened to add, remembering her manners.

A very nice man, but like all the men around here, over-the-hill and not very interesting. After all, old Mr. Sabrova didn't have jet-black hair, thick as an animal pelt, and sexy muscles that bulged right through the fabric of his crisp white shirt and snug dark slacks, nor did he have stormy gray eyes that hinted at mysteries unlike anything she'd ever encountered.

"You're going to have to wear a uniform, you know," she told him, suppressing a grin as she thought of how he'd look in the ridiculous getup Mr. Sabrova had favored.

"I'm used to uniforms. I've been a Navy SEAL

and a beat cop in my time.'' But then he remembered. This was a strange house with strange practices. He turned slowly and looked at her. ''What sort of uniform?'' he asked suspiciously.

''Oh, white with gold braid and epaulets on the shoulders and a red hat and—''

''No way.'' He laughed shortly. ''That's not *my* style.''

She gave him a skeptical look. ''That's the way we do things here. That's the way it's always been.''

''Tell you what. It may just be time to modernize this whole operation.''

She laughed softly. ''I can hardly wait to hear you tell that to the duchess.''

He gazed at her quizzically. ''Is there a 'mister duchess'?''

''Oh, yes. The duke. He's a darling. I adore him. But he doesn't matter. It's all her, believe me.''

He held his hand up to stop her from saying anything while he listened intently.

''They're gone,'' he said decisively. He opened the door a crack and looked into the hallway. Glancing back, he winked at her. ''Thanks for the memories,'' he said. ''See you around.'' And he slipped out into the hallway, closing the door silently behind him.

Kari stared at the closed door for a moment, then moved resolutely toward the telephone on the corner of the dresser. Picking up the receiver, she pressed a few numbers and put it to her ear.

"Blodnick here," said the gruff male voice at the other end.

She smiled. "Mr. Blodnick, it's Kari. I believe you have an appointment today with a man—an old friend of yours—about taking on the job as head of security."

"You're right. He's late."

"No, on the contrary, he was here quite on time. I'm afraid I detained him."

"You what?"

The shock in his voice was palpable, but she ignored it.

"If at all possible, I'd like to have him hired, please."

There was a pause, and the man cleared his throat. Then he said the only thing he could say. "Whatever you say, Princess."

"Oh, and, Mr. Blodnick. About the uniform. I think you should discuss designing something new for the security guards. Your friend may have some ideas on that score. It is a new millennium, you know. We need to get with the times, don't you think?"

"Sounds doable, Princess."

"Thank you, Mr. Blodnick."

She hung up the telephone and smiled happily. Suddenly she didn't feel sick at all. Maybe this summer wasn't going to be quite the boring disaster she'd expected it to be. It was, after all, going to be her last period of relative freedom. And when it was over, she would be marrying someone her aunt chose for her.

Something told her he wasn't going to be at all like the new head of security.

Her smile faded as she remembered that, and the familiar sensation of a fist closing down inside came over her. By winter she would be married and on her way back to Nabotavia, a place she didn't even remember.

"But that is weeks away," she told herself, closing her eyes and taking a deep, cleansing breath. "Weeks away."

Chapter Two

Jack tested the condition of the wrought-iron fence near where the hill rose behind the property and noted the results in his minirecorder. It was really too dark now to get a full picture, but he could see some of the more obvious features. He'd been head of security on this estate for all of six hours, and he'd already found a number of improvements that had to be made to bring the place up to standard, which was what he'd been told his goal would be. Upgrading conditions and managing a staff of five rotating guards were the main duties he'd signed on for. The pay was above average and included living quarters right here in the compound. It was a good job and he was glad he had it, if temporarily.

The estate was large, consisting of the main house, a few utility buildings, a five-car garage with chauf-

feur's quarters overhead, a garden house with the security office and the apartment where he would be
staying. The grounds were extensive, including a
small stand of redwoods that gave the sense of being
in a forest, a formal rose garden that seemed to be a
special showplace for the estate, emblematic to the
royal family themselves, a kitchen garden and three
small pools connected by waterfalls, ducks and koi.
Another waterfall recycled water into the swimming
pool. Everywhere there was the sound of water.

He still hadn't figured out exactly who this was he
was working for. Tim had been in a hurry to make a
meeting in L.A. and had promised to fill him in later.
He gathered these people were some sort of exiled
royalty from some little country in Europe—situated
somewhere between Austria and Hungary—he'd
never heard of before. They certainly employed a lot
of people, most of them from the same little country.
So far he'd seen three maids, a cook, a butler, two
gardeners and a chauffeur, plus, of course, the "companion" whose room he'd invaded.

Thinking of her, he glanced up at the house, his
gaze focusing immediately on the brightly lit window
of the room where he'd been, and the memory of how
soft and rounded she'd felt in his arms flashed in his
mind. Resolutely he pushed the image away. She was
dangerously attractive and deeply appealing, but he
wasn't in the market for that sort of thing. Getting
involved with a woman had messed him up one too
many times. If he hadn't learned his lesson by now,

there was no hope for him. He was going to have to keep his distance from that one. And that shouldn't be too hard to do. The security of the place needed a lot of work. He was going to be very busy.

And, turning to go back up toward the house, he nearly ran smack into the very woman he'd been trying to avoid thinking about.

"Whoa!" He jerked back, just missing her, and annoyed that he hadn't heard her approach. The ubiquitous waterfall sounds masked everything else. He was going to have to see about making some adjustments there.

"Hello," she said, glancing toward the house and stepping back farther into the shadows the long rose arbor made along the edge of the property. "I thought I might find you out here."

He frowned, not pleased to see her. She was too damn pretty for her own good. "I'm just going in," he said gruffly, and turned to go.

"Wait. I've brought you something."

He turned back and looked at what she was carrying, but he couldn't quite make out what it was in the darkness.

"I brought you a lemon tart from dinner. I know you didn't get one."

He hesitated, knowing he was being a fool. But a lemon tart—it was only his favorite food, and his stomach growled just to remind him that he was hungry as a bear. One little lemon tart. What could that hurt? Besides, it would be rude to cut her off when she was being so friendly. Reluctantly he turned back.

"Thanks," he said simply, and followed her back into the arbor to a bench where the light from the lanterns around the nearby swimming pool brightened the area. They both sat down, and she handed him the plate and a fork.

He took a bite, savored it, then gave her a lopsided grin. "Thanks a lot," he said sincerely. "This is really good."

She smiled back. She was glad she'd come out now. At first she hadn't been sure. All through dinner she'd watched for him out of the tall dining room windows, but she hadn't caught sight of him. So she'd decided to take a chance once her aunt was safely off to visit her friend who lived a few blocks away. She'd gone to the kitchen, snatched a lemon tart and come out searching. Luckily she'd found him right away.

"So, Mr. Jack Santini," she said, showing off that she'd found out what his name was. "You decided to take the job."

"A man's got to eat," he said, taking another bite of the tart as though to illustrate that very concept. "And from what I've seen so far, you people eat pretty well."

She supposed that was true. They employed a wonderful cook. The food here at her aunt's was certainly better than anything she'd ever been given at any of the many boarding schools she had attended. One of her goals for the summer was to learn to cook. What if it was true that good food was the way to a man's heart? Hmm...

She looked at him and felt a ripple of excitement flow through her. He was so attractive, so...well, so male. What could she do to get him to stay with her a little longer after he'd finished the dessert? Maybe she could get him to talk.

"Tell me about yourself," she said brightly. "Are you married?"

He took a last bite of the tart and gazed at her levelly. She was dressed in a sweater and slacks and had her hair tied back in a ponytail that looked completely appropriate. She seemed impossibly young. And young was something he had never seemed to be.

He wasn't sure if he'd always been such a pessimist, but lately it felt as though his life always had a sense of waiting for the ax to fall, wondering when things would get worse. And they usually did. Right now he was on suspension from the police department, cut off from the career as a police detective that he loved, taking this job to fill in the gap and hold him over until a hearing on his future was held.

It wasn't as if he was complaining. The suspension was his own fault. He knew very well what he'd done. Given the same circumstances, he very likely would do the same thing over again. His instincts always seemed to put him in position to go overboard protecting someone else—particularly if she was a woman—and end up hurting himself. He had to be careful not let that happen anymore.

And he had to be careful not to let anything he did here make things worse as far as his suspension went. And how could that happen? Well, he could let himself get involved in a flirtation with this pretty young thing. That ought to just about seal the deal on his doom. But he wasn't quite that stupid. Or that weak.

And she wanted to know if he was married. He gave her a sideways look and said, "Why would you care about a thing like that?"

"No reason. I'm just making small talk."

"Small talk." He couldn't help it. She made him want to laugh. "Okay, here's some fodder for your small talk. I'm thirty years old. I was born in San Diego, grew up all over the place. Was a Navy SEAL for a few years, then joined the Rancho Diego Police Department. I was engaged once, for about five minutes. But I've never been married. And I have no kids."

He left out a few things, such as the fact that his parents had died in a car accident when he was young and he'd been shuttled from one place to another, living with various relatives, until finally he'd ended up in a group home for problem teenagers. He understood that his early rootless existence was behind his strong need to find his identity in organizations such as the police force. But that understanding didn't make the need any less powerful.

"Whew." She whipped her head around as though

she'd just been hit with a strong wind. "I guess that takes care of that. Now I feel like I've known you all my life."

He handed her his empty plate, knowing it was time to get up and walk away. But that would be a little abrupt. He supposed he could spare a few minutes to be courteous. "You may know me, but I don't know you," he told her. "Your turn."

She blanched and looked away, using the moment to set the plate down on the bench beside her. She'd almost forgotten that he didn't know yet who she was. He would know soon enough—perhaps in minutes. But she wanted to prolong him not knowing as long as she could. She hated the way people changed once they were told she was royal.

Sometimes she wished she could shed that royalty like a used and useless second skin, cast it off like a worn-out dress. She'd been quite rebellious about it a few years ago as a teenager.

After all, to her, royalty meant such loneliness. Since the loss of her parents, when she was a baby, she'd always had her aunt and uncle. But her brothers had been raised elsewhere. The two oldest, Crown Prince Marco and Prince Garth, had been raised by another uncle at his family home in Arizona. Prince Damian, the closest to her in age, spent most of his early years living with their mother's twin sister and her family. She had only seen them all on special occasions. For most of her youngest years, she'd lived under the rule of a governess. Children were occasionally carted in to play with her, but the situation was hit-and-miss. She was excited when she went away to school at fourteen. Finally she would meet people of her own age.

But developing relationships was still hard as she moved to each school with a whole retinue, taking over entire sections of the dormitory like an occupying force. That, combined with the fact that she changed schools so often, meant that friendships were still tough.

She hoped things would be different once she was married. Though she hardly expected to find true love in an arranged marriage, she did expect her mate would be a friend, someone to talk to, someone to share life with. She'd settled down now. Her small flash of rebellion was in the past. She was sworn to do her duty and she was ready to fulfill her role. She only hoped she would marry a man she could like.

That was the current state of her affairs, of who she was, but Jack Santini didn't want to hear all of that.

"I'm not very interesting," she said quickly. "I'll tell you something about the family, though. What would you like to know?"

"Your name, for starters."

Her name. Well, that was easy. "Kari."

"Kari." He said it slowly, as though he wanted to remember it, and that made her smile. "Just Kari?" he added.

"Isn't that enough?"

"Most people have a last name, too."

She shook her head. "I've got too many of them. They would only confuse you." She turned to look at the swimming pool through the leaves of the rose vines. The light from the lanterns made ghostly reflections on the inky water. "But we were talking about the family. Aren't you curious about them?"

"The family." He considered for a moment. "Okay. Tell me what I should know."

"The Roseanovas are a very old family. They ruled Nabotavia for almost a thousand years. Then, twenty years ago they were overthrown by rebels. The December Radicals, they were called." She rolled her eyes to show what she thought of them. "The king and queen were killed...."

She stopped, surprised that her voice was quavering over that last statement. It was her own parents she was talking about. It had been so long ago, when she was just a baby, and she didn't remember them, except for what she knew from old pictures and stories. She'd thought she was used to that, but for some reason, her voice was betraying emotions she thought she'd tamed. Taking a deep breath, she went on. "And many others were forced to flee from the country."

"Including you."

"Oh, yes. Also the duke and the duchess, and—"

"And the princess? I've been told there really is a princess."

She nodded, eyes sparkling. "And you doubted me," she charged. "The princess was smuggled out

of the country, along with her three older brothers.''
Then she looked at him curiously. ''What did they
tell you about her?''

He shrugged and stretched back, leaning against the
railing with his legs extended out before him. ''Nothing. Tim was more concerned that I not get on the
wrong side of the duchess than anything else.'' He
cocked an eyebrow. ''Is that the duchess you were
talking about?''

She nodded. ''Yes.''

''So she's pretty hard to please, is she?''

Kari hesitated. She didn't want to say anything
against her aunt. After all, the woman had raised
her—in a way. How could she put this delicately?
''You know the wicked stepmother in the Cinderella
story?'' she ventured.

He grinned, his white teeth flashing in the gloom.
''Sure.''

She gave a soft laugh. ''She's sort of like an up-
dated version of her.''

He chuckled. ''And what are you? Cinderella? Do
they make you do all the dirty chores?''

''Not quite. But there are certain expectations and
standards that must be met.'' She waved the topic
away. ''But you'll see for yourself tomorrow. She's
planning to have Mr. Blodnick perform an introduction. Something of a royal audience,'' she added with
a gleam in her eye that was close to teasing.

He noticed. She was getting more and more familiar with him. He knew he ought to get up off the

bench and head for somewhere as far as possible away from this beguiling female. But for some reason he just couldn't do it. Instead he turned away again and sat staring off toward the swimming pool, telling himself not looking at her would be almost as good as leaving. And knowing he was lying.

"So I'm going to meet the people I'm working for," he noted with a shrug. "That's pretty routine, don't you think?"

"Oh, not at all. It's very important that the duchess and the princess approve of you."

"I've got no reason to think they won't," he said with complete confidence. "I know what I'm doing. And I'm a likable guy, after all."

She studied him critically, her head to the side. Likable was one thing. Absolutely gorgeous was another. What would her aunt think of having her guarded by a man like this? Wouldn't she have second thoughts? Wouldn't she notice that an electricity seemed to spark between them at times? And once she did notice, wouldn't she get rid of this man as quickly as possible?

The answer to most of those questions of course was yes. It was going to be up to Kari to find a way to make sure she didn't think them.

"Well, the duchess won't like you, no matter how nice you are, because the duchess doesn't like anyone," she told him pertly, overstating the case, but only a little. "But the princess...now that's another

matter.'' She pretended to think hard, her brow furled.
''What will the princess think of you?''

He had to turn and look at her. There was something odd about her tone of voice, and he couldn't
quite put his finger on what it was. He knew she was
teasing again, but he wasn't sure why.

''What's she like?'' he asked, watching her face.

''The princess?'' She shuddered. ''Oh, she's ugly
as a bulldog. She's slow and dull and she has no real
wit about her.''

He stared at her for a moment, then a reluctant
smile quirked the corners of his wide mouth. ''You're
a real good friend of hers, are you?''

''Oh, very,'' she said in all sincerity. ''We're close
as...as...as sisters.''

''Sisters.'' He nodded, and his smile took on a
more cynical twist. ''Funny, I heard she was pretty.''
He watched for her reaction.

And she gave him one, rolling her eyes. ''You
know how people are sometimes. They endow celebrities with beauty and talent they don't really have,
just because they *are* celebrities. Well, people do the
same thing with royalty.''

''Do they?''

''Oh, yes. I've seen men look at the princess and
not even notice that she squints and walks into walls
and that her feet stick out at funny angles.'' She nodded emphatically, her eyes shimmering with laughter.
''I've even heard people say she's beautiful.'' She
shrugged, hands out in a ''go figure'' gesture.

"Poor, demented souls." He was laughing at her now.

"Exactly!" She laughed back. "That's how blind people can be."

Their gazes connected and suddenly she was aware of how soft the air felt, how different from anything she'd ever noticed before. She sobered, still looking into his eyes and feeling very strange, almost like floating.

"Are you saying I'm blind, too?" he asked, though his voice seemed to have dropped an octave.

"Oh, no," she assured him. "I just wanted to warn you, so you could be prepared." She caught the hint of a clean, masculine scent and wondered if it were a flower blooming nearby or his aftershave. She wanted to get closer, just to see. "I wouldn't want you to fall into that trap," she added somewhat breathlessly.

"Why?" he asked her lazily, his eyes half-closed. "Are you afraid I'm going to fall for the princess?"

Her shrug had a sensual languor to it that made him think—for some reason—of naked bodies on satin sheets.

"You might," she murmured, her gaze locked with his. "Stranger things have happened."

The magnetic pull between them seemed to have a life of its own, generating heat and electricity that made Jack feel it was inevitable that they would kiss. The soft darkness, the sound of water, the scent of roses, all combined to draw them closer and closer.

But Jack had the sense and experience to know what was happening, and he knew it was wrong—and that he was the one who had to stop it. He started to straighten, to pull away, but Kari stopped him.

"Hold still," she said. "You've got a smudge on your face."

It was only a crumb from the pie crust on the lemon tart, caught by the barely visible beginnings of a growth of dark beard alongside his mouth. Her heart began to pound as she leaned forward to get it. What was she doing? She had no idea, but she wanted to touch him so badly. Reaching out, she brushed the crumb away, then let her fingers linger there as she looked up into his eyes, just inches away from hers. A change came over them as she watched. She saw a darkening, as though a cloud had covered the sun, and then she caught her breath. For the first time in her life, she saw raw desire in a man's eyes and knew it was aimed at her.

The strange thing was, it didn't frighten her at all. Instead, a thrill shivered through her, making her feel alive as she'd never felt before. Her hand turned, cupping his cheek with her palm and fingers, and she looked at his lips, suddenly needing his kiss as though it would keep her from dying. Her own lips parted and she drew closer...closer...her heart beating wildly, her blood singing in her veins.

Jack's groan came from deep within his soul and it came with an effort he was almost too overcome to make. Reaching up, he circled her wrist with his fingers and pushed her hand away.

"You'd better go in," he said roughly, hoping she didn't notice that his breath was coming too quickly, that his own heart was beating right along with hers. He didn't think he'd ever felt this aroused before without doing something about it. Why it had happened so quickly and so effortlessly with this woman he barely knew, he wasn't sure. He only knew he had to avoid the temptation she represented if he wanted to keep from ruining his own future—and that he had to protect her from himself.

That she was an innocent was obvious. That her naïveté seemed to excite him in a way he hadn't been excited in a long, long time was not something he was particularly proud of. His first instincts had been right on the money. He was going to have to avoid her at all costs.

Suddenly they were both aware of voices. They turned and looked toward the house. A figure filled the lit window of Kari's room.

"Oh-oh!" Kari jumped up from the bench, picking up the plate as she went. "I'm going to have to go in. The duchess is looking for me." She flashed him a quick, wavering smile. "Good night."

He watched her go and groaned again, leaning his head back against the railing. Five minutes with the woman and he was thinking about how she would fit into his bed. And she was the kind of woman that had "trouble" written all over her. If he was going to give in to the urge to mess around, it would have to be with a woman who had been there and done that and knew the score, not some sweet little innocent looking for someone to love. How had he let that happen? Whatever it had been—it couldn't happen again. If he had to get tough, that was exactly what he would have to do. But he had to stay away from Kari. That much was a given.

He was a little out of his depth here. What was he—an ordinary police detective, a guy who'd grown up in foster homes with no family of his own, who'd had to struggle to get an education and build a life for himself, with no background to depend on—doing here, working for royalty? Oh, well, it was just for the summer, just until he could get reinstated for his job. He supposed he ought to appreciate the experience. He would never have another one quite like it.

Chapter Three

"Karina, will you stop looking at yourself in the mirror?"

The duchess glared adamantly across her impressively decorated dressing room at her charge. They were prepared to go out to an engagement, but were waiting for Tim Blodnick to announce that he was downstairs and ready to introduce them to Jack Santini.

"You're developing an unhealthy interest in your own reflection."

Kari took one last look at the impeccably dressed woman in the mirror and sighed. For the first time in her life she actually cared how she looked in more than a passing way. She would have thought her aunt would be glad she was finally taking something of an interest.

The image was of a slim young woman wearing a

royal-blue silk sheath with princess seams and a scooped neckline. She had on white gloves and spectator pumps. A small pillbox hat with a skimpy veil for decoration sat perched atop hair that was carefully arranged in a comely twist. And, of course, she sported tasteful pearls. No princess of her age would go out without them. At least, that was what her aunt always told her.

She looked like a picture from a history book. What would happen if she ripped off these relics and put on a nice tight sweater and a leather skirt? Her aunt would have her committed, no doubt about it.

"First you tell me to take a look at myself more often and try to make my image conform to what a princess should look like," she commented. "Then you criticize me for doing exactly that."

The duchess turned and gave her an assessing look. The woman herself looked well groomed and elegant in an obviously expensive lime-green silk suit that suited her coloring. Her hair was cut short and chic and dyed an attractive shade of silver. She looked altogether imposing, which was precisely what she was.

"It is very important to get the look exactly right," she counseled her niece. "But it is just as important not to let anyone know it was any effort. Your royal style should flow naturally, like the waters of the Tannabee River that runs through the heart of Nabotavia." She made an elegant gesture with her hand. "Perfection is fundamental and imperative. But never allow anyone to see you attempting to achieve it."

Kari smiled to cover the annoyance she felt. She wanted to let it out, to rip the hat off and toss it out the window, to trade in her dress for jeans and a tummy-tickler T-shirt. She wanted to be a normal and very casual young woman, just like the young women she saw from the limousine window as she was whisked from one official engagement to another.

Well, she couldn't do that. But sometimes her sharp tongue was just too quick to be stopped. "I see," she said brightly. "In other words, all's fair in the quest for royal superiority. Lie, cheat and steal—just don't get caught."

The duchess turned away, looking in need of smelling salts. "Much too vulgar for a princess," she murmured faintly, but, glancing at her diamond-studded watch, she quickly regained her sharply efficient attitude.

"I hope Mr. Blodnick hurries along and brings this new fellow he's hired as head of security. I'm not sure I approve of this move he's made. I usually expect to meet the management-level employees before they are offered a contract."

Kari turned away and hummed a little tune trying to look innocent. If she told her aunt that she'd been behind the quick approval of the man, she knew very well her aunt would fire him on the spot. The duchess would be great at marshaling armies and taking over small countries, but she didn't have a lot of understanding in her soul.

She would certainly never understand what had happened in the arbor last night. But then, Kari didn't really understand it either. All she knew was that all she had to do was think about almost kissing Jack Santini and her breath stopped in her throat. She had been so forward! She knew very well that it had been her doing the seducing, not him. In fact, she didn't like to think about how he had reacted, because it made her worry that he'd been laughing at her the whole time. Had he thought she was silly?

No. Whenever she remembered the way he had groaned, as though he'd had to rip the sound out of somewhere deep and tortured, she got chills. She didn't think he'd been laughing. But still, she didn't know what he thought and that was making her nervous.

''Karina, please, don't slouch like a teenager.''

She straightened without really hearing what the woman was saying. That was actually her usual reaction to the constant stream of advice and reproach. She usually got along well enough with her aunt, but it was her uncle she loved. The duke was her father's half brother, and to her, an orphan left alone in a very scary world, he represented parental love in a way her aunt never could. Her aunt was the taskmaster, the instructor, the maker of hated rules and regulations. Her uncle was the man who had taught her how to whistle, how to find the Big Dipper on a clear night, how to tell robins from blue jays. He was the one who read bedtime stories to a sleepy little girl, who always had her favorite candy hidden in his coat pocket, who carried her up to bed when she fell asleep over her toys. And though he had retreated more and more from any sphere where his wife took charge, he was always available for Kari when she needed someone to talk to.

The telephone rang and the duchess took it. "He's ready," she told Kari. "Let's go down."

Kari hesitated, her pulse speeding up just a bit. She had to admit she was just a little nervous. She was looking forward to seeing Jack again, and yet she wasn't looking forward to his reaction once he realized she was the princess. She didn't think he'd guessed—although someone might have told him by now. Maybe when she walked into the room he would already know and she wouldn't have to see the look of shock in his eyes as he realized what she'd kept from him.

As she followed her aunt down the stairs, she realized she was dreading that. At first she'd thought it would be fun—that he would look surprised and she would laugh. But having gotten to know him a little better last night, she knew that wasn't what was going to happen. He wasn't going to like the fact that she'd tricked him.

"Duchess Irinia Roseanova, allow me to introduce Jack Santini, our new manager of estate security."

She came into the room just in time to see Tim present Jack to the duchess, but not in time to be addressed along with her. Jack's attention was all on her aunt and that was just as well. She hung back, waiting for him to look around and notice her.

"We've lived very quietly recently, Mr. Santini," the duchess was saying. "But all that is going to change as spring opens into summer. We have a number of entertainments planned, and we will need extra security during them.''

"What sort of entertainments do you have in mind?" he asked.

"We will be giving dinners, card parties, a tea or two and, of course, the ball.''

"A ball?''

"Yes. The ball will be held at the country club, not here on our premises. However, I'll expect you to be in charge of security for the ball, and that will entail quite a bit of work. We're expecting almost two hundred people to attend.''

They went on talking about plans, and Kari watched on tenterhooks. Jack was dressed in black slacks, a black long-sleeved shirt and a silver tie. She wondered if this would be the new uniform, and that made her smile. He was so very handsome. Still waiting, she tugged off her gloves and held them in one hand. When he was presented and he bent to kiss her fingers, she wanted his lips to touch flesh, not fabric.

And suddenly he was coming her way and looking right at her, and Tim was saying, "And I believe you've met the princess casually, but I'd now like to make a formal introduction. Princess Karina Alexandera Roseanova, may I present Jack Santini?''

Tim turned back to speak to the duchess, leaving Kari and Jack to deal with the rest of the introduction alone. She raised her gaze to meet Jack's and found it unreadable. That only made her more uneasy, so she held her head high and extended her left hand in a formal, if rather haughty, manner.

He took it gingerly, looked down at it, then back into her eyes. "What am I supposed to do with this limp fish?" he asked in a low voice just loud enough for her to hear.

She caught her breath. He was angry. Well, she supposed she couldn't blame him. But neither could she let on to her aunt that there was any sort of relationship between them.

"It is customary that you kiss my hand," she told him imperiously, keeping her gaze cool and distant.

Grabbing her hand more firmly, he used it to pull her closer and murmured, "I'd rather spank your bottom," before he let her go.

"Oh!"

Her cheeks colored and her blue eyes glittered and he immediately regretted what he'd done. But not very much. He was quite serious. The girl needed a little discipline. He felt like a fool and he was furious with her for leading him on and letting him say stupid things. Still, there was a facade here that had to be maintained.

He brushed her fingers with his lips and then dropped her hand like a hot potato.

"So happy to meet you, Princess," he said, sarcasm spicing his tone.

But then his gaze met hers again and he saw her remorse. His anger began to fade. After all, what had it really hurt for him to think she was just an employee for a time? Thank God he hadn't taken advantage of the kiss she'd offered him the night before. At least there was that.

"I'm glad to see that your squint has healed, Princess," he added, just to show her he was still annoyed, but wasn't going to hold it against her. "And that you are no longer walking into walls."

She bit back a smile, obviously relieved but still looking a bit contrite. "Yes, I'm doing very well," she said coolly, her nose in the air. "With therapy, I may even get my feet to go straight again."

The duchess turned from her talk with Tim and frowned in their direction. "Karina. Is something wrong?"

Kari sent a brilliant smile in her direction. "Oh, no, madam. Nothing at all."

They waited for the duchess to resume her talk with Tim, and then Jack leaned closer and said, "You could have told me the truth."

Her eyes flashed as she looked at him. "I did. You were the one who refused to believe it."

He knew she was right but he hated to admit it. Of course, if he'd only thought about it, he would have known. The clues were everywhere for him to see. As he thought back over their conversation the night before, he could see that she'd practically spelled it out for him. He was the one who'd been too dense to put two and two together. Well, what did it matter, anyway? Her being the princess only made it more imperative that he stay away from her. Maybe it was all to the good.

She turned to walk toward the windows, pulling her

gloves on as she went, and he followed her, no longer annoyed with her and rather captivated by the quaint picture she made, all decked out in her old-fashioned attire.

"You look like something out of the fifties," he told her softly as they stopped to gaze out over the lawn. "What's the deal with the little hat?"

She touched it and smiled. "That's the way we royalty are supposed to be, you know," she told him. "Timeless. Classic. Straight out of the past and walking boldly into the future."

She looked up at him, laughter in her eyes, and he found himself smiling down at her.

A princess. What the hell had he gotten himself into here?

But their moment was already over. Tim and the duchess were coming toward where they stood at the window, and the duchess was addressing him. He turned to face her.

"I'm glad to have met you, Mr. Santini," she was saying, looking very regal. "I'm sure you will do a splendid job, as long as you stick to the basics. Right now we're going to need someone to accompany us for the afternoon. We are going to a Ladies' League meeting. Princess Karina will be the guest of honor at their tea, where she will present a short speech on the history of Nabotavia and the latest developments from that part of the world. Even in such a benign setting, she must be guarded, you know."

"Very well, madam," Jack said mildly. He'd already known about this and was prepared. His gaze skimmed over Kari's and away again. "I've assigned Will Strator to accompany you. He should be waiting in the driveway at this very moment."

He didn't have to look at Kari to sense her disappointment. She'd thought he might be coming along. Well, he wasn't going to get caught in that game. He had other guards who could watch Kari when she went out in public. He wasn't going to do it.

"Goodbye," she murmured as she slipped past him. "You're missing a great speech."

She left her scent behind, and he inhaled it for a moment before turning away to get back to work. And then he wished he hadn't. Memorizing the perfume she wore would only make it worse when he thought of her at night. Because that was all he was going to do. No doubt about it. This was more of a hands-off situation than ever. The woman was a princess for God's sake. As if things weren't bad enough.

Three Days Later

"Oh, Mr. Santini."

Jack turned back. The duchess had just finished filling him in on some changes she wanted made to the alarm system and was calling him back as an afterthought.

"The princess has an appointment to make some dress selections at Goldmar's at two o'clock. She'll be going alone, as I have some visitors coming. But she'll need protection."

Jack gritted his teeth. Every man he had available

was already assigned. "I'm afraid we don't have anyone free at this time," he started to tell the duchess.

"Then you'll have to go with her," she said impatiently. "Protecting the princess is your first priority. Never forget that."

Of course it was, and he felt it as strongly as anyone. He knew she couldn't go out alone. He'd been briefed about the Nabotavian rebels and the threats that were periodically made against the family, and against Kari in particular. It was a turbulent time for the country, with the rebels losing favor with the population and a constitutional monarchy being restored. From what he gathered, there were numerous factions from the old country who would like nothing better than to get their hands on the popular princess in order to push their own agenda. Of course keeping her safe was the most important part of his job. He'd hoped the appointment might be canceled, but it didn't seem to be an option.

"Of course I'll handle it," he told her crisply. "I'll be ready at one-thirty."

In the three days since the introduction in the parlor, he'd managed to find ways to stay out of Kari's path for all that time. He was getting pretty good at knowing instinctively when she was liable to show up in any given area, and in making himself scarce at just the right moment. He'd even managed to stop thinking about her forty times an hour as he had at first. He was on the right track. As long as he kept his distance, the temptation she represented would fade more and more.

The worst had been the day it had been warmer than usual and a group of Nabotavians who lived in another part of the state had arrived for a visit. The party had included two young women about Kari's age, and the three of them had gone for a swim. Though he'd heard the laughter and the splashing, he hadn't thought much about it. But when he walked out of the guard office, there Kari had been, poised on the diving board, about to take a plunge into the water, wearing an alluring one-piece suit. She'd been calling to one of the others and hadn't noticed him, and that was lucky, because he'd turned to stone for a moment, unable to move, as he'd stared at her, every masculine response in his body coming alive and aching.

She'd been so beautiful in an innocent, untouched way. Her skin had gleamed golden in the sunlight, her hair a golden-blond halo around her pretty face. Her slim body was perfect, with her breasts swelling inside the swimsuit top; her long, graceful legs and those intoxicating curves. Desire had risen in him like smoke from a fire, and he'd choked on it.

He'd finally gotten himself under control and turned away, muttering every obscenity he could think of under his breath as he got out of there as quickly as he could. But the picture of her poised in the air like a bird would stay with him for the rest of his life, no matter how hard he tried to erase it.

So he approached their impending outing with some reluctance, but when he met Kari at the car, she gave him a brief smile and entered the large Cadillac, inviting him to sit in the back with her. He sank into the luxurious seating, trying to forget what he knew about the body beside him so modestly clothed in a chic linen pants suit. After only a quick glance her way, he sat looking straight ahead as the chauffeur began to guide the car out onto the city streets. They rode along in silence for some time, and he'd just about decided that she'd taken the hint to heart and realized that they shouldn't attempt to have any sort of relationship when she spoke.

"Why do you hate me?" she asked softly.

He looked at her, startled. She was staring straight ahead. He glanced at Mr. Barbera, the chauffeur. There was a Plexiglas barrier between the front and back seats, but he knew that didn't always mean that sound wasn't traveling from one side to the other.

"Don't worry, he can't hear us," she said, still staring ahead and letting her lips move only slightly as she spoke. "He's half-deaf. But he can see. And he will tell everything he sees to my aunt, you can count on it."

How reassuring. Jack sighed, wishing he were anywhere but here.

"I don't hate you," he said, following her example of moving his lips only as much as he absolutely had to and staring out the window while he spoke.

"You've been avoiding me like the plague."

"I'm not avoiding you," he lied. "I'm just trying to do my job."

"I thought we could be friends."

There was no particular overt emotion in her voice,

but he thought he heard something—some tiny tremor, some vague vibration—that made him look at her again.

"Kari...Princess." He turned his head away again. "Look. You're royalty. I'm the serf, or whatever. I work for you. We are on completely different levels. It's hard to be friends that way."

Her outrage at that statement made her careless, and she completely forgot to hide what she had to say, turning to him and demanding, "What! Did you grow up in Europe or something? You sound more like a Nabotavian than I do. We're in the U.S.A. Everyone is supposed to be equal."

He frowned, talking directly to her. "There are always levels, even if people pretend to ignore them. Be realistic."

They had arrived at the large exclusive department store and Mr. Barbera was pulling up before the entrance. A doorman rushed to get the car door. Without saying anything more, Jack got out and helped Kari to her feet. Giving the chauffeur a wave, she turned toward the store and he went with her.

"Anyway," she said in a conversational voice as they walked along through the fine jewelry department. "I'm not asking you to marry me. I just want you to be my friend."

They came to an elevator and stood side by side, waiting for the doors to open.

"You know you want more than a friend," he told her softly, watching to make sure they were not being overheard by any of the customers. After all, he shouldn't be talking this way to her. But he didn't have much choice.

"How do you know what I want?" she demanded, turning to look up at him, her blue eyes huge.

He hesitated. This really wasn't the time or the place. But once begun, this topic was pretty difficult to abandon until it had been dealt with. He looked down into her eyes and felt something twist in his chest. If only she weren't so damn appealing.

"The vibes between us tell it all," he told her shortly, willing her to understand without too much explanation.

"Vibes!" She said the word as though she scorned it.

The elevator doors opened and they went aboard. Jack pushed the button to close the door quickly so that they wouldn't have to share the elevator with anyone else. He had a feeling she would continue this conversation no matter who was listening.

Once they were underway, he turned to her. "Yes, vibes. You feel it, I feel it. If we hang around together too much, something is bound to happen."

Her eyes were even larger now, and they seemed to melt as he looked into them.

"Will it?" she said softly.

"Yes." Every part of him wanted to take her in his arms. Something about her looked so vulnerable right now. He wanted to reassure her, tell her not to worry. But he hardened his heart. "I've got more experience at this type of thing than you do. I know it will."

The doors opened on their floor. They stepped out. The showroom was before them, and a beautifully groomed woman was smiling in their direction. Kari looked around, then turned and grabbed his hand.

"Let's not argue anymore," she said, giving him a wobbly smile. "Let's just enjoy the afternoon."

He blinked. Didn't she get it? He was working here. He pulled away from her.

"I'll stay in the background and stand against the wall while you..."

"Oh, no you don't. You'll come on in with me." Her smile brightened as she took his arm. "They don't know I'm a princess. To these people, I'm just another spoiled girl from Beverly Hills. It would be perfectly natural for me to have my boyfriend along." Perfectly natural and perfectly normal. Things she would love to be. Things she really couldn't have. But just this once...

He was shaking his head, though he knew it wasn't going to make any difference. "Princess, I don't think this is a good idea."

"Please. I want you to."

He stared down into her beautiful eyes and swallowed hard. He should say no. He tried. But he couldn't do it.

"All right," he heard himself say.

She beamed up at him. "Good!" And she led him into the showroom.

Chapter Four

The showroom attendants were prepared for Kari and quickly accommodated her guest. A table had been set up in front of the stage. She and Jack sat down next to each other.

"We have a nice viewing ready for you, Miss Roseanova," the coolly efficient looking young woman told her. "Your aunt asked that you be shown a selection from a number of lines. If you would prefer to limit the number—"

"Oh, no. I want to see it all. Oh, and we'd like tea, please. And scones would be nice, don't you think?" Kari smiled at Jack, then at the helpful attendant. "Thank you very much."

Jack leaned close and muttered, "What are you doing?"

"I already know what dress I'm ordering," she told

him softly. "But the more I look at, the more time we'll have to talk."

"Talking isn't part of my job," he reminded her grimly, his gray gaze flickering in her direction and then away again.

"Maybe not, but keeping me happy is."

His face darkened, and she knew right away she'd said exactly the wrong thing. Catching her lower lip with her teeth, she winced, staring straight ahead. That had sounded bratty and immature and she deeply regretted it. Right then and there she vowed she would never let herself sound like that again. She tried to think of a way to take her words back, but it was too late as the first of the models began to mince across the stage.

The model paused, posing, but her gaze flickered over Jack before she got it under control. Kari stifled a chuckle. She nodded to the model and then to the attendant, who wrote down her wishes on the order slip. Kari took the opportunity to lean close to Jack and whisper to him.

"Do women always look at you like that?"

He raised an eyebrow innocently. "Like what?"

Her eyes sparkled. "You know very well what she was doing."

But another model had taken the stage, and it was time to examine the heavy silk gown she was displaying. One after another they came, while a background tape playing gentle standards filled in the atmosphere, but Kari hardly noticed. A few she ordered set aside, most she didn't, but her mind was much more on her companion than it was on the dresses.

He was sitting very still, and yet she thought she could feel that he was very alert, his senses on guard, his mind weighing everything. She had the urge to distract him, to make him pay more attention to Kari, the woman, rather than the princess who needed to be guarded. But she curbed her impulse. She wanted his respect as much as she wanted anything, and if that meant she would have to apply a little dignity to her bearing, that was what she would do.

Finally the attendant announced an intermission and the scones and tea were served on lovely porcelain china with sterling silver utensils. Kari took a sip of the hot liquid and smiled at the man by her side.

"You're bored to tears," she said calmly. "But you're very good at hiding it."

"I could never be bored around you, Princess," he said softly.

And it was true enough on a human level. Though he had some reservations about spending all this time merely sitting in a department store showroom, gazing at models and indulging a pretty princess, it did seem to be part of the job. This was a far cry from his usual routine, where periods of investigation and analysis were interspersed with violent episodes—short and dangerous but ultimately rewarding when criminals got the prosecution they deserved.

The rewards here were very different, he admitted to himself as he gazed at Kari's pretty face. Different...but just as dangerous.

"I'll tell you what *is* boring," he said as he bit into a scone. "The clothes you're looking at. I didn't know there were still stores that sold things my grandmother used to wear."

She sighed. "I know. That's why we shop here. No one else carries these relics." She rolled her eyes. "My aunt likes to keep me firmly in the past. I'm just lucky she can't find hoop skirts for sale anywhere close."

He looked at her speculatively. "There were some younger styles on mannequins on the floor we came in on. Why can't you look at some of those?"

"Oh, because my aunt…" Her voice trailed off and her blue eyes widened as she realized what she was about to say. He was right. Why couldn't she look at some more fashionable things? She'd fallen into the habit of letting her aunt dictate these matters to her. She sat up straighter. "What a good idea," she said, looking around for the attendant.

"You'd like to see something from our young adult collection?" the woman said when Kari rose and went across the room to ask. "Of course. Your aunt requested these more mature styles, and frankly we were quite surprised to see how young you were when you came in." She smiled and gave Kari a wink. "Don't you worry about a thing, my dear. We've got consultants who know what's hot. It will only take a few minutes to set it up. But we'll need some further measurements." She eyed the very conservative sweater set Kari was wearing. "And perhaps you'd like to go ahead and try on a few representative items, just to get a feel for the sort of thing that suits you.''

Suddenly a tedious task was becoming interesting. Kari felt as if she was going on an adventure. She looked over at the table and gave Jack a smile, then turned as two teenage girls came out from a side door with measuring tapes in hand.

"Would you like me to ask your young man to wait outside?" the older woman said.

"Oh, let her boyfriend stay," one of the girls who had a name tag that read Sheena said, laughing.

"We won't be doing anything too risqué," Mae, the other girl teased, giving Jack the eye in an open, friendly manner.

Kari looked across the room at Jack, and he met her gaze with resignation, just barely shaking his head to let her know he wasn't taking all this too seriously. She laughed softly and lifted her arms so that the others could begin to measure her.

She assumed they would just get her height, her waist, and maybe her shoulders, but soon she began to realize they were pulling the tape around every part of her, one saying the measurement while the other wrote down the number, and she began to feel a little more self-conscious.

"Get the breasts," Sheena called out to Mae in what Kari thought was an unnecessarily loud voice. "Take a deep breath, honey, and push your chest out. If you got 'em, flaunt 'em, I always say."

Mae pulled the tape tightly around the relevant items. "And you got 'em, honey." She called out a number that made Kari blush, followed by, "Woo-hoo!"

Her cheeks were hot. She glanced quickly over to see how Jack was taking this and found him staring relentlessly at the wall. At first she was hoping he hadn't been paying attention, but then she noticed the twitch at the corner of his mouth and realized he was working hard trying not to laugh. And that made *her* laugh.

Moments later she was behind a folding screen that had been set up for her, trying on clothes the likes of which she'd never seen before, with a lot of help from Mae and Sheena, both clucking over her like a pair of bantam hens.

Jack waited restlessly, wondering what he had put in motion here. From where he sat he couldn't see much, but he could hear a lot of disjointed comments, and he had to admit they were making him curious to see the finished product.

"No, honey, you don't wear a bra with that. The point is to look sexy. Let it all hang out."

"Ooh, add three inch heels with ankle straps…"

"I know it seems tight. Here, Mae and I will help pull it on. If we all three shove at once…"

"Oh, those cranberry hot-pants are fabulous on you! Come on, try this black metallic net top with them."

The outfits sounded intriguing. The only problem was, Kari wasn't coming out from behind the screen to show them off. Every now and then he could hear her soft voice in a demurral of one kind or another.

It was pretty obvious the clothes were a little far out for her at this juncture.

"Ohmigod!" Sheena cried at one point in a piercing voice that could have cracked open glaciers. "Look how cool she looks in the green velour spandex capri leggings with the see-through crop top!"

"Oh, yes! Eat your heart out Britney Spears!"

Jack reached out and poured himself more tea. As visions of Kari braless and in metallic spandex filled his head, his mouth seemed to be getting drier and drier, and at the same time sweat was popping out on his forehead. He pulled out a handkerchief to mop his face before he realized what was going on, and he had to shake his head, embarrassed for himself. His imagination was running wild. If she didn't come out from behind that screen soon, he was going to have to get up and go take a walk around the building.

"Ready?" she said at last, and he looked up to see her look out shyly, then emerge in a long, slinky dress that glittered like Las Vegas and clung like a second skin. "What do you think?" she asked, looking at him hopefully.

Oh, Baby! was what he thought. But he didn't say it. "Very nice," he said. "It's…ah…very nice." And he started doing some shallow breathing in order to hold off a meltdown as she walked slowly before him, turned and started back.

"You hate it," she said accusingly.

"No." He gave her a strained smile. "No, I definitely do not hate it. But I don't think you'd better buy it."

"Why not? Doesn't it look good?"

"It looks too good." He gave her a wistful look. "I'm supposed to be protecting you. I don't need the extra risk factor."

She paused, looking worried, then noticed that his eyes were dancing, and immediately she laughed. "You're bad," she said, waving a finger at him. "You are very, very bad."

He grinned at her and she went back behind the screen, changing into her own clothes and joining him again, despite the urgings of the two girls to try a few more. Rock music was blaring from the speakers now, and young women came dancing out in one fashionable outfit after another.

Kari leaned close and whispered, "My aunt won't like this," to Jack.

"Maybe it's about time she let you pick your own clothes," he murmured back.

She nodded. "Of course it is. I know it. The whole world knows it. Now how do we tell her?"

She went ahead and ordered a few items to be sent to the house for her to try on later. Jack watched her and liked what he saw—liked it too much. Her look, her scent, the sound of her voice—everything about her was turning him on in a way that reminded him of his teenage years. Uncontrollable lust wasn't a pretty thing and he wasn't crazy about it in any case. He liked control, liked to think he could manage himself and events around him. But for some reason the attraction he was experiencing with this young woman was like nothing he'd ever known before.

Forbidden fruit, he told himself. That had to be it. He knew he couldn't touch her so the need to touch her was building like a summer storm inside him. If he didn't watch out, he might become the most dangerous thing she faced in her daily life. And he was the one who was supposed to keep her safe.

To keep her safe. The words went straight into his soul. That was his job now. Suddenly he wondered if he was taking it seriously enough. She was quick and bright and self-assured, but there was a vulnerability that surfaced when he least expected it. And whenever he saw that, something in him responded and he wanted to pull her close and make sure no harm could touch her. But that was mostly a man-woman thing. Was he ignoring the most dangerous aspects of this project? Was she in real jeopardy?

"So what is next on the royal agenda?" he asked as they waited for the attendant to finish the tally and present the list of outfits that would be delivered the following day.

"The parties, of course."

"Why so many parties?"

She gave him the impish smile that always made the corners of his mouth curl into a responding smile despite all his best intentions. "To get me married. I'm supposed to try out all these men. They'll be bringing them over in herds."

His smile faded as the horror of the situation finally became clear to him. Summer at the Roseanovas was going to be a regular marriage market. She was going to be auctioned off to the equivalent of the highest bidder. This might be what royalty routinely did, but it sounded barbaric to him.

"And at some point you'll choose which one will be your husband?" he asked, frowning at her.

"Well, the duchess will choose. She will decide who is the most suitable."

He was speechless. How could she be so casual about it? He was outraged himself, and ready to threaten bodily injury to any man who got too close to her.

"But it doesn't really matter," she told him reassuringly, putting a hand on his arm as though she sensed his agitation. "I'm not marrying for love. It's my duty."

Her duty.

He pictured a gray-haired geezer with a lecherous grin taking this lovely young woman in his arms, kissing her, taking her to bed...and his stomach churned as adrenaline raced through his system. He wanted to hit something—preferably the jaw of the disgusting mythical bridegroom.

He cleared his throat, forcing back his natural reactions and attempting to maintain his cool in any way that might be possible.

"When do they start bringing them in?" he asked, hoping she didn't notice how strained his voice sounded.

"Who?"

"All these eligible bachelors they are going to be parading in front of you in order for your aunt to make her choice."

"Ahh." She nodded wisely. "Actually, the first dinner is tomorrow night."

He squared his shoulders as though preparing for an onslaught. "Okay," he muttered to himself. "No problem."

She made a face at him, but then continued on. "We'll start small. There will be three or four of them at the first dinner. But don't worry. My aunt has assured me these men aren't very important. We have invited them as a courtesy, so they will feel they've had their chance. But they won't be considered in the end."

"'Had their chance'?" He looked at her quizzically.

She laughed and preened. "Of course. I'm quite a prize, you know." Grinning, she made sure he understood she didn't take it all so very seriously. "I don't mean personally, of course. I mean what I represent."

But *he* meant personally. She was very much a prize. She was beautiful and lively and carried herself with a natural nobility that couldn't help but shine through. Any man would be lucky to get her hand in marriage.

So why was there a knot forming painfully in his gut? It made no sense. He tried to tell himself that things might get easier once the men started hanging around. At least her mind would be occupied. Yes, that was it. Get her busy. Then things would get back to normal.

But what was normal? The way the allure of her

perfume got caught in his head? The way her face haunted his dreams? The way he felt her presence beside him even when he didn't turn to look at her?

Maybe normal wasn't so safe, after all.

Jack was sometimes disconcerted by Princess Karina and her candid reactions, but when it came to his job as head of security of the estate, he was confident of being on solid ground. Here, he knew what he was doing. With the approval of the duchess, he ordered new security fencing, a new alarm system for the house proper to be turned on between midnight and six in the morning, and a cell phone for Kari.

The cell phone arrived the morning after their department store expedition. On his way to deliver it to the house, he found Kari sitting with a book in the very elaborate rose garden. The Roseanovas, he'd learned, used the rose as the symbol of their royal house. The rose garden was laid out as a map of Nabotavia, with paths standing in for rivers, making a maze. Kari was sitting where the capital, Kalavia, would be. The huge rose bush covered with deep red roses was supposed to stand for the castle where her family had lived since the Middle Ages.

She was a vision in the early light, with sunshine streaming through her hair and her face still a little sleepy as she looked up to greet him. He held out the cell phone.

"What am I supposed to do with this?" she asked, holding it between her thumb and forefinger as though it weren't clean enough to touch.

He maintained his composure, though she looked pretty comical. He'd promised himself he wasn't going to fall for her charms any longer—or at any rate, he wasn't going to let it show when he did feel that warm curl of attraction unfold in his chest. That always looked so doable when he was in his own apartment, preparing his plans. After all, he'd fulfilled tougher assignments in his time. But when he came face-to-face with her, plans tended to crumble.

He had accompanied her back from the showroom display the previous afternoon, only to find the duchess waiting as they walked in, a suspicious look on her face as she watched their interaction sharply. They were a bit later than expected, and he could understand her concern. But he'd quickly assessed the situation and engaged the duchess in conversation, keeping a cool head despite the fact that they were smuggling in popcorn for the duke.

The princess had told him about the popcorn as they were leaving the department store showroom, making their way back downstairs in the elevator.

"My uncle loves it," she'd explained. "And my aunt forbids him having any. She's very strict about his diet, you know. And she has some sort of idea in her head that popcorn is bad for his digestion."

"I'm sure she's only looking out for his best interests," he murmured, though he wasn't sure of it at all.

"Possibly," she responded breezily. "But I think he deserves a treat now and then, so I get him popcorn whenever I can sneak it in."

The elevator doors opened and she began to lead him toward the counter that stocked such things.

"It's got to be the candied kind," she said instructively. "And it's got to be in a vacuum pack, because of the smell, you know. That always gives it away. And if the duchess catches me…" She made a face that revealed dire consequences in a comical fashion.

He had to hold back a grin, but he allowed himself one comment as they came to a stop at the counter and began to wait for service. Looking at her sideways he murmured, "You're awfully sneaky, for a princess."

She laughed. "You don't understand royalty at all if you don't understand how sneaky the whole system is. To be royal is to put on an act. It's all a false front." She sobered, getting philosophical. "We have to try to be larger than life, because that is what people expect of us. If you just come across like an average, everyday person, people start to pout." She demonstrated, putting on a silly voice. "'What's the point? Who needs royalty like this?' I've even heard it said that the Russian revolution became possible when the people saw Czar Nicholas and realized he was just a scrawny little man. People began to say, 'Well, who's scared of a czar like that?'"

He had to laugh at her antics. She was absolutely adorable. He stood beside her and watched as she purchased her popcorn, feeling a wave of affection for her that made him groan inside.

But once they were home and faced with the suspicions of the duchess, he worked quickly, distracting her attention with a list of security concerns for her to deal with while Kari gave him a wink and slipped away, suitably disguised popcorn in hand, to visit her uncle.

There was no longer any doubt in his mind—the princess was a very special person. And she deserved every bit of creative protection he could manage to provide. Equipping her with a cell phone was only the beginning as far as he was concerned, and here she was, resisting his efforts.

"Hold it like this," he said firmly, taking her hand in his and showing her how to hold and flip it open, then immediately pulling away when he realized he was back to treating her like a pretty girl rather than a royal presence. Somehow he had to get it through his thick head that there was a wall between them, a wall he would be a fool to try to breach.

"The best thing to do would be to wear it at your waist. See, it has a clip at the back. That way you'll always have it with you."

"Is that really necessary?" she asked, still looking as though she would just as soon drop it in the nearest waste receptacle.

"It's just another element in our security system. It's meant to make you safer, to give you a means of communication in case anything should happen." He frowned at her. "What is your hesitation? Every girl your age in the civilized world carries one of these around with her at all times. Most wouldn't know how to function without one."

She shrugged, not at all convinced. "You still haven't told me what I am supposed to do with it."

"It will come in handy if you need to get a hold

of help quickly. And you can use it to call your girl-friends.''

She raised her head and met his gaze honestly. ''I don't have any girlfriends.''

She said it without irony, without bitterness, without guile. So much so that for just a moment he thought she must be joking.

''What are you talking about? I've never known a woman who didn't have friends. It's part of their nature.''

She shook her head. ''Not me,'' she said simply, a certain sadness shadowing her blue eyes.

He was still having trouble with this concept. ''What about those two girls who were over swimming with you the other day?''

One perfectly sculpted eyebrow rose. ''Were you watching us?''

''No, of course not.'' Suddenly his ears were burning again. What was it about her that made him do that? It had never happened with anyone else. ''But I did happen to see them with you,'' he went on doggedly, hoping she didn't notice the color of his ears.

She shrugged. ''I'd never met them before and I doubt I will see them again. I believe they were just passing through, though I didn't really get a chance for a good talk with either one of them. Besides, it would be too risky to make friends with anyone in the Nabotavian community. Too much chance for treachery.'' She shook her head. ''I'm quite serious, Jack. I have no real friends.'' A slight smile played at the corners of her mouth. ''I did have an imaginary friend when I was little. I called her Bambi.'' She looked at him quickly, wishing she could take that admission back. She'd never told anyone before. Was he laughing at her?

No. His eyes were stormy, and he was filled with a certain anger as he contemplated what her life must have been like growing up this way. What sort of archaic and sadistic system kept this lovely young woman from living a normal happy existence like that of others her age? What had all this protection and elitism done to her? And was it really worth it? No girlfriends, no life... And he thought *he'd* been deprived growing up with no family. Suddenly he realized that they had more of a common bond than he'd ever thought possible.

"Well, you should have a friend," he said tersely. "In fact, I'm going to look into getting you one."

She stared at him for a moment, and then a smile just barely crinkled the corners of her eyes. "I didn't know you could order them up," she said. "Darn! I would have bought one years ago if only I'd known."

He didn't smile. In fact, he felt more like he needed to hit something and he turned away from her.

But she followed, putting a hand on his arm to get his attention back. "You mustn't blame us for our old-fashioned ways," she told him earnestly, seemingly reading his mind and knowing how he felt about her upbringing. "We've lost our country. We hang on to as much of our traditions as we can manage. They are all we have left."

Of course. He knew that. Swallowing hard, he forced himself to remain casual and even attempted a look of unconcern. She had her life and he had his. There was no reason their two existences should touch in any form whatsoever, except in the most professional way.

It wasn't easy to figure out why she had this ability to reach in and take hold of his emotions the way she did. Regardless, he couldn't let it show. In fact, it was probably time he put some actual distance between them, before the duchess walked out into the yard and saw them talking. Instinctively he knew she wouldn't like it at all.

He looked down at her hand on his arm, and she removed it, flattening it against her own chest. His gaze followed, and for some reason he couldn't pull away. Her fingers were slim and tapered and looked beautiful against the lightly tanned skin showing above the scooped neck of her lace-edged top. The vision she made touched him, made him yearn for her. He ached to take her in his arms.

Their gazes met and held for a long, quivering moment. But as each second ticked away, he was gathering the strength to do what had to be done. And finally he gritted his teeth and looked away.

"I've got to get going," he said gruffly. "You practice with that cell phone. Get used to it. It won't hurt you to join the modern world, at least this little bit."

When he looked back, he found her smiling at him in a way so wise, he immediately feared she could read his mind and knew exactly what he was thinking. But she didn't make any comment, turning from him, picking up her book from the bench and starting toward the house.

"I guess I'd better get going, as well. I have a lot

to do to prepare for this evening.'' She turned back and gave him her impish grin. ''Tonight is the night. Madam Batalli is due soon to do my hair. Let's hope she manages to make me beautiful.''

He nodded, mixed feelings grinding through him. ''So you're pretty excited,'' he noted dryly.

''Well...sort of.'' She shrugged. ''This is the first step toward the beginning of the rest of my life. I'm about to launch, in a way. The way debutantes are presented. The way young ladies were introduced to society in the old days.''

He nodded again, fighting the impulse to say something to her. It would be better to let her go, he knew. He had no business imposing his thoughts. But he just couldn't leave it alone.

''Princess...'' He stopped, shoved his hand in his pocket and turned to go, then turned back. ''Listen, be careful, okay?'' he admonished awkwardly. ''I mean, about the man you pick. You deserve the best. Don't settle for anything less. Okay?''

She nodded, her eyes filled with the bright light of the sun. Suddenly she took a quick step toward him as he turned to go again.

''Wait...look,'' she said, making an elaborate show of attaching the cell phone to the waist of her slacks. ''Here, I'm putting it on. I'll be so much safer now, in case I get lost in the woods or fall down a rabbit hole or something like that.''

She looked up expectantly at him, like a child hoping for approbation. Then she sighed, as though she realized she was going over the top.

''I appreciate the attempt to protect my interests.

Really, I do. And I'll wear this faithfully as a token of my appreciation.'' She gave him a sharp salute, like a cute toy soldier at attention.

He bit back his own grin. ''Thank you, Princess,'' he said formally. ''Just remember to use it if you do find yourself in any sort of sticky situation.''

''Oh, I will,'' she said. Her eyes lit up as she thought of something. ''And once I memorize your number, I'll be able to call you anytime, day or night.''

He hesitated warily. ''Sure, if you're in trouble...''

''How about when I'm lonely?'' she asked softly, her eyes luminous. ''Or when I need some good advice?''

His face darkened. ''Princess...''

''I know, I know,'' she said lightly, turning away and starting for the house again, book in hand. ''I'm being frivolous.'' She looked back at him from the doorway. ''But I'm going to memorize your number, anyway.'' She put her hand over the cell phone at her waist and added, in a voice just above a whisper, ''I think you would make a wonderful friend.''

And then she was gone.

His heart twisted inside him, and he stood where he was, muttering every obscene swear word he could think of—anything to keep from feeling the emotions she triggered in him.

Chapter Five

Looking the current crop of suitors over later that evening, Jack tried to remain objective. If he was going to provide Princess Kari with the proper level of security, he had to understand what was going on around her. Emotions couldn't be allowed to cloud the issue.

He stayed in the background during dinner, blending in with the help and watching as the duchess and her guests were served an elaborate meal at the long, dark dining table. Huge candelabras lit the high-ceilinged room, casting shadows on the richly flocked walls. The duchess sat at the head of the table. Seven adults as stiff and mannered as she was were scattered up and down each side, and four young men sat between them, attention all on Kari, who sat at the other end. The conversation was polite. It seemed almost formulaic to Jack, as though each was reading from a script she'd learned for the occasion.

But that all changed as the party finished dessert and retired to the game room for liqueur in tiny crystal goblets and more animated conversation. The adults sank into plush chairs around a large felt-covered gaming table while the younger ones gathered at the far side of the room, encouraging Kari as she played a few light tunes on the piano.

All four of the young men were very handsome, though one had a dissolute look and another seemed bit vacant. They were all much younger than Jack had expected. There were no old lechers looking for a young bride here tonight. That should have been a relief, but somehow it didn't help. He still hated seeing them crowd around her, vying for her attention.

"She looks like Scarlett O'Hara at the barbecue," he muttered to himself as he stood, feeling restless, in the dim light of the patio off the gaming room.

A chuckle nearby told him he'd been overheard and he turned to find the duke coming up to stand at his elbow. "You hit the nail right on the head," the duke told him softly, nodding. "Look at her. Isn't she the most fetching thing you've ever seen?"

Jack turned back to take in the scene reluctantly. The older man's admiration was well-founded. Kari was wearing a violet dress that fitted her bodice like a glove, then flared out at the hips into a filmy cloud of transparent fabric that played teasingly about her long, lovely legs. It was one of the dresses they had looked at the day before, so he assumed her choices hadn't been completely vetoed by her aunt. Kari's hair was swept up into a cascade of curls that was old-fashioned but appealing, and her face was shining with joy. Jack had never seen a woman look lovelier. He was afraid to leave his gaze on her for too long, afraid a part of him would begin to burn inside. She was just as her uncle said, completely fetching.

The young men circling her were another matter, and the duke filled him in on their identities himself.

"Now Leonard Bachman's lineage goes back to the Holy Roman Empire," he noted, pointing out one with a decidedly superior look to him. "Eugene is one of the British royal cousins," he added, nodding toward the blonde. "Not very bright, I'm afraid, but awfully good at cricket. And Nigel is a very nice lad. I once thought I was in love with his mother."

That got Jack's attention. He smiled at the duke, really looking at him for the first time and realizing how sweet he looked for a man his age. His hair was either very blond or had turned a stunning shade of white, and was combed back in a debonair style that belonged to swells of another age.

"The one to watch out for is that redhead," the duke continued, unabashed. "He has a very wild reputation among the younger crowd. I don't like the look of him. He brings to mind a young Oscar Wilde."

Jack nodded. "I'd been thinking something along those lines myself," he murmured.

"Good. I'm glad you have an instinct for these things." The duke nodded his handsome head approvingly and patted Jack's shoulder. "I trust you'll be keeping a close watch on our young lady. And making sure none of these young swains get too fresh with her?"

Is that what I'm supposed to do?

He only thought the words, but the question was a good one. He knew he'd been hired to keep Kari safe, but no one had been very clear on the extent of that safety. Was he expected to make sure she didn't risk breaking her heart? Was that a part of it all?

I hadn't understood that morals patrol was part of the job.

Again he didn't say the words aloud but thought them as he muttered something agreeable instead.

The duke went on telling him anecdotes about each of the guests. The stories made Jack grin, and even laugh once, and he wondered why the man was being so friendly. He'd met him on occasion for only a few moments at a time, but he was acting as though they'd known each other for years. Something told him Kari was the reason. She must have mentioned him to her uncle. But what could she possibly have said that would make the man feel as though they were practically comrades?

He threw a casual glance in her direction. She was laughing, and the redheaded gallant was leaning toward her, touching her cheek, saying something that was obviously impertinent. Every muscle in Jack's body clenched. The young man drew back his hand, and Jack slowly, purposefully, made himself relax.

Whether the family wanted morals patrol or not, his instinct was doing the job on its own.

"Well, I suppose it is time to honor the scene with my royal presence. Frankly, I'd rather stay here chatting with you, but duty calls." The duke gave him a sad half smile. "As for my young lady, I'm sure you'll take good care of her," he said with a wink, then straightened his tie and set off to join the party.

Jack frowned, not sure what the duke had meant by that. Suddenly Kari's head lifted and her gaze met his across the room. She caught him off guard, and her smile shot straight into his heart. He saw a connection in it, a recognition that he should be in on her private joke. Suddenly he knew exactly what she was thinking just as though she'd whispered the words in his ear. She was having the time of her life but it wasn't serious—he wasn't to take it as such, and she wanted him to laugh at it with her. She wanted to share her joy with him.

He couldn't let that happen. The emotion knotting his stomach had nothing to do with humor. Telling himself to ignore this wasn't working. He was caught in a maze with no way out. Unless he took the initiative and made an escape route for himself. He took a deep breath. Time to do just that. Moving farther back into the shadows, he pulled out his walkie-talkie and called Greg Pinion, his right-hand man. It was time to hand the rest of the evening over to someone better equipped to handle the torture. He was getting out of here. A man could only take so much.

                    *   *   *

Kari bit her lip. Jack was leaving. She could tell. As he briefed Greg, she could read the signs. He was transferring the assignment and heading off to do something else.

Suddenly the delight drained out of the evening. Much of what she'd been doing had been an act meant to impress him. It had been fun, even thrilling for a time. There was certainly nothing boring about being admired. But more than that, she'd wanted Jack to see her as the center of a lot of male attention. She was sure that was a wicked thing to want, and now she was pretty sure it had backfired on her.

Of course, she was being foolish and she knew it. Much as she liked Jack, much as her pulse rate quickened whenever he was near, she knew there was no future for the two of them. She had gone through periods of feeling rebellious in the past, but that was all over now. She knew her destiny. She was going to marry and do her duty. She owed that to her parents and to her culture. In another few weeks she would be engaged to be married to an eligible nobleman of her country.

She caught her breath. That thought always made her feel as though she'd just fallen off a very high ledge. Married. How could she be married when she knew nothing—nothing at all—about men? She couldn't help being terrified of the whole situation.

"This isn't about love and kisses and romance," her aunt had told her often enough. "You don't need to know anything at all about men. That's irrelevant.

This is about duty to your family and your country. It is about securing the future of the nation, helping your brothers to make it stronger. That is what you were born for.''

Of course she would do her duty. But other girls got to date and flirt and have fun with boys they didn't intend to marry...didn't they? She was never going to be allowed to live like a normal person, but this one little thing...this friendship with a man who made her feel light-headed...couldn't she at least have this? Was that so horribly selfish?

She looked around at the faces of her admiring new acquaintances. Every one was well connected, handsome, charming. The man who would be picked as her spouse would be a lot like one of them, only probably a bit older—someone stable, ready to settle down, but of the right family and with the right connections. Someone eminently eligible for her hand, just as these were. Perfect for her.

This was what she'd been waiting for all this time. The days of being stuck with the old folks were gone. She was now allowed, even encouraged, to have fun with young men. She ought to be like a kid let loose in a candy store.

And yet compared to Jack these handsome suitors seemed colorless and uninteresting. It was lovely to be the center of their attention, but she'd had enough for tonight. She was ready to give up this pretense for the time being. She wanted to see Jack again. Ached to see him.

The handsome redhead was leaning close, murmuring sweet nothings meant to make her swoon, but she wasn't really listening to him. Her heart beat faster as she made her decision. Yes, she was going to see Jack again. Tonight.

Jack leaned back into the pillows he'd piled against the arm of the couch and yawned, turning off the television. Dressed only in slacks, he'd been flipping channels and finding nothing that could hold his interest. It was late. He'd been putting off going to bed but he'd waited long enough. Maybe now he would finally be able to fall asleep without thinking about...

He swore softly. No, he wasn't even going to let himself *think* about thinking about her.

This fascination with the girl was completely unlike him. He'd spent most of his life as a man's man, more at home with a group of buddies than with a girlfriend. He figured that was because of the way he'd grown up, in foster families and group homes, usually with a boy or two for a pal and very little contact with the opposite sex.

That had all changed in high school, of course, but though he'd dated a lot of pretty girls, he'd been more at home with his football teammates. Girls made him nervous. He just didn't understand what they expected. It seemed to him they said one thing when they really meant something else, and his head would swim as he tried to figure out what was going on.

The mystery girls posed faded as he hit his twenties. He even had a few fairly long-term relationships. But somehow his heart had never been truly touched.

And when each relationship ended, he didn't look back with any sort of remorse. Women were easy to get when you wanted one.

The single thing he did regret, however, was letting a woman mess with his life in a way that might turn out to be downright disastrous. It had already played havoc with his career. Now he was waiting to see if his partnership with Lucy Dunlap—and the mistake of trusting her—had turned his future to dust. By the end of the summer he would know.

There was a sound at his door, a knock so soft, at first he wasn't sure if he'd imagined it. He frowned. Someone at his door at this time of night could only mean trouble. Assuming it was one of the guards, he rose from the couch and sauntered to the door, ready to point out that a call on his cell phone would have been a quicker way to get his attention.

But he never made that little speech, because he pulled the door open and found Kari on his doorstep.

"Hi," she said in a voice meant to be muted to the outside world. "Let me in, quick."

Stunned, he did as she asked and immediately regretted it.

"You can't be here," he noted sternly, lurching back. "Don't close that door."

But she did, snapping it shut before he could reach it and then turning to grin at him. "Shh!" she said with a finger to her lips. "No one knows I'm here."

She'd dressed herself all in black, from her slinky turtleneck sweater to her soft jersey leggings. Her face was scrubbed clean of the makeup she'd worn earlier, and her hair was combed out and floating softly around her shoulders. Every time he saw her she looked more lovely than before. It was like a disease, and he was suffering from a rare and possibly fatal case of it.

"Why didn't Greg stop you?" he demanded, glowering at her. "He's supposed to be guarding the back of the house."

"I waited until he was distracted by something and I sneaked right past him," she said proudly.

"If he's that easy to fool, I'll have him fired in the morning."

Her eyes widened in horror. "Oh, no, don't do that. It wasn't his fault."

"If he can't do his job…"

"No, don't you see?" She gave him her most irresistible impish smile. "It isn't that he's so bad at what he does. It's all because I'm so good at what I do. You can't punish him for…for that…"

Her voice faded at the end because she'd finally taken in the condition she'd found him in. Her gaze trailed over his naked torso, lingering on the hard, chiseled muscles of his chest, his strong upper arms, the washboard panels tapering into his slacks.

"Oh, my," she said in a tiny voice.

He groaned and turned, rummaging in the couch, throwing pillows aside, looking for his shirt. "This is exactly why you shouldn't be here," he warned, finally spotting it and yanking it out to slip into. "You have no business coming to my apartment," he went on as he hastily worked with the buttons. "If the duchess knew you were here, she'd pack you off to a convent.''

''I had to come,'' she said in a strangled voice. She took a deep breath, then blinked hard a few times, regaining her equilibrium as he covered up his gorgeous flesh. ''I need your help.''

''What for?''

She looked at him expectantly, throwing out her hands. ''Aren't you going to ask me to sit down?'' she said. ''Isn't that what people usually do when someone comes to visit?''

He hesitated. He wanted her out of there as quickly as possible, but he knew darn well she wasn't going to budge until she'd said her piece.

''Have a seat, Princess,'' he said at last, biting out the words crisply. ''And tell me what you need help with.''

She sat gingerly on the edge of the couch, while he dropped to drape himself casually on the opposite arm, as far from her as he could possibly get. She noted that, then looked around at the simple living room, the small kitchen just off it, the hallway toward the bathroom and bedroom. Bookcases lined the walls, though there wasn't much filling them. The old security man had lived here for years, but when he'd left, he'd taken a lot of the furnishings and Jack hadn't replaced them with many personal items. She knew he was only here for the summer, but she was disappointed he hadn't set out more clues to himself and his life. She wanted to see what he liked to read, maybe some pictures of friends, a favorite item from his past. But there was nothing she could put her finger on. Jack seemed to enjoy being an enigma.

"It would be so much fun to have a place of my own," she said wistfully. "A place I could decorate my own way and have people over to visit." She sighed. "Don't you just love being on your own?"

He shook his head, his mouth twisted cynically. "The female urge to nest," he said. "It seems to be universal." His mouth hardened. "But this isn't getting us any closer to your problem."

"My problem?"

His brows drew together. "You said you needed help."

"Oh. Of course." She smiled at him. "This is going to sound a little strange. But it's actually quite serious. You see, I need to learn how to kiss."

He choked, which set off a short coughing fit.

She leaned toward him. "Do you need a good thump on the back?" she asked hopefully.

"No!" he said, leaning away from her. "I'm fine. It's just…" He coughed one last time and shook his head, looking at her in wonder, squinting as though that would help him see her better. He manufactured a glare, just to show her he was serious. "What did you really come here for?"

She thought for a second or two, then shrugged. "The kissing thing was it."

He groaned and she added defensively, "I thought it was a good idea. I think you ought to teach me how to kiss. Because I really need to know."

He looked at her uneasily. She was so pretty, so

impossibly desirable, and so completely unaware of the danger she could have been in. She shouldn't be saying things like this to a man like him. Still, he wasn't totally convinced that she wasn't pulling his leg.

"Why?" he asked suspiciously.

"Don't you think it's something I ought to know?" She didn't give him time to answer, talking fast. "I've been taught how to dance, how to make small talk, how to drive a car. Don't you think it would be best if I were taught the intricacies of kissing? After all, I might be doing quite a lot of it this summer."

He stared at her for a moment, then turned away, muttering something she couldn't quite make out. So she went on making her case.

"You know that song, 'Sweet Sixteen and Never Been Kissed'? You could change the lyrics for me." She let out a tragic sigh. "Bitter twenty-two and never even been touched by any man." Her face changed and she almost smiled. "Except you, of course," she added, dimpling playfully.

"Me?" His head whipped back and he stared at her. "What are you talking about?"

"When you came into my room that day. Remember? You grabbed me." She sighed dreamily. "It was great. I think about it every night before I fall asleep."

"Well, don't." Rising, he began to pace the room, running his hand through his thick hair as he did so. This was no good and could get a lot worse. He had to play it carefully. "Just forget about it."

She just smiled and he stopped before her, arms folded across his chest.

"Are you seriously trying to tell me you have made it twenty-two years without once being kissed?" he demanded.

"Of course."

He shook his head. "How could that be?"

"I've never been left alone with a man. I always have someone with me." She shrugged. "That makes it rather difficult to fool around."

He shook his head again, hardly knowing whether to believe her or not. The experience she was portraying was so far removed from that of the average young woman her age, it seemed like a fairy tale. But then, she *was* a princess, wasn't she? So fairy tales would seem to apply.

"There was no point in letting me date," she went on helpfully. "I always understood that perfectly well. Why should I go out with boys who have no chance of ever marrying me? What if I fell in love? It could be disastrous."

"It still could be," he noted softly, staring down into her beautiful eyes.

She held his gaze, head high, but there was an excitement quivering deep inside her. "I think I can handle it," she told him quietly.

He shook his head slowly. "You don't know what you're talking about," he told her. It took effort, but he forced himself to turn away and begin pacing again. What was he going to do with this girl?

She watched him, a slight smile tilting the corners

of her wide mouth. "You're probably right," she said. "But don't you see? That's just the problem." She waited a moment, but he kept pacing, hands shoved deep into his pockets, so she went on. "It occurred to me tonight that I really haven't had enough experience in handling men. I need help. My older brothers aren't here, so I can't turn to them. My uncle is hopeless and the duchess would just snap at me." She turned her palms up appealingly. "So I have no one else to turn to but you."

He stopped, turning to look at her. It was still an improbable scenario. Beautiful young princess appeals to lonely cop to teach her to kiss. No one else would believe it. Why should he?

"What happened tonight?" he asked her softly, his eyes searching hers, looking for evidence that there was more to this request than she was admitting to. "Did one of them try to…?"

"No, nothing like that," she said quickly. "But I want to be prepared, in case anyone ever does 'try' anything. I need to know what's possible, what to look out for. How can I defend myself if I don't understand what's going on?"

She was getting through to him. She could see the tiny seeds of doubt beginning to germinate. She was starting to persuade him to see it her way. Time to get back to the heart of the matter.

"But what I really need to know," she said softly as she looked up into his eyes, her own wide with innocence. "What I really need is lessons in how to kiss."

"Oh, no," he said, backing away from her. "There's no reason in the world you need to know how to kiss."

She rose, following him. "You wouldn't want me kissing some count or earl and having him think I'm just a callow schoolgirl who doesn't know what she's doing, would you?"

He stared at her, once again wary of being fooled by her innocent act. "Oh, come on, Princess. I imagine that's exactly what they want. Someone who's completely...untouched." He choked on the phrase and his mind was flashing words like *pure* and *virginal.* He had to turn away so she wouldn't see what that did to him.

"If you won't teach me how to kiss, I'm going to have to look for someone who will." Her eyes narrowed speculatively. "I suppose I could ask Count Boris," she mused.

He turned back, frowning fiercely. "Who the hell is Count Boris?" he growled.

She smiled at him. "The duchess's younger brother. He's coming for a visit soon. I haven't seen him since I was about ten years old, but I remember that he seemed very handsome to me at that time."

She waited, watching the conflicting emotions play in his dark gaze. It was all so blatant she was almost embarrassed. But she knew instinctively that she was never going to get anywhere if she left it up to him. So here she was, doing the best she could manage.

"What exactly is it you want to know about kiss-

ing?'' he asked her, though she could see it cost him
something to give in, even to this extent.

"I thought maybe...you could show me how?"

"Oh, no." He shook his head firmly. That was obviously out. Completely out. Wasn't going to happen.

"Well, at least you could give me some advice,"
she said sweetly.

"Advice?" He looked relieved. "Advice. Sure.
Why not? I'll give you some advice." He pointed at
the couch. "You go sit down. You make me nervous
standing so close. And I'll think up some advice to
give you."

She went back to the couch obediently, slipping out
of her shoes and curling her legs up under her, looking very comfortable. He stood on the other side of
the room, arms across his chest, gazing at her.

So now he was supposed to be some sort of expert.
What the hell did he know about man-woman relationships? Poor thing, she didn't realize he was the
last man she should be asking. You didn't get great
helpful hints from someone who had failed at what
you were aiming at. He could tell her what to avoid.
He could tell her relationships weren't worth the effort. He could tell her not to trust anyone. That was
pretty much the way he handled his own life. But
somehow he didn't want to steer her in the same direction. Maybe she would be lucky. Maybe she would
find something good in this rotten world. He didn't
want to ruin that for her.

"Okay, the first thing you have to realize is that as
a woman, you have all the power."

"The power?" She blinked in surprise. "How can that be? Men are bigger and stronger and..."

"Sure, men who are thugs can overpower you physically anytime they want to. But that's not the sort of power I'm talking about. With any normal man, it's going to be up to you to control things."

He stepped closer to where she sat, the subject suddenly as engrossing to him as it was to her. And that was odd because he'd never thought this through before. But now that he was considering it, there seemed to be a lot of theory floating around in his head, and he had to wonder how long that had been going on.

"You're beautiful, appealing and very sexy," he told her earnestly. "Men are hard-wired to react to that sort of thing. They can't even help themselves. Around a female like you, they're helpless."

She bit her lip to keep from snickering at him. Men helpless—what a concept. If men were so helpless and easy to control, why wasn't Jack kissing her right now? She took a deep breath and waited, listening intently.

"Which makes them very dangerous. Because a helpless man is going to feel cornered and is likely to do something stupid. So you have to learn to treat every man with a firm hand, but with some compassion at the same time." He frowned, shaking his head. "Is any of this making any sense?" he asked her. "What I mean is, you have to learn to play your cards very close to the vest, and to be aware of what kind of reaction you are getting at all times."

She laughed softly. "Oh, Jack, you're the quintessential law enforcement officer, aren't you? So suspicious of everyone.''

He didn't welcome her comment. ''Look, you asked my advice.''

''I did, indeed,'' she said quickly, looking suitably abashed. ''Sorry. Please continue.''

He made her wait a beat or two, then went back to pacing as he warmed to his subject. ''Okay, talking specifically about the prospective husbands—well, put it this way. Any guy worth his salt is going to want to kiss you. It's up to you to hold your kisses safe. They're worth a lot. It's up to you to decide who you value enough to squander them on.''

She dangled a foot over the edge of the couch. ''What if I decide I want to kiss them all?'' she asked breezily.

''No!'' He stopped short, frowning at her. ''No, because a kiss isn't just a kiss.''

She gazed at him quizzically. ''Then what is it?''

He thought for a moment, wanting to get this right. ''It's an invitation. It's a promise. It's a way a woman opens the door, even if just a tiny crack, into her soul.''

She gasped softly. She hadn't realized Jack could be so poetic. ''Just a little kiss can do all that?''

She watched him wide-eyed. She was beginning to understand what he'd meant. She thought she felt a little of the power he'd been talking about in the way she could feel that he was drawn to her. It was intoxicating. It made her think things possible she might not have dreamed of before coming here. What if…?

She rose and planted herself in his pacing path. He turned and almost ran into her, reaching out to steady her with his hands on her shoulders.

"I think you should show me that kiss now," she said softly.

The look that flashed in his eyes might have been alarm, or it might have been something more dangerous. She wasn't sure. At any rate he turned her down.

"I don't want to kiss you," he said flatly.

Her lips tilted at the corners. "Yes, you do," she said daringly. "I vote we be honest about this. Okay? You want to kiss me. And I very much want you to. So what's the holdup?"

He thought about turning away, but it had become impossible now. She was too close. Her scent was filling his head. And he couldn't seem to pry his fingers off her shoulders. But he had to try to keep this thing from steering off the cliff.

"Princess..."

"Scaredy-cat," she taunted softly, smiling up at him.

She felt so fragile in his hands, so deliciously pliable. Light as a breeze, sweet as a rose.

"No," he said, as much to himself as to her. Hell, he was strong enough to resist this. This was nothing. "No, we can't do this."

"Jack," she said, cocking her head to one side and looking deep into his eyes, "if you won't kiss me, someone else will be my first. Please be the one."

Resistance crumbled abruptly, and something close to pain was squeezing his heart. "Well, maybe just a small kiss," he heard himself saying. "A quick one. Just so you see…"

Oh, who was he kidding?

"No hands," he warned, releasing her shoulders. "No touching."

She clasped her hands behind her back and he held his hands in fists at his sides. She leaned toward him, and he leaned toward her. She closed her eyes.

The first thing that surprised her was that his lips were so soft. He was a hard man with a hard body and she'd expected hardness. But no. His lips were as soft as kitten fur and smooth as whipped cream. And yet it wasn't comfort she was feeling. Heat curled through her like smoke, fire began to lick in her veins, and every nerve ending seemed alive and aware as they had never been before.

She kept her hands clasped behind her but she arched toward him, instinctively wanting to feel her breasts against his chest. At the same time, her lips parted slightly and the tip of his tongue touched them, and then he jerked back, breathing quickly and scowling at her as though he was very sorry for what he had just done.

"I didn't mean to do that," he began, then swore softly, turning away.

She was standing there, all dewy and luminous, her lips still parted, and he knew she wanted more from him. And there was no denying every part of him wanted the same thing—and more. He grimaced, feeling like a man drowning in golden nectar, a man who had to claw his way back to the surface. But he was a man who usually did what he had to do, and he managed. And when he could breathe normally again, he turned on her sternly.

"Look, I think it's time for some plain talking. You want truth? Let's both face some facts." He pointed at her almost accusingly. "You are a princess. You're royal. You were born to be one of the elite." He ran his hand distractedly through his hair, setting it on edge. "I come from the opposite end of the spectrum. I'm nobody. I come from nowhere. I've got nothing."

She winced, hating that he was talking like this. "Jack..."

"In fact, the only reason I was available to take this job was because I'm on suspension from the police department. I'm being investigated. I might get fired."

That was news to her, and she didn't know what to say. Still, she made an attempt. "Jack, that doesn't matter. I can tell what kind of man you are."

"Can you?" He shook his head. "Sometimes I'm not too sure about that myself. You know where you come from. There are books full of your genealogy. I don't know anything about my background except that there's got to be an Italian in there somewhere. I was raised without roots, without history, without money." *Without love,* he could have added, but he would rather have died than say it. "We can't...I mean, you know there is no chance for there to be anything..."

Kari rolled her eyes toward the heavens and turned

with a sigh, slipping back into her shoes. She'd tried. But now she was getting angry.

"Save your breath," she told him evenly, tossing her hair over her shoulder as she stepped past him. "I'm not a foolish child. And I'm not falling in love with you. You take all this much too seriously." She stopped at the door, looking back. "I just wanted to learn how to kiss. That's all."

Pulling the door open with her head held high, she disappeared into the night.

Jack stared into the dark for a moment, then strode after her. He didn't say a word as he passed her, but went straight to where he knew Greg was standing sentry duty and engaged him in conversation, giving Kari cover to get into the house without being seen. And when he finally got back to his apartment and closed the door and leaned against it, closing his eyes and laughing softly, he realized one thing—she'd taken his lesson about power to heart, and she was a quick study. Maybe he wasn't going to have to worry about her social relations after all.

But there was something else, something that made his laughter fade quickly. He knew it was going to be a long and sleepless night as he fought his body every minute.

Chapter Six

"Stay away from Jack Santini. He's no good for you."

Kari looked down at her perfectly polished pink fingernails and chewed on her lower lip while she waited for Mr. Blodnick to finish his tirade.

"If I'd known something like this would happen, I'd never have hired him. But I darn well should have known, shouldn't I? After all, I knew all about his suspension from the department. That was over a woman, too. His partner, of all things. I should have kept that in mind…"

"Mr. Blodnick," she said quietly, having had her fill of his overreaction. "If you please."

"Oh." The man calmed himself quickly. "I'm sorry, Your Highness. But when you ask me a question like that—"

"Mr. Blodnick, nothing has happened. No transgressions are being contemplated. All is well." She pulled her robe more tightly around her shoulders. She was dressed for a swim, but had stopped by to ask him questions because she knew her aunt was out of the house at the moment and wouldn't notice. "I merely asked you to tell me what you know of Mr. Santini's background. Idle curiosity, nothing more. There is no need for you to let it upset you so."

"Your Highness...Princess...are you sure? Because if I were to be the cause of ruining your life, I would really feel bad about it."

Kari laughed and reached out to squeeze the man's hand with a great deal of affection. "I'm sure. Now tell me. What did Jack Santini do to deserve a suspension?"

He looked like a man being tortured on the rack. "Have you talked to the duchess about this?"

"Be serious. I'm the one who told you to hire him, aren't I? Do you think I would give her a chance to tell me how wrong I supposedly was?"

He shivered at the thought. "I wouldn't think so."

"Exactly. So come on, mister, spill the beans."

He shifted in his seat and looked very uncomfortable at being in the position of having beans to spill. "I don't really know the details. And I've only heard of it in the most general terms, so..." He coughed. "Well, from what I've heard, he let his feelings for his female partner get the better of him and ended up getting blamed for something she did."

His words cut into her hopes, but she wouldn't allow him to detect that. "I see," she said, all calm and casual.

"There is an ongoing investigation. And a hearing in late August. If he's cleared, he'll be back on the force in no time. But if the board rules against him..."

She nodded. "Was there a romance involved?" she asked, hoping her voice didn't betray how much this was costing her.

He hesitated. "You got me. All I know is, women are always falling for Jack. So I imagine it was something like that."

She smiled, rising from her chair. "Thank you, Mr. Blodnick. You've been very helpful."

He grimaced. "And you won't tell the duchess?"

Her short laugh held a trace of irony. "I'll never lie to her. But I certainly won't volunteer anything unless I'm forced to by circumstances."

"Good." He shook his head with a worried frown. "I'd hate to see him lose this job. I think his being employed here will look good to the board. Just in case he needs that extra boost. And him getting fired would look very bad."

There was no doubt about that.

But Kari left the man's office with a heavy heart. She had absolutely no right to be jealous, but human emotions were difficult to control, and she was feeling rather glum at the moment.

It had been almost a week since that night in Jack's apartment. He'd been avoiding her ever since. She knew he was right to do that. She knew that it was best for them both. They should just stay away from each other.

She'd been wrong to go to him that night. She'd been even more wrong to insist he teach her how to kiss. And yet, whenever she thought about it, she couldn't really regret it. It made her smile when she remembered how he'd tried to avoid kissing her. It made her gasp to remember what his kiss had felt like.

Still, he was right. They couldn't be together. There was no place for them as a twosome in this world. She needed to set her sights on her future, on the man who would be her partner as she returned to her country and began to serve her people the way she had been born and bred to do.

And there was a new angle. The more she was finding out about his situation, the more she realized that his position was quite precarious and could be threatened if anything happened to cause him to lose this job. Just from things she'd heard and things he'd said, she was putting two and two together and getting a rather scary scenario. It would be cruel to him to pursue him in any way. So she just had to stop it. Now, if only she could stop thinking about him as well.

Stepping out onto the veranda, heading for the pool enclosure, she stopped for a moment. She could see Jack in the distance, standing in front of the five-car garage, talking to one of his agents. At the other end of the property, she caught sight of her aunt, giving orders to one of the gardeners. Chin high, she ignored them both and went straight toward the swimming pool, dropping her robe on the deck and diving in without hesitation. She swam ten laps before she paused.

There, she thought. That's better. But she knew she was fooling herself.

She didn't know enough about men. That was the crux of the issue. Her brothers were always so far away, and her uncle was so often remote. After dressing, she quietly slipped down to the rooms the duke kept for himself and knocked on the door. Once he bade her enter, she opened the door and looked in.

"Hello, my favorite uncle," she said with forced cheer. "I've come to ask a favor. I need you to tell me something." She smiled at him tremulously. "Will you tell me about my father?"

Jack was carrying a ladder into the library the next day when he realized Kari was already in the room, sitting at a desk, books and papers spread out all around her.

"Hi," she said, looking up cheerfully.

"Oh." He stopped. He wanted to work on some wiring that had come loose in the alarm system, but he could do that some other time. "Sorry, I didn't know you were in here. I'll just go and let you have some privacy."

"No need to do that. I just came in here to transcribe some of my notes. You won't be bothering me." When he still hesitated, she flashed him a look of pure exasperation. "Don't worry. I'm not going to try and corner you to get another lesson in kissing or anything like that.'' Her mouth tilted in a slight smile. ''That was childish. Immature. Manipulative. And I'm sorry I did it.''

He turned to look at her questioningly, and her smile got rueful. ''Oh, rats,'' she said. ''That's a lie. I'm not sorry at all. But I know I should be, and I'm trying hard to be. It's just that, so far, it's not working.''

He couldn't help it—she made him laugh. And she made him want her with a yearning that was quick and deep and stronger than it should be. For just a moment he let himself dream, looking at her as she sat at the desk, her blond hair in disarray, her lacy blouse twisted, her short skirt revealing long, lean and gorgeous tanned legs that seemed to draw his gaze straight up to where it didn't belong.

What if she were just an ordinary woman? What would he be doing right now? Flirting, no doubt about it. Giving off signals. Looking for response. Wondering how long it was going to take to get her into his bed. Anticipating how sweet it was going to be to taste her nipples, how his hands were going to explore until he'd found all her most responsive secrets, how he would awaken her to things she'd never known before. At the same time, the need for her would build and build in him until it was almost unbearable, until he would slide into her body and take her all the way, and finally find a relief for himself so intense it would almost bring him to tears as her soft cries of pure wonder and delight filled his ears.

Whew. He blinked hard, forcing himself back to earth and looked at her quickly, hoping his thoughts hadn't been too obvious. But she didn't look alarmed. She was saying something about the notes she was compiling. He cleared his throat, still standing before her with the ladder in his hand.

"Notes?" he asked, scanning the books and papers she had spread out before her. "Are you giving another speech?"

"No. Thank goodness." She sat back in her chair, crossing her long legs and looking completely comfortable with herself and her circumstances. "Didn't I tell you about my three main goals for my summer?"

"No," he said, forcing his gaze to avoid looking at those lovely legs. "I don't remember anything like that." But then, he could barely remember his name at this point. He looked at the ladder he was holding. It took a moment to recall why he had it with him, but once he did, he went into action, setting it up along the far wall, greatly relieved to have found something to do besides standing there drooling all over the sexy princess who was supposedly in his care.

"Okay. I'll tell you now." She put down her pencil and rose, walking over to where he was beginning to climb up the ladder. "I have three big goals for my summer. Number one is to write a book about my mother's life. A biography. I'm actually using that as a device to explore a history of my country."

He was up high now. She looked very petite and

young from his upper perch. Still, he had to admit, the way she carried herself gave her a presence you just couldn't deny. No one would have to be told that she was royal. And from up here, her breasts looked so damn appealing...

"You remember that she was killed by the rebels when we escaped from Nabotavia. She and my father both."

He nodded as he reached into the vent with pliers. Maybe he could cut into a wire and get electrocuted, thus putting himself out of this misery. But misery wasn't really the right word for what he was feeling. Sweet torture was more like it. And if he were honest, he would have to admit it felt dangerously delicious, despite everything.

"That's why I want to find out all that I can about her and write it down. Before it's too late and everyone forgets."

He finally realized what she was talking about, and that caught him up short. Here she was discussing her murdered parents and he was off in fantasyland instead of giving the subject the respect it deserved. He quickly vowed to mend his ways.

"What about your father?" he asked by way of catching up as he threaded the wire into place.

"He's had a ton of books written about him," she said, wandering down the wall of floor-to-ceiling stacks and pulling out a book about the king, waving it at him, then shoving it back in. "But my mother hasn't. I want to use her story to fill in the lives of women of her time." She looked into space. "I want to write a memoir about Nabotavia, about how it used to be before the revolution. My uncle is helping me with it, but I'm also interviewing some of the older servants to get anecdotes from their lives, as well as some of my aunt's friends when they come to visit. I really want to get a lot of different perspectives." She turned back to see if he was still paying attention.

"How are you doing it?" he asked, snapping closed the opening he'd been working on.

"I have a little recorder I use. I just turn it on while talking to people. Then I transcribe the tapes later, go through and edit, pick out the parts I want to use. My uncle looks my work over and makes suggestions."

"Really." He was impressed, now that he was paying enough attention to understand what she was doing. His image of a pampered little princess whiling away her time eating bonbons and accepting flattery from the huddled masses was fading fast.

"Once I get it into a form I can live with, I'll have a few other Nabotavians of the old school look at it and tell me what they think. Eventually I hope to have it printed up and put into the national library."

"I think that's great." And he really meant it. She was quite ambitious in her way, and he admired that.

"Do you?" She glowed under his praise. "I hope it turns out to be something Nabotavia can be proud of. I live for my people, you know."

He winced. She'd finally hit a note that sounded sour to him.

"What are your other two goals?" he asked her,

changing the subject as he started back down the ladder.

She threw out her hands and dazzled him with a bright smile. "Number two is this—I want to learn to cook."

He stopped at the bottom to look hard at her. "Why would you want to learn that? You'll always have others to do that for you."

"That's exactly why I need to know. I don't want to be a silly princess who couldn't feed herself if anything went wrong." She slipped back onto the library table, sitting on the end, swinging her legs. "Things happen, you know. And I want to be prepared. And I don't want to be someone who gives orders and has no idea what others have to do to perform chores for her." She chuckled softly. "Besides, I don't think you've ever been at the mercy of a royal chef. It can be quite an experience. If he goes on a kick, say he reads that anchovy paste on everything brings good luck or something like that, you might just be faced with a week's worth of inedible food. I've seen it happen. Not a pretty sight. It's smart to be prepared for the worst."

He nodded, bending down to pack his gear into a toolbox. "And number three?" he asked.

"And number three, of course—I have to get married."

Straightening, he looked at her and nodded again. "Of course." His fingers curled around a pair of pliers. "How are things coming on that front?"

"Well, our next dinner is Friday night. The more

serious candidates are due to arrive. I'll be wearing one of the dresses I chose the other day and having my hair done in a special new style in the afternoon.''

"You're having your hair done again?'' It seemed to him that the hair dresser was a daily visitor lately.

She laughed at his naiveté. "I have to look my best, you know. Madam Batalli will be coming to help me before every party, and especially before the ball in August.''

"Really.'' He frowned thoughtfully, still holding the pliers. Madam Batalli was an older lady, almost elderly. One would think a princess would want to try some younger style ideas. "And all to catch yourself a royal husband.''

She went perfectly still, staring at him. "You don't approve.''

He lost it. If he'd only stopped for a moment and thought. After all, he was no one but an employee. He had no call to react the way he did. But by the time that realization had taken place in his mind, it was too late. The words were out.

"Damn right I don't approve. This is like some ritual out of the Dark Ages. This is like selling your oldest daughter to the highest bidder. I wish you'd reject it. I would think that a woman like you, with all you've got going, could tell them all to go to hell and walk out of here.''

Her head jerked back as though he'd slapped her. "Gee,'' she murmured. "Don't hold back. I wouldn't want you to feel as though your opinion had been overlooked.''

He grimaced, rubbing his neck. "Sorry," he said gruffly. "But you asked."

"Indeed I did." She gazed at him seriously. "So I take it you don't think much of royalty."

"I didn't say that," he replied. "It was useful once. I think royalty was nice while it lasted, but it's had its day and should get off the stage."

"But what if the people of a country want their royalty?" She shook her head. "It's a double-edged sword, you know. The people are locked into their traditions, and we're locked into providing something they want to have. I was born into a certain situation and I owe it to my people to fulfill my role."

He was beginning to wonder how he'd ended up in this position. It certainly wasn't a comfortable one. "Your people kicked you out," he noted dryly.

She whirled to face him. "No they didn't. That was only one small segment that took over. And now they are gone and the people seem to want us back."

"So you think you're really going back?" He'd heard something along these lines, that Nabotavia had held a plebiscite and the royalty was being begged to return. Funny how once he had the name of the little country in his mind he seemed to be hearing about it everywhere.

"Oh, yes. That's what this is all about. That's why I have to marry right away. By the end of the year, we'll all be going back. And it looks as though my oldest brother will be crowned as the new king."

Jack frowned, wondering what that would be like. "Does he want that?"

''Well, of course. It's his destiny. His destiny and his duty.'' She saw his skeptical look and went on a bit defensively. ''We were all raised with a sense of what our duty is, and I think that is a good thing. It helps to raise us above selfish concerns. Don't you find you become a better person once you commit yourself to a larger cause? Especially when it involves doing good for others.''

''I suppose so,'' he murmured doubtfully, but memories were floating into his mind, reminders of when he'd been a Navy SEAL and how he'd felt when he'd been active in the police force. She was right. He'd always been happiest when working for a bigger issue.

''You know about that,'' she said, as though she'd read his mind again. ''You're a cop.''

He glanced her way. ''Yes, I am.''

''Do you still feel a sense of duty to the police force, even though you're under suspension?''

His gaze hardened. He wished he hadn't told her about that. Still, it was hardly a national secret. ''Sure I do,'' he said speaking curtly. ''The situation I'm in was my fault, not theirs. I could have avoided it if I'd been smarter.''

''From what I've heard, you were protecting your partner.''

He groaned, looking away.

''I also heard your partner was a woman.'' She stopped right in front of him. ''Did you love her very much?''

He looked down into her eyes, wondering why she

was pushing this. "Princess, look. I know you live in a fairy-tale world, but most of us have to deal with a more mundane existence. Things don't follow the usual story lines."

She cocked her head to the side, regarding him with a piercing look. "There's nothing fairy-tale about my world. Just the names. Otherwise, it's very boring."

"So is being a cop. The cop shows on TV—they hype that up to make a good story. Real life is not like that."

"So you're saying you weren't madly in love with her?"

He almost had to smile at her dogged determination to get the straight scoop. "No, I was not madly in love with her."

He was in pretty heavy duty "like" there for a while, but he didn't have to tell her about that. Liking Lucy, feeling a lot of sympathy for her, all that had clouded his thinking at the time. And that was what ought to remind him of how important it was to keep a distance. He'd just about ruined his situation on the force by letting personal relationships get in the way of his duty. He'd be damned if he would let that happen again.

He started away, hesitated for a moment, then turned back. "I probably should warn you. I've ordered that the dogs be let loose to roam the estate during the night."

Her head came up and she stared at him. "The dogs?"

"Yes. The Great Danes that are kept in the kennel

behind the garage. I found out they were originally purchased to be guards, but no one ever followed through and actually trained them. So I've hired a trainer who says they can start right away.''

She nodded thoughtfully, her eyes cool as she gazed at him. "I see. So...is this because you want to guarantee I won't come visiting you at night?'' She cocked an eyebrow in that royal way she sometimes had. "Are these vicious beasts supposed to take the place of poor old Greg who 'couldn't do his job right'?''

He made sure that his expression didn't change. "It has nothing to do with that, Princess,'' he said.

"Really.'' She didn't believe him for a moment. "I see. Well, thank you for warning me. I'll be on my guard.''

He turned, ladder in hand, and almost ran into the duchess as she made her regal way into the library. She nodded to him curtly, then frowned as she looked at her niece.

Kari sighed. She would have liked a bit longer with Jack, but now he was out the door and there was no hope of clearing the air between them. And she was left with the duchess looking as though she'd walked in on a romantic tryst.

"Oh, Aunt, don't look so cross. We were only talking.''

The duchess looked skeptical as she dropped into a chair at the library table. "I'm not sure it was such a good idea to hire that man,'' she fretted. "I now hear that he has had problems in the past and is currently under suspicion of using his status as a police officer to cover criminal activity.''

''He's completely innocent,'' Kari blurted out, then regretted it as her aunt looked at her sharply.

''How on earth would you know that?''

''I just...Mr. Blodnick told me,'' she improvised quickly. ''And he has known him for years.''

The duchess drew her head back and narrowed her gaze. ''I think I'd better have a talk with our Mr. Blodnick.''

Kari's heart was in her throat. ''You're not going to have him fired!''

Her aunt turned and stared at her. ''Why is that so important to you? What's going on here?''

Kari knew she'd made a big mistake reacting as she had. Now she was going to have to summon all her acting powers if she was going to turn this around. Very carefully she composed herself and managed to look casual and unconcerned, if slightly offended. ''Oh, Aunt, there's nothing going on. Heavens, I've got enough on my mind right now. But I wouldn't want anyone fired just because rumors circulate about him.'' She smiled at her older relative. ''And I wouldn't want anyone fired because of me.''

''It wouldn't be because of you.''

Kari threw out her hands. ''Why not? He was hired because of me.''

''True.'' Her aunt seemed at least partially mollified. ''Anyway, I don't have time to deal with that this week. I'm going to be traveling to San Francisco overnight. I'll be back in time for our Friday night dinner, however.'' She sighed, looking at Kari. ''But you mustn't worry your head about these things. You just concentrate on readying yourself for matrimony, my dear. And the return to Nabotavia. Those are the only things you need to think about.'' She rose from her seat at the library table.

''By the way, my younger brother, Count Boris, will be arriving next week. He'll be staying with us for the rest of the summer.'' Her smile seemed to hold much pleasure at the thought of her brother arriving. ''He was quite fond of you when you were a child. I hope the two of you will still get along.''

Kari was breathing a sigh of relief and hardly paid any attention to this talk of Count Boris. ''I'm sure we'll do fine,'' she said airily, not giving it a second thought.

''Oh, yes,'' her aunt agreed, smiling as though she was quite pleased at the prospect. ''I'm sure you will.''

Chapter Seven

Princess Kari was in the kitchen the next morning when she got a surprise. Something was making a funny electronic sound, and she looked around the room for the source, then put her hand over the small bulge at her waist, realizing it was her cell phone. She'd been faithfully wearing it around for days without having any action at all.

"It's ringing!" she cried to no one in particular, since the room was empty except for her. She'd never had a real cell call before. Grabbing it, she flipped it open and said, "Hello?"

"Hi, Princess. It's Jack Santini."

"Jack!" Her heart leaped. "This is so exciting."

"What's wrong?"

His voice was filled with concern and she laughed. "No, it's just that you're my first call. Ever."

"Oh." He seemed to find that puzzling, but not interesting enough to pursue. "Are you alone?"

"Yes."

"Good. I've got some news. You know your hair appointment for this afternoon?"

Now it was her turn for puzzlement. "Yes."

"I'm afraid Madam Batalli can't make it today. I've found you someone new."

Kari frowned. "But I've had Madam Batalli since I was sixteen."

"All the more reason to try someone else. Don't worry. She's fine as far as security goes. Her name's Donna Blake. She's actually a good friend of mine."

"Who you just happened to have handy." Kari wasn't sure she liked this. "You haven't fired Madam Batalli have you?"

"No. Of course not. I can't do that. I just…sent her on a little vacation."

"What?"

"Never mind that now," he said quickly. "I just wanted to warn you. I think you'll like Donna. Here's her number." He rattled it off rapidly. "You can call her to confirm. She's waiting to hear from you."

"Jack…"

"Trust me. You'll like her. I've gotta go."

She clicked off, slightly confused but at the same time strangely happy. She'd had her first cell phone call and she liked it. Jack had actually called her.

"May it be the first of many," she declared out loud.

But the more she thought it over, the more her spirits drooped. Maybe this wasn't such a good thing after all. As she analyzed it, she began to think she might just know what Jack was doing. He figured if he contacted her by phone, he wouldn't have to risk any more face-to-face encounters. He was already calling out the dogs at night to keep her away and now he was using the phone to fend her off in the daytime. She had a sudden epiphany. Women used the phone to draw people closer. Men used phones to keep people at a distance.

So that's your angle, she thought, pursing her lips. Well, we'll just see about that Mr. Jack Santini. We may just have another card up our royal sleeve.

Pulling the cell phone off her waist, she pressed in his number, tapping her fingers against the counter while she waited for him to answer.

Jack hung up, letting out a long breath. She charmed him every time. She was so open, so innocent, so lacking in guile of any kind. It gnawed at him that he was now manipulating her as baldly as any woman had ever tried to manipulate him in the past. In some ways you might almost say he was sending in a spy. Well, not exactly a spy, but something almost as repugnant.

But that wasn't really fair. Donna was no spy. She was a darling and Kari needed a friend. As soon as he'd decided to try to provide her with one, Donna had leaped immediately to mind. He and she had both lived in the same group home the year before he'd joined the Navy. Though she'd been a few years younger, they'd struck up a friendship that had lasted ever since. They had even shared an apartment for a while, platonically, when he'd first been discharged from the Navy and she'd just finished cosmetology school. Donna had a basic decency and bright view of life that Kari might respond to. In his experience she had warmed the heart of everyone who had ever met her.

Kari had said she had no friends. Well, Donna would be a friend if Kari would let her be. He couldn't go so far as to manipulate the way the princess would feel about Donna, but he was pretty sure he knew how his old friend would feel about the princess. He couldn't imagine anyone not loving her at first sight.

Still, his conscience was nagging at him a little. The duchess wouldn't have approved, but she was out of town for the day—or Jack would never have tried to pull the switch this way. Maybe he was just being selfish, bringing in one of his own personal pals to be buddies with Kari. It was probably unethical as all get-out, but it wasn't necessarily illegal. He sighed. It was hell getting involved in a personal relationship, but here he was, stuck in one, whether he wanted to be or not.

His cell phone rang and he reached for it automatically.

"Hello?"

"Hi," Kari said. "It's me."

"No kidding." He couldn't help but smile at the sound of her voice.

"Since we're now in cell phone contact, I thought we ought to work on secret signals," she said pertly.

That opened his eyes. "What?"

"In case I get kidnapped or something. If I have my cell phone with me I could give you a call and tell you my location using code words if we have them set up ahead of time."

He had to smile at her enthusiasm, but at the same time he knew he had to squelch it. "The first thing that any competent kidnapper will do is strip you of your cell phone."

"Oh." She paused, but not for long. "Well, what if they're not competent? I'll bet the Sinigonians wouldn't have thought of doing that."

His brows drew together. "Who are the Sinigonians?"

"The people who kidnapped me before."

Shock catapulted him up off his chair. "You were kidnapped before? Why didn't anyone ever tell me?"

"Oh, it happened so long ago. It was no big deal."

No big deal. He swore softly, shaking his head, and when he spoke again, his voice was like struck steel. "Where are you?"

"I'm in the kitchen. But I'm very busy…"

"Don't move. I'll be there in less than a minute."

She sighed happily as she closed her phone and put it back at her waist. Sometimes things really did work out for the best. By the time he arrived in the doorway of the kitchen, she'd barely gotten back to work on the counter she was cleaning.

He stepped into the room and looked around suspiciously. The huge light-filled space gleamed with copper-bottomed pans and stainless steel appliances. Only the island butcher-block counter was a mess, covered with flour and the remnants of dough that Kari was cleaning. He looked at her as though he could hardly believe what he was seeing.

"Where is everybody? Do they leave you alone in here?"

"Very funny." She went back to scrubbing down the wooden counter. "Cook and I have been making the dough for dinner rolls. She's gone to take her midday nap, and I'm cleaning up."

"You're kidding."

"Why would I kid you about that? Here's the dough." She pulled out a large flat tray to show him the saffron-colored dough waiting to rise. She displayed it with all the pride of a creator. "Isn't it beautiful?"

"It's beautiful all right. I just can't believe…" But he looked at her flour-dredged hands, then her wide eyes, and cut his comment off without completing it. "So you're cleaning up."

"Yes," she said defiantly, going back to her scrubbing. "I'm cleaning up." She glanced up at him from under her tousled hair. "What do you think? That I'm making this up?"

"No. No, it's just that…well, you're a princess. You don't need to do this."

"Oh, yes I do," she said calmly. "Besides, I like doing it."

He watched her for a moment. Right now she could

have been any young woman in any kitchen in the country, doing chores that needed to be done. But no, he took that back. She was much more beautiful than any other young woman of his acquaintance, and the way she was scrubbing that counter, putting her whole body into it, she was also more hardworking. She was a puzzle. And she was also the cutest thing he'd ever seen.

He shook his head over her desire to play scullery maid, but decided to let it go. "Okay," he said crisply, crossing his arms at his chest. "Tell me about this kidnapping."

She shrugged, pushing back a stray hair with the back of her hand. "I told you it was long ago. No one has ever said anything about it to you because for the most part, I'm sure, they've all forgotten about it. It wasn't very significant, even at the time." She went back to scrubbing. "I was about thirteen, I think." She rinsed out a rag and began to wipe the counter dry. "It was the Sinigonian family. They are kind of the Keystone Kops of our homeland. They are always trying to gain advantage over the other factions, but they are just so incompetent. It never works out for them." She rinsed the rag again, hung it to dry, and turned to face him. "They only took me to their house in Santa Monica. My brothers came and rescued me before anything really happened."

Jack frowned. The entire operation sounded wacky, but he was considerably less alarmed than he had been when he'd first heard about it. He slumped onto a stool set at the counter, casually draping across it. "They didn't hurt you?" he asked her.

"Oh, no, not them." She plunked down on a bar stool next to the one he was sitting on, drying her hands on her apron. "They were very sweet to me, actually. Now the Davincas…that's a different story. You don't want to be kidnapped by them. They're a bunch of thugs. They took one princess and held her for ransom for weeks. They kept her in a vegetable cellar. It was horrible."

Jack shook his head. The Nabotavians seemed to be particularly enamored of nabbing royalty. "Were your kidnappers asking for a ransom?"

"Oh, no." She wrinkled her nose. "They only wanted me to marry their son, of course."

Jack gave her a look of outrage. "At thirteen?"

"The old-fashioned types think that's a great age. Catch her while she's young and too naive to complain, they say." She shrugged. "But they needn't have worried. My aunt has kept me young all these years." Her tone wasn't exactly bitter, but it was the closest thing to it. "I've been carefully nourished and coddled. I'm still like a thirteen-year-old girl. If you know what I mean." She held back her laughter. "Of course, I have recently been taught something about kissing, but not nearly enough to put me in the experienced category. Do you think?"

He avoided her gaze and steeled himself. He would be damned if he was going to let himself blush again. She was taunting him and he knew it. She was also tempting him, and he wasn't going to take the bait.

"But that is neither here nor there," she admitted breezily. "The most important thing—of supreme importance—is to keep the blood line pure." She gave a casual wave in the air. "After all, succession and all that."

He risked a look at her and then he couldn't look away. She was wearing tight, patterned leggings he'd seen her eyeing at the showing the other day, along with a lacy white blouse and the red rose pin that symbolized her royal house, a pin she always wore. Her clear skin seemed to glow with a magic sheen that made him want to kiss her. But then, just about everything made him want to kiss her.

"I suppose that's pretty important for keeping the royal boat stable in troubled waters," he said gruffly, trying to keep his focus.

"Absolutely." She smiled, knowing he understood. "That's what happened to my darling duke. He's my father's half brother, you know." She dropped her gaze as she went on. "He was illegitimate. His mother was a lady-in-waiting to my grandmother. And that means he can never be king, you see." She looked up again. "My brother Marco will succeed. And whoever marries me will be very highly placed in the hierarchy of things." She sighed. "Unless, of course, they try to marry me off to a royal from another country. Then who knows what will happen to me?"

He wasn't going to say what he thought of this whole rotten system. She was wedded to it and obviously thought she could live with it. He got crazy thinking about how easily she could give her life up to others to guide for her. He had moments of a wild fantasy of carrying her off himself. Luckily he wasn't insane enough to think something like that might work. She was what she was and he was what he was.

"And never the twain shall meet," he muttered to himself.

"What's that?" she asked, but he shook his head.

"So tell me," he said instead. "What happened to these people? Did you have them prosecuted? Are they in jail?"

"Oh, heavens no. They're harmless little folks. We Nabotavians mostly take care of our own."

He had to look away and swallow hard at that one. Come on, come on, he told himself impatiently. Just because their system is nuts doesn't mean you have to fix it for them. Just let it be.

But he had to find out a few things. "So you're telling me they could still be out there, plotting to snatch you again."

She put her head to the side, considering. "Oh, I doubt that. From what I've heard they've given up on me long ago. They've already married their son off to some lower level princess."

"Uh-huh. Just how many princesses do you people have?"

"Oh, tons of them. At least, there will be when everyone returns. They're all cousins who married other cousins. You know how that goes. It's a mess, believe me."

His wide mouth quirked at one corner as he

watched her. "So that's your problem," he said dryly. "Ever think you people might need to bring in some fresh blood?"

She looked up at him and smiled. "Sounds like a good idea to me," she said softly.

He grimaced and went on. "From the briefings I've had, it's been my impression that the group called December Radicals is the one to look out for."

"Yes. They're the ones who killed my parents." She sat back, all smiles extinguished. "For a while they had all the power. But they've lost it over recent years, and they've been trying to get it back." She shook her head. "But there's no hope for them now. The country is becoming a democracy ruled by a constitutional monarchy. However, I suppose it's best to remember, as you were telling me the other night, that it is when people feel cornered and helpless that they are the most dangerous."

He nodded thoughtfully. It was a disturbing thought. From what she'd told him, he gathered that the Sinigonians merely wanted a bride for their boy. The December Radicals probably had something else in mind, like blackmail, ransom and revenge. The only thing he knew for certain was that he must never give them a chance to get their hands on her. Them, or anyone else who didn't have her best interests at heart.

Suddenly, inexplicably, he felt overwhelmingly protective toward her, and it was not on a professional level. It had everything to do with her huge blue eyes and the trusting way she looked at him and very little to do with a paycheck at the end of the month. He wanted her in his arms the way a starving man wanted bread, with a deep, primitive need that threatened to choke him.

And she seemed to sense that things were veering into forbidden territory, because she slid off her stool and made it clear that it was time for him to go. He got up more slowly, his inner turmoil not as easy to turn off once it had started simmering.

She looked about the kitchen, then set her jaw and faced him squarely. "I'm not going to fall in love with you, you know," she told him. "So you can quit worrying right now."

"All right," he said, because he couldn't think of anything else to say about a statement that so thoroughly took his breath away.

"I guess I'd better go give this friend of yours a call," she was saying, "if I'm going to get my hair done in time for the dinner tonight."

"Oh. Good." He stopped and faced her, reluctant to go anywhere she wasn't going to be. "Donna's a peach. You'll like her."

Kari took a deep breath and asked, "What is she to you?"

"What do you mean?" But he saw in her eyes what she meant. "Oh, she's a friend. We've been friends since we were kids." He wanted to reassure her, then realized doing that would only make things worse. "We both ended up in the same group home after bouncing around from one foster family to another. So we have similar backgrounds that tie us together.''

''Unlike you and me,'' she said, her eyes dark.

''Unlike you and me,'' he agreed, his voice rough.

Suddenly she reached up and flattened the palm of her hand to his cheek. ''There's no one else like you,'' she said softly.

He ached to taste her lips. Reaching up, he covered her hand with his own, then took it and pressed a kiss into the center of her palm, his gaze holding hers, burning into hers. Something passed between them, some connection was made on a nonverbal level that made them both breathless. He dropped her hand and turned quickly, leaving the way he'd come, and she stood where she was, savoring the lingering sense of the kiss she'd captured in her hand.

What did it mean? She didn't know. She didn't want to know at this point. She only wanted to feel, not to think. Closing her eyes, she held her hand to her own face and smiled.

Then she remembered the telephone call she still had to make and her smile faded as she remembered this Donna person. She hated this jealous feeling she had. She'd had it about his partner and now she had it about his hairdresser friend. Mr. Blodnick was probably right—he was the sort of man who women fell for in droves. There were always going to be women around him. And it really had nothing to do with her. So why did it make her heart twist in agony?

* * *

Kari started out the hair session determined to dis-
like Donna, but in very little time she realized that
was going to be an untenable position. Donna's dark
hair was cut in a bob that left her with bangs barely
revealing bright green eyes that sparkled with interest
and the joy of life. She started right out acting as
though she'd known Kari all her life, without a hint
that she might in any way be in awe of royalty.

"Here's what we'll do," she told her new client
once they were alone in Kari's room. "While I'm
setting up my equipment, you go through your snap-
shots and other pictures for the last year or so and
pull out any you find where you think your hair
looked its best. Also, if you have any pictures from
magazines, or whatever, of hairstyles you'd be interested in trying, get those out, too. Then I'll sketch out
some ideas using your facial shape and your bone
structure as a foundation. And then we'll see what we
can come up with."

They spent the next two hours together, giggling
over pictures, trying out various outrageous styles,
then settling on something less flamboyant but very
different from the style Kari normally sported. All in
all, it was the sort of fun that Kari wasn't used to,
and she had to admit, she had a very good time. She
ended the session liking Donna a lot, despite her original reservations.

Still, she wondered about the relationship Jack and
this woman might have had in the past.

"So you've known Jack just about forever," she

said, being carefully casual, as they began packing Donna's equipment and implements away.

"Oh, yeah, we go way back," Donna replied, giving her a quick smile that revealed her understanding of how things were. She stopped and looked at Kari earnestly. "Look, hon, don't be embarrassed if you've got a crush on the guy. Not many girls who meet him can resist a bit of one, you know. He's so cute and so very, very manly." She gave her a wise and knowing look. "I know you know what I mean."

Kari couldn't help but smile. "How about you?" she asked curiously.

"Me?" Donna laughed. "He's like a brother to me. Do you have a brother?"

"Oh, yes. I have three of them."

"Then you know what it's like. In some ways we're almost too close. There's not enough mystery left between us. You know what I mean? I adore him, but not that way."

For some reason—maybe because she just wanted to so badly—Kari believed her. Just before Donna left, they had a last look in the mirror together, both nodding with approval. The "do" was sophisticated, yet young and lively, with curls cascading down one side of her head and small tendrils teasing her ear on the other side. Kari was excited. She felt like a different person.

"Oh, I hope you can come again sometime," she told Donna impulsively. "I mean, I love old Madam Batalli, but..."

"Don't you worry about the madam. She's on her way to the Caribbean."

Kari frowned. "Whatever do you mean?"

"Didn't you know? Jack got her a position on a cruise ship. Seems she's always wanted to travel and this is her chance. She won't be back until fall."

Kari stared at Donna. "Why would Jack...?"

"He didn't tell you?" Donna shrugged and smiled at her, then launched into a long explanation, talking so fast Kari could hardly keep up with her thoughts. "Well, here's the deal. Jack told me about your situation, how you have to marry some dude you hardly even know, because of your duty to your native country. And I really admire you for that. I know I couldn't do it. But he also told me that you have wealth and you are going to have power, but the one thing you don't have, because of your position, is friends. He said to me, 'Donna, every woman needs a friend.' And you know, he's right. It's genetic. It's born in us. But he said, 'You go be her friend, if she'll have you.' And I told him I'd give it a try. I'd have to see if we got along. And if I liked you." She grinned. "And I guess you could say I like you just fine." She shrugged. "So that's where we are. And if you decide you want me to come back, I'll sure do that. But it's up to you."

Kari didn't know what to think. She'd seldom met anyone quite this straightforward. "Is this sort of like hiring you to be my friend?" she asked warily.

Donna gave an explosive laugh. "No! You're hiring me to be your hairdresser. The friend thing comes free.'' Impulsively she reached out and gave Kari a hug. "Darling, I'd love to be your friend. And I'd love to be your hairdresser. But if this just doesn't work for you, I'll understand." She turned to go. "Just remember, anything you say to me will be strictly confidential. Even from Jack. It's part of the hairdresser's code." She laughed, and as Donna left, her heels clicking down the hallway, Kari smiled. That laugh was infectious.

"I may just have a friend," she whispered to herself in wonder. And that was fun. But the fact that Jack had done this for her was harder to think about. A part of her wanted to find the angle, wanted to puzzle out the reason he might have done such a thing. What did he have to gain? Was Donna here to watch her for Jack?

"Or is he just a wonderful, wonderful man?" In her heart she thought she knew.

Chapter Eight

The duchess hated Kari's new hairstyle. And she was furious to find that Madam Batalli was now working on a cruise ship. She'd come back from her overnight trip in a hurry to make it to the evening festivities, and she'd been presented with a fait accompli that she didn't agree with at all. She knew whom to blame.

"That Jack Santini man has got to go," she fumed. "I've been suspicious of him for quite some time and now he's overstepped his authority. We never should have hired him. I want him fired right away."

The atmosphere was electric with her criticism, but Kari's response stopped all that. She stood listening as her aunt went on and on, detailing how Jack was to be fired, and at last, when her aunt paused for breath, she made her statement.

"No."

The word echoed through the drawing room. The duchess stopped and stared at her. Tim Blodnick, who'd been jotting down notes on just how the firing was supposed to go, gaped at her, as well.

"I don't want him fired," she said calmly, facing them both with quiet dignity. "I think he's done a wonderful job and I want him to stay."

The duchess regained her composure quickly. "My dear young lady," she said icily. "I don't think you know what you're talking about. Older and wiser heads will make these decisions for you. We're only thinking of your own good, you know."

Kari shook her head stubbornly. "I'm sorry, Aunt, but I won't hear of it. I'm over twenty-one and can make my own decisions now. Jack Santini stays."

The duchess fussed for a few more moments, but her tone was unconvincing. She'd been shocked by what Kari had done, but it was obvious she'd known it would happen at some point and she was beginning to be resigned to it. After all, truth to tell, Kari *was* the princess, and for the first time in her life, she was pulling rank. She'd never even dreamed of doing such a thing before. But it felt very natural now that it was done.

And though she wouldn't stop and frame the thought in full, a part of her knew instinctively that Jack had become more important to her than just about anything else.

In some ways the evening was like a rerun of the week before. There was a new cast of characters, but the circumstances were similar. Even the conversation seemed like something heard before. But the dinner was up to the usual high standards. Kari made sure Jack got slipped a roll, one of the ones she had helped Cook prepare that morning, then waited for his verdict. When he gave her a surreptitious thumbs-up, she put her nose in the air with a "See? I told you so," display of hauteur. But when she peeked at him again, she caught him laughing, and that made her smile, as well.

Unfortunately, that incident provided the most interesting moment of the evening. This group of aspirants was older, more world-weary and not as prone to the sort of giddy courtship practiced by the younger set. Still, from the look in each eye she could tell they mostly thought she would make a pretty fine plum to be baked in their particular pie.

But that wasn't likely to happen. She found them all pretty boring. One was a future minister of health for the upcoming administration. Another was destined to manage the educational system for the newly reorganized country. A third was a sort of a rich playboy who had been married to a film star but was recently divorced. He drank too much wine and fell asleep during dessert and had to be carried to the couch.

The remaining gentlemen talked about politics and business—things she knew were important—things she knew she was going to have to begin paying attention to herself. But she didn't relish the idea. She was still too young for this, darn it! She needed a little more time. She needed some other sort of man. Someone like…

No, she wouldn't say it, not even to herself. But her gaze sought him out. He was standing in the shadows at the far end of the room, talking to her uncle, as he often did. But his gaze met hers immediately and he acknowledged her with a very slight, almost imperceptible wink. He looked as strong and handsome as any statue by Michelangelo, and it was quite clear his main object in life, at the moment, was to make sure she was safe. Watching him, she felt a surge of something hot and sweet that filled her soul, and her heart fluttered in her chest.

I'm in love, she thought. And the shock of it shivered through her.

No, she couldn't be. She couldn't let herself be.

Yes, I'm in love. I'm in love with a man who stirs my blood and is living his life to make mine better. A man who takes time out of his day to think about finding me a friend. How could I not love a man like that?

She'd told him only that afternoon that she wouldn't fall in love with him. But what else could she have said? If she'd told him the truth, he would have been worried about things he didn't need to worry about. Because it was clear as glass to her that she would do her duty, no matter what. Falling in love wasn't going to change anything.

The evening seemed to drag interminably. She was polite and she was cordial, but she was hardly engaged with her guests, and her aunt knew it. Still, she found to her surprise that she didn't care. She had a new sense of herself, and she was exploring that. She had little time and less interest in stepping back into her good-little-girl role. In some ways she'd entered a whole new world, and she wasn't sure how she was going to do there. But it was going to be interesting finding out.

Jack caught her look in his direction during the after-dinner session, when she stared across the room at him. It was odd the way he felt he could read her mind at times. He could tell that she thought she was in love with him. It had been coming for a long time, and he'd been dreading it. Nevertheless, he wasn't so sure the feeling wasn't mutual. He'd never felt about another women the way he felt about Kari. He'd never wanted one with this intensity, never cared about one with this much passion, never worried about one the way he worried about her. Her happiness was more important to him than his own. He didn't know whether that scared him or gave him some sense of pride—he only knew it was completely different for him and he wasn't really sure what he should be doing about it.

Kari surprised him again that night with another late visit after the suitors had gone, appearing at his door with both dogs at her side.

"Meet Marcus and Octavio," she told him blandly as he opened the door and registered shock at seeing her with the two of them, one nuzzling her hand, the other leaning his head against her hip and gazing up at her with pure doggy love. "They're great pals of mine—have been ever since they came here as puppies."

He wasn't unwilling to show his chagrin with a baleful smile. "I didn't know."

"Well, you know now." She returned his smile, her eyes shining. "But so what? I'm not the one they are supposed to be guarding this place against."

"No, but the fact that you have them licking your ankles and whining for smooches is not encouraging to me." He glared at them. "Come on, guys. Show some spirit. You're supposed to be warriors."

She laughed. "Oh, you leave them alone. They're just fine. They'll wait outside while I come in and talk to you."

His look turned playfully sardonic. "No, they won't have to—because you're not coming in."

"Oh, yes, I am." She placed a hand in the middle of his chest and gave him a shove. He didn't move much, but she got in, anyway, because his standing in her way was only for show, not for real. "Excuse me," she said, stepping around him. And he let her, turning to keep an eye on her as she entered his apartment.

"How did you get past Greg this time?" he asked, looking her over in approval. She was back in black, but she'd left her hair in the new style, and he liked it.

She gave him a direct look. "I walked right up to him and told him where I was going," she said. "And he said, 'Watch out for the dogs.' And I gave a whis-

tle and they came right away." She grinned at him.
"You know what? I think I'm going to like this be-
having like a grown-up thing. That little princess act
of mine had just about played itself out."

"I don't know," he said a little sadly. "I thought
it was pretty cute myself."

She smiled up at him and he winced, knowing he
was going to have to pull back from this interchange
if he didn't want it to start down a road he knew led
to a blind cliff.

"Grown-up or not, you don't belong here," he reminded her.

She nodded with regret. "I know. But I had to
come. I just wanted to thank you for bringing Donna
to me. I think we are going to be friends. And—"
her voice went lower and her gaze grew misty "—I
want to thank you for caring about me."

Her words conjured up an array of emotions in him,
some conflicting, all of them new and unexplored in
his life. Shoot, he might as well admit it. She scared
the hell out of him.

But he couldn't deny that she was right. He cared
about her. "How could I not?" he said softly.

They stood so close that her perfume was making
him dizzy, and yet he didn't dare touch her.

"Oh, Jack," she said with exquisite longing. "If
only…"

"Yes," he said quietly, holding the passion in
check. "If only."

The moment quivered between them and tears
filled her eyes.

Jack cursed softly, turning away. "Go to bed, Princess," he said with a voice that sounded like ground glass. "Get some sleep."

She nodded, blinking back the moisture. "See you in the morning," she said softly, and in a moment she was gone.

Jack closed his eyes, let his head fall back and slumped against the wall. It was going to be another long, long night.

Count Boris arrived a few days later, amid much hubbub. It was plain that the duchess doted on her little brother, and he seemed to enjoy being made a fuss of. Despite all that, Kari's first impression of Boris was good. He was tall and blond and handsome—the very picture of a Nabotavian noble. He met her willingly, kissed her on both cheeks, then stood back to admire her. He was friendly, attentive and made her smile. All in all, he wasn't so bad.

"What do *you* think of Count Boris?" she asked Jack later that evening when she ran into him as she was coming in from her daily swim. The afternoon was lovely and sultry and water clung to her eyelashes in sparkling beads.

He looked at her steadily for a moment, then shrugged. "I'd say he's definitely a major part of the plan," he said at last.

She blinked at him, caught off guard by his cynical tone. "What do you mean?"

"It's pretty obvious your aunt had this rigged from the start."

"You mean, for me to marry Boris? Oh, no. I don't think so." Kari frowned, thinking it over. "Why would she set up the parties with all these other men?"

"Window dressing."

She shook her head. "You're just being suspicious, as usual," she noted. "It seems to be a well-ingrained character flaw."

He shrugged again. "Maybe so. How old is this guy, anyway?"

"Oh, thirty-five or so. Not all that old." Her impish grin surfaced. "Why? Did you think they were going to hand me off to some old decrepit graybeard?"

His eyes narrowed. "The thought had crossed my mind."

She laughed, holding her robe together with one hand. "I would run away first," she said impulsively.

"Oh, yeah?" he responded, wishing she would loosen her grip on the robe. He would have loved to see her in that suit again. "Where would you run to?"

She sighed. "That's just it. I don't know anything about the world. You would have to help me."

The trouble was, such ideas were beginning to sound appealing to him. He'd seen the count and he'd seen the duchess looking at Kari and every instinct he possessed told him this was a setup. The guy seemed okay, but Jack didn't like the way he was being foisted on her. Hell, if push came to shove, he wouldn't mind giving her a hand at evading these people for a while.

Then he had to laugh at himself. Talk about euphemisms. He knew it was time to stop thinking along these lines, when he started referring to kidnapping as an evasive action. Kari's future was her own to shepherd. It was none of his business what she decided to do. But he knew that all the cards were in the hands of the people who wanted her to marry Boris. She'd been indoctrinated in this path from the time she was born. Who was *he* to get in the way of the grand scheme? Besides, doing anything crazy would guarantee his main objective—to get his job on the force back—would fail. And then where would he be?

Still, Kari's happiness was a factor. He couldn't deny that. He just couldn't figure out how to deal with it. But the thought of Boris walking off with her rankled deep inside him. On a certain level he would feel that way even if she suddenly decided she was madly in love with the count. He wouldn't like it.

Where had this dog-in-the-manger attitude come from? It wasn't like him. He wasn't usually the jealous type. If he were honest, he would admit that he hadn't often cared about anyone enough to give much of a damn about whether or not they stayed true to him. Why should this be any different? She wasn't his, she could never be his, and yet, something in his gut told him that she *was* his. And that just wasn't right. Somehow his job was getting confused with his personal emotions, and no good could come of it.

It was probably time he got out of here—quit this job and moved on. He wished the hearing would come sooner so he could get his life sorted out. In the meantime, he had to drill it into his own head that Kari was going to marry someone at the end of the summer, and it wouldn't be him.

The next few weeks were a constant round of dinners, afternoon teas and chamber music evenings for Kari—any excuse to gather a group of Nabotavian men together and run them past the princess, for her consideration. It was fun at first, but as time went by and they kept coming, it became tiring, and the men tended to blur together in her memory. Only Count Boris stood out, and he was nice, but he didn't excite her the way a certain other male icon did.

She was learning a lot about cooking, which was good. And she was making headway on her biography of her mother, devoting at least two hours a day to research, filling out little cards that she kept in a metal box, inputting details into a data base on her computer. It was a big job that would take her years. But all in all, she felt her summer was a productive one on many levels.

Still, her only real joy was getting away now and then for afternoon drives with Jack. She'd found the perfect ploy to arrange this, as she had to go to research libraries in outlying cities in order to find material for the biography. She would have Cook fix her a large box lunch the night before, and then she would take off early, before the duchess was up to stop her with invented errands to run or visitors to entertain. And she managed to convince Jack that he was the one who ought to go with her. And once he'd gone a time or two, she didn't have to argue any longer. He seemed to look forward to their trips as much as she did.

They seldom talked much as Mr. Barbera drove them along the freeways, then into the countryside, heading for libraries that always seemed to be in distant towns. Kari would then often have the chauffeur drop them at their destination. She would tell him to go see a movie or find a shady place to park and return to pick her up in three hours. That gave her time for an hour's worth of research—and two hours to stroll around the grounds or the town or the local park, with Jack.

And to talk. In the beginning they talked about what they were seeing and movies and books they'd read. But it wasn't long before they were beyond that. Kari had never had anyone to talk to about her hopes and fears and feelings. Mostly she talked and Jack listened. But he seemed to hear her. He even had a response now and then. And that was so new.

One golden sunny day they drove all the way to Santa Inez and spent an hour wandering the mission grounds. This time they left Mr. Barbera to doze in the courtyard by a Spanish fountain while the two of them took their lunch out under the huge old oak trees. They spent another hour talking softly, laughing a lot, and pretending there was nothing outside of the little world they made for each other.

Jack enjoyed these trips, but they were often more agony than ecstasy for him. Their relationship seemed stuck in a place it normally would not be. The way they responded to each other begged for another step to be taken. As it was, he was working very hard at not kissing her. He held her soft, slender hand now and then, and he often played with her fingers while they talked. That was dangerous enough, but to kiss...to have his mouth on hers, tasting her, taking in her essence, exploring her warmth...no, he couldn't do that without being tempted to go so much further.

So they talked about everything under the sun—life and art and music and why women talked all the time and why men didn't and whether liking rainy days made one a gloomy person at heart. He was surprised that he felt closer to her with just talking than he'd ever felt with women he'd had more physical relationships with. But then, in his experience, sex was often mere recreation. Getting to know Kari was something infinitely deeper.

Not that he wouldn't have liked a little lovemaking mixed in. Not that his body didn't remind him of that fact all the time. Still, something wise and cunning in his soul told him that making love with Kari right now would mess up his life—and hers—worse than anything else ever had. And that was the advice he was listening to.

Today he was lying back on the grass and she was sitting cross-legged beside him, her fingers playing idly in his hair. He'd just told her about the time he'd come home from junior high and found the foster family he was living with had moved away without telling him they were going. He'd lived on the street for weeks after that, until Children's Services finally found him again and put him in a new home. Funny, but he hadn't thought about that for years, and had certainly never told anyone before. Her interest seemed to dredge up memories without him even trying.

But eventually, as it always did, conversation came back to the marriage decision.

"So have you and your aunt decided yet?" he asked, looking up so that he could judge her reaction. "Is it going to be Boris?"

She sat back and sighed, looking cross. "I don't know. I know everyone wants us to pick Boris. But I don't think I could ever love him."

"No?"

"No."

A quiet feeling of satisfaction flowed in his veins, but it didn't last long. Left unspoken between them was who she could love, but they both knew who it was. Her eyes said it all. He looked away as satisfaction gave way to a wave of melancholy. This magic summer was almost over. In just a few weeks he'd developed feelings for this woman he'd never had for any other, and probably never would have. She was so special to him—special in his mind, special in his heart. And yet, very soon it would be over.

The hearing was tentatively scheduled for the day before the ball. On that day his future would be sealed, and by the next, so would hers be. Over those two days he would find out whether or not he was still on the force, she would find out whom she would

marry. Some man—some man other than he himself—would claim her for his own, would take her
into his bed, into his life. And Jack would be left
behind.

The melancholy turned into a surge of nausea, and
he had to get up and walk away for a moment, settling
his system down. He could hardly stand the thought
of losing her like that. And yet he didn't really have
her. You couldn't lose what was never yours in the
first place, could you? She wasn't his. She could
never be his. She belonged to Nabotavia. They had
both known that from the start.

She would probably be marrying good old Boris
and sailing for her homeland and a glorious home-
coming. Meanwhile, if he was lucky and was reinstated in his old job, he would be back in his lonely
apartment on Wilshire. There would be poker with
his friends on Friday nights and a date with some
interchangeable beauty on Saturday, but most of his
time would be spent with his nose to the grindstone,
just as it had before he'd met Kari.

And that was the good outcome. What if he didn't
get reinstated? There had been a time when he'd
thought his life might be over if that happened. There
might be nothing worth living for. But now he knew
that was nonsense. He'd found something infinitely
more important than making it back on the force. In
just a few weeks of knowing Kari, his life and his
outlook had changed immeasurably.

How could that be? It didn't seem possible. Knowing Kari had opened up a window onto a world he'd

never even known existed. Was that window just going to close again? Or would he go on and do something different, be something different, because of having known her? He didn't know. But he didn't want to think about going on without her.

Returning to where she sat, he dropped down to sit beside her. The sun was sparkling in her eyes, making them look as though they were shooting sparks all around her pretty face. He loved the look of her, the clean scent, the way she moved her hands when she talked. There were times when she looked so good to him, pain shot through his body. That wasn't normal, was it? He'd never felt that way with a woman before. But then, he'd never known a woman like Kari before.

"So you're not ready to commit to Boris just yet?" he asked, unable to stay away from the topic that hurt the most.

She shook her head. "He doesn't love me, you know."

"How do you know that?"

"I can tell. The way he looks at me." She gave him a lopsided smile, looking at him sideways. "Like I'm a car he's thinking about buying. And the only reason he's thinking about buying it is because he might look good riding around behind the wheel."

He laughed, but that only seemed to encourage her, and she went on with her analogy.

"Oh, he's thinking about making the purchase, but he's got to look over the numbers first, got to see if it will really be a good deal." She giggled, enjoying her own joke. "He'll probably consider haggling over the price. Ask for more accessories. Kick the tires."

"Hey." Reaching out, he curled an arm around her shoulders. "No kicking of the tires. Not on my girl."

My girl. He heard himself say it and noticed her tiny shiver of pleasure. She smiled up at him, but then he sobered, realizing that the underlying problem was no joking matter.

Summer was fast wrapping up, and with the end would come so many changes. Jack broke one of his own rules and kept her there in the shelter of his arms until it was time to get up and find Mr. Barbera and head for home again. He just couldn't let her go, she felt so warm and soft. There was comfort in that. Comfort, and a whole new level of sensual gratification.

A little more than a week before the ball, two of Kari's brothers arrived. The excitement over their arrival made the interest in Count Boris's visit pale by comparison. Maids scrubbed everything shiny, Cook baked special treats, Mr. Barbera waxed and polished all the cars, and Kari paced the halls, waiting for the signal that they were coming up the driveway.

And then they were in the foyer, two strong, handsome men, impeccably dressed, bearing all the dignity and swagger that royalty deserved to display, yet with the hint of a sense of humor showing and a warmth that belied their troubled background. Marco was the more wiry of the two, handsome in a rugged way, his face rather gaunt, as though he'd had troubles to bear—which he certainly had. Garth was gorgeous in a devil-may-care, confident way that drew women to him like moths to a flame. Kari ran into their arms, both at the same time. Oh, how she loved her brothers!

They were both older than she and had been raised in a different part of the country, but there was a bond between them that overcame all that, and whenever they were together, their shared sense of family shone through. And that happened again now. They spent an hour chatting formally with the duke and duchess in the parlor. The duchess then took the brothers on a tour of the estate, pointing out any changes since their last visit, while Kari went down to the kitchen to check on the progress toward the dinner and to relay requests for some favorite foods. A little later the three siblings burst out of the house like children on school break and huddled in the garden where they could talk and laugh and tease each other without being admonished by their aunt.

Finally Garth went off to check on the dogs, and Marco looked at Kari, getting serious. "What's this I hear about this fellow, Jack Santini?"

Some of the joy ran out of her day. She stopped to sniff a red rose. "I don't know. It would probably depend on who you heard it from."

"The duchess was my source," he said, crossing his arms over his chest and looking at her from the heights of his imperial prestige. "She made it quite clear that she thinks he's a bad influence on you."

"A bad influence!" Kari laughed, but she was only

covering up for the tremor in her fingers. Marco was
her oldest brother, a sort of father figure and symbol
of authority to her. She couldn't help but care what
he thought of her. "Oh, you know our aunt," she said
dismissively. "She tends toward extreme judgments
at times. She takes things too seriously."

"Indeed she does. But she's not crazy. And if she
thinks there's a problem, I'm going to have to look
into it."

"Oh, Marco." She turned and looked at him in
some distress.

His dark eyes took on a worried look. "What is it?
Do you have some sort of relationship with this
man?"

Her chin lifted. "Yes, I do. It's called a friendship." She sighed and patted his arm. "Don't worry,
dearest brother. I know my duty."

Crown Prince Marco was the one who had done
the most to instill in her a sense of what she owed
her culture, from the time she was a little girl. And
he led by example. His beloved wife had died two
years before, leaving him with two darling children,
and he had agreed to marry a princess of a competing
faction of Nabotavian power in order to facilitate the
return. Kari knew it was hard for him to even think
of marrying again, but he would do what was best for
them all. She'd always admired him so very much.
She would never do anything to disappoint him.

"I'm calling a meeting on the afternoon before the
ball," he said. "We'll get together and we'll discuss
the major candidates for your hand. It's time we made

a choice." He touched her cheek. "And you are prepared to abide by our decision?"

"Of course." She held her head high, but she couldn't meet his gaze and her cheeks colored. "This is what I was born and raised for. I will do what is expected of me. I'm ready to play my part in reestablishing our country. It's my destiny."

"Good. I'm so glad you've left that teenage rebellion stage behind."

Her eyes flashed. "Marco, I haven't been a teenager for a very long time. I'm a woman."

"Yes, I can see that. And a very beautiful one at that." He took her hands in his and smiled at her. "Princess Karina, our parents would be very proud of you."

"I'm glad to hear you say that." Her eyes suddenly shimmered with tears. "I miss them so much."

He pulled her into his arms, pressing her face to his chest and murmuring comfort to his little sister. "Kari, Kari, what a life you've had to lead. I'm sorry I haven't been here to help you through much of it. But it will all be worthwhile once we ride back into Nabotavia in triumph."

"If you say so," she said against his chest. "You know I trust you implicitly."

And she did.

Her brother Garth was a completely different matter. Garth had little of Marco's quiet reserve. Daring and impulsive, he had gained a reputation for his roving eye and cavalier wit. He was ready to return to Nabotavia as well, but Kari thought she detected a somewhat more reluctant state of mind. He didn't say anything specifically to her but she caught his look of irony at times, especially when Marco was waxing poetic about how wonderful it was going to be to go back.

And Garth quickly perceived, before they had been on the estate for twenty-four hours, how things stood between her and Jack. Despite that, Garth and Jack got along famously right from the start. While Marco treated Jack with suspicion and wariness, Garth took him on as a buddy he could hang out with, so much so that Kari had to admonish him to let Jack alone so that he could get some work done.

Garth was complimentary about the job Jack was doing.

"I must say I'm impressed with the security measures you've taken. The old estate is tight as a drum. It's like a different place." He'd gazed at Jack speculatively. "We could use this sort of creative thinking in Nabotavia. We'll be starting from scratch with the security forces. I've been researching the most modern techniques. If you have the time, I'd like to go over some of my ideas with you. See what you think."

Kari watched this exchange, proud of them both—her brother for the way he was open to new ideas and searching for answers wherever he might find them—and Jack for being so good at what he did that he inspired interest from her family members.

At a later encounter she heard Garth saying Jack ought to consider coming to Nabotavia to work. She was short of breath for a moment, then her excitement dimmed, realizing that might not be such a good idea after all. Later she asked Jack about it.

"Have you given any thought to what Garth said the other day? About coming with us to Nabotavia and taking charge of the security at the castle?"

He turned slowly to meet her gaze. His eyes were dark but every emotion was revealed in their murky depths. "No," he said shortly.

He didn't have to elaborate. She knew exactly what he meant. Being there, in sight but not being able to touch or to talk, would be a nightmare. She agreed with him. The answer had to be no.

Having her brothers around made the return to Nabotavia seem so much more real to her. All her life she'd heard about the beautiful little country with its snow-capped mountains and thick green meadows laced with clear running streams. Her uncle had once told her that the capital, Kalavia, had been as quaint and charming as a storybook town before the revolt. Would it still be as wonderful a place as she had always heard?

She hoped so. But never mind. If it wasn't, she and her brothers would soon make it so again. It was what they had been born to do.

Chapter Nine

The day of the ball was getting closer and closer. It was only a few days away when Kari began to wonder if she were losing her mind. She woke up one morning with a brand-new thought, and once she'd had it, she couldn't understand why she'd never thought of it before.

"Why do I have to get married, anyway?"

It was true. This was a new age. Women didn't do the things they'd done a hundred years ago. Just because she was going back to a country that was behind the times didn't mean she had to be back there with them. Did it? Had the rest of her family even considered this? What if she brought it up and made them see...

But no. She knew that wouldn't fly. Still, it gave her something to think about.

By that evening she'd admitted to herself that it

wasn't that she didn't want to marry at all—that was just a smoke screen—it was that the only man she ever wanted to marry was Jack. It was a relief to admit it. She wanted to marry Jack and hold him in her arms and have his children and live with him forever.

But it seemed so impossible. His life was so different from hers. Did she think she could just move into a little house with a picket fence and walk her children to kindergarten and all those normal things that people did? No, of course not. She could never live such a sweet and simple life. She would always need protection, because there would always be people trying to grab her for political influence, even if she claimed to have no part of Nabotavia any longer. She would always need more security than that sort of life could afford.

On the other hand, could she take him with her to Nabotavia? No. That wouldn't work, either. The princess marries the security guard—the system just wouldn't allow for it. The gap between their stations would be insurmountable in Nabotavia and there was no use pretending otherwise.

So she was back to her original premise of the day—not to marry at all. What would her family say if she presented them with that option? She rolled her eyes. She could hear the screaming and see the renting of garments now. No, it wouldn't go over. Still, she had to think of something. She only had another day or two to find a solution. Time was flying.

* * *

Kari was just getting out of the pool the next afternoon when Jack came right out onto the pool deck, something he'd never done before. She was surprised and, for just a moment, a little shy, because she was still in her suit and hadn't reached her wrap yet. But as his gaze devoured every inch of flesh she was showing, her own pride grew. The look in his eyes told her he liked what he saw. He waited while she pulled her robe around her, then held out a piece of mail he had received.

"I just got confirmation. The hearing is tomorrow. I'll be gone most of the day."

"Tomorrow," she said, pulling her robe tightly around her and tying it with a sash. "But that's the day before the ball."

He nodded, enjoying the way she looked with her hair wet and slicked back, her skin browning lightly in the sunshine. "I can't help the timing."

She nodded. She knew that. "So you'll know by tomorrow evening if you've been cleared or not?"

"Yes."

Shading her eyes against the sun, she stared at him for a long moment, then smiled. "Well, that will be a relief." With a hand on his arm, she led him into the arbor where they had met that first night. She didn't think they could be seen from the house once under the vines and she needed to look at him and maybe even talk to him more intimately than the glaring stage of the pool deck allowed for. "Jack, tell me what you think your chances are," she said as they both sank down to sit on the bench.

He gazed at her levelly, his gray eyes honest. "I've got to think they're good. I'm innocent." Reaching out, he took her hand in his. "And you know what's going to happen. If I'm exonerated, I'll be going back on the force right after the ball is over."

Her heart froze in her chest. "Oh, Jack."

"You won't need me anymore after the ball, anyway," he said, his hand tightening on hers. "You'll be all set with your new fiancé to take care of you."

"Jack." She let him see her pain and he responded with remorse.

"I'm sorry," he said, dropping her hand and looking away. "That was uncalled for."

She scooted closer to him on the bench and slipped her hand into the crook of his arm. "You've never told me what your suspension is all about," she said quietly.

He nodded, covering her hand with his own. "I know. And you deserve to be filled in." He hesitated, wincing a bit. "It's just that I'm not exactly proud of my behavior. I didn't do anything illegal, but I was stupid."

She waited, not saying anything. He looked down at her, took a deep breath and went on.

"It was a simple matter of being too cowardly to confront my partner about illegal activities she was obviously engaged in. I think my natural affection for her—and we were very good friends—blinded me to what she was doing. I was in a sort of denial. I just couldn't believe... Anyway, by the time I finally fully realized it, I had held off doing anything about it for too long.''

''What was she doing?''

''Stealing drugs. We'd make drug busts and all the confiscated material wouldn't end up in the evidence room where it belonged.''

''She was selling it?''

''It was a little more complicated than that. She had a brother who was addicted. I think she was giving it to him to sell to support his habit.'' He stretched his legs out in front of him. ''Anyway, by the time I'd decided I was going to have to turn her in, she'd already been spotted by internal affairs and they assumed I might be in on the thefts. There was no evidence against me, only the circumstantial elements.'' He shrugged. ''They did what they had to do, but I'm hoping the truth will set me free in the end.''

''Oh, I hope so, too!''

He smiled down at her, slightly awed by her blind faith in him. Why wasn't she suspicious? He could have made the whole thing—and especially his innocence—up. But she believed in him. ''For a princess you've got a very cute nose. Did you know that?''

''Thank you.'' Her eyes shone with laughter. ''For a cop you've got a very appealing mouth.''

He groaned, half laughing. ''So we're back on the kissing thing, are we?''

She nodded. ''I feel sadly lacking in the proper instruction,'' she noted wistfully. ''All I've had is one lesson. Hardly enough to become as adept as I'd like to be.''

His large hand cupped her cheek as he smiled down at her. ''Tell me this. Have you needed to put your lesson to use at all? Have any of the many applicants for your hand...?''

She laughed aloud. ''I've had a few clumsy attempts made,'' she told him. ''Remember the big industrialist with the walrus mustache? He kept whispering erotic suggestions in my ear during dinner and then he tried to kiss me as we walked out into the rose garden that night.''

Jack held back the impulse to find the man and tear out his heart on the spot. Very carefully he kept his anger under wraps and maintained a calm exterior.

''But all I felt was this bushy hair all over my face and I made a rude noise as I pushed him away. That seemed to offend him.'' She shrugged. ''Other than that, there was just the younger brother of the new minister of health and services. He caught me unawares and locked lips with me, but it felt so silly, I was laughing the whole time, and his feelings were hurt, too.'' She sighed. ''I seem to be a failure at kissing. Maybe I need more lessons.''

He grinned, pulling her close. ''Maybe you do.''

She lifted her face to his, and this time he didn't avoid the inevitable. He nibbled on her full lips for a moment, then used the tip of his tongue to go between them. She sighed softly, then gasped as he took possession of her mouth, opening to him and responding like a woman who badly needed to be loved.

"What the hell are we doing?" he muttered roughly as he pulled away, breathing hard after only a few seconds of the best kissing he'd ever had. "We're out in the open in broad daylight! Any gardener might have seen us, any delivery boy…"

She sighed, dropping her head against his shoulder. "That was even better than I thought it would be," she told him candidly. "The next time you kiss me—"

"There will be no next time." He frowned just to make sure she understood he meant it.

But she smiled. "Oh, yes there will. Next time, *I* get to say when we stop. Okay?" Dropping a quick kiss on his neck, she rose to her feet and turned toward the house. "Bye, Jack," she said, giving him a quick wave. And she headed for her room with a song in her heart.

Her cell phone rang late in the afternoon of the next day. She answered it quickly.

"I'm clear," Jack told her. "I'm back on the force as of Monday morning."

"Oh, Jack, that's wonderful." Despite the fact that this meant he would be leaving, she was filled with joy for him.

"I'll see you when I get back," he said. "I'm going out to celebrate with a few friends I haven't seen for a while."

"Of course. I'll talk to you when you return."

She rang off, filled with conflicting emotions. Luckily there was a lot to do in preparation for the ball, so she was too busy to think about it too much. But by the time night fell, she was on the lookout for him.

She watched for him by the hour, but he didn't appear. If she walked to the end of the upper hallway, she could see his apartment from the window. She checked every hour, then every half hour, and finally every ten minutes or so, but it was after midnight before she finally saw a light come on in his rooms. She slipped out of the house and made her way quickly to his door.

"Jack?"

He opened the door and she flew into his arms.

"I'm so happy for you," she said, holding him close. "You're getting back everything you've wanted so badly."

His arms wrapped around her and his face was in her hair. "Not quite."

He said it softly, but she heard and she closed her eyes, loving him. She could stay there with him forever, holding on to his hard, warm body. If she just kept her eyes closed, maybe the rest of the world would fade away and...

She turned her face up and his mouth was on hers before she had time to will it to happen. And then she found out what a kiss could really be—all hot and wet and sliding, all hunger and need and excitement, a fuse that lit off a fire in her body, a sense of animal delight that she hadn't known about.

She wrapped her arms around his neck, arching toward him. Suddenly she needed him to touch her breasts and she made that very plain. His hand slid inside her jersey top, slipping ever closer and she held her breath. When his fingers found their way inside her bra and curled around one swollen nipple, she gasped and an electric urgency crackled through her system, awakening parts she'd never known could feel like that. She moved her hips, yearning for him, wanting to feel her legs around him. Shuddering, she knew what her body needed with a knowledge as old as time itself.

"Maybe we should make love," she whispered breathlessly, rubbing her cheek against his, reveling in the roughness of his evening stubble.

He jerked back and stared at her. "What?" he demanded, as though he was sure he hadn't heard her right.

She searched his eyes, almost writhing with the way she wanted him. "Don't you want to?"

His head fell back and he groaned, still holding her by the shoulders as though he was afraid to let her go, afraid what she might do next.

"Of course I want to," he said gruffly. "But we can't."

She took air deep into her lungs, savoring her desire, not wanting to let it go. "I've never felt like this before. I don't know much about this sort of thing, but something deep inside tells me I want to feel you sort of...I don't know...take possession of me."

He shook his head, half laughing, half despairing. "Don't talk like that, Kari. You don't know what you're saying."

"Don't I?" she said wisely, smiling at him.

He hesitated, searching for a way to make her realize she was asking him for something he would be a jerk to give her. "And don't forget," he reminded her dryly. "You've got to be pure for your noble husband."

She shook her head, her hair swishing around her pretty face. "I don't care about that. Of course I probably have to marry someone. But I don't think he will really care much, either." This was no time to give him a lesson in royal affairs, but in fact she knew a lot of things she wasn't supposed to know. And she had no illusions. Anyone who married her from the marriage mart her aunt had set up would not be marrying her for love. "I'll give him everything that will be important for him to have, but I won't be able to give him my heart. That's already taken."

Jack looked down into her beautiful smile and didn't know what to say to her. How could she be so open, so full of love for him? Didn't she know how little he deserved it? Lacing fingers with hers, he led her to the couch and sat down with her, curling her into the protection of his arm and leaning down to kiss her beautiful little ear.

"My future life is back on track," he said. "I know what I'm going to be doing. Now how about yours?"

She sighed. "You're wondering who I will end up with."

"Exactly."

"I don't know." She glanced up at him and shook

her head. "The duchess has her favorite, but I'm not sure…"

"Boris," he said evenly, trying to maintain his natural logic and plain thinking. "They all want Boris. I suppose you'll do what's expected of you."

"Will I?" She shrugged. "What do you think I should do?"

"It's your life and your decision."

She nodded, considering, head to the side. "What if I chucked it all and ran away with you?"

His fingers tightened on hers. "You're not going to do that. You are a princess. You're going to do your duty. And I'm a cop, and I'm going back on the force. You're going back to Nabotavia. We've each got larger interests to serve. You told me yourself that is the best way."

She frowned, almost pouting. "I lied."

"No, you didn't. You told the exact truth. Much as it hurts now, there will come a time when we'll be glad we did the right thing."

She wasn't sure she believed that anymore. She'd believed it once. And it would be one thing if there was someone who would be hurt by their being together. But she didn't see that. People would be inconvenienced, maybe. Angered, surely. But no one would be really hurt if she didn't show up in Nabotavia with a consort by her side.

She knew she was being selfish. After all, look at what her brothers had been through. She'd had life so easy compared to them. Marco had the tragedy of losing his young wife, which would hang over him—

and his two little children—for the rest of his life. And there was Garth who gave every sign that there was some sort of inner demon that drove him, something related to the flight from Nabotavia. And then there was Damian, who always held himself a bit apart from the others. He had some secret pain he wouldn't reveal to anyone. By contrast, she'd had a sunny life, punctuated occasionally by fights with her aunt, but nothing serious. Now all that was expected of her was to marry and go to Nabotavia to live a life of luxury as a princess. Wasn't this what every little girl dreamed of?

Yes, every little girl dreamed of it—but not every woman.

"If there was a way, would you want me?" She asked in all humility, her eyes huge.

He looked into those eyes and cringed. He knew he could string her along if he wanted to. He could keep her hanging on for weeks, months, even years. They could have clandestine meetings, sneak phone calls. And maybe even a real tryst or two. But it wouldn't be fair to her. It might actually ruin her life to let her get caught up in something like that. It would be far kinder to break with her now. And bottom line, he would do what was best for her. Because she was all that mattered.

"There's no doubt I want you," he said softly. "I can't hide it. Every part of me aches for you." He took a deep breath. Now here came the hard part. "But it's not really a big deal. I've felt that way before," he lied, "and I'll feel that way again. There are other women." He was really lying now, and she might be able to hear it in his voice, but he had to go on with it. "It's just the old man-woman thing," he said gruffly. "I'll get over it. And so will you."

She'd turned her face to him, and her eyes were filled with shocked pain, but she didn't flinch from the hard things he was saying. "It's not like that with me," she said calmly. "I know I'm in love with you. I'll never love anyone else the way I love you."

"That's just not true," he told her seriously, almost angrily. "Don't say it."

"It's true for me right now and that is all I know." Reaching out, she took his hands in hers. "Okay, here goes. I'm making a formal proposal. Jack Santini, will you marry me?"

Hadn't she heard a word he'd said? Yes, she'd probably heard all too well. He didn't seem to be as adept at lying as he thought he was. She'd heard, but she hadn't believed him. Still, he had to make her see...

"You know that's impossible."

She squeezed his hands very tightly and searched the depths of his eyes. "I want you to tell me some way it would be possible." She shook her head slowly. "You're the magic man. You have all the answers. You tell me. What can I do? Is there something? Is there someplace we could go...?"

He turned his gaze away. He couldn't stand to see her so sincerely handing him her heart. Not when he just had to hand it right back.

"No matter what you decide, I think you have to

go back to Nabotavia,'' he told her quite seriously.
''You've been living for that your whole life. Your
whole family has. You can't just blow it off now at
the last moment. You have to go back.''

She closed her eyes and nodded. She knew he was
right. ''You could come, too,'' she tried.

But he was already shaking his head. ''You know
that's impossible.''

''Why?''

''Kari, we've gone over this before. I can't be your
groupie. I've got to have self-respect. I've got that on
the force. I wouldn't have it in Nabotavia.''

''So you're turning me down?''

He gathered all his nerve and looked her in the eye.
''Yes, Kari. I'm turning you down.''

She didn't say anything. Her face gave no hint of
her emotional state. He could only guess. ''When will
you be leaving?'' he asked her.

''Not until the end of the year.'' She bit her lower
lip, then asked, ''Will you come visit me before I
go?''

His gaze met hers and he slowly shook his head.
''Once you've made your choice, I don't think we'd
better see each other again.''

She nodded, rising suddenly, before he had a
chance to realize her intention. ''You're so sensible,
Jack,'' she said as she started for the door. ''Much
more sensible than I am.''

He rose and followed her. ''Kari, are you all
right?'' he asked, touching her cheek.

She gave him a wobbly smile as she started out the

door. "Oh, yes, I'm fine. But I do have to go." She smiled at him, her eyes already swimming in tears, despite her false bravado. "Goodbye, Jack," she said before she disappeared into the night.

The meeting was held in the library the next afternoon. All her family was there. Marco took charge, and he made the first speech, promoting Count Boris as the only logical choice.

"He's of a proper age," Marco noted. "He couldn't be from a better family. And he already has incentive to join with us. We won't have to worry about him trying to promote another faction. He's told me he has great affection for Kari and would be willing to do it."

Willing to do it! Kari bit her lip to keep from saying the words that came to mind.

"Of course I agree with you," the duchess said, beaming. "I think they will make a lovely couple."

"Whatever will make Kari happy," the duke said, though he looked rather resigned and not particularly enthusiastic.

"Why don't we see what Kari has to say about it?" Garth asked as his turn came.

"Thank you, Garth," she said slowly, looking from one face to another. "I just want to say that Boris is a very nice man and I like him very much." She nodded toward the duchess. "And I appreciate all of you being so concerned about my welfare. Really, I do. I love you all." She took a deep breath and forced herself to continue. "But I won't be marrying Boris," she said. "That won't be possible. You see, I'm in love with Jack Santini. And there is no way to change that."

All the faces staring at her exhibited shock of one form or another, but the duchess was the first to give it voice.

"I knew it! That gold digger. He's after her money, you can bet on it. I'll have him fired immediately. I'll…"

Marco put a hand on her arm, quieting her. "Tell me, Kari," he said in a voice too quiet, "what happened to your pledge to do your duty?"

His words were a dagger at her heart, but she didn't flinch. "I believe in duty, Marco. Duty should come before anything else, even personal happiness. I really believe that. But…I can't. I just can't take that next step." She took a deep breath and had to fight back tears. "I know I made you so many promises, Marco. And I was so sure I would keep them. But when the time came, things had changed. I'm so sorry."

The disappointment in his eyes cut like a knife, and she had to struggle to keep her breathing normal. The last thing in the world she wanted to do was make Marco feel that she wasn't keeping her end of their lifelong bargain. But she didn't have a lot of choice. She loved Jack. She couldn't pretend otherwise.

"You little fool, you'll never marry him!" the duchess cried.

Kari tried to smile. "You're right," she said tightly. "I've asked him. He's turned me down."

This time the shocked silence only lasted a few seconds, and then everybody was talking at once.

Kari rose and looked at them all. "So the bottom line is, I won't be getting married. I realize it would be impossible to cancel the ball at this point, so I suggest we don't tell anyone about this just yet. We can send regrets later in the week, if you like. Otherwise, let's just enjoy the party."

Turning, she left the room, head held high, and as she went, she realized this was the first time she'd left such a family meeting without waiting to be excused by Marco or the duchess first. That thought gave her at least one small glow of consolation.

Despite everything Kari was feeling, the ball was wonderful, setting the night on fire with shimmering lights and beautiful music and a sense of excitement in the air. Donna had performed miracles on her hair, setting it off with a diamond tiara and giving her gleaming cascades of curls that seemed to go on forever. Her dress was a spectacular blue silk, threaded with spun silver, with a plunging neckline and a cinched-in waist that showed off her figure nicely. She shimmered like an angel every time she moved.

And she moved a lot. She danced with so many men she was lost in a blur. All attention was on her, and that was exhilarating, even though she felt a twinge of guilt that it was built on the faulty premise that she would choose one of these attentive men as her mate. Still, she couldn't help but revel in being the belle of the ball. But one thing stayed with her the whole time—she was bound and determined she would get one dance with the man she loved.

Outside the building Jack was coordinating security. The ball was being held at a local country club, so he had the assistance of an extra set of agents but the headache of trying to mesh his forces with theirs. The building was beautiful, with high windows that flooded the greenery with light and verandahs as long and wide as the deck of a ship. From outside, he could easily see in, and he couldn't avoid seeing Kari. She was having a wonderful time. He kept telling himself that should make him happy. But it really didn't. Every time he saw her in the arms of another man, it seemed like another slashing wound in his heart.

Luckily, he didn't have to watch too often. His attention was distracted by his duties, and as often as not, by the duke, who came shuffling out every now and then for a chat.

The odd thing was, he really liked the old gentleman. Over the weeks they'd become quite friendly, and he'd heard all about the problems with the Nabotavian translation of Shakespeare the duke was working on, and how much he hated wearing the cravat the duchess insisted upon and how beautiful he thought his niece was tonight.

"I'll agree with you there," he'd told him.

The duke smiled rather sadly. "I know you do. It's a shame, really…"

His voice trailed off and then he looked at Jack. "Well, I've been to all the dinners, all summer long. Met all the suitors, each jockeying for position, hoping to catch the princess's eye. And I've got to agree with my niece. Not one of them can hold a candle to you, my lad.'' He patted his shoulder as he turned to start back to the party. ''Sorry to see you go.''

Jack stared after him, not sure what to make of his declaration. But then he saw Kari coming out of one of the long doors, and it slipped from his mind. It was just before midnight, and she'd managed to sneak away.

''Hi,'' she said, beaming at him.

He stood looking at her, his face displaying just how beautiful he found her. ''You really do look like a princess,'' he told her.

''A princess in need of a handsome prince,'' she said, raising her arms to him. ''Will you be my prince for one dance?''

He hesitated. ''Out here?''

''Why not? We can hear the music.''

He smiled at her, placing the walkie-talkie he'd been carrying on the nearest chair and erasing the distance between them in two quick steps. ''Your wish is my command,'' he murmured.

It was a slow song, a simple song, about love and longing called, ''I Love You in Moonlight,'' and the music was a perfect backdrop to their embrace. Once she was in his arms, she closed her eyes and let him sweep her up in the rhythm. She felt like Cinderella about to lose her slipper, like Belle dancing with the Beast. She was a princess and that meant she should be allowed a little time in a fairy-tale world. Shaking off reality, she sank into a dream and sailed away.

He held her close and buried his face in her hair, breathing as much of her as he could manage to capture, experiencing the curves of her body beneath the fabric, the sweetness of her skin. She seemed to melt against him, merging her body with his, soul to soul, heart to heart. For just this moment she was his, and he held her with tenderness and yet fiercely, ready to take on all comers, anyone who might come to claim her for their own, and for the first time he admitted to himself that he was in love.

She hadn't told him her choice and he hadn't heard it from anyone else. But maybe that was for the best. If he knew who it was and saw him here, face-to-face, there was no telling what emotional shape he might be in at the time and what he might do. Best not to know until he was away from here and from her. Then he was going to have to get used to it.

The song ended. Slowly they drew apart. She looked up at him, her smile gone. Raising her hand, she touched his cheek, and a look of pain passed through her eyes.

"Goodbye, Jack Santini," she said softly. "I hope you have a wonderful life. I hope you find someone wonderful to marry, and that you have many lovely children. I hope that you do well in your career and that your love for the police force is rewarded." Tears shone in her eyes. "You'll always be the only man I ever really loved."

He wanted to say something back, but he couldn't. There was a large and very painful lump in his throat. So he just watched as she turned and walked away.

Every part of him cried out for him to stop her, to make her come back, to tell her it was the same with him—that he would never love anyone else the way he loved her. But he knew that if he did that, he would be tying her into a lingering relationship that would cripple her chances for happiness. So he had to keep his mouth shut and let her believe that he didn't really care. And wondered why his eyes were stinging.

Chapter Ten

It was almost a month later before Jack heard Kari's name again. He'd been watching the papers, looking for an announcement of one sort or another, but there had been nothing. He'd assumed the Nabotavian community was just keeping a low profile on the matter.

He kept telling himself that was for the best, that the less he heard about her, the sooner he would stop thinking about her. But it didn't seem to be working. In fact, there were days when he thought about little else.

It was good to be back at work again. His new partner was a great guy. They got along well. Everyone had welcomed him back, and he'd been recommended as qualified to take the captain's exam when next it came up. Some of the senior officers had already assured him that he was slated for bigger things once he had the exam under his belt. Things were definitely looking good.

But he had to admit his experience working for Kari's family had broadened his outlook considerably. He wasn't sure how long he was going to be satisfied with his work on the force, now that he'd tried other things and found he had a certain knack for them. He was happy now, but he could foresee a bit of restlessness in his future.

He was feeling a little gloomy on the day he got the call that pulled him back into Kari's life. He was at his desk at the station house. His partner had gone out to get something to eat. The phone rang and he picked it up.

"Santini here."

"Jack." It was Garth's voice, and something in it hit his alarm button right away. "They've got Kari. They grabbed her today."

His hand tightened on the receiver. "Who?"

"I don't know. December Radicals, I suppose. She was on her way to a speaking engagement at the Pasadena Library but they were still in Beverly Hills when it happened. They shot Greg and Mr. Barbera and snatched Kari, drove off with her."

"Oh, my God." His stomach dropped and a coil of cold despair snaked through his gut. "When?"

"Just about ten minutes ago. The police have been called, but I thought maybe you could—"

"I'll get her back. Quick, give me all the details."

The details didn't help much. He was in his car only minutes later and moving without any real place to go, but he was in contact with the deputies who were on the case, and he could at least get closer to where the crime had occurred.

"Think!" he ordered himself. The last bunch who had taken her had put her in a house in Santa Monica. If only he knew who had her this time. It would certainly help.

His cell phone rang. Assuming it was one of the other officers he'd contacted, he flipped it open. "Santini," he barked into it.

No one spoke. He waited another beat or two, then gave an exasperated sound and began to hang up. But just before he did, something caught his attention. There was background noise, and then a voice, coming from far away. Frowning, he listened more intently. Then he realized the voice was female. And lastly, that it was Kari.

He pulled over and shut off the engine, still listening, trying to make out the words. Suddenly things were much clearer.

"I see we're going south on the San Diego Freeway," Kari was saying, her voice projecting, her words enunciating carefully. "Are we heading for the border? No, I'll bet it's that airport in Orange County, isn't it?"

"Hey! Shut her up."

The dull thud of flesh smashing into flesh set his jaw on edge, and then he heard her soft cry. The evidence that someone had hit her would have driven him crazy if he'd let it. But he kept his composure. He knew he would have to remain calm if he were going to get her back unharmed. So he turned to stone. He had to.

The voices were muffled again, unintelligible. But he had his destination now. "Airport," he muttered as he started his car again. "Smart girl."

And he would bet they weren't heading for the public terminal. They'd chartered a plane, had it warmed up and ready to go. He knew just where that plane would probably be.

Using his police band radio, he called in what he knew, then concentrated on the race to the airplane. If it was ready to go, there might not be time...

Reaching under the seat, he pulled out the magnetic flashing light, turned it on, opened his window and jammed it onto the roof of his car, then turned on his siren and began to cut through traffic like a knife through butter. Nothing was going to keep him away from that airplane.

He checked his shoulder holster to make sure his .38 was ready for action, but he wasn't going to use it if possible. Two people had already been shot, and he didn't want to risk something happening to Kari. Still, it had to be ready, just in case guile and strength weren't enough to do the job.

The airport was in his sight. He turned on a side street he knew of and headed for the cargo area. At first everything looked so peaceful and serene, he couldn't believe there was anything going on and thought he must have the wrong place. But then he saw them.

It was a small private jet and it was ready for take-off. A black car had driven right up to the ramp and people were getting out. He would never make it unless...

Gritting his teeth, he gunned the engine right through a barrier. Splintered wood flew in all directions, but he was focused straight ahead. Adrenaline pumping, he raced across the tarmac and screeched to a stop at the airplane, jumped out of his car and raced for the ramp.

He didn't stop to think. There was no time for that. He reached the first man and tossed him over the side of the ramp onto the tarmac where he landed with a dull thump and remained motionless. The next man was pulling Kari toward the door of the plane, but she was struggling and he took the steps two at a time and reached the man before he could stuff her in the door. A good right hook got him to let go of her. A little pounding got him to crumple to the steps in a heap. Someone else appeared in the door of the plane, but Jack didn't wait to see who it was. He'd grabbed Kari by now, swung her up into his arms and was dashing back down the stairs to his car, ignoring the incredible percussion of a gun firing behind him, ignoring the bullet he felt barely miss his ear. He heard sirens as he placed her in the passenger's seat and raced around to the driver's side. They were ready to take off as the squad cars arrived, tires squealing, lights and sirens blaring. But just before they left the area, Jack signaled to an officer he knew, just arriving.

"I've got the kidnap victim with me," he said, showing his badge. "I'm getting her out of here."

The officer said something, but Jack didn't wait to see what it was. In another two minutes they were a mile away.

"Are you okay?" he asked her gruffly, not turning to look for himself.

"I'm fine," she said breathlessly. "I can't believe how you just crashed in and took me like that."

Something in her voice flicked a switch in him and he was finally able to begin to relax, to let the adrenaline subside. "You're here, aren't you?"

"Sort of."

He let himself look at her and, just as he'd feared, his heart broke in two and he had to pull over. "Ohmigod, you look…"

"Like something the cat dragged in," she conceded. "I know. I was flailing around a lot." She grinned crookedly. "I think I gave one of them a bloody nose."

He wanted to cry but instead he grinned. "My little wildcat," he muttered. He couldn't stop looking at her, devouring her with his eyes.

"Yours?" She raised an eyebrow as she tucked some wayward hair behind her ear. "Why, whatever do you mean, kind sir?"

"I'll show you what I mean," he growled, reaching out to pull her into his arms with no hesitation, no second thoughts. She came willingly, laughing softly as he rained kisses on her face, turning her lips to his mouth, sighing as he began to devour her.

"Wait," he said suddenly, drawing back. "You aren't married, are you?"

"No." She shook her head. "I'm not even engaged."

"Good. But why not?"

"The night of the ball, I told them I wouldn't marry anyone but you."

He laughed softly. "You're crazy."

"I know." She reached up and caressed his cheek. "Crazy about you."

He kissed her gently, mindful of the bruises he knew she must have sustained. "I can't believe they didn't take that cell phone away from you."

"I know. They took my purse, they checked my pockets, but they didn't notice the phone attached to my waistband. It took me a while before I could worm my way around to where I could make the call. Luckily I had you on a preset."

"They didn't tie your hands?"

"No. They weren't nice," she said, putting a hand to where her jaw was starting to swell. "But they seemed to think I was a ninny princess who wouldn't have any resources of her own."

"Boy were they wrong."

She grinned, then shook her head as her eyes darkened. "I kept thinking…as I was riding in the car…I kept thinking, what if they kill me? I'd never get to see Jack again."

Groaning, he pulled her to him again and held her close, rocking her against his heart. A fierce new resolve was building in him. He wasn't going to let her go. He was going to be in her life somehow, if only to keep her safe.

The whole family was waiting as he pulled up in front of the house. There was a sense of celebration in the air as they all talked at once and all tried to hug Kari at once and then to hug Jack, as well.

"Dr. Manova is here," the duchess told her. "He's in the upstairs sitting room, waiting to check you over."

"I don't need a doctor to look at me," Kari claimed unconvincingly. "I'm fine."

They all glanced at the bruise on her jawline, then looked away again.

"It's standard procedure," Jack told her reassuringly. "We have to make sure."

"Oh!" She shivered with frustration. She didn't want to be away from him. There was no telling how long he would be staying, and her eyes couldn't get enough of looking at him. "Don't leave while I'm upstairs," she ordered him, holding on to his hand as though she would never let it go.

"I won't," he promised, nudging her toward the stairs.

"You'll stay for dinner?" she asked, lingering.

He gave her a lopsided grin. "Sure."

Finally satisfied, she ran up the stairs, while Jack turned to face the rest of the family. They wanted details, and he gave them as much as he could remember. He felt oddly at home here in this house where he'd spent so much of his summer. As he looked from the duke to Marco to Garth, and even at the duchess, he realized he felt comfortable with them, as well. They were good, decent people, regardless of the differences he might have had with them at times—and he felt nothing but warmth from every one of them now. He had a feeling that this family would go back to Nabotavia and turn it into a good and decent country. In a way he envied them such a clear-cut goal.

For the first time, he met Kari's brother Damian who was now staying at the Beverly Hills estate hoping to recover from a boating accident that had left him blind. Despite that disability, he had a look very much like the others in his family and Jack knew he was going to like him as well.

Marco asked to speak to him alone and he followed him into the study, sitting down across the desk from him.

"I have something I need to go over with you," Marco said. "We've discussed finding an appropriate way to thank you for what you've done today."

"Thank me! Hah!" Jack laughed shortly. "No need to thank me. I would have done it regardless of anything at all."

"We understand that. But it's beside the point. The fact is you've done something very important, and the nation of Nabotavia must find a way to thank you for it. We've decided that the most appropriate way would be to ask you to accept a knighthood."

"A what?" For just a moment he thought it must

be a joke. But as he looked at Marco, he could see that the man was completely serious.

"I am authorized to begin rewarding service to the crown. Yours will be the first knighthood of the new regime. Should you choose to accept it," he added quickly.

"Me? A knight?" Did the fairy tales never end with these people?

"Why not?" Marco smiled. "The police are a sort of paladin group, wouldn't you say? It seems only natural."

He shook his head. "I don't understand."

"There's nothing to understand," said Garth, coming in along with Damian to join them. "Just accept it. Become a knight. You'll be Sir Jack Santini."

That made Jack laugh. "You've got to be kidding."

"We don't kid about this stuff," Garth said with a grin. "Hey, come on. You'll be a knight of the Nabotavian realm. And as such, entitled to a certain status among our people."

Realization was slowly beginning to dawn in Jack's cloudy brain.

"And as someone of that status you will be eligible to be considered for the princess's hand in marriage," Garth added, just in case Jack hadn't let the facts sink in quite yet.

He shook his head, trying to clear up his thinking. Was Garth really saying what it sounded like he was saying?

"Don't worry, Jack," Garth added, laughing. "I

think you know by now that when there is royalty involved, everything is carefully planned out ahead of time. Spontaneity is not our game. We've considered this carefully and we all agree.''

Jack stared at him. "And exactly what is it we all agree on?"

He shrugged. "That we all love Kari very much."

Jack nodded slowly. "Yes, I'll agree to that," he said.

Damian grinned. "Take the knighthood, Jack. The rest is up to you."

Jack looked at Marco, then slowly, deliberately he rose to stand at a sort of attention before the desk. "Crown Prince Marco," he said in a clear voice, "I'd be honored to accept."

"Good." Marco rose. "I think we'll just go ahead with it, if you don't mind. We can have a public ceremony later, but I'm due in Dallas tomorrow, and Garth is going home to Arizona."

Jack shook his head. "This is your game," he told him. "I'll play by your rules."

Marco nodded. Going to a cherry wood cabinet, he took out a long, beautiful silver sword. "We'll dispense with the long version of the ceremony, if you don't mind." His smile was playful. "We'll skip the praying all night and the ritualistic assuming of the suit of armor, piece by piece. And we won't expect you to perform any tournament tricks just yet. We'll get right to the heart of the matter, shall we?"

"Let's."

Marco gestured for him to kneel, then rested the

sword on one shoulder. "In the name of the people and crown of Nabotavia I dub thee Sir Jack Santini, a knight of the realm. We trust you will protect the weak, honor women and right the wrongs you find in this world. Be brave and loyal and remember that you now represent Nabotavia in all you do." He tapped each shoulder with the sword, then nodded. "Arise, Sir Jack Santini. We welcome you."

Jack rose and looked around him. This was exactly the sort of thing he should be making fun of if he were to remain consistent. Instead he found himself flooded with an emotion he hadn't expected, and his eyes grew a little misty. He was a knight of Nabotavia. Now he would have to be a good guy for the rest of his life.

Even more scary, he was gong to ask Kari to marry him. Funny how that didn't seem as crazy as it might have just days before. All the walls he'd built up over the years were melting away. Now the crazy thing would be to imagine trying to live without her. For a few short summer months she'd brought joy and light to his life. Being away from her had taught him that those were elements he could no longer live without. He needed her like he needed air in his lungs and sunlight on his face. She was a part of him.

"Now that you're a knight," Garth said, putting an arm around his shoulders, "I'd like to talk to you about a job I'm thinking of offering you. Nabotavia is going to need someone to coordinate the various armed services and the homeland security and intelligence services. With your varied background, I thought you might be the one to help us pull all that together. How would you feel about the title minister of security?''

Jack started to laugh. Marco and Garth soon joined in, and by the time Kari came down to join them, they were out of breath and wheezing and unable to explain to her what the joke was. But they all knew, and a bond had been formed among the four of them, a bond that would take a lot to break.

Kari wasn't sure where things were going. She was only sure that this had been the most amazing day of her life. Jack was now a knight of the realm. What did it all mean? She wasn't sure, but she did know that he was being treated as an equal, not an employee, even by the duchess. That was confusing, but very, very gratifying. She thought back to the young girl she'd been at the beginning of the summer and she hardly recognized her. And now she was with the man she loved, and it seemed things might work out the way she'd always wanted. So much had changed.

Some detectives showed up to question her about the kidnapping. The men involved were all in custody and one of them was providing a lot of information. As suspected they were all members of the December Radicals. They had hoped to use her as a hostage. A number of their leaders had been captured during the liberation struggle the year before and they had been planning to use her as a bargaining chip in order to free them. The detectives took her statement and made an appointment for her to come tomorrow for further questioning. She went through it all with so much more confidence, just having Jack at her side. They contacted the hospital to check on Greg and Mr. Barbera, both of whom were being treated for minor wounds and were going to be released that same evening. That was a relief.

So there was a sense of celebration at their family dinner, and afterwards she and Jack went for a walk in the rose garden. He tucked her hand into the crook of his arm and held her close to his side.

"Remember when you asked me to marry you and I turned you down?" he said, looking down at her.

"I remember it well." The joy in her eyes dimmed.

"I was wondering…what if I were to reconsider?"

Her heart leaped, but she pursed her lips. "I don't know, Jack. That proposal was made in the exuberance of the moment. I'm not sure you can hold me to it."

He gave her a questioning look. "Are you taking it back?"

She pretended to consider. "I'll have to think about it."

He sighed. "Well, maybe it's just as well," he teased. "After all, now that I'm a knight of the realm, there's no telling how many princesses might want to marry me."

"Jack!"

"I mean, I suppose I shouldn't just fall for the first princess I see…."

"You devil!"

He laughed and wrapped her in his arms where she

snuggled in as though she would never leave. "I love you, Princess. I can't fight it any longer."

"I love you, too," she said, sighing with satisfaction. "Is it really true? Are we really going to get our own 'happily ever after'?"

"Yes. It's true." He kissed her, then looked at her lovingly. "And you're finally going to get those kissing lessons you've been asking for."

"Oh, good," she said. "Can we start right now?"

"Your wish, Most Royal Highness, is my command." And he proceeded to follow through on his promise.

*   *   *   *   *

The Forbidden Princess

DAY LECLAIRE

USA TODAY bestselling author **Day Leclaire** is a three-time winner of both a Colorado Award of Excellence and a Golden Quill Award. She's won *RT Book Reviews* Career Achievement and Love and Laughter Awards, a Holt Medallion and a Booksellers Best Award. She has also received an impressive ten nominations for the prestigious Romance Writers of America RITA® Award.

Day's romances touch the heart and make you care about her characters as much as she does. In Day's own words, "I adore writing romances, and can't think of a better way to spend each day." For more information, visit Day on her website, www. dayleclaire.com.

**Don't miss Day Leclaire's exciting new novel,
Dante's Temporary Fiancée, out in July
from Mills & Boon® Desire™.**

To Melissa Jeglinski, who felt my books might be
Desireable. Many thanks!

One

Merrick Montgomery studied the woman whose life he was about to destroy…and who could, ultimately, destroy his.

Alyssa Sutherland was stunning, he conceded. Sexy, even in the silver wedding dress she wore. He adjusted the binoculars to get a closer look. She sat without moving while a bevy of women fluttered around her like jewel-colored butterflies. Her features were as close to perfection as a man could desire and her figure—what he could see of it beneath the embellished gown she wore—threatened to rouse that desire to a fever pitch. Dappled sunlight touched the champagne blond of her hair, kissing it with the merest hint of rose.

He felt an inexplicable and powerful urge to fully bare her to his gaze, to see if her body mirrored the perfection of that face. Not that there was much doubt about what he'd uncover. Such was the gift nature bestowed on certain women—warm, breathtaking beauty combined with cold, avaricious natures.

Beneath her gown he'd find her flesh pale and un-blemished enough to make any man forget her true nature. She'd feel soft and supple against his calloused hands. Would she be built like a goddess, her hips a lush, feminine sanctuary? Or perhaps her gown hid a smaller, more boyish figure. He'd found such women to be strong and lithe in bed. Miniature dynamos.

Goddess or dynamo, it didn't matter. She'd sold herself to Brandt von Folke, which had forced his hand.

"Merrick."

The voice whispering in his ear brought him to his senses and his mouth tightened. He'd allowed the Su-therland woman to distract him from his goal and that angered him. It had never happened before. Not once in all the years he'd been head of the Royal Security Force. But this woman… He studied her one final time, ac-knowledging the intensity of her allure while deliber-ately setting it aside as nothing more than an obstacle. Her beauty would be a problem. It wasn't easily over-looked and threatened to draw attention to his actions, something he needed to prevent at all costs.

He readjusted his binoculars, sweeping them in a slow, wide arc around the courtyard where the woman sat. It only took him a moment to find what stood between him and his goal. There were eight guards in all. Six clearly visible and two on either side of the chapel doors. He checked his watch and then sent a quick hand signal to the men who accompanied him. They would move in in ten minutes.

Once again he fixed the powerful binoculars on the

Sutherland woman, tightening the focus until all he could see was the porcelain perfection of her face. She might have been lifeless for all the emotion she showed. Her eyes were downcast as though in thought, and he couldn't help but wonder what, if anything, went on behind that perfect oval mask. As he watched he caught the tiniest quiver of her mouth. Nervousness, perhaps? Second thoughts? No, not a chance. Not this woman. A prayer of thanksgiving for her coming triumph? Now that was more like it.

His mouth tightened. Pray, woman. Pray for all you're worth. Not that it would help. In a few more minutes he'd take this woman. He'd do whatever necessary to ensure that this day ended much differently from how she envisioned as she sat far below.

"It's time," Merrick announced. "No matter what, we make certain the woman doesn't marry Brandt von Folke. Understood?"

He didn't wait for agreement. His men were handpicked. They would follow his orders without question or hesitation. His mouth curled into a hard smile. There was no doubt what would happen next. His reasons were just. His need absolute. He was doing the wrong thing for all the right reasons. He was going to kidnap another man's bride for the most noble of causes.

Alyssa Sutherland sat silently amidst a sea of chaos. It took every ounce of her self-control to keep from jumping up and shrieking at the women surrounding her to leave her alone. To give her just two minutes in which she could sit quietly and try and catch her breath. To allow her the luxury of tears or breaking down in momentary hysteria or even to close her eyes and escape into a brief, blissful fantasy where someone would come and rescue her from this nightmare. Not that there was any likelihood of that happening.

Events for the past week had moved at a breakneck pace and she hadn't found a single minute to regain her equilibrium. Not a moment to think. Not to fight. Not to negotiate or protest or plead. Or run. She'd simply been told what to do and been expected to obey without argument.

And she had, though it went against every instinct and every aspect of her personality. Unfortunately, there had been no other choice.

"Princess Alyssa, it's almost time." The woman spoke in lightly accented English. But then all the people Alyssa had met so far had spoken English as fluently as their native tongue. "You should enter the chapel now."

She spared the woman—Lady Bethany Something, she recalled—a brief glance. "It's just Alyssa. I'm not a princess."

"Yes, Your Highness."

Alyssa closed her eyes in despair. Lowering her head, she struggled to maintain her composure. She could feel her mouth quiver, but it was beyond her ability to control it. "I need a moment," she whispered.

"I'm sorry, Your Highness. That isn't possible."

How many times in the past week had she been told the same thing? Too many to count. Always polite, always phrased with the utmost care and consideration and always the same underlying message: Not a chance in hell will you be permitted a single moment alone. You'll be guarded every single second that ticks off each endless hour of every hideous day. And yet...

They called her Princess Alyssa. They bowed and

curtsied and treated her as though she were made of spun glass and was twice as fragile. Their respect wasn't a pretense. She sensed an underlying sincerity she couldn't mistake. For the first time in over a week, a spark of hope ignited. Perhaps she could work their deference to her advantage.

Taking a deep breath, she lifted her chin and fixed Lady Bethany with a steely gaze. "I need a moment alone."

Lady Bethany fluttered, casting nervous glances over her shoulder. "I don't think—"

"I'm not asking you to think. I'm telling you that I need five minutes alone before I return to the chapel. I need to…to gather my thoughts. To prepare myself for the ceremony so I don't let down my—" she swallowed, struggling to speak through the distress gripping her throat "—my husband-to-be."

Lady Bethany's fluttering grew worse. "I don't think His Highness would approve. He ordered—*requested*—we remain with you at all times."

"The guard will see to my safety," Alyssa pressed, sensing victory.

"But His Highness—"

"Would agree to your making an exception on my wedding day." She infused her voice with "royal" demand. Not that she had a clue what that really meant. She could only give it her best shot and hope she hit the mark. "Why don't we send for Prince Brandt and see who's right?"

Apparently, it was the perfect tack to take. Her bluff worked. Lady Bethany blanched and stumbled back a step, dropping a hasty curtsey. "That won't be necessary, Your Highness. I'll ask the guards to escort you to the chapel when you're ready. Will five minutes be sufficient?"

Five minutes. Five short, precious minutes. How could she possibly prepare herself for what was to come in so little time? She inclined her head. "That will be fine, thank you." It would have to be.

Her bevy of ladies-in-waiting, as they'd described themselves, gathered into a hurried group, whispering in their native tongue of Verdonian—a language Alyssa didn't understand, which put her at a distinct disadvantage. Shooting quick, anxious looks over their shoulders, they withdrew into the chapel.

Drawing a deep breath, Alyssa stood and walked from the courtyard into the garden. The largest of the guards followed, putting enough distance between them that she didn't feel crowded, and positioned himself between her and the woods that bordered the garden. She crossed to the stone bench farthest from the chapel and all the prying eyes.

Earlier that morning it had rained, but now dappled sunlight filtered through the branches of the oaks, warming her chilled skin. Not long ago she'd caught a glimpse of a rainbow—a sign, her mother had always claimed, of better times to come.

"There's a pot of gold waitin' for us out there, Ally, baby," Angela Barstow had always insisted. "And one of these days, we're gonna find it."

"Not this time, Mom," Alyssa whispered.

They couldn't run away from their problems this time. No new starts. No new stepfathers. No being dragged from her bed in the middle of the night so her mother could sneak them out of whatever city they'd pitched their tent in. This time the trouble was too great to run from.

She fought against a wave of panic. She didn't have

long to gain control of her emotions. The seconds were ticking by. She could sense the restless movement of her guard and attempted to dismiss him from her mind. She drew in another breath, filling her lungs with the spring air that permeated what little she'd seen of the European country of Verdonia.

If this had been any other time, if the series of events that had brought her here had been different, she would have been enchanted by the beauty she'd encountered. But she was far from enchanted. She was alone and frightened and desperate to find a way out of this nightmare.

If only she hadn't gone chasing off to save Angela from her latest catastrophe. But the express envelope begging for help, along with the prepaid airline ticket to Verdonia, had been too much to ignore. So, Alyssa had postponed the start of her latest job and flown to the rescue. She couldn't have anticipated that she'd be snatched from the airport and carried off into the wilds of Verdonia anymore than she could have foreseen being forced into a marriage as a result of threats she didn't dare challenge—threats to her mother's well-being.

Somehow she'd become caught up in a political maelstrom, one she didn't understand. Her mother had tried to explain but there'd been so little time. From their frantic and painfully brief conversation, Alyssa had learned that everyone believed she was a princess of Verdonia, and that her marriage to Brandt von Folke would unite two of three warring principalities. It was a crazy mistake. Even so, she found herself at the very heart of the current turmoil. She'd simply been told her only option was to say "I do" or her mother would suffer the consequences.

"I beg your pardon, Your Highness. It's time."

Alyssa opened her eyes and stared at the burly guard hovering over her. Panic tightened her throat. "Already?"

"It's time," he repeated, though she caught a hint of sympathy in his gruff voice and kindly brown eyes.

Before she could plead for another moment of solitude, just a few precious extra seconds, a small whine sounded in her ear, whooshing past like a starving mosquito. A strange expression drifted across the guard's face as though he, too, had heard the odd noise. He made a small strangled sound and started to lift a hand to his neck, before dropping like a stone. With an exclamation of horror, Alyssa leaped to her feet.

She managed one quick step in his direction before an iron band wrapped around her arms and waist, lifting her off the ground and up against a tall, muscular male body. At the same moment, a large, powerful hand closed over her mouth, cutting off her incipient scream. She hung in his arms for an endless moment, a rush of sensations swamping her.

His scent washed over her. It held the confusingly civilized odor of cedar and spice. But underlying the crisp, delicious scent came something far more basic and dangerous, a primal pheromone that invaded her senses at the most carnal and instinctual level. An image of a lion flashed through her mind's eye, streaking across the African veld, claws extended, teeth bared, its powerful haunches contracting as it hurdled toward its prey…toward her.

Alyssa exploded into motion, kicking and twisting. It didn't have the least impact. He controlled her with frightening ease. The warmth of his breath stirred the curls alongside her temple and his laughter rumbled against her back.

"Calm yourself, Princess," he told her. "Fighting won't do you any good. It will simply wear you out and make my job all the easier."

His voice contained the distinctive lilt of most she'd met in Verdonia, though his was deeper and darker. Educated. The realization filtered through her terror. She struggled to control her panic and pay attention, to gather as many facts as possible in the hopes that she could somehow use the information to her advantage.

She stilled and he gave a grunt of satisfaction. Turning his head, he called out several soft words in his native language. They weren't aimed at her. She sensed others around her—not the guards—but men who worked in concert with the one who held her with such casual strength.

As soon as he'd satisfied himself that she'd given up her struggle, he melted into the shadows of the sur-rounding trees, carrying her from the garden outside the chapel's courtyard into the woods. She caught a glimpse of the men he'd spoken to before they were blocked from view by a stand of trees. All three were dressed in black, hooded and ominous in both appearance and size, and they moved with unmistakable purpose. What did they want? What were they planning? Dear heaven, she'd wanted a way out of the marriage, but not like this and not at the expense of her mother. Her mother! She tensed within her captor's hold, preparing to struggle again, but his grip tightened in warning.

"Don't." He lowered his head so his whisker-rough-ened jaw brushed her cheek. She shuddered at the deli-cately abrasive sensation. It might have been a lover's caress—would have been—if it hadn't come from a ruthless kidnapper. The dichotomy only further served to escalate her fear and she squirmed in reaction. "Keep struggling and I'll tie you up. Is that what you want?"

Oh, God, anything but that. Frantically, she shook her head. The movement dislodged her veil, sending it sliding over one eye. The finely tatted lace obscured her vision, increasing her terror. She'd always suffered from mild claustrophobia and the idea of being robbed of both her freedom of movement, as well as her sight, horrified her. Panic bubbled upward and she forced herself to focus on her breathing, to drag the air into her lungs bit by bit.

In the few moments it took to regain control of herself he carried her through the woods to a narrow country road. A pair of SUVs idled on the dirt shoulder, one black, the other a silver-gray. So far she'd counted four men, the one who'd spirited her off and the three from the courtyard who had yet to rejoin them. Now she heard a fifth member of her abductor's team emerge from one of the vehicles. Her heart sank. A single kidnapper, particularly one as powerful as the man who held her, made any attempt at escape next to impossible. But five against one killed all hope.

"It's time." Her abductor addressed the newest member. To Alyssa's relief he continued to speak in English, enabling her to follow the conversation. "You don't have to go through with this. You can still change your mind."

"I can't and I won't. There are…reasons."

At the sound of a woman's voice, Alyssa stiffened. From the corner of her eye she caught a flash of silver. She started to turn her head to look, but the man's grip on her tightened, preventing it.

"Quickly, Merrick," the woman murmured. *Merrick!*

Alyssa filed the name away for future reference. "We have only moments until her disappearance is discovered."

Ripping the voluminous veil from Alyssa's head, he tossed it to the woman. "Will this work?"

"It's perfect. From what I can tell our dresses are almost identical. The veil will conceal any discrepancies."

She said something else, something in Verdonian that caused Merrick to give a short, gruff laugh. His reply was unbelievably tender and gentle. Loving. At total odds with the ruthless kidnapper who'd just abducted her. There was a soft rustle of clothing that came from the direction of the woman and then the swift fall of her footsteps faded in the direction of the chapel.

Now they were alone and Merrick continued to restrain Alyssa within the protective shadow of the woods. Releasing the arm that anchored her to his chest, he set her on the ground and spun her around to face him. Her gaze inched upward past his thickly muscled chest to his face. She shuddered. It was as though the lion she'd pictured earlier had been reborn as a man.

Dark brown hair awash with streaks of every shade from umber to desert sand fell in heavy waves to frame strong, fierce features. Arching cheekbones underscored intense eyes, the brilliant gold irises ringed in dark brown. His razor-sharp nose had been broken at some point, but it only added to the unrelenting maleness of him, edging his appearance from the realm of stunningly handsome toward dangerously intriguing. More telling, his broad mouth had a scar that hooked the left side of his upper lip and slashed toward his cheek.

This was a man who'd lived a life of dangerous pursuits. Ruthlessness blazed in his eyes and was echoed in the grim lines etched into his features. Any hint of gentleness had been carved away long ago, honing his appearance to the bare essence of a man who eschewed softness and compassion and all things temperate, who couldn't be swayed by a woman's love, and certainly didn't compromise or yield, no matter how overwhelming the odds.

He backed her against a tree trunk, holding her with only his hand clamped to her mouth and the sheer force of his personality. The rough bark bit through her gown and clawed at her back. "I'll release you if you promise not to scream. Otherwise, I pull out the duct tape. Clear?"

She gave a careful nod. One by one his fingers lifted away, his hand hovering a mere breath from her mouth. Tilting her chin she forced herself to meet his leonine gaze without flinching. She wouldn't plead, she refused to beg. But she'd demand answers before she took another step.

"Why?" She breathed the single word from between numb lips, allowing a hint of outrage to underscore the question.

He shrugged, his black shirt pulling taut across broad, well-muscled shoulders. "You're a pawn. A pawn I intend to remove from the playing field."

Her heart pounded in her chest. How did he plan to remove her? Did he mean…by killing her? A bubble of nearly uncontrollable hysteria built inside her chest, pressing for release. "Isn't there some other way?" She forced the words past her constricted throat, despising the hint of entreaty they contained.

His expression remained unrelenting. Merciless. This wasn't a man who could be affected by a woman's tears. Nor pleading, nor demand, nor wiles. What would happen had been predetermined by him and she was helpless to change that.

"I can't allow the wedding to go on." He hesitated, and to her surprise a hint of distaste gleamed in his odd golden eyes before being ruthlessly extinguished. "I need your gown."

The demand caught her off-guard. "My what?"

"Your wedding gown. Take it off."

"But…why?"

"Wrong answer."

She shook her head. Her hair, loosened when he'd ripped the veil from her head, cascaded to her shoulders, cloaking her. "Then you won't like this one any better. I can't remove it."

She was right. He didn't like her answer. Hard furrows bracketed his mouth and tension rippled across his frame. The lion stirred. "Pay attention, Princess. Either you take it off or I do. Your choice."

For some reason his response angered her. She didn't have a clue what hidden wellspring it erupted from, or how it managed to overcome the fear that held her on the very edge of control. She simply recognized that she had two choices. She could give in to the fear and start screaming, knowing full well that once she started, she'd never be able to stop—not until he silenced her, perhaps permanently. Or she could choose to react to an impossible situation with a shred of dignity.

She looked Merrick square in the eye. "I'm telling you the truth. I can't remove my clothing. I've been sewn into my wedding gown. I gather it's the custom in this principality. So, if you're going to kill me, get it over with."

"Kill you?" Something flashed in his eyes. Surprise? Annoyance? Affront? "I have no intention of killing you. But I do need that dress. It'll draw too much attention to us. So, if you can't remove the damn thing, I will."

She heard the distinctive scrape of metal against leather and, unable to help herself, her gaze darted downward. He'd pulled a knife from a scabbard strapped to his leg. It was huge and serrated and gleamed wickedly even in the shadow of the massive oak. The breath hissed from her lungs and she discovered that she couldn't draw it in again. Darkness crept into the periphery of her vision but all she could focus on was that knife and the hand that held it—a hand that fisted around the textured grip with unmistakable competence and familiarity.

"No—"

She managed the word just as the knife descended in a sudden, swift arc, the edge biting into the bodice of her gown. For a brief instant she felt the repellent coldness of metal against the swell of her breast before it sliced downward through the silk straight to the hem. He shoved the ruined gown from her shoulders, allowing it to pool on the verdant tufts of grass at their feet.

She turned ashen, every scrap of color blanching from her skin as she struggled to suck air into her lungs.

Merrick watched her reaction with a bitter distaste for the necessity of his actions. He despised what he'd been forced to do, what he'd been forced to become because of von Folke. And yet, despite everything he'd done to her, her recovery was as swift as it was impressive. The panic and fear rapidly faded from her expression and renewed anger glittered in the intense blue of her eyes. He applauded her spirit, even as he realized it would make his job all the more difficult.

The instant her breathing stabilized, she attacked. "You son of a bitch."

He conceded the truth with a twisted smile. "So I've been told before."

She stood with her spine pressed against the rough tree trunk, her arms folded across her chest. Seeing her without her gown answered two of his earlier questions. She had, indeed, the creamy complexion he'd imagined, perfect in every regard. And she was more goddess than dynamo.

For such a petite woman her breasts were surprisingly full, overflowing the low cut demi-bra she attempted to conceal with her crossed arms. A tiny pink bow rested between the cups holding them together, though how it managed to remain tied defied explanation and tempted him beyond reason to release the pressure keeping all that bounty in place.

His gaze lowered and he almost smiled. Damned if she wasn't wearing a petticoat, no doubt another custom of the region. But then, he supposed it was necessary given the gown she'd worn. The layers of white silk and tulle belled around her, whispering in agitation in the light breeze.

His amusement faded. Time to set the tone for their relationship from this point forward. Distaste filled him again, but he forced himself to do what he knew he must. "Don't move," he ordered.

He lifted the knife again, giving her a full ten seconds to fixate on it before driving it through the voluminous skirting at her hip and deep into the tree trunk, pinning her in place. Then he reached down and snatched up the shredded wedding gown, crumpling it in his fist. Deliberately turning his back on her, he carried the gown to the silver SUV and tossed it inside. His men would dispose of it.

Merrick paused, interested to see what the Sutherland woman would do next. Her choice would determine how they spent the rest of their time together. He didn't have to wait long for his answer. Nor was he surprised by her decision. The sound of rending silk signaled her response.

Turning around, he was just in time to see her stumble free of the knife and run—as best she could given her three-inch heels—back into the woods, her petticoats fluttering behind her. To his relief, it didn't occur to her to scream. He retrieved his knife before giving chase, running in swift and silent pursuit. Her hair streamed behind her like a golden flag of surrender and her breath came in frightened pants. She'd kicked off her shoes at some point and the tear in her petticoats where she'd ripped free of the knife gave her plenty of legroom, allowing her to run more easily and making her far more fleet than he'd anticipated.

Merrick gritted his teeth. Miri's disguise would only hold up for so long. Before von Folke discovered the deception, he needed to have his princess whisked far away from here. Putting on an extra bit of speed, he closed the distance between them. He waited for her to take a couple more steps so that he could control their fall, and then he launched himself at her.

He twisted so he'd take the brunt of the landing. Hitting the earth with a thud, he skidded a foot or two in the leaf litter and tree bracken before coming to rest in a grassy section free of rocks and sticks. He wrapped one arm around her body and the other around her neck, controlling her air supply. She struggled for a brief minute before giving up the fight with a soft moan of surrender.

"You don't listen very well." He spoke close to her ear. "That's going to cost you, Princess."

"You don't understand." His choke hold prevented her from speaking above a whisper. "I have to get back to the chapel. I have to go through with the marriage. If I don't—"

"If you don't, you won't get to be Her Royal Highness, Queen of Verdonia. Is that it?"

"No! You don't understand. My mother. He has my mother."

"If your mother is anything like you, I'm sure she'll be able to fend for herself."

He released his choke hold and rolled, reversing their positions, which might have been a mistake. Seeing her splayed beneath him against the grass-sweetened earth, her tousled hair fanned around her beautiful, treacherous face was more provocative than he could have imagined. And though honor kept him from touching, he sure as hell could look.

Her petticoats belled around her, nipping in at her narrow waist. The tear in the endless layers of tulle allowed him to catch a glimpse of a lace garter and silk stockings—stockings that seemed to glisten along every endless inch of her leg. And then there was the practically nonexistent bra she wore with the tiny bow that tempted a man almost beyond endurance, begging him to tug at the ends and allow the feminine scrap to drift from her body.

Merrick's body clenched, reacting to a powerful need with frightening predictability. He was infuriated to discover that it was beyond his ability to control the automatic response. Not even a lifetime of training enabled him to overcome the temptation of this particular woman. It defied explanation.

Beneath her silver wedding gown she'd been dressed to seduce, to provoke the ultimate possession, to make a man forget everything but the desperate need to mate.

She stared at him with wide aquamarine eyes and in that insane moment he saw what it would be like to have her. He saw them locked together in the most primitive dance of all. A give and take that went much further than mere sex. He saw the ultimate possession, a sharing he'd never dared allow himself with any of the women he'd had in his life. White-hot passion. Basic driving need. A mindless surrender. Blind trust—something he'd never known in all his twenty-nine years. He saw every last detail in eyes rich with promise.

And he wanted as he'd never wanted before.

He forced words past a throat gone bone dry. "Von Folke must have caught one glimpse of you and thought all his dreams had come true."

To his surprise she shuddered. "If he was attracted to me, he never showed it." She squirmed beneath him, which thrust her breasts and pelvis up against him in a provocative brush and swirl. "Please let me up."

He wanted to refuse her request, wanted it with a raging fervor that proved to him that man was still at heart a creature of wanton instinct, an unleashed animal lurking beneath a thin veneer of civilized behavior, ruled by emotions barely kept in check and not always within his ability to control. He fought with every ounce of willpower. Endless seconds ticked by before intellect finally managed to overcome base desire.

"Very well, Princess." Or maybe intellect hadn't fully won out because he found himself saying, "But I warned that running would cost you. Time to pay."

With that, he took advantage of her parted lips and dipped downward, possessing the most lush, sumptuous mouth he'd sampled in many a year.

Two

Alyssa sank beneath the powerful onslaught of Merrick's kiss. She'd never felt anything so all-consuming, so fierce and passionate. This wasn't remotely similar to what she'd experienced during her lighthearted collegiate years, untutored kisses that tasted of beer and youthful enthusiasm. Nor did it resemble the well-practiced embraces from the men she'd dated in the years since, embraces tainted with calculation and ambition.

This was an experienced man with an experienced man's skill and knowledge. A dark desire underscored his breaching of her lips and the sweeping possession of his mouth and tongue. He consumed her, igniting a fire she'd never known existed until he'd fanned it to life.

Heat pooled in the pit of her stomach, a finger of flame scorching a path downward to the most intimate part of her and she moaned in protest. She shouldn't want this—*didn't* want this. And yet she remained still beneath him, offering no resistance. His fingers forked into her hair, tilting her head so he could deepen the kiss. He softened it, coaxing where before he'd subdued, tempting instead of demanding. Teasing. Enticing. Daring her to respond.

And she did respond, her blasted curiosity getting the better of her.

Her mind screamed in protest while her body softened to accommodate a taking she didn't want, yet somehow couldn't resist. Her jaw unclenched and her lips relaxed beneath his, parting to offer easier access. Maybe she surrendered so readily because it would keep him off guard and allow for the possibility of escape when he least expected it. But in her heart of hearts she knew the excuse was sheer self-deception. She couldn't explain her response to Merrick. She reacted to him in ways she hadn't with any other man, in primal ways that overrode rational thought and intellect in favor of reckless impulse and base desire.

And it horrified her even as it thrilled her.

One of his hands slid from her hair and followed the line of her throat to her shoulder before settling on her breast. That single brushing stroke branded her, marking her his in some inescapable way. He cupped her in his palm, his thumb grazing her rigid nipple through the thin layer of silk.

Her breath escaped in a soft cry of shock, the sound absorbed by his mouth. His hand shifted, hovering above the bow that held the cups of her bra together. Before he could pluck the silk ribbons free, the urgent clatter of church bells rang through the forest while a pipe organ bellowed forth the first few triumphant notes of the wedding march prelude. The change in Merrick was instantaneous. He levered himself off of Alyssa in a flash, his scar standing out bone-white against his tanned face.

"What the hell…?" With a quick shake of his head, he focused on her, the passion scoring his face dying a rapid death. "Clever, Ms. Sutherland. Very clever. You'll do whatever necessary, even seduce the enemy, to make sure you wear the crown of Verdonia, won't you?"

The breath hissed from her lungs and she glared at him as she shoved herself upright. "Seduce you? How dare—"

To her surprise, he whipped off his shirt and thrust it at her. Beneath it he wore a black stretch T-shirt that clung to his muscular form, emphasizing every hard bulge and angle. "Put this on."

"*You* kissed *me,* not the other way around," she reminded him as she thrust her arms into the over-long sleeves.

"And you fought me every inch of the way, didn't you?"

Hot color flooded her cheeks while the unpalatable truth of his accusation held her silent. She searched for a sufficiently quelling retort as her fingers fumbled with the buttons of his shirt. Not that she came up with anything. Perhaps she had so much difficulty because his distinctive scent clung to the black cotton, distracting her with his crisp, woodsy fragrance. Or perhaps it was because she kept sneaking quick glances at Merrick— or rather how Merrick filled his impressive T-shirt.

Regardless, she worked each button into each hole with a stubborn doggedness until she'd fastened her way straight to her neck. The instant she'd finished, he reached into his back pocket and to her horror pulled out a flat roll of duct tape. Before she could utter a single word of protest, he'd slapped a piece across her mouth and wound another length around her wrists.

"Note to self," he muttered, his mouth twisting into a humorless smile, "from now on, no kissing the bad guys."

She shook her head in furious denial, her angry protests stifled by the tape, though she didn't doubt for one moment that he understood the gist of what she'd attempted to impart, if not the full flavor. Standing, he lifted her with ease and slung her over his shoulder. A strong, calloused hand held her in place, gripping the backs of her thighs. She shuddered beneath the intimate contact even though it came through layers of tulle, hating herself for the sizzle of heat that vied with her terror at her predicament.

Within minutes he'd retraced the path they'd taken in her desperate flight through the forest, carrying her with long, swift strides to the SUV that idled on the side of the road. Opening the back door, he tipped her onto the floor.

"Keep silent and still," he instructed. "Don't make me take more drastic measures than I have already. Nod if you understand, Princess."

She fought a silent inner battle for five full seconds. With no choice but to acquiesce, she jerked her head up and down. Satisfied, he tossed a blanket loosely over her and closed the door. An instant later the driver's door opened and he climbed in. Without wasting another moment he put the car into gear, driving swiftly from the scene of her capture.

They continued for what seemed like hours, the route twisting and turning, the roads rough and bumpy. She could tell that many were either dirt or gravel. As the sun crept lower and lower in the sky, she worried endlessly about what was happening back at the chapel.

It hadn't been difficult for her to figure out that the woman who'd been part of Merrick's group had taken Alyssa's place. But how long would the woman's disguise work? Even more imperative—why had Alyssa been kidnapped and what did Merrick plan to do with her? Clearly, Verdonia had political problems in which she'd somehow become embroiled. Her abduction must be related to those problems.

Of even more concern was what Prince Brandt had done when he'd discovered the switch in brides. Had he taken his fury out on her mother? Was her mother safe? Although the prince hadn't leveled any specific threat against her when she'd been brought to his palace, the implication had been loud and clear. If Alyssa didn't marry him, her mother would meet with an unfortunate accident.

She closed her eyes, fighting her tears. So now what? She had to find a means of escape, that much was obvious, though even if she succeeded in freeing herself, how could she rescue her mother? The worrisome questions swirled through her mind, increasing her fear and desperation while offering no practical solutions.

During the interminable journey, a single goal formed, burning in the forefront of her mind, and she latched onto it with unwavering determination. She had to escape and return to Prince Brandt, no matter what that entailed. But how? Slowly, an idea grew through her fear and worry.

There was little question that her abductor was attracted to her, even if he fought hard to resist that attraction. She'd seen the desire in those extraordinary eyes of his, the hunger that had risen unbidden to score his face when his hand hovered over the tiny pink ribbon holding her bra in place. It had been strong enough an attraction for him to act on, despite the circumstances and the clear need for haste. Assuming nothing better presented itself, she could attempt to seduce him in order to free herself, no matter how distasteful she found the prospect. Then, once she'd returned to Prince Brandt, she'd marry him if doing so ensured her mother's safety.

It was a frightening plan, one that just a short week ago would never have occurred to her. But she hadn't come up with a better idea, and right now time was her enemy.

She wriggled in place, the floor of the SUV uncomfortable. Unable to stand it for another moment, she inched onto the backseat, shoving the blanket under her head as a pillow. Over the next several minutes, she surreptitiously peeled the duct tape off her mouth, wincing as the glue left her sensitive skin raw and chapped.

She took several slow, deep breaths, gathering her courage to speak. "You have to take me back," she finally called to Merrick.

He didn't seem surprised to hear her speak. But then, if he'd wanted to permanently confine her, he would have wrapped the duct tape around her head instead of slapping a short strip across her mouth. And he'd have taped her wrists behind her instead of in front of her. She grimaced, wishing she'd thought of that a couple of hours ago.

"You aren't going back."

She sat upright. "Why not? Why have you abducted me?"

"Lie down," he snapped. "Keep out of sight or I'll gag you again."

She stretched out along the backseat, unwilling to put his threat to the test. Not that anyone driving by could have

seen her. Twilight was full upon them. "You don't understand. I *have* to go back. It's a matter of life or death."

"Very melodramatic, Princess." He made a sharp turn
that almost sent her plummeting to the floor again. "But
my reasons for taking you are equally imperative."

"Please." She choked on the word, despising the need
to beg. But she'd do whatever necessary if it meant
getting to her mother. "I'm not being melodramatic."

"This is not the time for that particular discussion."
The SUV came to a sudden halt and this time she did
roll onto the floor, landing on her hands and knees.
"Welcome to your new home."

Before Alyssa could get up, Merrick opened the door
and lifted her out, setting her on her feet. She shook her
hair from her face and forced herself to confront him.
Shoeless, wearing little more than his shirt and a
rumpled petticoat, she'd never felt more vulnerable in
her life. Not that she'd allow that to undermine her determination. "You have to listen to me. There's more
than a marriage at stake here."

"I know far better than you what's at stake," he bit
out, holding her in place with a hand on her arm. "This
is my country, Princess. You come here and upset the
political balance. All I'm doing is resetting that balance
by removing you from the equation."

"I didn't choose to come back here," she argued.
"And I don't care about your country's political problems. I only care about—"

She broke off at his expression and if his grip hadn't
tightened just then, she'd have fallen back a step. In the
little light that remained she could see a fierce anger turn
his eyes to burnished gold, warning that she should have
selected her words more judiciously. He leaned in, huge

and intimidating, his comment little more than a whisper in the sultry night air.

"Interesting that you care so little for Verdonia when you're intent on becoming her queen. But somehow I'm not surprised. Your type sells herself for fame and fortune. Money and attention, that's all you care about. The throne. The crown. The jewels." He emphasized his point by flicking her earlobe with his index finger where a heavy amethyst and diamond earring hung. The pair were a gift Prince Brandt had insisted she wear for their wedding. "You have no concern for the people or their problems, only for yourself."

His comments threw her. They didn't make a bit of sense, but instinct warned she'd do well to listen rather than question or argue. He released her arm and assisted her toward a small house set beneath a stand of towering pines, steadying her as she picked her way around a scattering of stones gleefully intent on torturing her bare feet. The structure was a pretty A-frame, what she could see of it through the gathering darkness. The roofline and shutters were decorated with gingerbread trim painted a crisp white that stood in sharp relief against the charcoal stain of the siding. High above, a balcony jutted out from the second level and no doubt offered a spectacular view of the surrounding area.

"Where are we?" she asked.

He paused by the front door and removed a set of keys from his pocket. "In Avernos, on the border of Celestia."

A fat lot of help that was. Maybe if she knew where Avernos or Celestia were, she'd have a clue. But she didn't. The names weren't the least bit familiar. "Why are we here? Why did you abduct me? What are you going to do with me?" So much for listening rather than peppering him with questions.

He shoved the front door open without replying and ushered her inside, flipping on an overhead light. She looked around, filled with a reluctant curiosity. Directly in front of her a staircase led to the second level. To her left she caught a glimpse of a great room complete with a stone fireplace and wall-to-wall shelving overflowing with books. A dining room occupied the right side of the house and she could see a doorway leading to a kitchen at the far end.

Merrick gestured toward the kitchen. "Let's get something to eat."

"I'd rather not."

"No?" He lifted an eyebrow. "We could pick up where we left off earlier, if you'd prefer."

An image of them in the woods flashed through her mind, of his mouth on hers. Of his hands on her. Of heated desire and helpless surrender. Her throat went dry and she moistened her lips in response. Lord, she could still taste his distinctive flavor. Worse, she felt a craving to taste it again. "No kissing the bad guys, remember?"

A grin slashed across his face, changing his appearance. Where before he'd been harsh and remote, his features were now rearranged into an expression she found quite stunning. A tug of forbidden desire swept over her, causing her to stumble backward. He must have noticed her awareness of him, or at the very least sensed the shimmer of sexual tension humming between them, because his smile grew.

"You sure?"

"Positive."

She tugged at the tape that restrained her hands. What

a fool she was, she conceded bitterly. She'd wasted endless time in the car imagining herself capable of seducing this man. It had seemed reasonable at the time, even straightforward. But she'd never bothered to consider how she'd set about accomplishing such an impossible task. Should she simply touch him, drape her taped arms around his neck? Would that even be sufficient to provoke him to make the next move, or would she have to push it further still? Was she supposed to initiate a kiss or just offer her mouth for his possession?

None of those issues had been addressed when she'd come up with her idiotic plan. And even if she enticed him to kiss her again, what would be her next step? Did she allow him to fondle her, to remove the shirt he'd given her and untie the little bow that held her bra in place? She shivered as her imagination took it one step further—the final, terrifying step. Did she let him make love to her? And once she had him focused on her sexually, how did that help her get away? It would only work if she knocked him out, or something.

Standing in front of him, confronting all that innate masculine strength and power forced her to concede how futile her plan was, not to mention foolhardy. For one thing, she suspected he'd instantly figure out what she was up to, which wouldn't be beneficial to her overall health and well-being. And for another, her reaction to him warned that he'd have more success seducing her than the other way around. How could she keep her wits about her when every time she came within arm's length of him her body sizzled with desperate heat?

Her mouth tightened. Just because her body responded to him in such an unwelcome way didn't mean

she had to act on that response. If seducing him wouldn't
work, she'd have to remain alert to other possibilities.

"Well, Princess?" he prompted. "I assume your
silence means you'd prefer to eat."

"If the choice is food or picking up where we left off,
then yes, I prefer to eat." He laughed at her dry tone, the
sound deep and dangerous and far too attractive for her
peace of mind. "Will you at least explain why you're
doing this?" she asked.

He dismissed her question with a shrug. Planting his
hand at the base of her spine, he guided her in the direction of the kitchen. "You know why. Don't play
games with me, Princess."

"Games?" She turned on him in outrage. "Let me
assure you I don't consider any part of this a game."

Once in the kitchen, he pointed to one of two chairs
tucked beneath a small butcher-block table that had
been positioned beside a wide picture window. In the
final glow of twilight, she could just make out a fenced
garden overrun with flowers, weeds, and to one side, a
collection of indeterminate vegetables.

"Sit, Princess. It's pointless to keep up this pretence
of ignorance."

"I wish it were a pretence. I wish all of this was."

Feeling the rising panic, she took a deep breath,
striving for calm. Pulling out the chair he'd indicated,
she curled up in it, drawing her knees against her chest
beneath the voluminous petticoats. Her pink-tipped toes
peeked through the rips in her stockings and she studied
the smudges of dirt marring them as she considered
how best to get through to Merrick. If she didn't get
answers soon, she wouldn't have the necessary information to plan her escape, an escape that—second by

second—became increasingly more important if she were to save her mother.

"Why does everyone keep calling me Princess Alyssa?" she asked. "I'm not a princess."

Merrick paused in the act of removing a selection of meats, cheeses and fruit from the refrigerator and turned to study her. "You're Princess Alyssa, Duchess of Celestia."

"No. I'm Alyssa Sutherland, soon to be Assistant VP of Human Relations for Bank International."

He ignored her attempt at humor. "You left Verdonia when you were just over a year old." He placed the selection of food in front of her, along with a crusty loaf of bread and several bottles of sparkling water. "Your mother, an American college student who'd met the prince while on vacation, married and divorced him in the span of two short years. A bit of a scandal at the time. Apparently living the life of a princess wasn't the fairy tale she'd envisioned. After the divorce, she took you back to the United States, leaving your father and your older half brother behind."

Alyssa hesitated. "She told me some of that years ago. But my father wasn't a prince anymore than I'm a princess."

"It would appear your mother neglected to mention a few pertinent details about your background."

For the first time a twinge of doubt assailed her. What had her mother said in the few minutes they'd been permitted to speak? She'd been incoherent, tearfully apologizing for tricking Alyssa into coming to Verdonia and for not finding a way to warn her about the mess she'd managed to entangle them in.

There had also been something about how she'd fled the country twenty years earlier, never suspecting

Alyssa would be expected to assume her brother's responsibilities—a brother she hadn't even known existed. The one thing that had been abundantly clear was that in order to keep her mother safe, Alyssa would have to marry Prince Brandt.

She tried again. "Everyone thinks I'm a princess. I assure you, I'm not. This is all some hideous mistake."

He saluted her with a sardonic smile. "Am I supposed to believe your story and let you go? Good try, but it won't work."

"No, I thought you'd realize that you have the wrong person and help me figure out what's going on." Her feet hit the floor with a small thud. "I'm telling you there's been a mistake. I'm no more a princess than I am this Duchess of Celdonia."

"Celestia. Verdonia is the country, Celestia is one of her three principalities. And there's no mistake." He tilted his head to one side. "Fair warning, this tactic isn't going to work."

"It's not a tactic." Frustration edged her words. "I don't know what's going on."

"Enough!"

Something in the roughly stated word had her swallowing nervously. "Fine." She waited a beat and then whispered, "He has my mother, Merrick. He's holding her hostage. That's why I agreed to marry him."

Merrick stifled a groan. It was her tone more than anything else that stopped him in his tracks; the soft, American-accented voice was filled with fear and anguish. He vaguely recalled her mentioning her mother while they were in the woods, but he'd assumed it had been another ploy to gain her release. He kept his expression implacable as he joined her at the table but inside he was filled with rage at von Folke's ruthless-ness. "Regrettable."

"I have to know what's going on. Please." Her mouth worked for a moment. "Can you explain it to me so I understand?"

"Eat. You'll need your strength."

He fought a brief inner battle while she picked at the meal he'd provided, weighing his belief that she was in on von Folke's plan against the possibility that she was an innocent victim in all this. If she were telling the truth, it was only fair that he explain the situation. Honor demanded as much.

He left her long enough to fetch a map from the great room. When he returned, he spread it across the table, anchoring the corners with the bottles of water. Next, he removed a fillet knife from a butcher block on the kitchen counter and after first slicing the duct tape binding her wrists so she had more freedom to eat, he used it to trace the outline of the country.

"This is Verdonia. It's divided into three principalities."

She studied it with all apparent interest as she massaged her wrists. "Where are we?"

He shook his head. "Not a chance, Princess."

"In general. You said we were on the border of Celestia and...and—"

He tapped the upper portion of the map. "We're just inside the border of Avernos. Mountainous and riddled with amethyst mines. The gems provide the economic backbone of Verdonia. This principality's ruled by von Folke." He broke off a chunk of bread and ate it before shifting the knife downward to the very bottom of the map. "The most southern principality is Verdon, the fi-nancial heart of Verdonia."

She glanced at him. "And the principality in the middle?"

He outlined the S-shaped bit of land that curled between the northern and southern principalities, cupping each in turn. "Celestia. Traditionally the artisans who work the amethyst have come from this principality. Until ten days ago, your half brother ruled here."

She leaned forward and was forced to shove a tumble of unruly curls behind one ear in order to get a better look. In the few hours since he'd first seen her, she'd been transformed from regal princess to rumpled seductress, both of whom appealed far more than he cared to admit. His awareness of her disturbed him. It was one thing to take her, but committing such a dishonorable act, even for honorable reasons, had been the most difficult decision he'd ever made. But to compound it by lusting after von Folke's intended bride.... Touching her, making love to her.... Damn it to hell!

He shoved a plate of cheese in her direction and didn't say anything further until she'd helped herself to some. She nibbled at it with a marked lack of enthusiasm before cracking the seal on one of the bottles of water. Tipping back her head, she took a long drink, unwittingly revealing the creamy line of skin that ran the length of her neck.

The memory of how she'd looked in the forest earlier rose unbidden to his mind. She'd lay sprawled in a lush pocket of ripe grass and summer leaves, like a sacrifice to the heathen gods of old, the scent of her lightly perfumed skin mingling with the odor of rich, fertile soil. Dappled sunlight had gilded her creamy skin, while the mystery of womankind had gleamed in eyes the color of aquamarines, tempting him to plumb its many secrets. And he'd wanted her. Wanted her more than he'd wanted any other woman. If it hadn't been for the church bells…

His mouth tightened. He'd come close to sacrificing both honor and duty in that moment. Too close.

She eyed him quizzically. "You haven't explained what's happened to my brother. How's he involved in all this?"

He didn't see any benefit in withholding the information. "My sources inform me he was paid a lot of money by von Folke to abdicate his position," he replied. "When that happened, the title fell to you. Where before you were Princess Alyssa, now you're also duchess of Celestia. Or you will be once church and state make it official."

Alarm flashed across her face. "I don't want the position."

"Don't you?"

He could tell his skepticism annoyed her, but she impressed him by holding onto her temper, though she spoke with a clipped edge to her voice. "Even assuming all of this is true, why would Prince Brandt have paid my brother to abdicate?"

"Two weeks ago the king of Verdonia died."

"Oh. I'm sorry." She hesitated briefly. "I don't mean to sound crass, but what has his death got to do with any of this?"

"Verdonia has a rather unusual system for replacing their monarchs. It calls for the people to vote in an election, choosing from the eligible royals from each principality."

"And there are three eligible royals?"

"Were three," he corrected. "With your brother's abdication we're down to two. There's Prince Lander, duke of Verdon—"

"That's…that's the southernmost principality, right? The one that governs the finances?"

"Correct. And the other contender for the throne is von Folke. If you were over twenty-five at the time of the election, you'd be eligible to rule, as well."

"Wait a minute. Are you saying that if my twenty-fifth birthday had fallen a few minutes sooner, I'd be a contender for the throne? *Me?*" If she were feigning shock, it was a stellar performance. "No. No, thank you. I have no interest in ruling Verdonia."

He shot her a sharp look. "Interesting that you're so quick to refuse when marrying von Folke will accomplish precisely that."

She stared at him, narrow-eyed, for a long, silent moment. "How?"

He stabbed the knife into the paper heart of Celestia, driving the point deep into the butcher-block table. "The popular vote, remember?"

He only had to wait an instant for comprehension to dawn. Her brows drew together. "If I really am a princess and duchess of Celestia and I marry Prince Brandt…" Her breath caught. "He'd win the popular vote of the entire country, wouldn't he?"

"Yes. To be honest, it's a brilliant plan. The principality of Avernos—von Folke's people—would vote in his favor. And with Celestia's princess married to von Folke—that's you—honor and loyalty would force the citizens of Celestia to vote for him, as well. Verdon would fall to Lander, but it wouldn't matter because von Folke would walk away with a two-thirds win."

"Which you want to prevent from happening." It wasn't a question, but closer to an accusation. "Why?"

He studied her grimly. "I'll do whatever it takes to

ensure a fair election. I'm honor bound to protect all of Verdonia, not just any one principality."

"Isn't who becomes king up to the people of your country to decide?" she argued.

He leaned in, crowding her. "Von Folke is the one who chose to tip the balance. He upset the natural order of things—with your help. I'm merely righting that wrong."

Apprehension flashed across her face before she managed to regain control. "By getting rid of me?"

He offered a humorless smile. "In a manner of speaking. The election is in a little more than four months. Once it's over, you'll be free to marry whomever you wish."

It took her several seconds to process his words. The instant she had, her breath escaped in a horrified hiss and she shook her head. "You can't be serious. Four months? *No!* I won't let you keep me here that long."

"And just how are you planning to stop me?"

"Like this!"

He had to admit, she surprised him, something that hadn't happened since he'd first begun his training as a callow youth. She fisted her hands around the filet knife embedded in the table and yanked it free, thrusting the razor-sharp tip toward his throat. She paused just shy of cutting him.

"My mother doesn't have four months. You're taking me back to Prince Brandt right now."

Even with a knife at his throat, he couldn't help marveling. God, she was beautiful. Vibrant. Infuriated. Infuriating. He deliberately leaned closer until the razor-sharp point pricked the base of his throat. "Listen up, Princess. Nothing you say or do will convince me to return you to him. There's only one place I'm willing to take you."

She glared at him for a split second before her gaze shifted downward to where the knife had nicked him. She shuddered at the sight of the blood she'd drawn. "And where is that?"

"My bed, of course." In one easy move he knocked her hand aside, sending the knife clattering against the wall and then to the floor. Before she could do more than utter a soft cry of protest, he swept her into his arms and lifted her high against his chest. "Consider it your home for the next four months."

Three

Merrick wasn't the least bit surprised that Alyssa fought him, though this time she struggled even more fiercely than when he'd initially abducted her.

"Stop it, Alyssa. You'll only hurt yourself waging a battle you can't win."

"I don't care. I'll fight you until my last breath." She clipped him with her fist. "I won't let you do this."

"I'm afraid you can't stop me."

He carried her from the kitchen to the steps leading to the bedroom and took them with swift efficiency, despite his struggling armful. Depositing Alyssa on her feet at the top of the stairs, he reached around her and thrust open the door on one side of the landing. Instantly she tried to skitter away. He gathered her back up and held her wriggling body tight against his. Damn, but he needed to put some distance between them. She'd become far too great a distraction, something he didn't need when tomorrow promised to be even more challenging than today.

"I don't want to hurt you, Princess," he warned. "But you will do as I say when I say it, or you'll spend the next four months tied to a bedpost."

"You can't honestly believe that I won't fight, that I'll just let you—" She clamped her mouth shut, unable to utter the hideous words.

"You'll sleep in my bed for however long we're together." He captured her chin and tipped it upward, forcing her to look at him. "Allow me to emphasize the word *sleep*."

She stared at him, her eyes wide and dilated. "Not…not—"

"No. *Not*," he repeated calmly. "Just sleep. Tomorrow's going to be a long day. I'd like to close my eyes for a few hours between now and then and I need to make certain you won't try anything foolish. Like escape."

"Why did you make me think—" Her voice broke and she waved her hand in an impatient gesture. "You know."

"Because you had a knife at my throat and I was angry." Even though the confession came hard, he didn't shy away from taking full responsibility. He let that sink in before adding, "But I wasn't lying, Alyssa. You will be sharing my bed for the next four months, though what happens in that bed is up to you."

She reared back as if he'd struck her. "Nothing will happen there!"

He didn't bother arguing. Time would prove her right or wrong more readily than anything he could say. Turning her to face the open doorway, he gave her a gentle shove toward it. Under other circumstances her expression of surprise and confusion when she found herself standing outside a bathroom would have been amusing.

"Get cleaned up. Shower if you wish. You can also help yourself to any of the toiletries you find. There's a robe hanging on the back of the door. Put it on before you leave the bathroom."

She bristled. "And if I don't?"

He deliberately chose to misunderstand. "Come to bed naked. I won't object."

"I meant, what if I don't come out at all?" Her fighting spirit had clearly been revitalized. "I'll...I'll sleep in the bathtub."

"You can try, but since the door has no lock you won't be very successful." He checked his watch. "You have thirty minutes. Use it wisely. When your time is up, I'm coming in after you."

"You wouldn't!" The response was an automatic one. Even she realized as much, because she shook her head. "Of course you would. But then, raiding the bathroom while I'm in the shower would be the least of the offenses you've committed against me, wouldn't it?"

He simply looked at her. Men rarely opposed him; women never did. And those few men who dared balk at his orders only did so once. But then, they knew who he was. Alyssa's unwavering defiance impressed the hell out of him. Even as she acquiesced to his demand, her expression and posture warned that she did so under protest.

When he remained mute, frustration vied with her anger. "You're a total bastard, you know that, Merrick?"

"Yes, as a matter of fact, I do."

Actually, the term was mild. As commander of the Royal Security Force, his life was comprised of making impossible decisions that had dire effects on the people with whom he came into contact. Worse, he had to live with the ramifications of his decisions. He didn't doubt for a minute that the actions he'd taken today, and would continue to take over the next four months, would produce the most painful results to date.

With a look of utter contempt, Alyssa turned her back on him and slammed the door in his face. He took it without flinching.

Score one for the princess.

She emerged from the bathroom thirty minutes later, timing it to the very last second, and he straightened from where he'd been lounging against the hallway wall. Despite her earlier threat, she wore the bathrobe he'd left for her and had washed her hair, which hung down her back in damp, heavy curls. Her face was scrubbed clean and to his consternation she looked all of twelve. Or she would have if it hadn't been for the womanly curves that turned floor-length terry cloth into a garment every bit as seductive as the scraps of silk and lace she'd been wearing earlier. How she managed it he couldn't begin to guess, but it guaranteed him a near sleepless night.

She stalked to the bedroom doorway, only a slight hitch in her stride betraying that she wasn't as amenable about the night ahead as she pretended. He followed, watching in exasperation as she crossed to a chair on the far side of the room and curled up in it.

He shut the bedroom door and locked it, steeling himself for yet another pitched battle. "Get in the bed, Alyssa."

"No, thanks. I'm good here."

"I can't allow that. I need to sleep and I won't be able to if I'm constantly watching to make sure you stay put."

She snuggled deeper into the chair, burrowing in for the duration. "You won't get much rest, anyway. I'm…I'm a very restless sleeper. I toss and turn all night long."

He almost smiled at the blatant lie. Or he would have if she hadn't been right about one unfortunate fact. It didn't appear he'd be getting much sleep. But it wouldn't have anything to do with her restlessness. "I'll manage." He pointed toward the double bed. "Get in."

She took several deep breaths before obeying. Leaving the safety of the chair, she approached the four-poster with all the caution of a mouse sneaking up on a baited trap and stood beside the bed for several long moments. Just when he was on the verge of picking her up and tossing her in, she pulled back the covers and slid between the sheets, curling up in as minute a ball as possible on the very edge of the mattress.

Hell. The next few hours were going to be some of the most difficult of his life. He circled the bed and yanked his black ops T-shirt over his head, tossing it onto the chair she'd abandoned. His boots came next, hitting the floor with a distinctive thud before he released his belt buckle and unzipped his trousers. He saw her stiffen at the distinctive rasp of the zipper and he could hear the nervous intake and exhalation of her breath.

Stripped down to his boxers, Merrick joined Alyssa in bed. She made a pathetically small mound on the farthest side of the mattress, no doubt attempting to remain as still and inconspicuous as possible in the hopes he'd leave her alone. Releasing his breath in a sigh, he hooked his arm around her and tucked her close, spooning her back against his chest. She remained stiff as a board, refusing to accommodate the alignment of curve to angle.

As for thinking she was pathetic, he was forced to hastily revise his opinion. Though she didn't struggle, somehow the dainty, fragile woman he held within his arms had managed to transform herself into hardened steel, gouging bony elbows into the few vulnerable parts of his body. Steel-tipped fingers dug into the arm anchoring her in place, and even her heels and toes had became lethal weapons. The only place she remained soft and cushioned was her backside, though he didn't doubt she would change that if she could. But at least it offered some small shielding against the rest of her anatomy.

"Do you have to touch me?" she whispered, squirming. "Isn't it enough that I'm in the same bed with you?"

Dear God, if she didn't hold still there'd be hell to pay. "It's necessary," he explained with impressive patience. "This way if you attempt to escape, I'll know. And I'll stop you."

Her breath trembled from her lungs. "I won't attempt to escape."

"Yes, you will. You think your mother needs you. So you'll continue to try and get away, just as I'll continue to stop you."

She shifted again and he stifled a groan, only half succeeding. "There's nothing I can do about it," she snapped. "I did warn you. I'm not used to sleeping like this."

"Tonight would have found you in some man's bed sleeping just like this, whether it was with von Folke or with me." Though with von Folke there would have been a lot more involved than talking and sleeping. He'd have wanted to consummate their union in order to make the marriage legally binding as per Verdonian law. For some reason the mere idea of anyone else putting his hands on Alyssa roused Merrick to a white-hot fury. "Or are you forgetting this would have been your wedding night?"

He didn't know what prompted him to ask the question, but to his surprise she shuddered. "I had forgotten," she confessed. Then her voice dropped to a whisper so soft, he barely caught it. "Being with him... It would have been far worse."

He didn't cut her any slack. "If that's how you felt, you should have refused to marry him. I doubt he'd have hurt your mother."

Her elbow clipped him in the gut and this time he suspected it was deliberate. "You didn't see his expression. I did. Prince Brandt will do whatever it takes to get me to the altar."

"If it means winning the throne, you're right. He'll say whatever he must to force your agreement. But even a man like von Folke has lines he won't cross. I suspect murder is one of them."

"People cross lines all the time when they're desperate." Her voice held a note of cool conviction. "One of my stepfathers was an auditor and I worked for him the summer between high school and college. That's how I became interested in finance in the first place. I could always sense when someone had been cooking the books. You can almost smell their desperation. If I were auditing Prince Brandt, I'd be checking his accounts very carefully."

Interesting. "Are you saying he's embezzling money?"

"No. I'm saying he's desperate. I have no idea why. But I can sense it, even though he's working really hard to keep a lid on things. Whether it's related to finances or not, I can't tell."

She fell silent after that, leaving Merrick free to sift

through her observations. Something was up. Too bad he couldn't be certain what. He didn't doubt that von Folke would go to almost any extent to wear the crown. Avarice. Power. Prominence. All were substantial motivators. But why would a man be desperate to become king? Desperation implied a driving need rather than a burning desire. Why would a man *need* to be king?

He'd already checked von Folke out. Maybe it was time to dig a little deeper. A full profile, he decided, including—he smiled—any books that might have been cooked.

Alyssa had finally settled, for which he was eternally grateful. Moonlight crept through the doors leading out onto the balcony and slipped into bed with them, frosting their entwined forms with silver. The crown of her head rested beneath his chin and silken strands of her hair snagged along his whisker-roughened jawline. He inhaled, filling his lungs with the odor of the herbal shampoo she'd used. He could also catch a hint of a lighter, more irresistible aroma, though whether it came from her soap or the natural scent of her body, he couldn't be sure. Either way, the fragrant perfume soaked into his pores, permeating his senses in a way he knew would forever be a part of him.

"That women who was with you earlier," she said, catching him by surprise. "What were you saying to each other? The part in Verdonian, I mean."

He lifted onto his elbow and drew her head to one side so he could look at her. The moonlight muted her vibrant coloring, turning her hair to silver and darkening her eyes to black. Her features took on a pearly glow, given depth and definition by the charcoal shadows sinking into the gentle planes and angles of her face. Watching her closely, he bit out a swift comment in Verdonian. She responded by staring at him in utter bewilderment.

"You don't speak the language, do you?" He shook his head in disbelief. "You come here expecting to be our queen and you can't even speak to your people in their native tongue?"

"Why should I?" she retorted indignantly. "I didn't know I was part Verdonian until last week."

"I would think if you were going to rule a country you might want to communicate with your subjects. What would you do if English wasn't our second language?"

"If I'd known that's what was going to happen to me, I would have learned Verdonian." Exasperation edged her words. "What did you say to me? How do you know I wasn't pretending I didn't understand? You think I'm pretending about everything else."

"Because my comment was unforgivably coarse." Unable to resist, he stroked his thumb along the sweeping arch of her cheekbone. "If you'd understood, you'd have reacted." Slapped him, most likely.

"Oh." She rolled away from him, not protesting this time when he spooned her into their earlier position. "You still haven't answered my question. What did she say to make you laugh?"

"She called me a bear cub. It can also mean a stuffed animal."

"A teddy bear?"

"A teddy bear. Yes."

Silence descended for several more minutes, though he wasn't the least bit surprised when she spoke again. "That woman—the one who called you a teddy bear— she took my place, didn't she?"

"That was the plan."

"Who is she?"

"My sister, Miri."

Alyssa turned her head again, this time of her own volition, and gazed at him in confusion. "Aren't you worried about what Prince Brandt will do to her when he discovers the deception?"

"Yes." He was incredibly worried.

"Then why did you let her do it?"

He hadn't wanted to but she'd insisted, threatening to reveal his plans if he didn't allow her to participate in the abduction. "It was necessary," Merrick limited himself to saying.

"She mentioned there were reasons for what she did," Alyssa said slowly. She settled onto her back. "Were they the same reasons you have? To make sure the elections are fair?"

He hesitated. He'd assumed that'd been what Miri had meant at the time, but since then he'd had several long hours to reconsider her words. Something in her tone had disturbed him, though he'd been unable to pinpoint what. With anyone else, he'd have managed it, had been trained to do precisely that. But his feelings for Miri interfered with his training, clouding his logic with emotion.

He narrowed his gaze on Alyssa. She'd proven herself a shrewd judge of character when it came to von Folke. Perhaps she'd picked up on whatever he'd missed. "Something's bothering you about what Miri said. What?"

Alyssa shrugged and her robe parted to reveal the soft skin of her throat and shoulders. "Her comment sounded...personal."

Personal. The longer he thought about it, the more certain he became that Alyssa was correct. He could see it now—the quiet despair in Miri's green eyes, the stalwart determination in her stance, the way she'd flinched when von Folke's name had been mentioned in connection with Alyssa's. Hell. Why hadn't he seen it before? He should have. Another concern to contemplate during the endless hours of the night.

"Go to sleep," he told Alyssa. He needed to think without distraction—and she'd already proven herself a huge one. "Tomorrow is going to be difficult enough as it is."

"Why?"

He sighed. "You ask a lot of questions, Princess."

"Yes, I do. And here's one more…" She rolled over to face him and her subtle perfume invaded his senses once again, threatening his sanity. "Are you certain you want to go through with this?"

It wasn't the first time the question had been posed, and Merrick didn't hesitate in his response. "The future of Verdonia depends on it."

She moistened her lips, choosing her words with care. "Eventually you'll be caught. You realize that, don't you? What will happen to you when you are? Will you be sent to prison?"

"Maybe. Or banished. It depends on who catches me."

"But if you send me back—"

So. She'd found a new angle of attack, one he cut off without compunction. "Enough, Alyssa. Prison or banishment, I'll deal with the consequences when they occur."

"What about Prince Brandt? What will he do to you? You said there were lines he wouldn't cross. Are you willing to bet your life on that?"

"He won't be pleased that I've taken away his best chance at the throne." That had to be the understatement of the century. "Not that it matters. Whatever occurs as a result of my actions is an acceptable penalty."

"You can't be serious."

"I'm quite serious." He lifted an eyebrow. "Don't tell me you're worried about me?"

"Of course not." But he caught the flicker of concern that gave lie to her claim. The temptation to touch her became too much and he stroked his hand along the curve of her cheek and down the length of her neck. She shivered beneath the caress.

"Don't," she whispered.

He spoke without volition, drawn to tell her the truth regardless of the consequences. "I'm honor bound to protect Verdonia from you."

"Am I such a threat?"

"A threat to my country." His mouth twisted into a ghost of a smile. "But a far worse threat to my honor."

As though to prove it, he lowered his head and captured her lips. They were every bit as soft and lush as he remembered, honey sweet and welcoming. A half-hearted protest slid from her mouth to his and he absorbed it, wanting to absorb all of her in every way possible.

How could she have been willing to give herself to von Folke? Didn't she realize it was criminal? More criminal than his abduction of her, and he told her as much with sharp, swift kisses. Then he sank back between her lips, reacquainting himself with every warm inch within.

He knew her mouth now. Laid claim to it. Drank from it. Possessed it, just as he planned to possess her. She went boneless in his arms, a surrendering that was every bit as wrong as it was overwhelmingly right.

The instant he released her mouth she whispered his name and it shivered between them into the velvety silence of the night. "You promised," she said.

"What did I promise?"

"That you wouldn't."

"Wouldn't what?"

Her head moved restlessly on the pillow. "I can't remember."

"Neither can I." Nor did he want to.

He found her mouth again and there was no more talking. Lips clung, then parted before unerringly finding each other again. Hands brushed, tangled, then released. Sweet murmurs filled the room, broken words that shouldn't have any meaning, but somehow spoke volumes.

Desire fired his blood, filling his heart and mind, crowding out rational thought. He needed more. Wanted the woman in his arms as he'd never wanted anything before. Clothes impeded him, taunting him, as they came between him and the warm, soft skin he so desperately craved. Skin that teased him with an irresistible perfume that had burrowed deep into his subconscious.

He found the belt that kept Alyssa from him. The knot fought his efforts to release it. And then it gave up the struggle, just as the woman had. He parted the coarse terrycloth and found the silken flesh within, soft and fragrant and burning hot.

"I swear, I'll make this good for you."

But the second he'd said the words, he knew he'd lost her. She stiffened within his arms and the desperate heat that had burned in her eyes only moments before faded, replaced with horrified distress. The princess had awoken from her enchantment and discovered she wasn't with Prince Charming. Far from it.

Her breath came in short, ragged gasps. "I want you to stop."

Desire rode Merrick hard and it took every ounce of effort to pull back from the edge. "Easy, Princess. I've stopped."

But his assurances had little effect. Panic held her in its grip and wouldn't let go gently. "You claim you're honor bound to protect all of Verdonia. Doesn't that protection extend to me, as well?" she demanded. "Or does your code of honor allow you to rape helpless women?"

She couldn't have chosen a more effective insult. He tamped down on his anger with only limited success. "It wouldn't be rape, and you damn well know it."

"Maybe not. But it wouldn't be honorable, either. Not when I'm being held prisoner. And not when you can't be certain I haven't given in because I fear the consequences if I don't."

He swore, long and violently. He'd never had his honor called into question. Not ever. Even so, he knew she was right, which disgusted him all the more. If matters weren't so desperate, he'd never have abducted her in the first place. He told her there were lines a man didn't cross. But hadn't he just stepped over one of them? Hell, he'd run full tilt over it, which bothered him more than he was willing to admit. Honor was everything to him, as was duty. He'd had a lifetime's training in each and in one fell swoop, had destroyed both. But no matter how far he'd sunk, forcing himself on a woman was unimaginable.

Sweeping the edges of her robe closed, he secured the belt, making certain every inch of her was covered, from neck to ankle. "Turn over," he ordered. "No more talking."

And no more touching. He needed every remaining

hour to recharge his batteries because he could predict exactly what sort of trouble the morning would bring.

Eventually his prediction was proven all too correct. At dawn the next day Merrick awoke—as he was certain he would—with guns pointed at his head.

Four

Alyssa stirred, switching from soft, sweet dreams to heart-pounding alertness in a single breath. She didn't understand what caused the sudden burst of fear. She only knew that it slapped through her, causing her pulse to race and a bitter metallic burn to scald her tongue. She started to speak but Merrick's arm tightened in clear warning and she fell silent.

"Don't move, sweetheart." Merrick whispered the instruction, his mouth nuzzled close to her ear. "I'll protect you. Just do exactly what I say. And…trust me."

Trust him? Of course she trusted him. The thought was immediate, instinctive and totally wrong. In the next instant, her brain kicked into gear and she remembered who he was, what he'd done. How his actions had put her mother's life in jeopardy. And she remembered a lifetime of her mother's warnings—never trust a man.

They'll always betray you. No, she didn't trust him.
Not in the least.

"Squeeze my hand if you're ready."

With no other choice, she did as he instructed and he
shifted her within his arms, just the gentlest of movements, as if they were lovers easing into a more comfortable position. And then he seemed to explode. One
instant she was held in the sweetest of embraces and the
next she found herself cocooned in pillows with her
face pressed against Merrick's broad back.

He'd somehow grown during the night, turning into
a human wall. It was the only explanation for how he'd
become twice as tall and broad as he'd been just hours
ago. The muscles across his back were roped into taut
steely cables, contracting smoothly in preparation
for…for what, she wasn't quite certain, other than it
would undoubtedly be violent. She dared one quick peek
around her human Stonehenge and stopped breathing.

There were six of them. Each wore the sort of black
special ops gear that her abductors had the previous
day. And each held an assault rifle pointed directly at
Merrick's head. She shuddered. Not good. Not good at
all. She could sense Merrick's compulsion to act, which
would have only one horrific outcome. She needed to
put an end to their little standoff, and fast, before matters
escalated out of control. Without giving herself time to
consider, she rolled out from behind him and scrambled
to the far side of the mattress.

One of the gunmen caught her by the shoulders and
dragged her from the bed, his grip painfully tight.
"Ouch! Let go of me. I'm surrendering, you idiot. See?"
She held her palms up and out. "This means surrender."

Merrick hadn't moved from his crouched position on

the bed. He simply cut his eyes toward the man who held her and said, "Take your hands off her."

He issued the order in a soft voice, barely above a whisper. But something in the tone had the ability to liquefy bone. Everyone froze for a brief instant and the man she'd been grappling with released her. Amazing. Then the leader of the group barked out an order and she was once again wrapped up in a crushing hold. Worse, Merrick received the brunt of the leader's displeasure, taking a fist to the jaw.

She cried out in protest, not that anyone listened to her. The assailants pulled Merrick from the bed. It required four of them to secure him and she took a vicious pleasure in that. If they didn't have guns, she suspected that even six to one odds would bring into question the outcome of this little sortie. She'd have put every last penny she owned on Merrick. Unfortunately, guns were an issue and he must have realized as much because he stopped struggling.

He stood immobile a short distance from her, topping the four men surrounding him by a good three or four inches. She'd heard the term "noble savage" before but until that moment she'd never fully appreciated the meaning. Dressed in black boxers and endless muscle, he exuded elemental male at its finest and most noble. But the expression on his face read pure savage. He addressed the leader of the assailants in Verdonian, a man she suddenly recognized as Tolken, von Folke's right-hand man. Her heart sank. Not assailants, she realized, but a rescue party.

"Yes, old friend, I know what's at stake," Tolken replied in English, apparently in response to Merrick's question. "And it's the only reason you're still alive."

Merrick's eyes filled with fierce conviction. "This is wrong, Tolk. You know that. Our people should be free to choose who they want for their king, not have it orchestrated for them. How many times did we discuss that very issue in university?"

"Silence!"

The order came from one of the men holding Merrick, who followed with a fist to the gut. Not that it had much impact, Alyssa realized, biting back a cry of protest. Lord, the man must have steel-belted abs. Tolken rapped out a reprimand and the man who'd hit Merrick stepped back, looking sullen.

"You'll have to excuse his manners," Tolken said. "He's understandably upset. You took something that didn't belong to you and there is a price to be paid for that. Consider those two blows a down payment."

It was too much. Alyssa fought the man restraining her. Or did he think he was protecting her? Not that it mattered. She didn't like being held by him any better than she liked the attack on Merrick. "He's unarmed. You have no right to hit him."

It was pointless to struggle, but she didn't care. She wanted their attention on her. It never occurred to her to wonder why she'd be so intent on protecting her abductor. She only knew she didn't want him harmed. She kicked at her captor, her heels pounding against vulnerable knees and ankles while she sharpened her fingernails on defenseless skin.

The recipient of her attack must have had enough of her antics. He gripped her wrists in one hand and lifted his other, planning to backhand her. "Stop, you fool!" Tolken commanded, furious. "Have you lost your mind? That's Princess Alyssa, the duchess of Celestia."

Merrick didn't wait to see whether the order was obeyed. Though his arms were pinioned, his legs were free and he put them to good use, lashing out with his foot and knocking the man to the floor. It earned him another fist. Dropping to his knees, he shook his hair from his face and fixed his gaze on Tolken.

"If your man touches her, or even attempts to touch her again, he's dead."

Once again, the words were barely above a whisper, and once again they had an immediate effect on the rescue party. It was subtle, but more noticeable this time, perhaps because she was in a better position to observe. Every one of them stiffened, including Tolken, coming to attention the way subordinates do in the presence of a superior.

As soon as Merrick saw he had their full attention, he added, "And if I don't succeed in killing him, von Folke will."

Tolken hesitated only a moment. She could see the inner battle he fought played out in the souring of his expression. Part of him wanting to defy Merrick's demand, to establish who was in control. The other part recognized the validity of those two simple threats. With a harsh curse, he barked out another order, this one in Verdonian, an order that had the man holding her scurrying from the room. They must not have considered her much of a threat because no one else attempted to secure her. It was a reasonable assessment. She wasn't a threat…at least not in a physical sense.

Merrick maintained eye contact with Tolken, not sparing her so much as a glance. "She won't go with you until she knows her mother's safe."

She didn't miss a beat. "He's right. I'm not leaving here until I talk to her."

Tolken dismissed her with barely a glance. "You will leave when we tell you. As for your mother, Prince Brandt will allow you to speak to her when he sees fit."

"Your Highness," she retorted icily.

The man frowned. "What?"

"You will address me as Your Highness, or as ma'am. But don't you ever again speak to me in that dismissive tone. Not if you value your current position."

Shock slid across Tolken's face, followed by a wash of mottled red. His hands collapsed into fists—fists itching to wrap around her neck if she didn't miss her guess. No doubt Merrick could sympathize. As though aware of his regard, she spared him a brief glance and he gave the barest nod.

"Get my mother on the phone. Now."

"I can't do that, Your Highness," Tolken said through gritted teeth.

Folding her arms across her chest, she dropped to the edge of the mattress. "Then I'm not going anywhere." One of his men took a step toward her and she shot him a warning look, deciding to follow Merrick's lead. "Don't even think about it. I may not have the power to stop you right now, but as Prince Brandt's wife, I plan to have a long and vindictive memory. If you dare put your hands on me again, I'll make you pay. And I'll make sure it's both inventive and painful."

To her surprise the man believed her. He stopped in his tracks glancing helplessly from her to Tolken. Behind him Merrick's lips twitched, forcing her to struggle at maintaining her "ice princess" demeanor. Damn the man. Didn't he understand how difficult she found all this? They had guns, for crying out loud. Prince Brandt held her mother hostage. And she'd been abducted—twice in two days. It wasn't a game and it sure as hell wasn't amusing, no matter how absurd the situation had become.

The stalemate lasted for endless seconds before Tolken caved. Plunging a hand into his pocket, he yanked out a cell phone and placed a call. Alyssa was fairly certain he spoke directly to Prince Brandt. They conversed for several minutes in Verdonian before he handed her the phone.

"Ally? Baby, is that you?"

Static sounded in her ear, but Alyssa could still make out her mother's distinctive voice and it brought tears to her eyes. "Hi, Mom. Are you okay?"

"What's going on?" Fear rippled through her question. "What's happened? Why is everyone so angry? Where are you?"

"Everything's fine, Mom." She used her most soothing tone, one that came naturally whenever she spoke to her mother. After all, she'd had a lifetime worth of experience calming her, reassuring her, taking care of her the best she knew how. "I'll be there soon. I promise." Before she could say more, Tolken yanked the phone from her hand. "I wasn't finished," she protested.

"Don't push your luck, Your Highness. We've done as you asked. Now you will come with us without any further argument or discussion." He put the phone to his ear and spoke for another moment before breaking the connection. Thrusting the phone into his pocket, he addressed his men. "Our top priority is retrieving the princess and ensuring her safe return to His Highness."

Alyssa struggled to maintain her composure while they spoke around her, referring to her as though she were a package. A possession. That's all she'd been since the moment she'd stepped foot in this blasted country and she was getting darned sick and tired of it.

"What about the commander?" one of the men asked, nodding toward Merrick.

Alyssa sat up straighter. Commander? Commander of what? Not that she had the opportunity to ask, not while they were busy determining Merrick's fate. She shot him an apprehensive glance. He didn't seem the least concerned. She remembered comparing him to a lion when she'd caught her first glimpse of him. Perhaps she'd been mistaken. He was more of a leopard than a lion, she decided, all lean muscle built for power and speed. There was also a ruthlessness about him, she associated more with leopards than lions, a deadly intent. A crouching watchfulness that preceded explosive action.

His eyes glittered a hard, winter-bright gold, watchful and determined. Whether these men knew it or not, they'd already lost. This man didn't fail, no matter how huge the odds or how dangerous the mission. She took a fierce pleasure in the knowledge before realizing that should Merrick succeed, she would lose. He'd prevent her from returning to her mother by any and all means at his disposal. How was it possible that every instinct urged her to trust him when it put her mother's life in jeopardy?

But no matter how hard she tried to picture him as the enemy, what she recalled most strongly were his arms wrapped tight around her and his hands and mouth offering the most intense pleasure she'd ever experienced. "Trust me," he'd said. She wanted to. God help her, she wanted to. And perhaps she would, if it weren't for her mother.

Tolken had reached his decision and he confronted Merrick. "I know you, old friend. It's too risky to bring you back on the helicopter with us. We'll secure you here on the premises." He stabbed a finger at three of the four remaining guards. "You will remain behind and guard him. He can be retrieved later and dealt with at that point. You will make sure he doesn't escape. His Highness will be most disappointed if you fail to do so."

"Prepare to be disappointed," Merrick murmured. "I won't be here when you return."

One of the men still surrounding Merrick raised his hand, but a single glance at Alyssa had him thinking better of it. Still, it prompted her to sweep to her feet. "Enough! I won't have a man beaten in my presence. In fact, you will keep your hands off him until he's turned over to Prince Brandt. Is that clear?" She didn't dare wait for a response since she didn't know how much longer she could maintain her bluff of future retribution. She turned to Tolken. "I need clothing, including shoes."

"Of course, Your Highness." He looked discomfited. "I—"

"Closet and dresser," Merrick said. "You'll find everything you need."

Tolken signaled his men to secure Merrick and leave. Alarmed, Alyssa took a swift step in his direction, only to stop short when she realized the inappropriateness of her actions. She stared at him in dismay, bewildered when he returned her gaze with one of calm confidence. A half smile hooked the corner of his mouth, his scar giving him a mischievous appearance that sat at odds with his warrior nature.

She didn't understand it. They were going to take him away now. They'd tie him up while they returned her to Prince Brandt. Once on the prince's turf Merrick would

be punished, severely, she suspected. And there was
nothing she could do about it, nothing at all, not if she
wanted to protect her mother.

She should hate Merrick for what he'd done, but she
didn't. For some strange reason, she wanted to protect
him every bit as much as she wanted to protect her
mother. How could that be? He'd abducted her. Stripped
her. Bound and gagged her. He thought she was moti-
vated by greed and ambition. He'd taken her captive.
Forced her to share a bed with him. Held her in his
arms. Kissed her until she couldn't see straight. Touched
her in ways no man had ever touched her. She ought to
congratulate Tolken and his storm troopers. Offer
profuse thanks. Instead, she wished them all a swift
journey straight to hell.

The man who'd been sent away earlier appeared in
the doorway. "Sir, the helicopter's arrived. We can
depart at any time."

Tolken jerked his head in Merrick's direction. "Take
him," he instructed. "See if there's a root cellar and
secure him there. The rest of you wait for me by the car."

Without another word, they escorted Merrick from
the room, the men filing out one by one until only
Tolken remained. Yanking open the closet door, he
removed the slacks and blouse and tossed them to
Alyssa. "I'll be waiting outside the door to escort you
to the helicopter as soon as you're dressed." He paused
in front of her. "And I believe these belong to you. A
wedding gift from His Highness, weren't they?"

He opened his hand and held out the amethyst and
diamond earrings Prince Brandt had given her the
day before. Had it only been yesterday? Good grief.
She vaguely recalled leaving the earrings in the

bathroom when she'd showered. Color tinted her cheeks at the hint of reprimand in Tolken's voice. But what did he expect? For her to wear them to bed…with Merrick? The ludicrousness of the whole sorry mess struck her and hysterical laughter vied with embarrassment.

Lifting her chin, she regarded him with as much composure as she could manage. "Thanks." She accepted the earrings and, since he continued to stand there and wait, put them on.

He gave a nod of approval and stepped into the hallway. The instant the door closed, she crossed to the small dresser shoved against one of the walls and checked the drawers. Sure enough, she found under-clothes with the tags still on them. Had Merrick chosen them, or had his sister, Miri? Not that it mattered.

The plain cotton underpants and matching bra fit reasonably well, though the bra felt a trifle snug. To her relief, they'd gotten the size of the blouse right, the soft taupe a color she often chose to wear. The plain slacks, several shades darker than the blouse, also fit well, if a little loose at the waist. She suspected the clothes had been chosen for their simplicity and in the hopes that the wearer wouldn't attract any undue attention. Under-standable, if regrettable. Had the circumstances been different, she'd have wanted to attract as much attention as possible. Next, she found a pair of sandals in the closet. They were a tad large, but the various straps and buckles could be tightened to compensate.

Glancing in the mirror, she groaned. No wonder Tolken had treated her with so little respect. She looked like a woman who'd made a rambunctious night of it. Checking the rest of the drawers, she lucked onto a comb and used the remaining few minutes taming the curls billowing around her face. That's what came from going to bed with wet hair.

Finished, she opened the door, surprised to discover that Tolken wasn't waiting for her after all, but another man stood in his place. "Where's your boss?" she asked.

"I'm to escort you to the helicopter," he replied.

"What about Merrick?"

He didn't answer, but jerked his head toward the steps. She preceded him down and crossed to the front door. She managed a swift glance toward both the kitchen and the great room before she exited the house, but didn't see anyone. Perhaps they'd found that root cellar Tolken had referred to and were busy tying up Merrick. It was a depressing thought.

Outside, more men stood around the vehicle waiting to transport her to the helicopter. As soon as she settled inside they drove a short distance to a narrow valley tucked between the mountains. A large black chopper squatted in the middle. Off to one side a half dozen men were lounging on the ground in a small group while another half dozen stood guard, their weapons at the ready. She didn't have time to do more than glance at the contingent before being helped into the helicopter. Tolken had brought far more men than she'd realized. Clearly, Prince Brandt wasn't taking any chances. He wanted her back and would use every resource available to ensure it.

She glanced up to thank the man who'd assisted her onboard and stared at Merrick in utter disbelief. "What? How…?"

He smiled, taking far too much enjoyment in her astonishment. "I had men surrounding the house. They liberated me."

She fought to make sense of it all. "But, that means…. You knew Tolken would find me?"

"I had a pretty good idea. I had my men stationed, ready for that possibility."

"It was all a setup?" she demanded. "You knew in advance that Tolken and his men would raid the house? You knew we'd wake up with guns pointed at our heads?" At his nod of confirmation, the full impact of his admission struck and unbridled fury took over. "How could you put yourself at risk like that? If one of those idiots had been a little more trigger-happy you could have died! How could you be so foolish?"

He gave her an odd look. "And you," he pointed out. "I put you at risk, as well."

She waved that aside. "They wouldn't have hurt me. Prince Brandt would have had their heads if I'd been harmed. But you… Damn it, Merrick. I'm sure they considered you expendable. Those men were out for blood. Yours, if I'm not mistaken. They—" Her voice broke. "They beat you."

He dismissed that with a casual shrug. "Fortunately for us Tolken had them well under control, a fact I was counting on since we'd both been trained by the same man—a man who abhorred unnecessary bloodshed." He held out his hand. "Now, if you don't mind, hand over your earrings."

The change of subject baffled her. "Why?"

"Tolken found you thanks to them." He hesitated. "You'll be pleased to know they've also helped prove your innocence."

Too much had happened in too short a time. She didn't understand anything anymore. When he made a move toward her, she held up her hands. "Stop. Just stop a minute and explain it to me in short, easy-to-digest monosyllabic words. Use sentences and paragraphs only if there's no other option."

He assisted her into one of the seats. Tucking her hair out of the way, he proceeded to strip her of the earrings. He held them up. "Von Folke gave these to you?"

She nodded. "As a wedding gift."

"They have a tracking device embedded in them." He allowed that to sink in before adding, "It confirms the story you've been telling me about being forced to marry von Folke. He wouldn't have needed to plant a tracking device on you if you'd chosen to marry him of your own free will. It only would have been necessary if he'd been concerned that you might try and run."

Outrage left her breathless. "That's how Tolken found us? I was...I was *bugged*?"

"Yes."

"And you knew they'd come for me?"

He shrugged. "Suspected. Hoped." Crossing to the open doorway of the helicopter, he tossed the earrings to one of his men. "If Tolk came after you, I could secure him and his men long enough for us to disappear. It worked. Now you and I will head out and Tolken will return to von Folke empty-handed."

"But, isn't this his helicopter?"

Merrick grinned. "Kind of him to lend it to us for our escape, isn't it?"

"But, isn't it bugged or...or have some sort of tracking device on it, too?"

"It is and it does. Too bad it's been disabled or he'd

know where we were going." Turning, he signaled the pilot. "Now, if you'll fasten your seat belt, Princess, we'll take off."

The blades began to whip around. "Please don't do this." She had to shout to be heard over the growing roar of the engines and blades. "Please. Just let me go with Tolken."

"Sorry, Princess. I can't. I'm afraid you're stuck with me for the duration."

The noise grew too loud to allow for further conversation. After a few minutes, the chopper lifted off and banked to the south. They climbed over the ridge of mountains separating Avernos from Celestia, a feature Alyssa remembered seeing on the map the previous evening. It didn't take long until they were on the other side and she caught her breath at the beauty of the rolling green hills spread before them. Rain clouds drifted off and the sun broke through, sending a rainbow spearing toward earth. She'd been born there, she marveled. She'd come from this place.

Eventually, the helicopter set down in another field, bordered by a dirt road. A car was parked off to one side along the grassy verge. As soon as she and Merrick had exited the craft, the chopper departed, winging northward once again.

"You had this all carefully planned, didn't you?" she asked as soon as the noise had faded enough to speak.

"It's my job to plan carefully."

Alyssa planted herself in front of the man who'd abducted her for the second day in a row, facing him with a fierceness born of equal parts exhaustion and anger. "Who are you?" she demanded. "I mean, really."

"We were never formally introduced, were we?"

She folded her arms across her chest. "No. This might be a good time."

He surprised her by sketching an elegant little bow. "Merrick Montgomery, at your service, Princess."

Not only a leopard, but a graceful one with old-world manners. She didn't want to notice such things. She wanted him to be rotten and evil so she could focus on escape, instead of being distracted by how he looked and moved, spoke and smelled. And kissed. Those kisses had been the ultimate distraction.

"This is ridiculous," she muttered.

He nodded in agreement. "Bordering on the bizarre."

"You still haven't told me what you do. How did you become caught up in all this?"

"I'm commander of Verdonia's Royal Security Force." At her blank look, he clarified, "It's the security contingent for the country as a whole, rather than any one principality."

"Like the army or something?"

"Or something. A specialized armed forces."

That explained Tolken and his men's demeanor toward Merrick, as though they were subordinates addressing a superior. It also explained their apprehension. What the hell had she become involved in? And how could she get herself and her mother out of it? "Well, Commander, would you mind explaining to me how snatching an innocent woman is part of your job description?"

"It's my job to see to the safety and protection of my country and its citizens. That includes you and your mother, something I'll deal with before much longer." He started across the field toward the car. He didn't even check to see if she followed, though considering she had nowhere else to go, it was a bit of a no-brainer.

"Now let's start at the beginning, Alyssa. How and why did you come to Verdonia?"

He spoke English with a near perfect accent. But it still held a gentle lilt most noticeable when he said her name. Was there nothing about the man she could despise? "I was about to start a new job."

He nodded. "Assistant Vice President of Human Relations for Bank International in New York City."

"Do you remember my saying that, or did you have me investigated?"

"Both."

Did they have a dossier on her? She found the idea unnerving. Did he know about all her jobs? About how, since college, she'd bounced across the country, from position to position, always looking for the "perfect" one? The perfect place to finally, finally put down roots? Did he know about her mother's background, as well? Oh God.

"My mother—Angela Barstow—sent me an express envelope. It contained a brief note begging me to help her out of a jam she'd gotten herself into. And she sent an airline ticket." Alyssa shrugged. "What could I do? I flew out to help."

"This jam, as you call it—what was it?"

Alyssa frowned. "She didn't say. She and my current stepfather recently broke up and she often runs away after—" She broke off, aware she'd said too much. "She thought an extended trip to Europe might give her time to get over him. I don't know why she returned to Verdonia. Maybe she got it in her head to visit my half brother for some reason. Perhaps she wanted to visit my father's grave."

Merrick swiveled to face her. "Is it possible she set you up deliberately? Could she be working with von Folke?"

Five

Alyssa glared at Merrick. "My mother working with von Folke? Not a chance," she retorted without hesitation. "She's the least devious woman I know. She's…helpless. That's why I need to get to her as soon as possible."

With a noncommittal nod, he continued on to a white sedan and opened the passenger door. "That's not going to happen, Princess. You're going to have to trust me when I say that von Folke won't do anything to harm her."

Instead of climbing in the car, she slammed the door shut. "I'm supposed to trust you?" she demanded. "How can you even suggest such a thing? What have you done to inspire my trust?"

"Not a damn thing." Merrick dropped his hands to Alyssa's shoulders. "Since you haven't known me long enough to trust me, consider this…. Tolken and his men know I've taken you against your will. I made that clear to them. They also know that you were willing to return to von Folke. Hell, you were eager to. The fact that you weren't able to isn't your fault and everyone will recognize that fact. There's no advantage to hurting your mother. It won't help his cause."

It made sense, but she didn't dare risk her mother's life based on Merrick's brand of logic. "You can't be certain. Not a hundred percent certain," she argued.

"I can, and I am. Right now von Folke has a certain level of sympathy. Someone has stolen his bride and that has the potential for swinging votes his way—assuming he makes that information public knowledge. I'm betting he'll keep it quiet for the time being. There are too many variables beyond his control to risk any sort of general announcement."

"What variables?"

Merrick ticked off on his fingers. "If it comes out that you were forced to the altar, his credibility is called into question. If we make it public that von Folke's holding your mother in order to ensure your compliance. If the point is made that by forcing you to marry him, he would win the throne. All of these variables are out of his control and of substantial risk to him. No, he'll remain silent. Instead, he'll send men after us in the hopes of recapturing you without creating an uproar."

"Aren't you concerned about that?"

"We have a few advantages of our own. Tolken is…" He frowned, seeming to struggle for the right words. "You have state law enforcement in your country, do you not?"

"Yes. Local police. State troopers."

"Tolken is like that. As von Folke's right-hand man, he enforces the peace within the principality of Avernos. You also have law enforcement that supercedes the state level?"

"Of course. Federal agencies."

"I am the equivalent of that. It would be frowned upon for Tolken to come into Celestia and attempt to enforce the law. When he comes—and he will—it'll be on tiptoe, whereas I only have to tiptoe if it's to my advantage."

"Okay, I get it. Commander tops the principality police." She returned to the issue that worried her the most. "I still don't see how that guarantees my mother's safety."

"The only way von Folke succeeds is if you're willing to marry him. If you return and discover your mother's been harmed, I can't see you agreeing to cooperate with his plans. It's in his best interest to keep your mother healthy."

"And if he decides his plan is a bust?" she protested. "Don't you think he'll want to get rid of everyone who knows what he attempted?"

"Including you and me?" He gave it a moment's consideration. "All the more reason to stay well away from him until after the election."

"At which point he can take his anger out on my mother."

He fought to hang onto his patience. "I'll find a way to free your mother."

"How?" she demanded.

"Again, you'll have to trust me."

She wanted to. She wanted to more than she cared to admit. Every instinct she possessed urged her to allow him to take control of the situation, to yield to his superior strength and conviction. But she didn't dare. "I can't," she said at last.

"Why?"

She hesitated, not certain she wanted to reveal such personal information. But something in his eyes held her, demanding the truth. And she found herself telling him, opening herself in a way she hadn't with any other man. "I spent a lifetime watching my mother run from one bad situation—and man—straight into the arms of another. Each time she trusted the new man in her life and gave up all her power and control, allowing her new husband to dictate how and what and when and why. And each one betrayed that trust, leaving her worse off than she'd been before."

"Hell, Princess." He was seriously taken aback. "How many stepfathers have you had?"

She waved his question aside. "That's not important."

"I disagree. I think it may be very important."

She shook her head, refusing to betray her mother. "The bottom line is that long ago I promised myself I'd never repeat the same mistakes she made. I'd stand on my own two feet. Control my own life. Make my own decisions. And the main decision would be to never allow any man to tell me what to do or how to live my life."

"And now you have a man doing just that." He blew out a harsh breath. "Tough break."

"It has been. Until now." She paced away from the car, gazing toward the mountains that bordered Prince Brandt's principality. "So far I've lived my life my way. I haven't let any man control me. I'm tired of playing the victim. One way or another, I'm going to take control again, to determine my own fate."

"Good for you. In four months, you can get right back to doing that."

She spun to face him. "Not in four months. Right now. I'm going to find a way to rescue my mother. You can either help or get out of the way. But I'm not going into hiding for the next four months and leave my mother to Prince Brandt's mercy. You can't guard me every second. Sooner or later I'll find an opportunity to escape and I intend to seize it with both hands."

"Thanks for the warning. I'll make sure I don't give you that opportunity." He opened the car door again. "Please. Get in."

"And if I refuse?"

"I'd rather you didn't."

"But if I do?"

His expression remained adamant. She could no more move him than the mountains at her back. "I plan to succeed," he stated.

"No matter who gets sacrificed?"

He didn't answer. He didn't have to. "Please. Get in the car." He waited until she'd reluctantly complied before leaning in to fasten her seatbelt. "In case it hasn't occurred to you, if you'd married von Folke you'd have given up even more control than you have with me. He'd have seen to that. This solution may not be *much* better. But it is better."

She had no response to that.

"And, Princess?"

"What?" she whispered.

His expression softened. "Welcome home."

Alyssa turned her head and stared out the front windshield while Merrick watched in concern. She'd done a fair job at concealing her thoughts from him, but her mouth quivered ever so slightly. He remembered her looking just like that when he'd studied her through the binoculars the day before. At the time he'd thought of her as a lifeless doll, that betraying quiver a result of either nerves or triumph. He knew better now. She might be trying to hide the fact, but he could tell that being in Celestia, knowing her roots were here, had made an impact.

She flicked a swift glance in his direction and then away again. "Where are we going?"

"I have a place nearby where we can spend the night. We can't stay there longer than a day. Tolken may figure out where we are." He grimaced. "It depends on how good his memory is."

"What is this place?"

"A farm that belongs to my grandparents. The place is vacant while they visit my brother in Mt. Roche. That's the capital city of Verdonia."

"So you have both a brother, as well as your sister, Miri. What's his name?"

He hesitated. Would she recognize it? He couldn't afford to take the risk. "It's not important." Before she could comment, he changed the subject. "You're not going to like this next part," he informed her.

"Really?" She lifted an eyebrow. "And which part up to now have I liked?"

Score another point for the princess. "For the rest of the time we're together we'll be sharing a bed, the same as last night."

"No," she rejected the plan. "I can't do that. Not again."

"Why?" Fool. He knew damn well why. They'd only spent one night in bed together and he hadn't been able to keep his hands off her even for the space of those few hours. How was he supposed to succeed in leaving her untouched for weeks...months? "Was it because of that kiss?"

Her gaze jerked up to meet his and he read the answer without her saying a word. Her eyes were an incredible shade of blue, startling in their intensity, even more so with memories of the previous night darkening the color. Her lips parted and he could hear the quickening of her breath. He leaned closer, drawn to that mouth, that amazing, lush mouth. He'd never sampled anything like it, anything so addictive, so intoxicating. He wanted more. He wanted to drink her down until all he could taste was her, until his hands knew her body more intimately than his own, until the air filling his lungs was saturated with her scent and the sound of her voice became the only music his ears could comprehend.

The confines of the car seemed to close in around them, shrinking until only the two of them existed. He reached for her, cupping her head in his hands. Her hair slid through his fingers, the curls knotting around them, anchoring him in place. Not that he wanted to go anywhere. He leaned in until their lips brushed. Parted. Brushed again, harder this time. Sealed. She moaned, a rich, helpless sound that rumbled deep in her throat, like a cat's purr. She didn't even seem to realize she'd made it, a fact he found unbelievably erotic.

Her hands slipped to his chest and she gathered up fistfuls of his shirt. For an instant she relaxed into the embrace, welcoming his touch. Her head nestled into the crook of his shoulder and wayward strands of silky hair clung to his jaw, giving off the faintest aroma of exotic flowers mixed with tangy citrus. And then she released his shirt and her arms encircled him. He could feel her urgency, one that fed his.

Her kiss was filled with a desperate passion, as though snatching life-giving sustenance before the onslaught of a drought. She consumed him with abandonment, greedily drinking in everything he had to offer. And that's all it took to set him off. The combustion was as violent as it was immediate, a flash fire sweeping through him and igniting the overwhelming compulsion to make this woman his on every possible level. He pushed her against the door, angling her mouth for a deeper kiss. Their tongues joined in a sweet, hot duel. Tangling. Warring. Caressing.

This was wrong. Oh, so wrong. Not that he gave a damn. If they'd been anywhere other than in a two-seater with a stick shift threatening mayhem between them, he'd have taken her right there against the door and to hell with the consequences. The only thing that stopped him was the expression in her eyes. A fierce conflict raged in them, physical desire in a pitched battle with rationality. Want clashing with common sense.

He couldn't say how long they teetered on the knife's edge, caught between a mindless, delicious fall into insanity and the far less satisfying retreat toward reason. He could take her, could have her body and use it until he was sated. But it wouldn't be enough. He didn't want just her body. He wanted far more, he suddenly realized. And he wouldn't be satisfied until he had every piece of her. If that happened here and now, so much the better. He could convince her that what had started out as an abduction had become something else altogether. Personal. Vital. Necessary to both of them. Still, he forced himself to make it a fair fight and eased back a scant inch.

She accepted the out he offered and pulled back, gasping for air, staring at him with glazed, bewildered eyes. "Why does this keep happening?"

"Because I'm irresistible?"

She disengaged herself from his embrace and the curls wrapped around his fingers tightened in protest before reluctantly setting him free. "Every time you touch me I come undone." She glanced down at herself and the breath hissed from her lungs. She plucked at her blouse. "Look at me. This is exactly what I'm talking about. How did you manage to do that?"

To his amusement, half the buttons were unfastened. "I don't know how that happened. I thought I'd been cupping your head the entire time."

She fumbled with the buttons. "You have to stop trying to seduce me. It's not fair. It's only supposed to work in reverse. Not in…in… Not this way."

Her comment intrigued him. "You mean, it's accept-able if you seduce me?" He could only come up with one reason why she'd attempt that. The corner of his mouth kicked upward. "You think seducing me will give you an opportunity to escape?"

"If that's what it takes, then yes," she snapped. "Not that I'd have succeeded."

"You might have." He opened his arms. "I'm willing to let you give it a try if you want."

"Oh, ha ha. Very funny. But I've already thought it through. It wouldn't work."

"Why not?" He was genuinely curious.

"Simple. What happens after I seduce you?"

"I go deaf and blind?"

Her mouth twitched before she managed to suppress it. "If I thought you would, I might be willing. Because the only way I'd manage to give you the slip would be if you really did go deaf and blind. And even then, I'd need a three day head start."

He snagged another of her wayward curls and twined it around his finger again, forcing her to look at him. "If I ever get you in my bed for real, if I ever make love to

you—proper love to you—I'd never let you go,
Princess. I'd keep you wrapped up so tight you wouldn't
know where you ended and I began."

She jerked back. It was too much too soon and she
reacted with a feminine alarm as old as time. The female
preparing to flee from the pursuing male. The scent of
want mingled with the fear of domination. As badly as she
needed to retreat, it didn't come close to how badly he
wanted to give chase. Every instinct he possessed urged
him to take her. Now. To forge a bond before she escaped.

She must have read his intent because her hand
groped for the door handle, clinging to it as though it
were a life raft. "I think we should go now." She spoke
with an authority that didn't quite ring true. Moistening
her lips, she tried again. "But I have a condition of my
own before we do."

He buried a smile. He could guess what that condition would be. "Which is?"

"You don't kiss me again. No touching. No sexual
overtures. I need to feel safe."

His amusement died, replaced with regret. Is that
what he did to her? Made her feel unsafe? But then, how
could it be otherwise? He'd abducted the woman. Tied
her up. Forced himself on her—even if she had responded with a passion that blew him away. And he'd
been unable to resolve the issue with her mother, something that left her frantic with worry.

"You are safe," he informed her gently. "You have my
word."

"Fine. Then we can go."

"As soon as you fasten your seatbelt."

She groaned. "I didn't realize I'd unfastened it. Buttons.
Seatbelts. You're a regular magician, aren't you?"

"If I were, I wouldn't bother with buttons and seat-belts. Anyone can unfasten those." He turned the key in the ignition. "I'd find it far more interesting to unfasten you from the inside out."

She didn't reply, but confusion warred with alarm. Leaving her to consider his words, he shifted the car into gear and drove to the farm. He gave her time to explore, keeping his distance so she had an opportunity to come to terms with her situation without his breathing down her neck. Dusk had settled around them when they met in the kitchen for their evening dinner.

"Who's taking care of the farm while your grandparents are away?" Alyssa asked toward the end of the meal.

Had she hoped for rescue from that direction? If so, she'd be sorely disappointed. "There are caretakers who live not far away. I warned them I'd be here tonight." Merrick topped off her glass of homemade buckthorn wine, a wine his grandparents only served to their most honored guests. Much to his relief, Alyssa had been effusive with her praise of the exotic brew, taking to the unusual flavor as though born to it. "They won't inter-fere," he added pointedly.

She accepted the information with a stoic nod. "I've been wondering… What happens to Celestia when I return home? Who will inherit it after me?"

"No one."

She frowned and genuine concern lit her eyes. "Didn't my father have any relatives? Distant cousins or a twice removed niece or nephew or something? The succession can't just end with my brother."

"No." He waited a beat. "But it can and does end with you."

Her frown deepened. "Then, what happens to Celestia?"

He took a sip of the golden wine before replying. "According to law, it'll be divided in half and absorbed by the other two principalities. One portion will go to Avernos, the other to Verdon."

Her distress wasn't feigned. "That seems so wrong."

He shrugged. "It's within your power to prevent."

She started shaking her head before he even finished his sentence. "I can't. My home is in New York. I have an apartment. Responsibilities. I start a new job in another two—"

He winced as she broke off. He could tell she'd only just realized that being held by him for the next four months put more things at risk than just her mother. No doubt she'd lose her job, as well. She'd been thrust into a situation not of her choosing, her entire life turned upside down courtesy of the political upheaval in Verdonia. And there was nothing he could do to change that. At least, not until he could figure out what was behind von Folke's desperate maneuvering.

As much as he regretted the sacrifices her abduction created, he didn't for one minute regret her presence in Verdonia. In the short time they'd been together he'd come to realize that she belonged here. More, he realized she belonged with him.

Now all he had to do was convince her of that.

One look was sufficient to warn it would take a hell of a lot of convincing. Alyssa stood, her smile strained, darkness eclipsing the brilliance of her eyes. "I think it's time for me to turn in," she announced in a painfully polite voice. When he would have stood, as well, she held up a hand. "Could you give me a few minutes? I need some time to myself. I promise I won't try and escape."

"Of course. I'll get our luggage from the car."

"We have luggage?" She laughed, the sound heart-breaking. "You do plan ahead, don't you? At least, for most things."

She left the kitchen and a few minutes later he heard her enter the bedroom. The door closed with a gentle click, leaving Merrick swearing beneath his breath. Damn it to hell. He'd never meant for this to happen. The decision that had seemed so obvious and clear cut a week ago had become complicated beyond belief now that he'd executed it. What he needed was time to think, to review his options, as well as review possible alternatives he hadn't previously considered.

Exiting the house, he removed the luggage and delivered it to Alyssa before retreating to the kitchen. He sat in one of the ladder-back chairs, remembering the summers he and his brother had spent here. Little had changed since then. The heart oak kitchen table remained the same, with only a burn mark from one of his grandfather William's cigars to mar the scoured surface. He could still recall his grandmother scolding her husband for his inattentiveness and the way he'd reduced her to breathless laughter by apologizing with a smacking kiss. The wide plank flooring was just as spotless now as then, as were the whitewashed walls. And every appliance had been polished to a satin sheen.

He poured himself a final glass of wine and carried it out to the front porch to William's rocker. His "thinking chair" as he'd often referred to it. Sipping the wine, Merrick allowed the minutes to ease by. The consequences of his actions weighed heavily, the potential outcomes haunting him. He'd forsaken all he'd held dear, all he'd spent a lifetime creating. Had he made the right decision? Was his purpose just and honorable? Or had he subconsciously allowed personal aspirations to guide his choices?

After two full hours of contemplation, he still didn't have an answer. Giving it up as a lost cause, he returned to the bedroom, groping his way in the dark. After a quick shower, he climbed into bed. If he'd been any sort of a gentleman, he'd have left Alyssa alone. But he couldn't. He needed her. He slid an arm beneath her and tucked her close. He heard her breath sigh into the night as she settled into his embrace.

"I'm sorry," he murmured. "I didn't intend for you to lose your job or to put your mother in harm's way. If I could change any of it, I would."

"You can change it. You choose not to."

He couldn't deny the accusation. "True. Will they hold your job for you?"

"Doubtful. Not for four months." She spoke dispassionately, but he heard the underlying ripple of pain and anger.

"The outcome would have been the same even if I hadn't abducted you. You realize that, don't you?" She stilled in his arms. Apparently that hadn't occurred to her. He gave her the hard, cold truth—at least the truth as he saw it. "If I hadn't interfered you'd now be married to von Folke and your job would still have been sacrificed. This way you'll be free in four months, free to return home and pursue your career once again. I suspect von Folke would have kept you tied to him for a year or two. Possibly longer."

"I…I hadn't thought of that." She fell silent for a long moment. "I don't know what I'm going to do…after."

"You could stay in Verdonia."

Her laugh held a bitter edge. "Pretend to be Princess Alyssa, duchess of Celestia?"

"You are Princess Alyssa, duchess of Celestia. You have degrees in psychology and business administration, with experience in international finance. Your education is tailor-made for the position," he argued.

"I don't belong here."

"You could."

She fell silent for a long time. Then, "Was he your friend?"

The switch in topic caught him by surprise. "Who?" But he already knew.

"Tolken. You sounded…" She paused to consider. "You sounded familiar with each other. More than familiar. Friends. No, more like friends turned enemies."

She continued to amaze him with her insight. "Yes, he was my friend. He was my best friend."

"Until yesterday?"

He exhaled. "Until I put my hands on you. The friendship ended in that moment."

"So much sacrificed by so many," she murmured.

He found the reminder tortuous. "Sleep, Princess. Tomorrow's a long day."

"Where are we going?"

"We need to keep moving. But at least you'll see more of your land."

She twisted within his arms. "Not my land."

"Deny it if you will. But you belong to Celestia every bit as much as she belongs to you."

"And who do you belong to?"

"No one. Nothing. At least, not anymore."

It was a painful truth to face. Though his roots sank

deep into the rich Verdonian soil, they didn't run deep enough to survive this. Von Folke would see to it that he paid dearly for his actions. At the very least, he'd be expelled from Verdonia, a pariah to his people. More likely he'd be imprisoned.

"What will you do?" she asked.

"Finish what I started."

"And then?"

"Face the consequences." After all, he had no other choice. Not anymore.

The next day, Merrick made tracks southward toward Glynith, the capital city of Celestia. He had to work hard to maintain a low profile. He was a public figure and easily recognized. But either Alyssa didn't pick up on the deference they offered him or she put it down to his being the commander of the Royal Security Force.

He'd arranged for several safe houses, though the first they headed for wasn't far from the Celestian capital. He'd debated just driving up into the hills and staying at the anonymous cabin he'd rented there. But he preferred a place that offered more avenues of escape while he waited for von Folke's next move.

He soon discovered that the worst part of the abduction wasn't the wait, but the endless nights. How he ever thought he could spend four full months sleeping with Alyssa, wrapped so tightly together that every luscious inch of her body was pressed against every hard-as-tempered-steel inch of him, he didn't know. After just one week exhaustion rode him almost as hard as shameless desire. Not that she noticed.

The instant he crawled into bed with her and tugged her close, she fell into a deep, abandoned sleep, accepting his embrace as though they belonged in each other's arms. It was almost as if they were two parts of a whole, separate and adrift from dawn until dusk, complete only at night, where within the velvety darkness it felt safe to express emotions they kept well hidden in the harshness of daylight.

To his relief, she didn't follow through on her threat to take off the first chance that presented itself, not that he gave her the opportunity. He guarded her every second of every day. But by the end of their eighth day together, Merrick was sick of staring at the four walls of their rooms and twitching from the effort of keeping his hands off Alyssa, neither of which boded well for the endless weeks ahead of them. She must have felt something similar, because when he suggested a short excursion through the capital city, she leaped at the offer, promising the world in exchange for the chance to be outside.

Driving through the busy streets of Glynith, he pointed out key landmarks, including the royal residence. "Not as impressive as the one in Verdon or Avernos," he observed. "But it serves its purpose."

"It's huge," she replied faintly. "It's so strange to think that my mother once lived there."

He regarded her in amusement. "So did you."

"And I had a father and a brother I can't even remember. I wish..." She swiveled in her seat. "Did you know them? What were they like?"

"I never met your father, but he was considered a good man, committed to Celestia and her people. He came from farm stock, like my grandparents, and loved the land."

Bittersweet emotion swept across her expression. "And my brother?"

"Also a good man. I find it hard to believe that he'd have taken money to abdicate. Perhaps von Folke brought other pressures to bear."

"I can't imagine living your entire life in one place." And yet, he heard an intense longing quivering in her voice. How different would her life have been if she'd grown up here? Had put down roots here? Did she ever wonder? "What about Miri? Has there been any news?"

His mouth compressed. "None. Tolk doesn't have her or he'd have said something when he found us."

"But you can't be sure."

"He wouldn't harm Miri." There wasn't a shred of doubt in his mind. "But, the few times I've called home, no one's heard from her."

And the fear and concern were tearing him apart. What had Alyssa said about so much sacrificed by so many? Here was another sacrifice—one laid firmly at his feet. His noble intentions seemed far less noble all of the sudden. He had so many to protect, so much at stake— more than his future, or Alyssa's new job, or even the safety of Miri and Angela Barstow. There was an entire country to consider. And until he found out what secret von Folke concealed and why he'd become so desperate to gain the throne, Merrick had to put the welfare of the country ahead of the few. He'd put out feelers, but so far he hadn't discovered anything pertinent.

Neither of them wanted to return to their rooms after the drive and Merrick decided to take one more risk and allow them a brief walk through one of the commercial sections near their apartment. A local jewelers window held Alyssa's attention the longest, and she returned a second time on their way back to their rental.

"My favorite is this one." Alyssa pointed to a deep

purplish-blue amethyst with flashes of brilliant red at its center.

Merrick smiled. "You have excellent taste. That particular stone is called a Verdonia Royal. The color is unique to our country and quite rare, like a Siberian amethyst, only with more blue than red. The most common are these ones," he said and indicated a pinkish-lavender stone. "The Celestia Blush. Outside of Verdonia this color is often called a 'Rose de France' but our name has historic significance, so we tend to use it rather than the other."

"And this ring?" She pointed to the centerpiece of the display. "I love it."

They'd caught the eye of the proprietor who waved them in. Before Merrick could stop her, Alyssa opened the door and entered the shop. Hell. Adjusting his sunglasses, he settled the American-styled ball cap he'd recently acquired lower on his forehead and prayed he looked as much like a tourist as Alyssa. Then, he followed her in.

It was too much to hope that the store owner wouldn't recognize him, but the instant he did, Merrick gave a single shake of his head without alerting Alyssa. The owner, a man named Marston, nodded in silent understanding, clearly willing to cooperate if Merrick wished to remain anonymous. Satisfied, he leaned against a nearby counter and watched the two interact.

"Every once in a while the mines cough up a few of the Royals," Marston explained as he slid the ring on Alyssa's finger. It fit perfectly. "They're highly prized and only used in the best pieces. Like this ring."

"It's beautiful. Is this white gold or platinum?"

"The ring is platinum." He spared Merrick a brief

glance and after receiving a nod, rolled into a more fulsome description. "The antique Edwardian setting features a three carat Royal as its center stone and a blue diamond and Blush on either side, each perfectly balanced, and weighing in at 2.1 carats apiece. The broad gallery is bead set with .44 carats of European cut diamonds. Finished with fully mille grained edges, the pierced openwork gives this ring an unsurpassed elegance." He blinked up at Alyssa through wire-rimmed glasses. "Would you like to know what the ring says?"

Alyssa lifted an eyebrow. "The ring says something? Tell me. I'd love to know."

"Our finest pieces are always designed to express a particular sentiment. In this case, the Verdonia Royal symbolizes the union of soul mates. Aside from the unique color, that's why it's so highly prized and so rare. It's considered very bad luck to give or accept one if it's not for true love. But this ring also has a diamond and a Blush. The diamond represents many different things, but mainly strength, love, and eternity. As for the Blush, it was used in olden days to seal agreements and contracts." He pointed to the pattern formed by the pierced openwork of the ring. "And then, see this?"

Alyssa examined the banding more closely. "Why does that pattern seem so familiar?"

Merrick took a look and smiled. "Because it's the shape of Celestia. Historically, Celestia has always been the fulcrum between Verdon and Avernos, unifying the two opposing forces into one country."

Alyssa exclaimed in delight. "So, the pattern represents the unification of the three separate stones into one, right?"

Marston nodded. "Very astute. The designer named

it Fairytale because that's what the ring is. It's a fairy tale with a happily-ever-after ending all in one. Soul mates united in an unbreakable bond of eternal love. That's what it means."

"It's an incredible piece," Alyssa marveled. "I don't think I've ever seen anything like it."

Marston grimaced. "Unfortunately we haven't been able to purchase any stones of this caliber for years. Even the Blushes have become rare. The problem has grown worse over the last few months. Rumor has it that the amethyst supply is drying up." He threw Merrick a hopeful look. "Perhaps you could shed some light on the source of the problem? Are the mines played out, as some have suggested? Or is it simply a means to drive the international price up by creating an artificial shortage?"

Merrick shook his head. "I can't answer that. I wish I could. But I can assure you that we're aware of the problem and it's being looked into very carefully."

A small sound came from the doorway between the retail section of the shop and the back room. An older woman stood there, wide-eyed. "Your Highness," she said with a gasp and swept him a deep curtsey. "We're honored to have you in our store."

Alyssa stiffened. "Your Highness?" she repeated sharply.

The woman offered an understanding smile. "I can tell from your accent that you're an American, so perhaps you don't recognize His Highness. This is Prince Merrick."

"No." Alyssa took a swift step backward. "He's commander of Verdonia's Royal Security Force."

The woman nodded. "That's right. The commander is Prince Merrick Montgomery. His older brother,

Prince Lander, could very well be our next king." Her gaze flitted back and forth between the two and a hint of uncertainty crept into her voice. "I'm sorry. Have I said something wrong?"

"I believe His Highness is incognito, my dear," Marston explained gently.

Before the woman could do more than stammer out an apology, Alyssa slipped the ring from her finger and carefully returned it to the velvet tray. Then turning on her heel, she darted from the store.

Six

Alyssa flew out of the jewelry shop and down the street that led deeper into the commercial district. Instinct was driving her and she simply acted, determined to get as far away from Merrick as quickly as possible. To lose herself in the twisting jumble of avenues that spidered out in all directions.

She'd been deceived. Merrick had deceived her. The thought echoed the painful tattooing of her heart and pounding beat of her racing footsteps. That woman had called him "Your Highness." She'd said that Merrick was a Montgomery, that he and Prince Lander were brothers. And who just happened to be Prince Brandt von Folke's rival for the throne of Verdonia? Prince Lander.

All Merrick's fine talk about wanting the best for his country had been nothing but a lie. Everything he'd done had been to benefit his brother. He'd had an ulterior motive for preventing her marriage, right from the start. If she'd gone through with the wedding, Celestia and Avernos would have voted for Prince Brandt and he'd be king. By stopping the ceremony, Merrick's brother still had a shot at the throne. So much for the better good of Verdonia. More like the better good of the Montgomerys.

She kept up a rapid jog, taking turns at random, forced to slow to a brisk walk when she developed a stitch in her side. The breath heaved in and out of her lungs. How could she have been so stupid? She'd seen the respect with which people treated Merrick. Had caught the casual familiarity with which he referred to Prince Brandt. His air of authority. The way von Folke's men had reacted to him. It simply hadn't occurred to her that it was anything more than the appropriate deference offered to the commander of the Royal Security Force. Now that she knew better, she needed to get away.

Ahead of her she saw a uniformed officer. Was he the local authority? If so, perhaps he could help her reach the American embassy. Before she'd taken more than a single step in his direction, a heavy arm encircled her waist, yanking her against a hard, masculine body—a very familiar hard, masculine body. At the same time a hand whipped across her mouth, cutting off her incipient shriek.

"Not a word," Merrick murmured close to her ear.

He pulled her backward into a pitch-black alleyway. Up ahead the officer paused to speak to someone, and when the man turned his face into the glow from an overhead streetlight, she realized it was Tolken. She stiffened within Merrick's hold.

"I see you recognize our friend." Merrick's voice

was a mere whisper of sound. "It appears Tolk's given up tiptoeing and is being a little more aggressive in his search. That tells me it's time for us to find a new hiding place." His grasp tightened. "Pay attention, Princess. When I tell you to move, you move. Nod if you understand and agree."

A tear escaped before she could prevent it, plopping onto the hand he kept locked over her mouth. His reaction to that single drop of moisture was subtle, but confined within such a close embrace, she felt him stiffen and heard the slight hiss of breath escaping his lungs. It sounded like a sigh of regret. No sooner had the thought entered her head than she rejected it. No. That wasn't possible. People as ruthless as Merrick didn't experience regret.

"You haven't responded, Princess. I'd hate to do this the hard way. Now, will you obey me?"

She nodded in agreement, yet even then, his hold didn't slacken. He maneuvered them backward, deeper into the alley. How he could see, she didn't have a clue. But somehow he managed to avoid the obstacles blocking their path. A few yards further on they reached the opposite end of the alley, which opened onto a dimly lit side street.

"I'm going to uncover your mouth. If you make a single sound, I promise you'll regret it. When I release you, we're going to head back to where I parked the car. We maintain a brisk pace. We walk with purpose, but don't run. Two lovers eager to return home. Clear?"

She nodded again and he removed his hand, ready to silence her again if she so much as breathed wrong. When she simply stood there, he tucked her distinctive hair beneath her blouse and lifted the collar. Sliding his arm from her waist to her shoulders, he tucked her close against him so she was almost concealed from curious eyes and urged her onto the sidewalk. He kept to back streets, emerging close to the jewelry shop. Another block and they reached the parking lot where he'd left the car. The entire way she didn't dare make a sound. But the instant she'd slipped into the passenger seat, she turned on him.

"You lied to me, you bastard. You didn't tell me you were Prince Lander's brother!"

Without a word, he started the engine and thrust the car into gear.

"Don't you have anything to say?" she demanded.

"Not here and not now."

They sped past their apartment without pausing and she twisted in her seat, watching it vanish behind them. "Where…where are we going? Why aren't we returning to the apartment?"

"Too risky. We're moving on. I have another safe house that's not too far from here. We'll spend the night there before heading into the hills."

"But our clothes—"

"Are replaceable. Everything we need I have on me."

She fell silent at that, too upset and emotionally drained to do more than stare out the side window. There was so much she wanted to say in reply, but words failed her. Perhaps it was due to the exhaustion dogging her. More likely it was because she knew if she tried to speak again she'd end up in tears. The drive seemed endless as they darted up and down narrow, winding streets, at times backtracking and circling. After an hour he'd satisfied himself that they weren't being followed and pulled into a drive that lead up a steep embankment.

At the crest of the hill stood a large house with an impressive view of the city.

As soon as they were ensconced inside, he walked her through the place, checking windows and doors as he went. Checking escape routes, she supposed. The home was beautifully appointed, far superior to the apartment they'd shared.

"Whose place is this?" she roused herself enough to ask.

"No one I know personally. No one Tolk can trace to me."

"He found us sooner than you expected, didn't he?"

"Yes."

She could tell that fact had him worried and she couldn't decide if the knowledge brought her a certain level of satisfaction, or if she joined him in his concern. They returned to the living area and Merrick crossed to a well-appointed wet bar.

"We need to talk," he announced, pouring drinks.

"What's the point? You lied. End of discussion."

"You deserve an explanation." He handed her a snifter half-filled with amber liquid. "Here. You look like you could use this."

She cupped the glass in her hands and inhaled the rich, nutty scent as she gazed at him across the wide brim of the cut crystal snifter. "Is brandy the official antidote for betrayal?" she asked.

"You'll have to let me know."

She lifted the glass. "In that case...to trust," she said and took a healthy swallow.

"I apologize, Alyssa. I should have told you who I am."

Her mouth curved in a bitter smile. "And who are you, exactly?"

"Exactly who Marston's wife claimed I was. Merrick Montgomery."

"Don't you mean Prince Merrick? Younger brother of Prince Lander, duke of Verdon." She lifted an eyebrow. "Do I have that right?"

"Yes."

"The same Prince Lander who's competing with Prince Brandt for the throne?"

A muscle jerked in his cheek. "Yes," he said again.

"It would seem your antidote isn't working." She swirled the brandy around the balloon of the snifter. "I still feel betrayed."

"I'm sorry."

"I believed you," she whispered. He didn't say anything and she took another gulp of brandy, choking as the aged wine took a bite out of the back of her throat. "I actually believed you had an altruistic motive for what you were doing. But instead every last action has been to ensure your brother becomes king. What a fool I am. You'd think I'd have learned from my mother's mistakes. Never trust a man, especially one with an agenda."

His anger flashed, hot and potent, causing her to stumble back a step. "Do you think I haven't questioned my own motives?" He tossed back his brandy, as well, though he handled it far better than she had. "That I haven't worried that they might be less than pure?"

She turned her back on him and strode to the French doors that accessed a large balcony. Thrusting them open, she stepped outside. Glynith stretched out far below, the glittering lights of the various buildings turning the city into a virtual fairyland, filling her with a yearning she didn't understand.

She sensed Merrick's approach and spoke without

turning around. "You may have questioned your motives, but it sure as hell didn't stop you from abducting me."

"No, it didn't." He dropped his snifter onto a small table at one end of the balcony, the fragile crystal ringing in protest. "Because it all boiled down to one vital consideration. What was best for Verdonia."

"And your brother's the best choice, is that it?"

"No."

She turned her head, startled to discover Merrick standing almost on top of her. She fought to conceal how everything about him affected her. Profoundly. The deep roughness of his voice. His musky scent. Even the size and shape of his hands captivated her on the most basic, primitive level. Her gaze lifted to the sensuous curve of his mouth. His distinctive scar hooked his lip into a half smile. She could still remember how that scar felt beneath her own mouth and she drew a deep breath, forcing herself to ignore everything but getting through the next few moments.

"If your brother isn't the best choice, then why did you abduct me?"

He took the brandy from her hand and set her glass on the table alongside his. "The best choice is whomever the people of Verdonia choose in the upcoming election. But it's their call. Not von Folke's. Not Lander's. Not mine or yours. It's for all of Verdonia to determine. That's what I'm fighting for."

She hated that his words made sense, that they struck a chord that resonated deep within. He stood for a deeply rooted community, for individuals joined together in purpose. It was something she'd longed for all her life. Instead, she'd always hovered on the outside, her nose pressed to the proverbial glass. "And now?

What happens next? Do we continue our four-month pilgrimage?"

"That's no longer possible. Trust is a two-way street, Alyssa. Neither of us trusts the other. So, it's time to take more drastic action."

She swallowed, wishing she had more of that brandy. "I'm afraid to ask what that might be."

"I always had a plan B. I just hoped not to have to use it." His mouth curved in an ironic smile. "We're going to marry."

It took two tries to catch her breath sufficiently to speak. "We're what?"

"Going to get married."

She shook her head. "You've lost your mind."

"Think about it, Alyssa. If I marry you, von Folke can't."

"You've hit on the perfect solution. The perfect way," she marveled, then added furiously, "the perfect way to get my mother killed."

"If we marry, he can't use you as a pawn. You're free. We'll wait a decent interval and then divorce. As for your mother—" he scrubbed a hand across his jaw "—if you marry me, I'll leave immediately afterward to rescue her."

That stopped her. "Are you serious?"

"Dead serious."

"You…you would do that?"

"I would have done it already if I'd believed she were in any real danger." He cocked an eyebrow. "Do we have an agreement? Will you marry me?"

She wished she had time to think it through, to give it more than two seconds' worth of consideration. But she was out of both options and time. She snatched a quick breath and took the plunge. "Yes. I'll marry you."

"Excellent." His satisfaction at her response vied with some other emotion, one she hesitated to put a name to. One that held a frightening element of the personal attached to it. "Then I suggest we seal our bargain."

The words hung between them for an endless moment. The driving thunder of her pulse matched the harsh give and take of his breath. He took a step in her direction, closing the scant few inches separating them. Resolve darkened his eyes and he reached for her, mating their bodies, locking them together in a fit that could only be described as sheer perfection.

There was nothing tentative about his taking, it came lightning fast and deliciously accurate. He knew precisely how to touch her, how to kiss her, how to steal every thought from her head except the burning need for gratification. Desire struck, a sharp, lustful craving that demanded satisfaction. He plundered her mouth, initiating the sweetest of duels.

She surrendered without hesitation. No. Not a surrender. A battle for supremacy. Then not a battle at all, but a giving, one to the other. His tongue tangled with hers, teasing, playing, demanding. His hands followed the length of her spine, his fingers splaying across the curve of her buttocks, fitting her into his palms. He lifted her, pulling her tight against him. She could feel his arousal pressing against her belly and it ignited her own desire, intensifying it. Spurring it to unbearable heights.

She forked her fingers deep into his hair, tilting his head to a more accessible angle. Catching his bottom lip between her teeth, she tugged urgently, before falling into his kiss again. Time and place vanished. All that remained was the harsh sound of breathing, the rustle of clothing, the slide of flesh against flesh. More than anything she wanted him to hike up her skirt and rip through the modest layer of cotton that kept her from him. To drive into her and give her the relief she craved. She'd been alone all her life. Endless, empty days and nights. A life of running from, but never to. She wanted to stop running. To fill that emptiness, fill it in the most basic, carnal way possible. If her mouth hadn't been otherwise occupied, she would have asked for it, demanded it. Begged.

And it was that image—of her pleading to be taken on the balcony of a stranger's home as mindless lust overrode common sense—that acted like a splash of cold water. She shuddered. What the hell was she doing? How could she have been so foolish? Worse, how could she have compromised herself with such ease and so little thought? Had she learned nothing from her mother's example? From Merrick's betrayal? She untangled herself from their embrace, ashamed that she couldn't resist snatching a final, hungry kiss before pushing at his shoulders.

"No more." The words were as much plea as demand. "This is a mistake and I've made enough mistakes in my life without compounding them."

She could see him debate whether or not to push, to take advantage of her momentary weakness. To her relief, he contented himself with feathering a final kiss across her mouth before releasing her. "Consider our bargain sealed."

She moistened her swollen lips with the tip of her tongue. His taste lingered, unsettling her, and she struggled to come up with a way out of the agreement she'd been foolish enough to enter. "About that—"

He lifted an eyebrow, clearly amused. "Going to break your word already?"

She was tempted. Sorely tempted. She'd gotten herself caught in a dangerous situation, one she should have walked away from the minute she'd sensed the trap. But she'd have done anything, agreed to anything, if it meant saving her mother. Now she'd struck a deal with the devil and she didn't doubt for a minute that he'd hold her to it.

"Don't worry, I'll stick. You just make sure you play by the rules from now on."

His grin slashed through the dark. "I'm not here to play by them, Princess. My job is to make them up as we go along."

He'd gotten her with that one and she turned away without another word. She stalked back into the living room, his soft laughter following her, tripping through her, rousing emotions she'd thought were long dead. She wasn't here for romance, she reminded herself. She was here bargaining for her mother's safety. Falling in love wasn't part of the plan. Nor was falling in lust. Regaining control of her life was the end goal and she'd be smart to remember it.

It took her a few minutes to remember where the bedroom was located and once she'd found it, she shut herself inside, praying Merrick would give her time before joining her. Closing her eyes in helpless despair, she leaned against the door and forced herself to admit the truth. She wanted to be swept away by his touch, to drown beneath his kisses. To sink into the powerful surge of his lovemaking before floating on the glorious tide of release that would surely follow. Why? Why did she react to him? Why this man over all the others she'd met in recent years?

She wandered through the darkened room, caught in

the restless ebb and flow of her own emotions. Eventually she found herself standing beside the huge bed. Images flashed through her mind. Male and female, naked. Darkness and light, intertwined on a bed of silk. The first tentative strokes. Gentle. Tender. Soft, urgent cries of need. The slow give and take of the mating ritual. A sweet loving.

Loving.

She spun away from the bed. What in the world was wrong with her? No. Not loving. Sex was one thing. Love, something entirely different. She could use one, enjoy it, without being imprisoned by the other. She lowered her head, dragging in air. Damn it! A single crazed kiss and her hormones were all stirred up and desperate for release. What had happened to her self-control? What had happened to her focus and determination?

She had one single goal—to rescue her mother and return home—and she'd do well to remember that.

"What the hell do you think you're doing?"

Merrick winced as he opened the door a little wider to allow his brother, Lander, access to the safe house. "I don't know what you're talking about." That seemed the smartest response, at least until he had time to find out how much big brother knew.

"I'm talking about the abduction of Princess Alyssa Sutherland."

Damn. Apparently he knew a lot. Too much, in fact. "Who talked?"

"Miri." Lander brushed past him and paced across the living room, as large and aggressive as ever, the embodiment of his nickname—the Lion of Mt. Roche. "She's on the Caribbean island of Mazoné, probably because she knows our mother will wring her neck when she finds out what the pair of you have been up to."

"Thank God she's—" *Safe.* Merrick bit off the word. Probably not the best thing to say to an overly protective older brother. "I'll deal with Mother."

"Good luck with that." He faced Merrick, his arms folded across his chest. "Now where is the princess? She's going back to Avernos right now, even if I have to take her there myself."

Merrick swore beneath his breath. "She's asleep and she's not going anywhere. In fact, you don't want her going anywhere. If you return Alyssa to von Folke, you'll lose the election."

Lander cut him off with a cutting sweep of his hand. "Then I lose the election."

"Don't interfere," Merrick warned. "Alyssa and I are getting married. End of discussion. When we do, it'll put paid to von Folke's scheme and the election will be based on merit rather than regional loyalty."

Lander appeared skeptical. "I can't believe Princess Alyssa is agreeable to such a drastic solution."

"Trust me. When it comes down to a choice between me and von Folke, she's agreeable."

"You swear she's willing?" Lander pressed. "You're not forcing her the way Brandt was?"

Merrick fought back a wave of indignation. "Hell no, I'm not forcing her. I'm not von Folke." Though he couldn't in all honesty claim she was a hundred percent willing. Amenable, perhaps. If he stretched it. "We reached an agreement. She marries me in exchange for my rescuing her mother."

"Son of a—von Folke again?"

"Yes." Merrick took a step in the direction of the door. "You need to go. I don't want anyone to find out we've been in communication."

Lander speared his fingers through his brown and gold mane of hair and glared with hazel eyes that were more green than gold. "I'm not going to be able to talk you out of this craziness, am I?"

Merrick shook his head. "Not a chance."

"Do you realize all you're sacrificing?" Lander asked urgently. "You don't have to do this. Not for me."

"Yes, I know precisely what I'm sacrificing. And yes, I have to do this. By tomorrow it'll be a done deal." He offered a crooked smile. "Just so you know, I consider it well worth the consequences."

Lander cleared his throat. "Thanks."

Merrick executed a slight bow. "My pleasure and my duty, Your Highness."

"Oh, knock it off," his brother said in embarrassment. "Here, I have something for you." He pulled out a computer CD in a plastic case and handed it over. "You requested a set of blueprints to von Folke's palace. I offered to play courier."

Merrick frowned in concern. "You shouldn't have brought these anymore than you should be here. I'm trying to keep you out of this. I want you to have plausible deniability."

"You're kidding yourself if you think that's possible. I could shout deniability from dawn until dusk, and no one would believe it. You're my brother. The assumption will be that I'm in on the abduction and any other actions you take from here on." His face settled into grim lines. "Not that I care. We're not the ones who set this game in motion. Von Folke will have a tough time crying foul play when it's revealed that he's been cheating from the start. Was he really forcing her to marry him? You're certain?"

"Positive. Once Alyssa found out he was holding her mother, she didn't feel she had a choice other than to go through with the ceremony. If I hadn't taken action, they'd be married by now." Merrick gestured toward a small study off the living room. "Come on. There's a computer in there. Let's take a look at what's on the disk."

Lander followed him, leaning against the desk to watch. "I've been going over the situation ever since I found out about von Folke's plan," he said while they waited for the computer to boot up. "I can't figure why he'd pull such a stunt. It's out of character for him."

"I have a feeling it's connected with the amethyst supply drying up. I can't help wondering if something's happened with the mines."

Lander shook his head. "Why would he keep a problem with the mines a secret?"

Merrick considered the various possibilities. "I'm not sure. For political leverage? If it became common knowledge that the mines were tapped out and he hadn't given the country adequate warning, there'd be hell to pay come the election." He slipped the CD into its slot and pulled up the menu. "Okay. Let's see if we can figure the best way for me to get into the palace, nab Alyssa's mother and get out again with our skins intact."

Lander traced his finger along an underground passageway that ran between the interior courtyard of the palace and the chapel. "What about taking this route? You could slip in through the woods near the chapel, take the passageway to the palace and be right on top of them before they knew what hit them."

"Assuming he hasn't blocked it off."

"Hmm. If he has, you'll have to approach from this side." Lander gestured toward the south entrance. "Trickier."

Merrick began jotting down notes, sketching out the bare bones of a plan. "I'll send one of my men in tonight to see which is the most viable choice."

Lander straightened. "So, when's the wedding?"

"What? Oh. Tomorrow."

"We could just...make her disappear for a few months. You don't have to go to the extreme of marrying her."

Merrick tossed aside his pen and stood. "Too risky. She could escape. Von Folke could find her. The variables are endless. Marriage is the only way to make certain he doesn't get his hands on her and finish what he started."

Lander shot his brother a hard look. "Does she know the marriage will have to be consummated in order for it to be legal in Verdonia?"

"It hasn't come up," Merrick answered shortly.

"You're not going to tell her, are you?"

"It won't be an issue."

Lander stared in disbelief. "Are you sleeping with her already?"

Merrick bristled. "That's none of your business."

"I think it is. Damn it! You don't need me to tell you how inappropriate that is. Do you have feelings for this woman? You can't be thinking of turning this into a real marriage."

"Don't be ridiculous," Merrick snapped. "My concern—my only concern—is for Verdonia. Marrying Alyssa is a means to an end, nothing more."

Lander's eyes narrowed. "That had to be the biggest

load of crap I've ever heard. You can stand there and tell me you don't care about this woman, but I'm your brother. I know when you're lying, even when it's to yourself."

Anger swept through Merrick, possibly because Lander's comment hit a little too close to home. "There's more than a relationship at stake. More than even an election. With Alyssa's brother, Erik, abdicating, the principality is in desperate need of its princess. If Alyssa doesn't stay, it means the end of Celestia. I intend to keep that from happening."

"Or maybe you want a justifiable excuse for taking her to bed," Lander suggested dryly.

Merrick didn't have an answer to that. As much as he wanted to deny it, he couldn't. Not totally. Lander was right. In order for their marriage to be considered legal, it had to be consummated. If von Folke suspected there was a loophole somewhere, he could still cause trouble. But the marriage also gave Merrick the excuse he needed to make love to Alyssa. Once they were husband and wife, he wouldn't have any other choice if he wanted the ceremony to be legally binding. Nor would she. Still, he hoped she'd choose to remain in Verdonia and accept her rightful position. Celestia needed her. It wouldn't survive without her.

The real question was…was he making the decision to marry her for the better good of Verdonia? Or was his true motivation something far less honorable?

Seven

The morning of Alyssa's wedding dawned clear and warm, filled with the scent of springtime yielding to summer. The marriage had been planned for early evening when the church would be closed to parishioners and Alyssa couldn't help but remember preparing for a far different ceremony just two short weeks ago. On that occasion she'd been terrified and alone. She'd also feared her bridegroom, been sick with worry about her mother and unsuccessful at discovering a way out of her predicament.

This time she felt far differently, a fact that left her uncertain and confused. She should hate Merrick for twisting her arm to get her to the altar. After all, he was no better than Prince Brandt, right? But no matter how hard she tried to convince herself of that fact, it didn't quite work. Merrick wasn't Brandt and never would be. Although his motives weren't pure, they were noble.

From the moment he'd announced his plan to marry her, events had screamed by at breakneck speed. He'd chosen the venue and had a gown, veil and shoes delivered by one of his men. Even a set of wedding bands had shown up. She didn't bother contesting any of his plans. How could she? It would have been like attempting to derail a runaway train with a toothpick.

As the afternoon deepened, she dressed in the gown he'd selected, a simple three-quarter length ivory silk with a wide, sweeping skirt and fitted bodice. A hip-length mantilla veil looked stunning with it, which she chose to carry, rather than wear and risk damaging on the drive.

The chapel Merrick had chosen was glorious—small, intimate, reverent. The floors were flagstone, worn smooth from years of faithful usage. Stained glass lit the interior with a rainbow of glowing light. The pews and altar were lovingly polished to a high sheen, and the faintest hint of beeswax and lemon complimented the scent of the flowers and candles.

Once again Alyssa was struck with how differently she reacted to everything in comparison to last time. Nervousness gripped her, an excited fluttering deep in the pit of her stomach. Not fear. She remembered that sensation all too clearly. Could it be…anticipation?

She shook her head. No. That wasn't possible. She didn't want to marry Merrick. She'd agreed for one reason and one reason only—to save her mother. She'd made a bargain, one she'd honor no matter what. But it wasn't a bargain she anticipated with any degree of excitement. It couldn't be.

"This is for you." One of the staff members at the church handed Alyssa a hand-tied bridal bouquet, a medley of herbs, ivy and curling sticks and twigs. "It's a traditional bouquet. The herbs are to ward off evil spirits and endow the bride with fertility. The birch twigs are for protection and wisdom, the holly branches represent holiness. And the ivy is to ensure fidelity."

Alyssa ran a finger along the sprigs of lavender. "And this?"

"The national flower. It promises a marriage filled with luck and love."

It was a sweet gesture, if a pointless one. Or so she thought until she joined Merrick in front of the altar. She didn't think she'd ever seen him look more handsome and the sight of him stirred emotions she shouldn't be experiencing. The final glorious rays of sunlight warmed the chapel, filling it with a rainbow of color as soft as a prayer.

Taking both her hands in his, Merrick bent and kissed her. "It'll all work out," he whispered. "I swear it."

His words affected her more deeply than she cared to let on, filling her with a desperate yearning. What would have happened if they'd met under different circumstances? If she'd grown up here and met him as part of her royal duties? Would she have fallen in love with him? Would they have been celebrating a real wedding instead of this charade? Or would they have settled for a brief, intense affair before going their separate ways? The fact that she couldn't answer any of those questions left her nerves jangling.

Afterward, she didn't recall much of the ceremony. From the instant Merrick touched her and their eyes connected, time slowed. She didn't remember looking away, not once, but allowed herself to be held by his fierce golden stare, empowered by it. The one moment that burned itself into her memory was when he repeated his vows, his voice strong and sure, and slipped the wedding ring onto her finger.

She caught her breath at the beauty of the platinum band he'd chosen, a circlet studded with alternating diamonds, Verdonia Royals and Celestia Blushes. Before she could say a word, he bent and took her mouth in an endless kiss. It was in that timeless moment that she realized her feelings for Merrick had undergone a radical change.

And that she was in serious trouble.

Alyssa had no idea what happened immediately after the ceremony. A part of her retreated, stunned by the re-alization she'd made when Merrick kissed her. She'd allowed feelings for him to slip beneath her guard. She cared about him.

She didn't know when or why it had happened. She didn't even know how it was possible after all they'd been through. She simply felt…harmony. A rightness. A belonging. A wild passion that went deeper than anything she'd ever felt for any other man. She burned with it, bled from it. Was consumed by it. And, ulti-mately, she turned from it, refusing to deal with the consequences of those emotions.

They returned to the house tucked into the hills over-looking Glynith, where she'd first agreed to marry him. Silence reigned, neither willing—or able?—to speak. She entered the darkened room and stood in the middle of the living area, still dressed in her wedding finery. She removed her veil, meticulously folded it and set it on the back of the couch. And that's when all her doubts came storming back.

"What have we done?" Alyssa murmured.

"You're just wondering that now?"

She spared Merrick a quick glance, alarmed to discover him in the process of stripping off his suit. "What are you doing?"

"Getting comfortable." He tossed his jacket aside and approached. "Would you like help getting out of your wedding gown?"

She took a quick step backward. "And then what?" She couldn't believe she'd asked the question, despite the fact that it been plaguing her for the past hour or more. "I mean—"

"I know what you meant," he replied mildly.

"I'm sorry." He maintained his distance, but he was still too close for comfort. Everything about him overwhelmed her, filled her with a sense of risk. "I guess I'm not handling this well."

His eyes grew watchful. "Then chances are you aren't going to handle this next part any better." A predatory smile edged his mouth. "After we get out of our clothes, I plan to make you my wife in every sense of the word, even if it's for only one night."

Oh God. He'd said it. He'd actually said the words. Part of her trembled with anticipation, the other with apprehension. Apprehension won. "Not a chance."

"I think there's every chance. You want me as much as I want you." He stepped closer. Too close. "We've shared a bed every night for almost two weeks and it's been sheer torture. Do you deny it?"

"We're attracted to each other," she began, but the expression darkening his face had her faltering. "Okay, fine. I want you. Are you satisfied?" Maybe that accounted for the feelings she'd experienced during the ceremony. Simple desire. Not caring. Not an emotional connection. Lust. It was the only possible explanation.

"There's only one way we'll both be satisfied and you damn well know it. Or are you afraid?" His eyes narrowed. "Is that it, Princess? Are you afraid to take the final step, afraid of what will happen if you do?"

Her chin shot up. "Where do you want it? Here? On the table over there, maybe?" She scuffed a toe in the carpet. "This looks soft enough. Maybe you'd prefer it down and dirty."

She'd pushed him too far. She saw the crack in his self-control, watched as it fragmented and splintered. Before she could do more than take a single stumbling step backward, he snatched her high in his arms. "Personally, I prefer the comfort of a bed."

"Merrick, wait—"

"I've waited as long as I intend to. Tonight we finish it."

Without another word, he carried her down the short hallway and into the bedroom. The skirt of her gown flowed over his arm and trailed behind, a fluttering flag of virginal surrender. Striding to the center of the darkened room, he set her down. She took a quick, desperate look around. Even unlit, she could tell the bedroom was extremely masculine—too masculine. She wanted lightness and femininity and romance—a playful fantasy that softened the harsh reality. This...this was pure male. Unbridled male. Sharp and potent and darkly dangerous. Just like Merrick. She spun around, intent on escape and plowed directly into him.

"Shh," he soothed, gathering her close. "Easy."

"I've changed my mind. I can't." She shot an uneasy look in the direction of the bed. "I just can't."

"Let's see if I can help you with that." He caught her left hand in his and ran his thumb across her wedding band. It gleamed in the subdued lighting. "We made promises tonight. Do you remember them?"

"I promised…" Her chin wobbled. "I promised to love. To honor and cherish."

"As did I." His voice deepened, turning to gravel. "Don't you understand? This ring symbolizes the first chapter in a book you've set aside before even beginning. Don't leave it unread. What's happened so far is no more than the prologue. And then what, Princess? Where does the tale go from there?"

Her breathing grew harsh, labored. "Nowhere."

"That's not true and you know it. It can go anywhere you want. We create the story. We determine the direction. We can even start over if you want and rewrite the beginning." He lifted her hand and kissed her ring. "Or we can move in a new direction. Start fresh on a new page. The choice is yours."

"What about your choices?" She laced her fingers with his, turning their locked hands into the moonlight streaming through the windows. His wedding band splintered the gentle glow, shooting off sparks of silver and gold. "What happens to you when this is all over?"

He hesitated for the briefest moment. "My choices are more limited."

"What do you mean?"

"This can only have one ending for me. Von Folke will see to that."

Alyssa's vision blurred. "You mean jail."

"Most likely." He brushed her cheek with his thumb, erasing the tears she hadn't been able to control. A cloud drifted across the moon, casting their rings into shadows. The glitter dimmed, then winked out. A prediction of their future? "Look at me, Alyssa."

She did as he demanded and saw the calm certainty in his gaze. "I'm not afraid to make love to you." The truth came tumbling out. "I'm afraid of what will happen afterward. What it'll do to us. How it'll change us."

"Trust me."

Those two simple words hung between them. And then the clouds passed and moonbeams once again pierced the dimness, stabbing the room with tines of silver. He stepped back from her into one of the shards, the moon's gilding leeching him of all color. Only the blacks and whites and grays remained, shades of darkness and light, of ambiguity and clarity.

Without a word, he unbuttoned his shirt and shrugged it off his shoulders. It dropped into shadow. Holding her with his gaze, he unzipped his trousers, the metallic sound harsh and grating in the silence of the room. His trousers parted and her mouth went dry. She could barely think above the fierce pounding of her heart. In one fluid motion, he stripped away the last of his clothing before drawing himself to his full height. Totally nude, sculpted by the moonlight, he made for an impressive sight. He stood motionless, allowing her to look her fill.

He had one of the most spectacular physiques she'd ever seen. His shoulders and arms were powerfully masculine, able to bear the heaviest of weights. And yet it struck her that those same arms would also be gentle enough to cradle a helpless infant. The dichotomy moved her more deeply than she thought possible. Her gaze dipped lower, to a chest lightly furred with crisp brown hair just deep enough to sink her fingers into. A narrow line speared downward, like spilled ink, splitting washboard abs on its path to his groin. He was fully aroused, yet made no effort to act on that arousal.

"Why are you doing this?" she whispered.

"So you can see you have nothing to fear." His gaze grew tender. "Whatever you want, it's yours."

"Just tonight." She choked on the words. "It can only be for tonight. You know that, don't you?"

"Then it's just for tonight." He stepped from the light into darkness, finding her where the gloom held her ensnared. "But when tomorrow comes, you may discover that one night isn't enough."

She wanted what he offered, but fear and uncertainty froze her in place. "Tomorrow doesn't belong to us. You've already warned me about that. Von Folke—"

"Will be dealt with. And who knows, perhaps it'll all work out." He planted his feet and spread his arms wide, an oak of a man—strong and sturdy and protective. His heart and soul was rooted deep in the soil of Verdonia, a fact she envied more than she could have believed possible. "Just come with me. Stay with me. Take a chance."

His words sang with endless promise, bewitching her, offering to turn dreams into reality. She gave in to their enchantment. She stepped into his arms and fell from darkness into light.

Alyssa slid her hands across Merrick's chest in a quiet prelude to their mating dance. For the first few minutes they barely touched, just a tentative brush of hands. A whisper of a kiss. Lips joining. Clinging. Parting. Then rejoining. The soft exhalation of desire across heated skin.

This time she was the one wearing too many clothes and she fought to curb her impatience. She didn't want anything separating them, nothing that would prevent them from touching flesh to flesh. And yet, this wasn't an occasion to hurry. She wanted to linger over each and every step, to sear into her memory every moment as it happened.

He found the cloth buttons holding her gown in place, and one by one released them. She lifted her arms, savoring the drag of flesh-warmed silk followed by the cool sweep of air. Her slip came next, skating down her hips to pool at her feet. He dropped to his knees, lifting first one foot free, then the other, leaving her standing in nothing but a bra and thong. Sliding his hands around her thighs, he held her steady as he trailed feather-light kisses from knee to thigh, wandering ever higher until he'd reached the shadowed apex.

His breath was warm through the triangle of silk that concealed her. Hooking his fingers into the elastic band at her hips, he tugged. Her panties drifted downward, seeming to vanish of their own volition. And then he took her, his kiss the most intimate she'd ever received. She threw back her head and dug her fingers into his hair, her throat working frantically.

"Easy, Princess," Merrick murmured against her. "We have all the time in the world."

"Okay. Fine. I just—" She shuddered. "I need to finish getting naked. I need to finish getting naked right now. And then I need you naked on top of me. Or under. I'm not particular."

She felt his smile against her heated flesh. "I can help with that."

All of a sudden she didn't want to savor each moment. She wanted to seize every last one, burn through each second in a swift, glorious blaze. She couldn't handle slow, let alone leisurely. Fast and desperate appealed far more.

"Hurry." He slid his hands from her thighs upward, cupping her, and she practically danced in place. "No, I mean it. *Hurry!*"

But he didn't hurry. Instead, he parted her with his thumbs and blew ever so gently, a mere whisper of sensation before he kissed her again. And that was all it took. She exploded in his arms, unraveling helplessly. A keening wail built in her throat, trapped there for an endless moment before escaping. She hung, suspended in paradise until finally her knees gave out and she collapsed into his waiting arms.

Merrick swept her up, carried her to the bed and spread her across a velvet-soft bedspread. "Why?" Alyssa demanded.

He didn't pretend to misunderstand. "It gave you pleasure." His hand slid behind her back and released her bra. "And that gave me pleasure."

"In that case, prepare yourself," she warned him as he tossed the scrap of silk outside the oasis of the bed. "Your pleasure quotient is about to go through the roof. I'm going to see to that."

Rising to her knees, she slid her arms around his neck and kissed him, a hard, urgent, open-mouthed kiss. To her amazement, desire flamed again, thrumming through her with stunning urgency. It was as though the past several minutes had never happened, as though this was the first time they'd touched, the first time they'd kissed, the first time they'd shared a moment of intimacy. She pressed closer and wrapped herself around him. It was like sliding into a pool of molten heat.

Merrick groaned. "You're killing me, Princess."

"I don't want to kill you, not unless it's to love you to death."

He tipped her onto her back. "I think I can live with that."

Her quick laugh must have provided him with a beacon to her mouth because he honed in on her parted lips with pinpoint accuracy. Sealing them with his own, he drank her in. First fast and needy, then slow and tender, before haste consumed them in a frantic burst of uncontrollable hunger. He snatched a final swift kiss and began sampling her as though she were a buffet of delicacies spread out for his tasting pleasure. Her shoulders. Her neck. Followed by the painfully sensitive tips of her breasts. He ignored her urgent pleas, feasted there while his hands took over, touching, probing, teasing, wallowing in a banquet of tactile indulgence.

The tension grew within her again. Desperate. Demanding. Frenzied. An explosion building toward a new eruption. She shoved at his shoulders, forcing him to give ground. Stabbing her fingers into his hair, she pulled him back to her mouth, consumed him in one fierce, biting kiss before wriggling her hands between them. She found him, fully aroused, steel wrapped in velvet. Scissoring her legs around him, she pulled him inward. Took him. Absorbed him.

Loved him.

He surged to the very core of her, hard and heavy, almost painfully so. She could feel him trying to hold back, to ease his passage into her body and she arched, her muscles drawn taut.

"Don't stop." The breath burned in and out of her lungs. "Even if it kills me. Even if it kills you. Just don't ever stop."

He moved then, mating their bodies in a primal give and take, stroking to the harmony of their own private song. Fire burst all around them, flames licking at her skin, burning through her blood, gnawing at her bones. She could see the brilliance of it, hear its angry crackle, feel the heat exploding within. A scream built, clawing at her throat. She could sense the release approach, more powerful than anything she'd felt before. It slammed into her, the power of it smashing through every barrier. She flew apart, disintegrating into pieces so small they could never be gathered up again.

From a great distance she heard a voice. The voice of her soul mate. "Alyssa." That single word whispered through the air, barely audible. And yet, it did the impossible.

It brought her home.

Merrick woke to complete darkness, uncertain what had disturbed him. It only took an instant to realize what it was. His arms were empty and his bed cold. He sat up, searching the darkness for Alyssa.

The curtains by the balcony stirred, alerting him to her whereabouts. Tossing aside the tangled sheet, he padded nude across the room. The French door to the balcony stood ajar and he stepped outside into the soft, dewy air. He found Alyssa there, leaning against the railing, the bathrobe she'd wrapped around herself fluttering in the breeze. She gazed out at the city where the full moon dipped low in the sky. Its silvery life's blood flowed across Celestia, a river of light pouring across her homeland.

He knew the instant she became aware of him. Without a word, she untied the robe and allowed it to slip off her shoulders. He came up behind her and slid his arms around her waist, tugging her close. Flesh slid against flesh, warm and vibrant and life-affirming. Alyssa twisted in his arms, grasping his shoulders. Cupping her bottom, he lifted her and in one easy thrust, sheathed himself in her heat. Turning, he braced her against the French door.

Then slowly, ever so slowly, he moved with her to a rhythm only the two of them could hear. She arched in reaction, drawing his hands to her breasts, tilting her head back against the cool glass in silent ecstasy. The moonlight painted her with a loving brush, turning her skin luminescent. She glowed with an unearthly passion, a passion that pierced him to the soul. Consumed him. Threatened to destroy him. They clung to each other, riding to the edge, teetering there, poised on the brink of an endless fall. She gathered him up with moonlit eyes, before leaning in and pressing her lips to his ear.

"You're right," she whispered. "One night's not enough."

And then she exploded in his arms.

Eight

Merrick woke early the next morning. Pre-dawn light eased into the room, gilding his wife in a soft, rosy glow.

His wife.

Just the thought filled him with pure masculine possessiveness. Alyssa was his woman, joined to him in every way possible. When he'd first suggested marriage, it had been with the thought of forming an alliance. A contract. He'd wanted her, he couldn't deny that. But it had been a purely physical want, nothing more. He'd intended for their wedding night to consummate their contract, to close all legal loopholes. Now he wasn't as certain of his motivations.

He closed his eyes. Damn. What was he going to do? Their relationship didn't have a hope in hell of succeeding. Too many factors interfered. Little things such as he lived in Verdonia and she in the States. He'd abducted her and put her mother at risk. Most prob-

lematic of all, he was headed for prison, she for a new
job in New York City. Not the most promising foundation for a successful marriage.

The early morning light strengthened, a warning that
time was passing. As much as he hated the idea, he
should leave. He'd made a promise to his wife, a promise
to rescue her mother immediately after their marriage,
and come hell or high water, he'd honor that promise.

Yet as urgently as he needed to head out, he gave
himself a few final minutes to study the sleeping face
of his wife. From the first, he'd found her beauty startling. In an aesthetic sense, it was. But in the weeks he'd
known her, he'd found her character even more beautiful, giving depth and dimension to the physical.

He leaned over and kissed her, lingering, slipping
within. She moaned, her mouth softening, parting, responding even in her sleep. Her eyes flickered opened,
reflecting the sunlight, the color deepening to the sultry
blue of a warm summer sky.

"Good morning." Dreams still clung to her voice,
filling it with a delicious huskiness. "You're awake early."

"Good morning, wife," he greeted her with a slow
smile. "Welcome to our first day of married life."

Unable to resist, he lowered his head and kissed her
again. Cupping the nape of her neck, he nudged her into
a deeper embrace. Her arms encircled him and after a
long moment, she pulled back just long enough to look at
him. He thought she was going to speak, but instead she
slid her fingers into his hair and tugged his head back down
to hers. He didn't need any further encouragement. He
gave in to her, gave everything. Not that he had any choice.
Half measures weren't part of his nature. But he was honor
bound, bound to obligations he could no longer postpone.

He swept unruly curls from her face. "It's time for me to leave."

"Leave?" The hint of sleepy passion ebbed from her voice. "Where are we going?"

"To Avernos."

"Avernos?"

He didn't know whether to laugh or groan at her look of utter bewilderment. He wished he could take credit for her having forgotten, that he could believe she'd been so enthralled by their lovemaking that it had driven every other thought from her head. But he knew the more likely cause was exhaustion. He hated to remind her, to put their relationship back onto a business footing, especially after the night of passion they'd shared.

"Your mother, remember?" When she continued to stare blankly, he added, "Our bargain?"

"Our— Oh, good Lord!" A deep blush blossomed across her cheekbones and she shot him a chagrined look. "One kiss and you drive every intelligent thought out of my head," she admitted.

Her embarrassed honesty had him fighting back a grin of sheer masculine delight. She had forgotten and it hadn't been due to exhaustion. At least he could take comfort in that much when he left. "I've made arrangements for you to stay with some of my men. They'll protect you while I'm gone."

It took a second for his words to sink in. The minute they did, she bolted upright in the bed. The sheet dropped to her waist, and she snatched it up again, tucking it beneath her arms.

"You're leaving without me? No way. I'm coming, too."

He shook his head before she'd even gotten the words

out. "Too risky. It'll be faster and easier for me to slip in, grab your mother and slip out again on my own."

"She won't go with you unless I'm there," Alyssa argued. "You'll need me to convince her."

How should he phrase this? "I'll convince her the same way I convinced you."

He should have chosen a more diplomatic way of wording his explanation, perhaps something in the nature of a flat-out lie. Rage lit her eyes. "You're going to abduct my mother?" she demanded in disbelief. "You're going to terrorize her the way you did me? That's just great. Brilliant plan, Prince Charming."

He gritted his teeth. "I may not have any other choice."

"You can't do that. She's not like me. She doesn't get angry in scary situations. She'll be terrified."

"Only until I get her clear of the area." Didn't she understand? He'd been trained for this, damn it! He knew what he was doing. "I'll explain everything to her then."

"Please, Merrick. Don't do this. There's only one of you. You're one man against all of Prince Brandt's forces. Against a royally ticked off Tolken, in case you've forgotten. And you'll be abducting a struggling uncooperative woman who will be crying and screaming the entire way. Somehow I don't think that's going to work. Unless, of course, you plan on holding a knife to her throat." Her eyes widened in sudden alarm. "Oh my God. Is that your plan? To use a knife on my mother?"

Hell. Didn't she know him better than that by now? "Of course it isn't. If it'll help satisfy you, I'll arrange to bring a few men with me. But I still can't risk taking you."

"Can't risk…? And just what am I supposed to do when you're captured?" she protested. "Spend the rest of my life hiding out with your men?"

Morning had fully broken and brilliant light flooded through the window, washing over her. It struck her jeweled wedding band and splintered, shooting miniature rainbows of color in every direction. A conflicting combination of pleasure and sorrow surged through him. The ring looked right on her finger, as though it belonged. It was a declaration, a promise, a pledge for the future. His jaw firmed. A future they'd see together, no matter what it took.

She stood, struggling to wrap herself in the length of soft Egyptian cotton sheet. "It only makes sense to bring me with you," she argued as she worked the knot.

Merrick snagged a pair of jeans from his overnight bag. "Maybe to you. Not to me."

"But we're married." She thrust a tumble of curls from her eyes. "There's nothing Prince Brandt can do anymore. You've stopped him."

"You don't know the man. There's plenty von Folke can—and will—do."

She folded her arms across her chest and the knotted sheet slipped a tantalizing inch. "Then he can and he will, whether I'm with you or not."

"I can't risk that. I can't risk you," he corrected.

"Right back at you, husband."

Husband. She'd called him husband. He approached and grasped the ends of the loosened sheet. With quick, economical movements he retied it. "Lyssa. Princess." He smiled. "Wife. You have to trust me."

"I do. It's just—"

"No, not just. No debate." He cupped her face, forcing her to look at him. "Yes or no. Do you trust me?"

Her mouth quivered. "You have no idea what you're asking."

"I know precisely what I'm asking. And you haven't answered my question." He feathered a kiss across her mouth. "Listen to your heart. What does it tell you?"

The answer he wanted hovered on her lips and glowed in the sudden softening of her eyes. The events of the life she'd shared with her mother had forced her to erect self-protective barriers, to regard others with deep suspicion. To distrust. But now those barriers trembled, their foundation shifting and he knew that he was close to breaching them.

"Merrick—"

His cell phone rang before Alyssa could say anything further. He was tempted to let it ring, to force her to answer his question. But only a limited number of people knew where they were. And they'd been told to contact him only in case of an emergency. He crossed the room and snatched up the receiver. "Montgomery."

"They've found you," his man informed him, a hint of urgency underscoring his words. "Von Folke's man, Tolken. He's on his way to the safe house. Please, Your Highness, you must leave immediately."

"What? What's happened?" Alyssa demanded the instant he cut the connection.

"Tolken. He's on his way here." Merrick grabbed the overnight bag and dumped the contents onto the bed. "Get dressed. Fast."

She didn't waste time talking. Ripping off the sheet, she started throwing on clothes. In less than a minute she was ready to go. Merrick spared precious extra seconds rolling up her wedding gown and stuffing it into the bag.

"What are you doing?" she asked. "We have to hurry."

"We're not leaving your wedding dress."

"Sentiment?"

He spared her a brief look. "Don't get misty-eyed on me. I don't want to leave any evidence behind of our marriage. No point in giving them an edge." At her stricken look, he added. "Okay, so maybe there's a little bit of sentiment involved. Grab your veil and head for the car. I need to clean out the study."

In under five minutes they were on the road and racing away from Glynith. He deliberately headed north toward Avernos, hoping Tolken would expect them to travel south to Verdon since it was Montgomery-controlled.

"What now?" Alyssa asked.

"I'll arrange to rendezvous with one of my men and pick up the equipment I'll need to rescue your mother. He'll take you with him to another safe house. With a bit of luck your mother and I will join you there within twenty-four hours."

"Let me come with you." She spoke urgently and he suspected tears weren't far off. "I can help."

"No, you can't."

A quick glance confirmed the tears—tears she seemed determined to keep from falling. "We're married now, Merrick. If we approach Prince Brandt with that fact, maybe he'll let us take Mom home without any hassle."

"I have no intention of approaching von Folke, let alone confronting him about our marriage. If I had my way we wouldn't come within a hundred miles of the man." He shot her a concerned look. "I'd keep you a solid thousand miles away, if I could."

She managed a smile, though he could tell it took an effort. She fell silent after that and two hours later they reached the rendezvous spot. To his frustration, his man wasn't there. Nor did he answer his cell phone or show up in the three hours they sat and waited. Finally, Merrick started the engine.

"Change of plan, Princess."

"I'm coming with you?"

"You're coming with me."

"What about the supplies you need?"

"I know a place I can get them. But this worries me."

They crossed the border between Celestia and Avernos in the early hours of the morning. Merrick parked near the location of Alyssa's abduction. Once he had the car secured, he reached into the back for the equipment he'd purchased. His wife stood patiently by while he helped her strap on a pair of night vision goggles and instructed her on their operation. Then he led the way through the woods toward the chapel.

On the edge of the woods, he caught Alyssa's arm and drew her to a stop. "I doubt there's anyone around at this hour. But we don't want to take any chances. So, no talking once we leave the woods. We're going in low and careful. I take point. You follow. Agreed?" At her nod, he continued. "There's an underground passage-way near the chapel that leads to an interior courtyard. Are you familiar with it?"

"Yes. The private rooms of the palace surround it. They're keeping my mother in one of the courtyard bedrooms."

"Do you know which one?"

She frowned. "I might be able to figure it out once we're there, assuming they haven't moved her. They kept us separated most of the time. I only had the op-portunity to see her once. Considering how upset we both were…" She trailed off and bit her lip.

He wrapped his arm around her and pulled her into

a swift embrace. "Don't worry. We'll find her." Of course, then they'd have to get away again, backtrack to the car and drive like maniacs for the border. All in a day's work. "Okay, let's go. Once we get to the palace courtyard I'll need you to show me which room is hers."

The first part went more smoothly than he could have hoped. The chapel appeared deserted and they found the door to the passageway without any problem. It was locked, of course, but he didn't detect any sort of alarm system, cameras or motion detectors, which surprised him. The lock proved a minor obstacle. He had it picked and open in less than a minute. The next phase of the operation promised to be trickier.

They emerged on the palace side and he signaled Alyssa to wait while he checked the exit. He still couldn't find any sign of an alarm system and that bothered him more than he cared to admit. Every instinct he possessed warned that their incursion had been too easy. That it was a trap. More than anything, he wanted to turn around and get Alyssa the hell out of here. But he knew, without a single doubt, that the only way she'd leave without her mother was the same way he'd removed her last time—by physical force.

The landscaping of the courtyard offered plenty of cover. Trees and shrubs abounded. He made a swift reconnaissance of the area, familiarizing himself with the layout. There were two doors that accessed the building and here he finally found an alarm system. He examined it carefully and it only added to his growing suspicion.

Hell. He couldn't see Tolken using something this basic. Not when a pair of wire clippers and a remote device could disarm it. They'd both been trained better than that. He returned to the passageway.

"What's wrong?" she whispered the minute he crouched beside her.

"It's a trap."

"Where? How?"

"The alarm system is too dated. I can punch through it in no time."

"But that's good."

He sighed. "They know we're coming and they're waiting for us. We should leave."

"Not without my mother." And then she played the one card he couldn't trump. "You promised. You gave me your word."

"I did. And I'll keep it. But I want you out of harm's way."

Her mouth tightened. "You mean, you want me to return to the car."

"And leave if I'm not back within thirty minutes."

She shook her head. "Good try, but I'm staying."

"Alyssa—"

"We're wasting time, Merrick. Let's get in there, grab my mom and get the hell out before we're discovered."

He could feel her anxiety, sense how close to the edge she'd slipped. If they had any hope of succeeding, they needed to act. Now. Catching her hand in his, he lifted it and kissed her ring. It sparkled in the subdued light, a rainbow flash of joy that mirrored his memories of their wedding night. It helped center him, filling him with determination.

"Okay, Princess. Listen up. Once we're in the court-yard, I'm going to give you a moment to get your bearings. There are two doors. One will be to your left, the other directly in front of you. See if you can remember which is closest to the room where they were keeping your mother. Ready?"

At her nod, they exited the passageway and slipped into the deep shadow of an ornamental cherry tree that overhung a koi pond. She scanned the area and then pointed toward the door to their left. As promised, he disabled the alarm in minutes. He went through the door first, ready for anything.

The corridor was empty. Not good. It only heightened his sense of dread. This wasn't going to end well. He knew it with a gut-deep certainty. The worst part was putting Alyssa at risk, which was why he'd deliberately left his weapon behind. At the first sign of trouble, he intended to surrender. In the meantime, he'd let it play out and hope he could negotiate a reasonable resolution if the situation went sour.

She tugged at his arm and pointed to a room farther down the corridor. He nodded in acknowledgement. Keeping her behind him, he approached the door she'd indicated. Ever so carefully he turned the knob. It held firm. Precious seconds were eaten up as he picked the lock. The deadbolt snicked home and he eased the door open. The room lay in total darkness and yet with his night vision goggles he could see a woman standing rigid in the middle of the room. The only thing she lacked was a sign hung around her neck that read, "cheese."

Before he could stop her, Alyssa brushed past him and darted toward the woman. "Mom!"

He swore. Instantly, the lights flashed on, blinding him. He tore off his goggles, not that it helped. His vision was gone and all he could do was brace himself for the inevitable. They took him down. Hard. They'd left nothing to chance this time. There were a full dozen men who moved with a fluid coordination that warned that their attack had been expertly planned and executed. He didn't fight them. There was no point. They finally dragged him to his feet, not too bruised, his hands cuffed behind him.

Tolken stood beside the two women, both of whom were weeping as they embraced. "This was the second most foolish thing you've ever done, Your Highness," he commented.

"And the first?" As if he didn't know.

"Abducting Princess Alyssa, of course."

Merrick would miss their friendship, could hear the finality of its passing in Tolk's voice. "I'd have to disagree with you there." He attempted a smile, then winced as it tugged at his newly split lip. "That may have been the smartest thing I've ever done."

"You will change your mind after Prince Brandt is through with you."

Merrick's smile faded. "Or he'll change his when I'm done with him."

Tolken escorted Merrick and the two women through the palace. They ended up in a large, richly appointed office. Von Folke sat behind his desk, nursing a drink. He stood as they filed into the room, studying each of them in turn. His attention settled on Alyssa.

"Are you all right, my dear? Montgomery didn't harm you?"

His undisguised warmth surprised her, as did the tenderness underscoring his words. What in the world was going on? "I'm fine, thank you," she replied cautiously.

His gaze shifted to Merrick and all warmth and tenderness vanished. Raw fury gleamed in the inky darkness of his eyes, fury he barely held in check. "You stole my wife, you son of a bitch."

Alyssa shuddered. She'd heard a similar tone used only once before. Ironically, it had come from Merrick when Tolken and his men had burst into their bedroom that first morning at the cottage and one of the guards had dared to put his hands on her.

"I stole your bride," Merrick corrected. "There's a difference."

Brandt lunged before his men could stop him. He grabbed Merrick by the throat and slammed his back against the wall. "She isn't just my bride, you bastard. She's my wife. You dare deny it?"

"Your *wife?* Hell, yes, I deny it." To Alyssa's relief, Merrick didn't fight back. She suspected if he had, Prince Brandt would have taken him apart, piece by precious piece. "What are you talking about?"

"You snuck into my home in the middle of the night and you took her from me. She was with you when my men found her. In your bed." A primal rage exuded from von Folke. "You may have taken advantage of her since our wedding night but that doesn't change the fact that she's *my* wife. You put your hands on my woman. And I will see that you burn in hell for that."

Merrick's eyes narrowed. "Yes, I abducted her, but not in the middle of the night." He spoke slow and clear, a hint of cold arrogance bleeding into his words. "And FYI... She's not your wife."

Brandt's hand fisted and for a split second Alyssa was certain he intended to use it to pound Merrick's face. Gathering himself, he released Merrick and took a step back, the breath heaving in and out of his lungs. His fight for control was impressive to watch. Bit by bit he regained command of himself, banking the fierce anger that held him in its grip in order to consider the situation logically.

"I've never before known you to flat-out lie, Merrick," he said after several endless minutes had passed. "In consideration of our former association and out of respect for the faithfulness with which you have served our country, I'll give you a single opportunity to justify your actions. After that, I promise you, life will become very painful."

In response, Merrick pulled himself up into a military stance, wincing as he did so. "First, you didn't marry Alyssa Sutherland. I can't be any clearer than that. As for justifying my actions, you know damn well why I took her from you." His voice held undisguised condemnation. "The people of Verdonia deserve a fair election, not one orchestrated by you. I was honor bound to stop you, and I did. End of story."

"I have no intention of debating politics with you. That can wait for a more opportune time. At this point, all that matters is the harm you've brought to my wife and the lies you're telling about her." Brandt stalked across the room and took a stance at Alyssa's side. "I married this woman two weeks and one day ago. Bishop Varney performed the ceremony. Afterward, she retired to her room where she remained…attended to the entire time."

"You mean, under guard?"

The taunt sent dark color sweeping across Brandt's cheekbones. "I was with her that night. I should know who I married." He laced Alyssa's hand in his. "She even wears my ring."

She lifted the hand he held for everyone to see. Her amethyst and diamond studded wedding band glittered in the subdued light. "You're mistaken, Prince Brandt."

He gripped her fingers, staring in disbelief. "What have you done with the wedding ring I gave you?" he demanded.

"You never gave me one."

"Explain!"

"Merrick's right. I never made it to the ceremony. He abducted— I mean, I escaped with him before the wedding took place."

"That's not possible." Brandt said the words automatically, but they lacked his former heat. "You were there. At the ceremony. We said our vows."

She shook her head. "I wasn't. I never married you."

"The earrings. The tracking device." He struggled as though finding his footing on shifting sand. "That's how we located you after Montgomery's abduction later that night."

"You gave me those earrings before we married," she reminded him. "Think back. Did you see them on at any other point? During the ceremony? Afterward? When we were together on our wedding night?"

He shook his head, his mouth compressing. "How do I know you aren't lying?"

"I have no way of proving what I say, if that's what you mean. But I assure you, I'm not lying. I've only ever married one man and it wasn't you."

"Who?" His infuriated gaze shifted. "Montgomery? You married *him*?"

Merrick took the opportunity to shrug off the guards restraining him. "Yes, she married me. Now take your damn hands off my wife!"

Brandt stilled, his expression icing over. "Every-one out." He signaled to the guards. "Escort Mrs. Barstow to her room. Princess Alyssa will remain behind."

"No!" Angela cried. "I want to be with my daughter."

Brandt dropped a hand to her shoulder and gave it a gentle squeeze. "It's only for a short time." To Alyssa's surprise, the prince's manner had softened perceptibly. "Please don't worry. This will all end very soon and then you may return home."

"Do you promise?"

He inclined his head. "I promise." He glanced at Tolken. "You and Prince Merrick stay, as well."

They waited while Alyssa's mother and the guards exited the room. The door clicked loudly in the sudden silence. "Hold him," Brandt ordered Tolken, indicat-ing Merrick.

As soon as Merrick was secured, he turned to Alyssa. "Allow me to apologize in advance, Princess. But I need to verify your claim."

Her alarmed gaze slammed into Merrick's. "How?"

Brandt gestured toward her jeans. "Unzip them."

Merrick's howl of fury raised the hair on the back of her neck. He fought Tolken, fought with a wild reckless-ness that terrified her. It took all Tolken's strength to restrain him. If it hadn't been for the cuffs, he wouldn't have succeeded.

"Stop!" Alyssa cried. "Merrick, don't. It's not worth it."

His eyes were crazed, the gold burning so bright it hurt to look at them. "I swear to God, von Folke, if you touch her, I'll kill you."

"He's not going to touch me. I won't let him." She ripped at the snap of her jeans and yanked down the zipper. She glared at Prince Brandt. "There, I've done it. Now, what do you want?"

He stood in front of her, blocking her from the view of the other two men. "Show me your left hip. The woman I married had a tattoo there."

She did as he requested, tugging the denim along her side down an uncomfortable few inches. An embarrassed flush stained her cheeks. "Satisfied?"

"The other hip, if you will." As soon as she'd complied, he stepped back, thinking hard. "There are such things as temporary tattoos, are there not?"

"Yes," Alyssa acknowledged, refastening her jeans.

"Then there's no way to be certain yours wasn't temporary, unless…" He faced her with stony resolve. "Again I must apologize, Alyssa. If there were any other way, I'd take it."

"What are you going to do?" she asked warily.

A slight smile softened the harshness of his features. "Make your husband—assuming he is your husband—extremely angry."

Her chin shot up. "And me, as well, I suspect."

He inclined his head. "And you, as well."

He didn't give her time to retreat. Cupping her face between his hands, he bent down and, with Merrick's curses ringing in their ears, he kissed her. He took his time, tracing her lips with his, first gently and then with a hint of passion. She stood, enduring it, praying all the while that Tolken was a hell of a lot stronger than Merrick.

After an endless moment, Brandt straightened and took a step back. Then he turned and faced Merrick. "It would appear your wife is telling the truth. She's not the woman I married." His attention shifted to Tolken. "Your men have some explaining to do."

"Yes, Your Highness. I'll get the facts as soon as we're done here."

"Give me a timeline, Montgomery," Brandt ordered. "When, where, how."

"Very well." Merrick shrugged free of Tolken's grasp. "May twentieth, thirteen-thirty. I infiltrated the woods behind the chapel garden. Your bride and one of her guards moved from the courtyard into the garden. I disabled him and—" A hard, fierce smile tugging at the scar on the side of his mouth. His anger had subsided, though not by much. She could still hear the remnants of it, undermining the tattered scraps of his self-control. "And liberated your bride-to-be."

"I cooperated fully," Alyssa insisted.

Brandt held up his hand. "Good try. But considering your mother was my…guest, I doubt you'd have willingly left without her."

"Merrick insisted you wouldn't harm her."

"Did he?" The question held a trace of amusement. "And you believed him?"

"Yes."

"Admirable." He gestured to Merrick. "Continue. You forgot to mention the men you had with you."

"I operated on my own."

"A lie, but an understandable one, given the circumstances." He addressed Tolken, not bothering to conceal his intense displeasure. "Clearly, one of your men neglected to report this. You'll find out who and deal with it."

"I used a modified tranquilizer dart," Merrick offered. "The subject is only rendered unconscious for a short time. He could have believed he'd fainted or blacked out for some reason, and since your bride was still present and safe when he came to, he was too embarrassed to report it. Regardless, I drove Alyssa to the safe house where your men found us the next morning."

"At which point you—how did you refer to it before? Ah, yes. You *liberated* my helicopter and flew to Celestia."

Merrick inclined his head. "We appreciated the loan."

Alyssa stifled a groan. "For God's sake, do you have to go out of your way to provoke him?"

"When did the two of you marry?" Brandt asked.

"Two days ago."

"I assume you can prove the legality of it?"

"I can."

"In that case, I only have one final question."

Merrick bared his teeth in a mock grin. "Always happy to help."

"Just out of curiosity…" Brandt strolled closer, the expression in his eyes causing Alyssa to shudder. "Whom did I marry?"

Nine

Merrick shrugged. "Some woman I picked up. I don't remember her name."

"Try."

He pretended to consider. "Sorry, doesn't come to me."

"Perhaps time in a jail cell will assist your memory."

Merrick planted his feet as though in preparation for a blow. "Don't count on it."

Brandt stopped in front of him. "I married this woman you 'picked up' believing her to be Alyssa. I took her to my bed and made love to her." He lifted an eyebrow. "You react to that. Interesting. So, you do know her. And for some reason you don't care for the fact that we were intimate. I'd suspect she were a former lover of yours, except for one small detail."

"What's that?" Merrick asked through gritted teeth.

"My mysterious bride was a virgin."

Merrick's fury burst through his self-control. "How dare you put your hands on her. You had no right!"

"I had every right. She's my wife." He leaned forward, speaking in a low, intense voice. "Do you think I took her by force? If so, think again. Now tell me who she is and why you're protecting her."

Merrick gathered himself. "It's my job. I got her into this situation. It's my responsibility to ensure that no harm comes to her."

"Then you shouldn't have put her in harm's way." Brandt stepped back and signaled Tolken. "Take Prince Merrick and his wife to the Amethyst Suite. And Tolken?" His black eyes held a warning. "Make sure it's secured. No more surprises."

Merrick paused by the door, determined to have the last word. "She left you, Brandt." He tossed the comment over his shoulder. "Your wife could have stayed. But she didn't. You might want to think about that."

Apparently, he wasn't to have the last word, after all. "And you might want to wish your own bride a fond farewell," Brandt shot back. "Because I intend to make certain that this is the last night you spend with her for a very long time to come."

Alyssa and Merrick were escorted to their room. As soon as the door locked behind them, she walked into her husband's arms. "This is all my fault."

"No," he corrected. "It's von Folke's."

"You warned me it was a trap. I should have listened to you."

"Okay, that's true."

She shook her head in disbelief. "Amazing. Here we are, captured, locked in a room, the threat of jail hanging over your head. How can you make light of it?"

"What would you rather I do?"

"Hold me." He tightened his arms around her, willing to do whatever necessary to ease her mind. "You were right about one thing."

"I'm right about most things," he informed her with impressive modesty. "Which one did you have in mind?"

"Did you see how Prince Brandt treated my mother? He was so…gentle with her. So careful. She usually has that affect on people, but even so I suspect he'd never have hurt her. You told me he wouldn't, but I didn't believe you."

"You couldn't take the risk. I understand that."

"I'm so sorry, Merrick." Her arms encircled his neck. "I can't bear the thought that you'll be condemned to prison because of me. What are we going to do?"

"Give von Folke time to come to terms with what's happened." He released his breath in a long sigh. "Which will give me time to come to terms with it, as well."

"That won't be easy." She hesitated, lowering her voice to a soft murmur. "What about Miri?"

"We keep silent about her. Do you hear me, Alyssa? Not a single word to von Folke."

She frowned. "You're not going to tell him who he married?"

Was she kidding? "Not a chance. I don't want him anywhere near my sister any more than I want him near my wife."

Alyssa hesitated, and he could tell she was picking her way through their conversation. "She stayed with him, Merrick. If Prince Brandt is telling the truth, she chose to sleep with him. Did you tell her to do that?"

He jerked back as though she'd struck him. "Hell, no! How could you even suggest such a thing?"

"I didn't think you had," she hastened to placate. "But the point is, it happened. She wouldn't have slept with him just to give us more of a head start, would she?"

"No."

Her hands dropped to his shoulders, massaging the clenched muscles. "Is that a 'No, I hope not because I can't handle the guilt if she did' or 'No, it's not in her nature to ever do such a thing'? I hate to ask the question, but does Miri have as strong a sense of duty as you? Would she have slept with Prince Brandt for king and country?"

He swore, long and virulently. "Yes, she has a strong sense of duty. No, I hope to God she wouldn't do anything as foolish as to sleep with von Folke in order to give us extra time to get away, or even worse, out of obligation."

He didn't dare consider the possibility that there might be another reason, not when he was holding on to his temper by a thread. Still, he couldn't help remembering the conversation he and Alyssa had the night he'd abducted her—the one where they'd discussed the possibility that there'd been a personal aspect to Miri's insistence on participating in the abduction.

"So, what now?" Alyssa asked.

"Now we do as von Folke suggested. We make the most of the time we have left together."

"Don't say that," she protested in alarm. "You're not going to prison, not if I have anything to say about it. I'll deny I was abducted. They can't prove I didn't go with you willingly."

"This isn't the United States." He tried to break it to her gently. "Despite the fact that you're Princess Alyssa, duchess of Celestia, von Folke governs this part of

Verdonia. His word is law. He can throw me in prison, if that's what he chooses and there's little anyone can do about it. My best guess is he'll leave me to rot in jail for a while before banishing me."

"But just from Avernos, right? Surely, he can't banish you from the entire country?"

"He can—and will—if he takes the throne."

"No! I won't allow that to happen."

He regarded her with regret. "You won't be able to stop it." He brushed a kiss across her brow. "Since we can't predict what tomorrow will bring, there's no point in worrying about it now. We still have tonight. Let's not waste our few remaining hours."

Tears filled her eyes. "What if I want more than just one night?"

"Our relationship was never meant to be permanent. That was our agreement, remember?" He tilted his head to one side, hoping against hope. "Or has that changed?"

"And…and if it has?" Her chin shot up and a hint of defiance gleamed in her eyes. "What if I said I wanted more than a temporary relationship?"

He had to hear the words. "How much more?"

She took a deep breath and he could feel her square her shoulders. "What if I said I wanted our marriage to be a real one? What would you say then?"

He hardened himself against her pleading gaze. "I'd say that wasn't enough. I want more from my wife, from the woman I commit to spend the rest of my life with."

A tremor rippled through her. "Then…what if I said I loved you? What if I told you that I love you more than I thought it possible to love another person?"

He closed his eyes, wanting to shout in triumph. "Are you asking? Or are you saying the words?"

"I love you, Merrick." No hesitation this time. No doubt. No ambiguity. Just a hint of wonder and a infinite quantity of joy.

"That's all I need to hear." He cupped her face. "I love you, too, Princess. You are my beginning, my middle and my end. More than anything, I want to spend the rest of my life with you."

Dragging his head down to hers, she took his mouth in an urgent, hungry kiss, one that devastated the senses. Her hands caught at his T-shirt, shoving it up and out of her way until she hit hot, bare skin.

Her desperation poured over him in waves, her need ripe and edgy. Demanding a response. Teetering out of control. She so clearly wanted to lose herself in him. He followed her lead, taking his mouth off hers only long enough to yank her thin cotton shirt over her head and toss it aside.

She was beautifully naked underneath, her breasts milky white and topped with sweet raspberry buds that begged to be tasted. He took a quick biting sample and she went rigid in his arms. A thin, keening wail caught in her throat and she vibrated with a frenzied yearning that nearly proved his undoing. He slid his hands along endlessly bared skin to the snap of her jeans, ripping it open.

"I've never wanted a man the way I want you." She swept a hand down his chest until her hand hovered at the heavy bulge beneath his belt buckle. "I can't seem to help myself. I can't seem to get enough. I want more."

"No problem." It took every ounce of self-possession not to grind himself against her hand. He settled for leaning more fully into her, mating them as completely as possible without immediate access to a bed, far fewer clothes and the time and energy to indulge in every hot and sweaty fantasy the two of them could invent. "For you, I have a limitless supply."

"No." Her head moved restlessly back and forth. "This isn't just about sex. That wouldn't be enough for me."

"Really? I thought it was pretty good, myself."

She fixed her gaze on him, her eyes huge and dilated. "Sex...that's for anyone, anywhere. That's easy. I've never been willing to accept easy. I've always wanted more."

He stilled, understanding what she was trying to say. "But you've been too afraid to grab more, haven't you, Princess?"

She trembled with the effort to speak, to trust him enough to open her heart. "I've spent a lifetime running. My mother taught me that lesson well." Her throat worked for an endless moment, and when the words came they were heavy with pain. "I'm afraid to stop."

"Then pause. Just for one night." He soothed her with a kiss, eased her heartache the only way he knew how. "Savor the moment. You can always run tomorrow."

"You don't understand, because you've always had it. A home. Roots. Security." She leaned into him and closed her eyes, almost chanting the words. "I don't belong. I've never belonged."

"Is it that you don't belong, or have you turned away from the one thing you want most of all because you were too afraid to take a risk?" He pushed ever so gently. "Tell me which it is."

Tears squeezed from beneath her tightly closed lids. "I'm afraid," she whispered. "I want to belong. But I can't risk it. So, I tell myself I can't have it. That I don't even want it."

The answer was so simple. Didn't she see? "It's

already yours, my love. You do belong. You belong with me. Now and forever."

He speared his fingers into her hair and lifted her face to his. Her beautiful, tragic face. He kissed away the pain etched alongside her mouth, across her eyebrows, nuzzling the muscle-tense juncture of neck and shoulder, before briefly sampling the raspberries and cream. He trailed his hands up her exposed arms to her shoulders, watching her shiver. Watching her nipples peak with desire while her gold-tipped lashes fluttered open once again. Her skin felt like silk, the sheen from her desire tinting it with the barest hint of sultry rose.

His touch sparked an immediate response. With a sigh of relief she opened to him, gave herself without question or hesitation. And he took what she so unstintingly offered. He lowered his head and captured her mouth once again. Her lips parted beneath his in helpless invitation and she softened against him. It was such a gentle taking, the way he slipped between her lips, the sweep and swirl of his tongue a blatant imitation of a more physical joining. It told her how it could be, if she would just let down her guard and open to him. She responded, tentatively at first, and then with growing ardor.

Instantly, the gentleness shifted and became more passionate. Fierce. Raw. Their desire spinning out of control. Without breaking contact with her mouth, he cupped her bottom and lifted. Her legs parted of their own accord, wrapping around him, allowing him to settle in the warm juncture of her jean-clad thighs. His clothes were a delicious abrasion, the friction of his slow undulations driving her toward the brink. She rocked in tempo with him for an endless minute of pure delicious lust before freezing.

"Please." She tightened her hold, preventing him from moving, while she dragged air into her lungs. "I'm going to lose it."

He brushed his fingertips across her beaded nipples, edging her closer still. "I hope to heaven this suite has a bedroom."

She swallowed, fighting for control, teetering so close to oblivion that he knew the least little movement would send her over. "Find it. Fast. Or it'll be too late."

"It's already too late. We'll do it here and now."

His mouth crushed hers, practically swallowing her whole, as he tipped her onto the floor. Hands got in the way, his as he tackled her jeans, hers as she tackled his. Clothes ripped loose, discarded with blistering haste. The urgency built, pounding at them, firing their blood, reducing them to the most basic, primal essence. Through the roar in his ears he heard her whimper, the breathless plea, the blatant demand. Or maybe they came from him.

The scent of her filled his lungs, the sweet, hot musky odor that was so uniquely hers. It roused him to a fever pitch, proving to him yet again that in this regard, nature forever dominated intellect. He found her ready for him, burning wet, and he filled her, driving into her, sending her up and over. She crashed down, brutally hard, only to scream upward once again as he rode the pain and pleasure.

It had never been like this. Never. "More. More. More!" The words were ripped from him. A desperate mantra that beat out the pace. The music sang through them both, soaring to a final endless note before dying to silence.

The breath shuddered from her lungs and she stared

at him, dazed. "That was…that was—" She trembled. "I haven't a clue what that was. But you better be able to play it again."

"Oh, yeah." Maybe. If he lived that long.

Eventually they found the bed and fell into it, exhausted. She clung to him and he read the silent message. She was terrified that any minute now Tolken and his men would come to the door and drag him away. He could only reassure her with his touch. He held her, stroked her, soothed her. The light fragmented off his wedding band, catching her eye and her arms tightened around him in response.

"You're my husband." She said the words, fiercely, laying claim.

"For as long as you choose."

Her fingers traced his features, a delicate exploration before feathering into his hair. "He'll come for you soon."

His shoulders lifted. "We have a little longer."

"I don't think I can handle it when they take you." The admission came hard. "I want you in my life. More than that, I need you."

"I can give you what you need. No question." He said it with absolute assurance.

She smiled, her mouth trembling from laughter to tears. "You don't know what I need or want. You might think you do. But you don't."

The tenor had grown serious and he rolled onto his side to face her. "Then tell me," he urged. "Tell me so I'll know."

She met his gaze and he read the temptation hovering there along with the reluctance. "If you were smart," she whispered, "you'd let me go. I'm not the type to stick around."

"I can't. I won't." He felt the brief yielding of her body and pressed home his advantage. "You say you love me, that you want to be with me. You have a home in Celestia. You have people who love you and need you there. So, stay." To his frustration, he instantly realized he'd miscalculated, a rare misstep.

She stiffened within his arms, wariness creeping into her gaze. "Is this how you negotiate? Use whatever advantage will get you what you want?"

"Yes." He couldn't help smiling. "Though if it makes you feel any better, I only use my sexual advantage on you."

Exhaling roughly, she flopped onto her back. "Of course. After all, it's worked like a charm up until now, hasn't it?" She scrubbed the heels of her hands across her face as though waking from a deep sleep. "What am I thinking? I'm not the type who stays. I can't believe I'm even considering the possibility."

He couldn't resist a final caress, one that left her shivering in reaction. "What did she do to you, Alyssa?"

She didn't pretend confusion, he gave her credit for that much. "It's not my mother's fault. Not totally. I could have chosen a different path instead of following in her footsteps."

"Explain it to me."

"You haven't noticed her hands, have you?" She shook her head before he could answer. "No, you wouldn't have. There hasn't really been an opportunity for you to."

Merrick frowned, picturing Angela during that brief time they'd been in the room together. He'd observed her, of course, and had automatically filed away a quick, detailed image in his mind. An occupational hazard.

She'd been slight of build and fair like Alyssa. Paler. Fragile. Eyes the same slice-of-heaven blue. But her features were sharper. Drawn. She'd stood perfectly still, arms at her sides, as though reluctant to draw attention to herself. But he couldn't recall anything specific about her hands.

"No, I didn't notice," he admitted. "What about them?"

"They were broken as a child. Deliberately. Finger by finger."

"Oh God."

"The details aren't important. Let's just say that whatever type of abuse you can imagine happening to her probably did."

Anger filled him, an impotent rage over the helplessness of children trapped in the keeping of deviant, amoral adults. "Was she removed from her parents' custody?"

"Yes. Foster homes followed. A series of them. I don't think she was abused there. At least, she's never hinted at it. She just wasn't helped. When she turned sixteen, she took off."

He closed his eyes. "And so the running began."

"Exactly. She's spent most of her life looking for love and never finding it, always hoping she'd discover salvation around the next corner." Alyssa's mouth twisted. "Or with the next man. Most of her husbands have been older. Substitute father figures, if I had to guess."

It fit. "Like Prince Frederick."

"He was a father figure?" He'd surprised her. "Older than Mom?"

"Twenty, twenty-five years older."

Her brow wrinkled. "I guess my brother must be older, too."

"Forty-five, at least."

"I didn't realize." She released a gusty breath. "So, the pattern was set, even then."

"Apparently." He took a moment to digest everything she'd told him before asking his next question. "Okay, I understand your mother and what motivates her. But how do you fit into all this?"

"I love her," Alyssa stated simply. "I've been the one constant in her life. We've been on the run from the minute I was born, with brief layovers along the way. A couple of cockeyed optimists searching for the pot of gold at the end of the rainbow. At least, that's how she always described it to me."

"So, it's all about honor and duty with you, too. Not to mention protecting those you love." Judging by her stunned expression that had never occurred to her before. "And now? Where do you go from here?"

"I'm so tired, Merrick." Her voice dropped, filled with a yearning that tore at his heart. "I'd like to stop, maybe stay somewhere awhile. Let that rainbow find me for a change."

He brushed a tumble of curls from her eyes. "Maybe stay longer than a while?" he asked tenderly. "How does forever-after sound?"

"That might have been a possibility, if it weren't for one small problem." She smiled, a wobbly effort too painful for words. "The one person I'd have been willing to stay for won't be here, not if Prince Brandt throws you in jail. Now, how's that for irony?"

"Then maybe I can give you something to remember me by."

He left her arms long enough to find his trousers and remove a small velvet pouch from the pocket. He dumped out the contents and returned to the bed, gathering her close once again. Taking her hand in his, he slipped a ring on her finger.

"This is for you," he told her.

The subdued light flashed off Fairytale, the ring she'd admired at the Marston's shop. A ring that symbolized soul mates united in an unbreakable bond of eternal love. With a small exclamation of disbelief, she turned in his arms and clung to him. "How? When? Why?"

A slow smile lit his face. "Why? Because it was meant for you and only you. The how and when were a little trickier. But I found a way." His smile faded. "I'd planned to choose the perfect time to give this to you, but I'm not sure there's going to be one."

She gathered his face in her hands and kissed him. "Then we'll make this the perfect time. Here and now."

And as one by one their final minutes together ticked away, she made those moments more perfect than any that had come before.

Prince Brandt sent for Alyssa early the next morning. She was escorted once again to his office. She didn't know quite what to expect, though she could guess what he wanted.

"Please. Sit." He held her chair with an inborn graciousness. "We need to talk."

"About what?"

"First, I wish to apologize to you. I pulled you into a situation not of your making or of your concern. It was wrong of me."

"You tried to force me to marry you," she replied bluntly. "And you used my mother in order to ensure my agreement. That wasn't just wrong. It was outrageous."

"There were reasons. Valid reasons." He said it without remorse.

Anger swept through her. "Because you want to be king? You consider that a valid reason?"

He started to reply, then hesitated. "I can't go into it at this point. Perhaps someday in the future." He regarded her in silence for a moment and then spoke with surprising frankness. "You were a pawn, Alyssa, a pawn I chose to use without taking into account how it would affect your life."

"You mean without caring."

He inclined his head. "Without caring." This time he did show a hint of regret. "If there had been any other way, I would have taken it. But there wasn't. There still isn't."

"You can't really intend to throw Merrick in prison," she said, hoping to take advantage of his momentary change in disposition. "You abducted me, remember? If anything, his could be considered a rescue mission."

Brandt shrugged that off. "My principality, my rules. His prison sentence stands."

"So, what now?" She struggled to keep her distress from showing. "Is this the point where you threaten me if I don't tell you who you married?"

"I was thinking more in the nature of a bribe." He cocked a sooty eyebrow. "Would that work any better? You and your mother on the next plane to New York, Merrick at your side? Any interest?"

"I'll pass, thanks."

He sighed. "Don't tell me Montgomery has brainwashed you with his notion of honor and duty."

She tilted her head to one side. "You know, a few hours ago you might have scored with that one. But my husband pointed out an interesting fact to me. I do believe in honor and duty, in protecting the ones I love. Otherwise I wouldn't be sitting here right now, intent on saving my mother and my husband." She smiled coldly. "So, no. He didn't brainwash me. I was pretty much there already."

"Honor and duty? Really?" He looked mildly intrigued. "Are you serious?"

"Dead serious."

"Let me guess." Laughter gathered in his eyes. "You plan on saving Verdonia from the evil prince."

"Hey, if the royal shoe fits."

"And you plan to swear on your honor that Montgomery didn't abduct you."

"Absolutely."

"You cooperated with him."

"All the way."

"In order to avoid marrying me."

"Can you blame me?"

"So when the opportunity presented itself, you ran off with Montgomery."

"I did."

"And let Miri take your place."

"Yes. No. *No!*" She stumbled to a halt, staring at him in barely controlled panic. She debated backtracking, saying something—anything—to cover up her mistake. But she could see it was far too late. He'd bluffed; she'd fallen for it. She closed her eyes, guilt overwhelming her, and spoke through numb lips. "How did you know?"

"I was pretty much there already," he replied, tossing her own words back at her. "But I appreciate the confirmation. Now, one final question. Where is she?"

"I don't know." She opened her eyes, blinking against tears. "That's the truth."

"Yes. I can see it is. You don't lie very well, Ms. Sutherland."

"You say that like it's a bad thing."

"In my position, it can be. You'll see what I mean in a minute." He picked up the phone and punched a button. "Bring them."

She regarded him with undisguised bitterness. "You'll never know how delighted I am that we never married."

"You may find this hard to believe, but so am I, despite the agenda that made our alliance so critical."

He leaned across his desk toward her. She found his features too austere for her taste, though she couldn't deny they were compelling. And when he smiled with gentle warmth, as he did now, he was downright stunning.

"Don't take it too badly. Despite your husband's ridiculously protective nature, there are few women he'd feel the need to defend with quite such passion and ferocity. His mother. His wife." Something shifted within his gaze, an emotion that he swiftly banked. "His sister. It only required calm logic to reach the appropriate conclusion." He gave a harsh, self-deprecating laugh. "Though I'm forced to admit it took me most of the night to manage calm, let alone logic."

"And why is that, Prince Brandt?"

"Because of Miri," he surprised her by admitting. "And then, once the obvious occurred to me, I needed someone to confirm my guess about her."

Alyssa flinched. What he meant was someone foolish enough to confirm his guess. Before she could snarl a response, Tolken entered the room, followed by Merrick and her mother, as well as a handful of guards.

Prince Brandt stood. "You'll all be pleased to know that Alyssa and I have reached an accord." He gave

Alyssa a courtly bow. "Thank you, Princess, for your assistance identifying Miri as my wife. The three of you will be driven immediately to the airport where I've arranged for first-class seats from Verdonia to JFK."

Merrick, whirled to face her, took one look at the guilt she was certain was written all over her face and charged toward her. He was stymied by the timely intervention of the guards. "What the hell did you do?" he demanded, frantically struggling against his captors. "You told him, didn't you? Why, Alyssa? Why would you do such a thing?"

Ten

Alyssa shook her head, frantic to explain, eaten up with guilt. "It's not what you think."

But before she could explain further, Prince Brandt interrupted. "Part of me envies your future, Montgomery. To live in the United Sates, playing house-husband while your beautiful, intelligent, *cooperative* wife takes over as Assistant Vice President of Human Relations at Bank International. Quite the life of leisure. Far better than a jail sentence, don't you agree?"

"Take off these handcuffs and I'll show you how well I agree with you."

Brandt shook his head. "Perhaps we'll save that for another time and place." He picked up a packet and handed it to Tolken. "Here are the tickets. The ladies will be riding in the limousine I have waiting. I'm afraid I don't quite trust you to behave well enough for such an elegant vehicle, Montgomery. Tolken and a few of his men will escort you in a van better suited to the transportation of felons. Not quite as comfortable, but I'm sure you understand the necessity. Just as I'm sure you understand the necessity of the handcuffs remaining on until you're safely aboard the plane."

"I'm not leaving Verdonia."

"I thought you might say that." Brandt smiled. "So, I've arranged for a jail cell for your wife and mother-in-law should you refuse. Your choice, Montgomery."

"You can't do that," Alyssa protested. Her gaze flickered from Brandt to Merrick, and back again. "You can't, can you? Everyone keeps telling me I'm a princess. That ought to count for something."

Brandt shrugged. "Once again…my principality, my rules. I might not be able to lock you up forever, but I can hold you long enough."

Merrick shot her one brief look. "My wife in jail. Tempting."

"But you'll pass, won't you?" said Brandt.

To Alyssa's distress, Merrick had to think about it before nodding. "If it means she'll be out of Verdonia permanently, then yes. I'll pass." Before anyone could prevent him, he took one swift step in her direction. "It's a good thing you run well, Princess. Because when I get free, you better be able to run faster and farther than I can." His gaze, pure molten gold, pinned her in place. "Trust me on this one, you don't want me to catch you."

"Merrick—"

Without sparing her so much as another glance, he crossed to the door and addressed Tolken. "What are we waiting for? Let's get the hell out of here."

* * *

"She betrayed you, old friend."

"Shut up, Tolk." The van rumbled onto the highway and gathered speed.

"Don't feel bad. Women are notorious for being weak."

"Some women, perhaps," Merrick conceded. "Not Alyssa."

"So you're saying she's strong enough to resist Prince Brandt's questioning?" Tolken nodded. "That would indicate she chose to betray you. Outrageous. Definitely not the sort of woman to rule Celestia. Verdonia is better off rid of her."

Merrick ground his teeth. "That's not what I meant."

"Tell me. What did you mean?" When a response wasn't forthcoming, he suggested, "Perhaps her betrayal is your fault."

"What the hell are you talking about now?"

"You abducted her for the greater good. Do I have that right? I'm sure you set an excellent example. No doubt she betrayed Miri for a similar reason. Of course in this case it was for her greater good and that of her mother." Tolken lifted a shoulder. "Well...and yours."

Merrick deliberately changed the subject. "I won't get on that plane. You realize that, don't you?"

"I realize it'll take force. It's a good thing I have plenty of that available."

"Even if you succeed, I'll return."

"With your wife?" Tolken tilted his head to one side. "Or without?"

There was no question. "Without."

"In that case, I've been authorized by Prince Brandt to offer you a deal."

"What deal?" Merrick asked warily.

"Simple. Resign your position as commander of the Royal Security Force and return to Verdon. Stay there. Quietly. Live a long and peaceful life out of the public eye. If you do that, Prince Brandt is willing to pretend this incident never took place."

Merrick gave a short laugh. "What you mean is, if I don't tell on him, he won't tell on me. It wouldn't be to his advantage for any of this to be made public, would it? Not before the election." He stared moodily out the window of the van. "What about Alyssa?"

"What about her? She'll return to New York. Not that there's anything Prince Brandt could do if she elected to stay in Verdonia, despite his threats. Especially since the airport is on Celestian soil." He curled his lip. "Just as well she goes, if you ask me. She wasn't suited to play the part of a princess."

"You know nothing about her." The retort burst from Merrick. It felt good to explode, better yet to siphon off some of the anger sloshing around inside him.

Tolken grunted. "I know one thing. She's capable of betraying her husband. No doubt she hid that trait from you. I'm sure you'd never have married her, otherwise. A very devious woman, your wife."

"Just shut the hell up, Tolk, she's not like that. She believes in honor and duty as much as I do. She protects the people she loves. She risked everything to save her mother. Sacrificed everything."

It took a second for him to hear his own words. The minute he did, he groaned. Oh, man. He was a first-class idiot. His head dropped toward his chest. Dammit, dammit, dammit. He did need to resign his position. No one this stupid should be allowed to live, let alone be in charge of a national security force.

"You could be right," Tolken was saying. "I'm not familiar with that aspect of her character. There is one thing I know for certain."

Merrick lifted his head, finally, finally starting to put the pieces together. "And what's that?"

"Your wife is a rotten poker player, whereas Prince Brandt is a master."

Merrick stared blankly. It took a full minute before the implication sank in. And then he said, "Get me out of these handcuffs and give me your cell phone, Tolk. Hurry. I have a plane to stop."

Tolken smiled. "About damn time."

They arrived at the airport and Prince Brandt's guards escorted Alyssa and her mother through security. She delayed as long as she could, constantly checking over her shoulder for Merrick. But he never showed. Once through the checkpoint, they were ushered to a private lounge where she paced off the next two hours, minute by endless minute, step by dragging step.

And still he didn't come.

"I don't understand it," she burst out. "They weren't that far behind us. They should be here by now."

"Maybe they're holding him in the van until it's time to board," her mother said, trying to soothe her. "They probably don't want you having the opportunity to scream at each other ahead of time."

Alyssa spun to face her guards. "You must have cell phones. Can't you call Tolken and find out where they are?"

"My apologies, Your Highness. I'm not permitted to do that," was all one would say.

Another hour passed and a knock sounded at the

door. Alyssa flew across the room, waiting breathlessly for Merrick to join them. But instead of her husband, an airport official entered. "You may board now," he informed them.

Deaf to her protests, the guard escorted Alyssa and her mother from the lounge to the boarding gate and then down the gangway leading to the plane. "Wait. Please." She had to try one more time. "I need to speak to Merrick."

"You can do that when he boards, Your Highness."

"You don't understand." She fought to keep from weeping. "He's not coming. I know he's not. He thinks I betrayed him. And he needs to protect his sister. He won't leave Verdonia."

"I assure you, Your Highness, he won't have a choice."

They were shown to their first-class seats in the front of the plane where Angela handed her daughter a third tissue to help mop up her tears. "Listen, baby, as long as you're already crying, there's something I need to tell you." She glanced around, then lowered her voice, whispering, "It's about your father."

"I already know," Alyssa replied, fighting to regain control of herself. "Merrick told me that he was older than you."

"No. That's not it. I mean, there's that. But there's something else that I should have told you long ago. I did marry Freddy because he was older and because he was safe. We only knew each other a week before we did a Las Vegas." She twisted her ruined hands together. "But that's not what I have to explain to you."

No doubt there was a point to her mother's confession, but Alyssa wasn't sure what it might be. Still, it was a relief to focus on her mother, to put her needs first.

Anything to take her mind off Merrick. She dried the last of her tears and gave Angela her full attention. "What is it, Mom? What do you have to tell me?"

Her mother bowed her head. "It's about what happened when Freddy and I came here. By then it was too late to change anything. We were already married and I couldn't just leave him. I mean, how would that look after just a week?"

"So, you didn't run?"

"I couldn't. Mainly because I didn't have a plan in place at that point. Besides..." Her voice dropped to a mere whisper. "That's...that's when I met him."

A coldness crept into the pit of Alyssa's stomach. "Met who?"

"Freddy's son, Erik." Angela's eyes slowly lifted and fixed on her daughter. "Your father."

Alyssa could only stare for a long minute in stunned disbelief. "You're saying..." She drew in a deep breath. "Are you telling me that my brother is actually my father?"

"Yes, to the father part. No, to the brother." Angela's brow crinkled. "Although since he was technically my stepson at the time, maybe he would be both your brother and your father. I get a headache just thinking about it."

"Mom—"

Her face crumpled. "I'm sorry. I'm not doing this very well."

"Is this somehow connected to why you're here in Verdonia?"

"Uh-huh." Her lashes flickered as she glanced at Alyssa, and then away again. She cleared her throat. "After I left Jim, I decided to fly out to Verdonia. I'd heard that Freddy died a few years back and I thought maybe…maybe Erik and I…" She bowed her head, trailing off miserably. "I wanted to see him again."

"And did you?"

"Yeah. Yeah, I saw him, all right."

"Good grief, Mom. What did he say? What did he do when you showed up?"

"Oh, he abdicated."

Alyssa struggled to breathe. "You went to visit Prince Erik, duke of Celestia and he up and abdicated? Just like that?"

"Sort of. He said something about finding these important documents and needing to fix things, or some such. He said if he abdicated, you could rule Celestia and that when he returned he and I could marry. Only…" Her eyes overflowed. "Only Erik disappeared and Prince Brandt arrived and invited me to stay with him. With Erik gone, I didn't know what to do. So, I went with Prince Brandt. As soon as he learned that Erik had abdicated and that you would rule Celestia in his place, that's when everything went to hell in a handbasket. He came up with that crazy scheme to marry you."

It was Alyssa's turn to supply the tissues. "You can still find Prince Erik. You can be with him now."

"No, it's too late."

"Only if you let it be too late."

Angela shook her head. "I've made a mess of my life. I allowed my past to ruin my future. I let it dictate my choices." She faced her daughter, the river of mascara and tears slowing. "That doesn't have to happen to you. You're so much stronger than I am, just like your father. You can take a chance. Have the future you always dreamed of having."

"No, I—"

"Listen to me, Ally." She used a tone Alyssa had never heard before, that of a determined mother. "I want you to leave. Now."

"What are you talking about?"

"I want you to get off this plane and live your dreams." She swiped the dampness from her cheeks. "Don't think about it. Do it. Get up and walk away."

"I can't leave you behind," Alyssa protested. "You need me."

"Not anymore. I've held you back for too long. We've gotten our roles all mixed up. I'm supposed to be the parent. You're supposed to be the child. And yet I've always let you take care of me."

"I wanted to, Mom. It was my choice." She gripped her mother's poor, broken hands, lifted them to her mouth and kissed them. "I love you."

"Ever since I was a child I wanted someone to take care of me. To love me unconditionally. You always did that." Angela broke down for a brief moment again before gathering herself back up. "But it wasn't fair of me to let you. It was wrong and I won't allow it to go on any longer."

"There's no point in getting off the plane. Merrick thinks I betrayed him."

"Then you'll have to set him straight." She released Alyssa's hands. "Take off your wedding rings."

"I don't understand."

"Take them off. There'll be an inscription inside of them."

"How do you know?" Alyssa asked, even as she found herself tugging off the rings.

"It's a Verdonian tradition, a rather sweet one, actually. A private message between husband and wife.

Read what yours says. If it's something pitiful, like, 'You're my hoochy momma' or 'It'll be fun while it lasts' then you know it wasn't meant to be and we'll hit New York City and buy shoes or something." She leaned forward. "But if it's special, really special, then you have to promise me you'll get off the plane. Do we have a deal?"

"Okay, yes. It's a deal."

Alyssa held Fairytale to the light, turning the ring until she could make out the flowing script inside and started to cry.

"Oh God. It says hoochy momma, doesn't it?"

Alyssa shook her head. "No, no it doesn't. I've got to get off, Mom. I have to go now." She half rose in her seat before realization dawned. "The guards. They're not going to let me off the plane."

"Of course they will."

"No, they'll stop me."

"Think, Alyssa, think. If there's one thing I'm good at, it's getting out of a tight spot. And this one isn't even all that tight." Her mother smiled slyly. "You just have to tell them who you are."

"Tell them—" Of course. Alyssa didn't hesitate. She gave her mother a fierce hug. "Come with me. Do it, Mom. You can have the dream, too. We can find out what happened to Prince Erik. And maybe you can have your happily-ever-after ending, as well."

She didn't wait for her mother's decision. It was hers to make. Alyssa had her own life to live, her own future to fight for. She swept to the doorway. The guards were still posted there. They immediately moved to block the exit.

She drew herself up to her full height. "I am Princess Alyssa, duchess of Celestia," she announced in her most ringing, royally-ticked-off tone of voice. "And you *will* move out of my way."

She'd rattled them, she could tell. They glanced helplessly at each other, uncertain how to respond. Before they could decide, a man in uniform appeared from the front of the plane, either the captain or co-captain, she wasn't sure which.

"Did you say you're Princess Alyssa?"

"I am."

"We've been denied clearance until you're removed from the plane." Annoyed disbelief touched the man's face. "We've been accused of abducting Celestia's princess. So, if you wouldn't mind disembarking…"

"I'd be happy to."

The guards weren't given an option at that point and they reluctantly moved aside. A few minutes later, Alyssa stepped back onto Verdonian soil. To her absolute delight, her mother joined her. She reentered the airport only to be greeted by a wave of people. Clearly, someone had revealed her identity. The minute they saw her, they began to cheer. And when she paused in front of them, every last man, woman and child swept into deep bows and curtsies.

It took her two tries to get the words out. "Thank you," she finally said. "You have no idea how much this means to me."

"Will you be staying, Princess?" one of the women asked shyly.

Alyssa smiled. "Where else would I go? It's my home." And that was the simple truth, she realized.

"And your husband?" a husky voice sounded in her ear. "What about him?"

She spun around. Merrick stood behind her. For a

long moment they didn't move, each greedily drinking in the other. There were so many questions she wanted to ask, so much she wanted to say. Apologies to make. Explanations to give. Wounds to heal. But none of it mattered. Not right then. Not when she looked into those beloved golden eyes and saw the fierce glow of undisguised love.

She took one step toward him. Then another. And then she raced into his waiting arms. He practically inhaled her, kissing her mouth, her eyes, her jaw before finding her mouth again. They were hard, fierce kisses. Urgent kisses. Greedy and needy. Telling her without words how desperately he wanted her. And then the tenor changed.

He kissed her gently, a river of passion flowing deeply beneath. A balm. A benediction. A husband gifting his wife. "I didn't tell him," she said, breathless and dazed. "I swear to you, I didn't."

"I figured that out. It took a while, but I got there."

"I couldn't leave Verdonia. Couldn't leave you."

"I figured that out, too." He cupped her face with his magician's hands. "You still haven't answered my question. You have a husband, Princess. What are you going to do about him?"

Her chin wobbled. "*My home is within your heart. At least, according to this Fairytale I read not long ago. Unless your ring has a better suggestion.*"

"Just one."

"Which is?"

A hint of color darkened his cheekbones. "It's trite."

She grinned through her tears. "I can't wait to hear this. Come on, warrior man. What does it say?"

He snatched his wife into his arms, lifting her high

against his chest. More cheers broke out around them. "It says, *Two souls destined to live as one.*"

She wrapped her arms around his neck and buried her face against his shoulder until she'd recovered sufficiently to speak. "Let's go home, Merrick."

"Is this your home, Princess? Have you finally found your roots?"

"A home. Roots. Heck, I've even found a father." She laughed at his stunned expression. "I'll explain that part later."

To her delight, Merrick's brother was waiting for them outside the airport. One look was all it took to see the resemblance, both in autocratic manner and old-world graciousness. She looked forward to getting to know her brother-in-law a little better, to form an opinion about the man who would be king. There was hint of a warrior about him, a trait that must run in the family, though the rough edges were a bit more polished than with Merrick.

To her surprise, it didn't take long for Lander to put her at ease, and he had her mother charmed within minutes. He also drove them back to Glynith, and though it rained almost the entire way, Alyssa neither noticed nor cared. There were too many other matters of far greater importance to address.

"How did you figure out I hadn't betrayed you?" she asked Merrick at one point.

"Tolken helped with that." He flicked her nose with the tip of his finger. "Surprises you, doesn't it? Once I calmed down enough to think straight I realized you would never have given up Miri, not even for my freedom. Certainly not for your own."

"Not even for my mother's," she confirmed. "I'd have

given him almost anything else, but not that. It was too high a price to pay."

"There's the palace," Angela broke in. Wistfulness underscored her comment. A whisper of bittersweet memories.

Merrick peered out the window, squinting as the sun broke through the rain clouds. He wrapped his arm around his wife. "We can't take up residence there until after church and state have made your position official. But that shouldn't be too long a wait."

"And you? What will you do?"

"I've decided to keep my current job. After my dealings with von Folke, I think Verdonia needs a tough watchdog." He inclined his head toward the palace. "I'll just relocate my base of operations."

Alyssa stared at her new home. This was it. Permanent. No more running. A hint of apprehension rippled through her. Staying involved so much responsibility. How would she manage to handle it all? If it hadn't been for Merrick's presence, she would have been tempted to order Lander to turn the car around and return them to the airport.

And then she saw it. Watched as it formed right before her eyes. From its roots, deep in Celestian soil, a rainbow arched across the sky, a brilliant sweep of color, so dazzling it hurt the eyes. And from where she sat it seemed to burst apart right on top of the palace. Merrick saw it, too. He turned to her, a crooked grin tugging at the corner of his mouth, clearly understanding the significance.

Alyssa caught her mother's hand and directed her attention out the window. "Look, Mom. You were right. Our rainbow was out there. After all these years we finally found it."

And then she met her husband's steady gaze, one that glittered like the sun. She'd discovered what was at the end of her rainbow and it was infinitely more precious than mere gold. She curled deeper into Merrick's embrace. "Take me home," she whispered.

"On one condition."

"Which is?"

"That you promise to live happily ever after."

She pretended to consider. "There's only one way that'll work." Her expression softened. "And that's with you at my side."

He lowered his head and kissed her. "Welcome home, my love. Welcome home."

* * * * *

Royal Affairs – luxurious and bound by duty yet still captive to desire!

Royal Affairs: Desert Princes & Defiant Virgins

Available 3rd June 2011

Royal Affairs: Princesses & Protectors

Available 1st July 2011

Royal Affairs: Mistresses & Marriages

Available 5th August 2011

Royal Affairs: Revenge Secrets & Seduction

Available 2nd September 2011